THE SCREAM PLAYED ON

Perry found Cyndi where she had hidden, under some Anne Klein originals on her mommy's closet floor. She was dragged out easily. Noisily.

Beautifully.

Then his friends came in, and they held her down on the thick white shag. The music downstairs was still pounding up through the floorboards. The screaming had long since died off. "Gonna be my baby tonight," he said, and then helped himself to a few of the things she would no longer be needing.

Her t-shirt.

Her eyes.

The
SCReAM

John Skipp & Craig Spector

SPECTRA

BANTAM BOOKS
TORONTO • NEW YORK • LONDON • SYDNEY • AUCKLAND

THE SCREAM
A Bantam Book / February 1988

Grateful acknowledgment is made for permission to reprint the following:

"It's No Game," copyright © 1980 by Jones Music. Used by permission. "Here Comes the Flood," by Peter Gabriel. Used with permission of Peter Gabriel Ltd. Administered in USA & Canada by Run It Music, Inc. All rights reserved. "Once in a Lifetime," by The Talking Heads. Copyright © 1980, 1981 Bleu Disque Music Co. Inc., Index Music, & E. G. Music Ltd. Used by permission of WB Music Corp. All rights reserved. "Billion Dollar Babies," by Alice Cooper courtesy of Alive Enterprises. "Mother Stands for Comfort" (Kate Bush), copyright © 1985 by KATE BUSH MUSIC LTD. All rights for the US and Canada controlled by SCREEN GEMS-EMI MUSIC INC. "The Working Hour," copyright © 1985 Virgin Music (Publishers) Ltd. and 10 Music Ltd. All rights controlled by Virgin-Nymph Music Inc. Excerpt from THE THIRD WAVE by Alvin Toffler, copyright © 1980 by Alvin Toffler. By permission of William Morrow & Company. "Just One Victory" by Todd Rundgren, copyright © 1972 by Fiction Music, Inc., Todd Rundgren and Screen Gems Music.

ISBN 0-553-26798-1

Published simultaneously in the United States and Canada

PRINTED IN THE UNITED STATES OF AMERICA

KR   0 9 8 7 6 5 4 3 2 1

For Jim and Tammy

ACKNOWLEDGMENTS

T he authors have long been accused of writing acknowledgment pages worthy of an Academy Awards acceptance speech, and show no sign of curbing this impulse. Oh, well. We'd like to express our deepest thanks to the following people for their friendship, support and/or endurance:

Lou, Janna and the fun folks at Bantam, Adele, Richard and Richard of ALA, Beth and Tappan for the deluxe *TK/BAM!* mix, Doug Winter for handy backward masking tips, Marc at JFK and Donna at Spectrum for the tours, the guys in Iron Maiden for the great show, Linda and the folks at Broadway Shakespeare & Company for being there the day the Mac died, Marcia and Ray for the MIDI raps, Fern Drilling for Lamaze coaching, Frank Zappa and his people for the Z-Pak, Marianne and Lori for love, insights, and infinite patience, and a very special thanks to George Ihm for his technical advice and historical anecdotes. Their help made this book what it is today. Lord, have mercy upon them.

We'd also like to thank Lucius Shepard, Dave-boy Schow, Stephen Meade, Turtle Beach, Leslie and Adam, Matt, Alli, Steve, Tony, Brian, Sally Vicious, Pete and Gail, Jim and Lois, our families and, once again, everyone we mentioned in the last books.

We quite possibly couldn't have done it without you. Thanks.

"In Germany they came first for the Communists and I didn't speak up because I wasn't a Communist. Then they came for the Jews, and I didn't speak up because I wasn't a Jew. Then they came for the trade unionists, and I didn't speak up because I wasn't a trade unionist. Then they came for the Catholics, and I didn't speak up because I was a Protestant. Then they came for me—and by that time no one was left to speak up."

—Pastor Martin Niemöller

"This is the working hour.
We are paid by those
Who learn by our mistakes."
—Tears for Fears

CYNDI'S PARTY

"Blessed are the meek,
For they shall inherit the earth."
—Jesus Christ

"If I'm too rough, tell me
I'm so scared your little head
Will come off in my hands."
—Alice Cooper

THURSDAY, JULY 12
DIAMOND BAR, CALIFORNIA

Perry's eyes were gone, but that didn't really matter. The old biblical quote had been set on its head. Perry had no eyes, yet he still could see.
Let Jesus suck on that one for a while.

Dr. Wyler's Wreck Room was a California dream of exposed brick and stucco, adobe reds and desert-sand tans. On the far side of fifty, and the man had style. The Wyler home was typical for the Diamond Bar area: a gracious, comfortably elegant split-level that oozed organically upward mobility and San Gabriel Valley chic. Every line, every curve was clean and crisp and new; every room was tastefully decorated in opulent woods, burnished brass and natural fabrics.

But the sprawling downstairs rec room was the best. There was a well-stocked wet bar across from the wall-to-wall sliding glass patio doors that led to the pool; there was a Neiman Marcus dart board and tapestries woven by some nameless Mexican peasant on either flanking wall. Matte black CapriTrack lighting above, oak parquet floor below, potted midget palm trees and ficus trees to either side. The giant Sony Trinitron that filled damned near one whole corner of the room glowed like a portal to another dimension. The little driftwood *nouveau rustic* "Wreck Room" sign hung askew above enough matching leather sofa modules to accommodate six swinging couples, and the far corner of the playland held the most luxurious expanse of veld-green pool table that Steve Beeker's seventeen years had yet born witness to.

It was a great place for a party.

Too bad Dr. Wyler and his wife could not attend.

In the Wreck Room, the post-concert funzies were out of

control. No surprises there. *Fifteen drug-crazed Screamers,* Steve noted, *doth not a Tupperware party make.* They were dancing to the sonic boom of the Bang + Olufson stereo, making out or passing out in the corners. They were spilling drinks and leaving little cigarette burns on the modular sofas, the green felt plateau, the burnished wood of the bar and the floor. They were wired on coke and smoke and tequila and beer.

Most of all, they were wired on The Scream.

"Best fuckin' concert I ever seen!" Deke bellowed, and Steve was inclined to agree. Just more quietly. He prided himself on being a bit more thoughtful than most of the headbangers he hung out with. But the music they loved was the music *he* loved; and it was nice to know that even someone as monosyllabic as Deke could appreciate The Scream.

Steve looked over at the viddy: MTV was doing its heavy rotation number on The Scream's cut "Filet of Soul", from their double-platinum debut album. The band had opened the first show of their coast-to-coast MegaTour with it, less than three hours ago. The video was great, in itself: all sex and drugs and rock and roll, the way it should be.

But the visuals *inside* his head were better. If he closed his eyes, and was very very still, he could almost transport himself back . . .

. . . *to the sixth row, center, staring straight up what little there was of Tara Payne's skirt as she hip-ground her way to the edge of the stage. He could see the slash of razor-thin Mylar that obscured the oriental perfection of her features; he could see the wild black sweat-sheened hair that whipped like a thousand razor-tipped serpents. Her fine-boned beauty was almost painful to behold, and her face was matched only by her form. He had never seen so many curves move so well on one body. Every gesture was snake-and-mouse time; sixty seconds in and he was ready to die.*

The band thundered up through the changes: Rod Royale, the imperious lead guitarist, dressed like a crown prince of darkness in studded leather and lace, cock-strutting his way across the stage as twin brother Alex did his Amadeus-gone-mad number on the banks of synths and Gene and Terry laid down the law in tight-knit syncopation on the bass and drums.

Theirs was the undisputed claim as the tightest band in

*the lexicon of postmetal cyber-thrash, but they were much
more than that. They were more than a fashion, more than
a credo. They were magic. They were a way of fucking
life.*

When Rod and Alex played, yes.

But especially when Tara sang.

*On the video, she was just beginning her leap to the
kill . . .*

> "I want your body.
> No bones about it.
> Want you to know that
> I can't live without it."

Steve Beeker opened his eyes, caught himself in the
mirror behind the bar. He was pleased to note that he didn't
look nearly as loaded as he felt. The wraparound shades
helped, of course; so did distance from the mirror, and the long
dark locks that fell artfully across his face. At the ripe old age
of seventeen, he was a five-year veteran of the drug abuse
wars. He could handle his shit.

Or hide what he couldn't handle.

Which was more than he could say for some of the
boppers at this party: his adorable hostess, in particular. Cyndi
Wyler careened past his reflection, Eddie propping her up, her
lithe limbs like rubber.

"Barbie Meets Gumby," Eddie muttered, and laughed.
Steve smiled and shook his head. It was true. Like the party,
she was out of control.

Cyndi Wyler was the fifteen-year-old daughter of the doc.
Leaving her alone for the weekend might not have been the
wisest idea. Blond and built like a Nordic pinup goddess, she
was all tits and tan and even, perfect teeth. Had the I.Q. of a
toaster oven. All in all, the most likely candidate for statutory
rape that Steve could imagine.

Especially in the loving hands of Eddie Hansen: The Cock
Without a Conscience. Watching him in action was like watching
a panther toy with its lunch: the outcome was a foregone
conclusion. Steve hoped that they would name one of the
kittens after him.

"Yo, Eddie!" he yelled. Eddie turned. Cyndi did a centrifugal Snap-The-Whip, teetering at the end of her escort's arm. Her blue eyes were blank and shiny bright.

"*Now* what," Eddie droned, his face a death's head picture of gaunt, practiced arrogance. His hair was high and black, trailing down long in the back and shaved to the roots above his temples, in direct tribute to The Screamer look perfected by Rod and Alex. It gave his features a cadaverous appearance, offsetting the coldest smoldering eyes in Diamond Bar High. He turned on one hip, expertly flipping the trailing edge of his black canvas longcoat back over one leather-clad leg. What his garb didn't state outright, his shit-eating grin completed. He was young, vicious, amoral, and genuinely enjoying himself. He was a Screamer to the bone.

"You're not going to sexually abuse that poor girl, are you?"

"Kinda looks that way, don't it?"

"Promishesh, promishesh," elucidated Cyndi. She giggled, lost her balance, and gravity made its move. "Oops!" she added, then landed face-first in Eddie's armpit and giggled some more.

"So long as she knows what she's doing," Steve counseled.

"Look at it this way, dude. Either she'll love it or she won't remember a thing."

"Or *both*!" she cried, then began to howl with laughter. Her arms clung weakly to Eddie's chest. She quivered and quaked. He shrugged. Steve echoed the gesture.

"Better get her to bed, before she throws up"—Steve grinned ruefully as Eddie nodded and turned away, his tootsie in tow—"you miserable shit," Steve concluded, just loud enough to hear. Eddie laughed and headed up the stairs.

The bitch of it was, Eddie really *was* a shit. Not in the twenty-four-hour-a-day sense: he was funny, he was cool, he was gracious with his drugs. It was mostly in the way he treated girls and other perceived inferiors: humor 'em, use 'em, wad 'em up, and chuck 'em.

John Masey came up beside Steve, his bleary gaze following the couple up the stairs. He was dressed in gear almost identical to Steve's or Eddie's or any of the two dozen other Screamers in attendance, but somehow it hung all askew. It was fairly clear that Masey was doomed to trudge through life, perpetually harnessed with the "wrong way" caption to Eddie's "right way," and he damned well knew it.

"Sorta gets to you, doesn't it?" he said, swigging off a Grolsch bottle. "Fucker gets *all* the fine little foxes."

"I like to picture him in thirty years, with a watermelon gut and no hair."

Masey laughed. He was high enough to picture it. "Just a good thing Dempsey's not here. You know how the little creep is about Cyndi."

"Yeah."

Oh, yeah. Steve knew how Perry Dempsey was, alright. He could still clearly see the flicker off the knife's bright blade, even from a three-week distance.

"Why do *you* think he's not here?" Masey asked.

"What do you mean?"

The point of the knife had placed a deep dry dimple in the soft flesh under Beeker's chin and held it there, for what had seemed like a very long time. "Eddie ditched him at the concert. Lost him in the crowd."

Beeker smiled and looked amazed. It was common knowledge to everyone in Diamond Bar that little Perry Dempsey had a man-sized chubby for Cyndi Wyler. "Wow," he said. "What did he tell Cyndi?"

" 'Perry found another ride.' "

Steve laughed. Three weeks ago, he hadn't found it funny at all. *I don't know what I'd do if anybody ever hurt her*, Perry had said in his quivery little voice. Steve had chuckled noncommittally, waiting for him to buzz off.

I might do this.

And the knife came up.

Steve, to his credit, had diffused the weirdness: not reacting at all save to reply ever-so-calmly, *I don't think that would be a very good idea.*

It had worked, somehow. So much for the entertainment value of insane jealousy. The knife had held momentarily, grazing the softly stubbled skin beneath his jawline, as if weighing the wisdom of ploughing upward.

Steve waited.

The knife came down. Perry smiled, looking drunk or drugged or even a little chagrined as he shuffled away. He'd just jumped another notch on his peer group's Dipshit Scale.

"Eddie's one slick sonofabitch, that's for sure," Masey said.

"And Dempsey's one stupid one," Steve replied, remembering the laugh that had accompanied the knife's bloodless slide back into its sheath. Nobody home, one night-light in the basement. Mortimer Snerd *cum* Henry Lee Lucas.

And all of that for one harmless bit of flirting that wasn't even leading anywhere. Sitting on the stairs, three weeks ago, at Deke's house. Playing with her hair a little, kneading the tequila-loose flesh of her shoulders, making only the fuzziest come-ons in naughty-joke form . . . no big deal, right?

Wrong-o, buster. Not if your name was Perry "Psycho" Dempsey, the I-Was-a-Teenage-Norman Bates of Diamond Bar, California. Then it didn't even matter that the girl whose honor you were defending couldn't stand to be around you; it was just full speed ahead, point-first, through the shower curtain . . .

"Well, fuck it," John Masey said, clapping a hand on Steve's shoulder. Steve jolted back to the present. "I'm gonna grab me a brewsky and hit the Jacuzzi."

"Sounds good."

"Fuckin' A."

They slapped skin in the high-five way that had replaced power grips as the funny handshake of its age, and Masey headed for the bar.

Well, that was certainly meaningful, Steve told himself. The loving couple was long gone from view. Perry was probably still wandering around in the coliseum parking lot, waving his knife at the shadows. Unless Mommy and Daddy found him first, that is. If that happened, he'd probably be crucified.

Steve turned to the picture window, looked out. A slate path wound through the center of the backyard. He could see the sauna, the Japanese rock garden, the Jaccuzi and the swimming pool beyond. Again: Dr. Wyler was not lacking in style. It looked like there were some naked young people by the pool. That seemed like his best bet.

It was one o'clock. The night was young.

And getting older by the minute.

* * *

Mary Hatch was the first one to spot the bone-white Cadillac tooling up Ranchero Drive.

She was, at fifteen, tall for her age, and just beginning to fill out. Her breasts would probably never be large, but they were bound to get bigger than the thimbles she sported now. Her hips, on the other hand, seemed motherhood bound: high and wide enough to squeeze out a nine-pounder without even breaking a sweat. Breeder's hips, her mother called 'em, and they ran in the maternal gene pool along with her height and her hair and her green-eyed nearsightedness. Breeder's hips. Thanks, Mom. Looked like shit in a bikini.

But her legs, ahhh . . . Said legs were long and lean, like her upper half; and even though she thought her features too angular and her behind way too wide, she still got hit on enough to be convinced that she was attractive.

Mary Hatch was in the bushes, attempting a technique few women ever truly master: How to Pee Standing Up. She was not enjoying a tremendous amount of success when the Caddy careened into view.

She heard it first, actually; her eyesight was not so terrific, her glasses were down by the side of the pool, and best of all, she was tripping her brains out. But Ranchero was the only well-lit street on the hill; she just followed the distant rumbling until the tiny white blur near the bottom caught her attention.

This part of Diamond Bar tended to be quiet at night, Mary knew. She'd lived three doors up the hill from the Wylers' for the past seven years. Most of the neighbors rolled up their driveways by eleven, all the rest by twelve. That was certainly one reason why she found herself squinting at it.

The rest was somewhat more difficult to peg. But its effect was far more resonant.

The car made her nervous.

Mary glanced back over at the pool, her urinary scribbling forsaken. She couldn't make out any of the naked shapes . . . they were, to her, as formless and fuzzy as cloud formations . . . but seeing them popped an unnerving gestalt impression, full-blown, into her drug-enhanced imagination.

Big shape. Little shapes.

Water. Danger.

Shark. The word went off like a thirty-foot Great White Gong inside her head. *Shark.* She closed her eyes, and the pictures became instantly clearer: pictures of rending flesh and screaming, of dark dark water boiling in the heat of extinguishing life. She watched the pictures for two full seconds. That was more than enough.

She was no longer nervous.

She was scared.

Goose bumps were crawling over most of her all-too naked self. She felt a sudden, strong desire to be tucked, safe and warm, in her own little bed. Undressed, so close to the water, she felt more than vulnerable: she felt like a worm on a hook.

And the car was coming closer.

The last few drops of pee speckled her inner calves and thighs; she'd stopped paying attention. *Great*, said a voice in her mind. *Now you're pissing yourself.* Her irritation was vague, overwhelmed by mounting panic. She was thinking about her clothes, her glasses, and her friends. She was thinking about how far away they seemed, how hard to assemble and escape with. . . .

No, she told herself abruptly, sternly. *This is stupid. You're on drugs. How do you spell paranoia? LSD, and C-O-C-A-I-N-E.* It was the voice of Reason.

It was not at all convincing.

And the car was coming closer.

Mary sidestepped the moisture she'd laid and crept to the edge of the yard. There the hedges were highest, effectively slicing the Wylers off from the Cronenbergs next door. It hadn't been in the scheme of things to surround the place with redwood fence: it would have screwed with the topography, cut off the view down the hill. With territorial rights still a high priority, Dr. Wyler had taken the alternate logical step of surrounding the hedges with an all-but-invisible electric fence, which he sometimes boosted to a genuinely dangerous and highly illegal voltage. She'd seen the effects of it four years ago, when Cyndi's dog Astro had taken a flying, Frisbee-chasing leap into the wire and the Hereafter. Not pretty. She steered clear of it, grabbing safe hedge branches like periscope handles.

Watching the car.

Coming closer.

And closer.

Until details of the vehicle came obliquely into focus: big, white, convertible, with a slew of dark figures jutting up from the seats. She saw these things, as best she could, in the moments before the car reached the Wyler driveway.

Then she glanced at her clothes, her glasses, her friends.

And waited where she was.

In the hedges.

Naked.

Alone.

The bedroom was engaged in a carousel spin, lurching in slow motion through a sea of Cuervo Gold. Cyndi closed her eyes to blot it out, but the darkness was even worse. She was the axis at the center of this merry-go-round, and she wanted very badly to get off.

But she couldn't, because Eddie was holding her down, pinning her body to the designer Cannon sheets of her parents' king-size bed. He was three years older, four inches taller, and the almost fifty pounds he had on her was mostly muscle. He was also not nearly as drunk as she was; chances were good that the room wasn't spinning for him.

These were fairly decisive advantages. He had parlayed them into the removal of her oversized black pig-suede shirt, the hiking of her bright yellow sleeveless T-shirt past her nipples, and the unbuttoning of her peg-leg paisley pants. These were now attempting to slide off her hips, through no effort of her own.

She was starting to figure out, though dimly, that maybe Eddie wasn't the greatest dude in the world, and that he might not have her best interests at heart. He was gorgeous, yes, and most of her friends would gladly lube on command for his attention. But that didn't change the fact that he looked like he was about to ride her, and no mention of contraception had been made.

This wasn't her first time. That wasn't the point.

She was starting to reconsider.

Cyndi looked up. In the dim and swimming light, it was extremely hard to see his face. The fact that he had twelve of them, doing a Ferris wheel spin around her vision's periphery, didn't help. She could see the outline of his spiky black hair, the faint gleam off his wraparound shades, the even fainter gleam of his carnivorous grin. Somehow, it failed to reassure her.

"Eddie," she said. The word came out muffled, tongue-tied by tequila. He ignored it. His attention was on the pants he slid down past her ass, en route to her ankles. His fingers left trails of murky sensation that tingled her naked thighs. Arousal and trepidation mingled: a single schizophrenic, slowly spinning in the fog.

"Eddie." Louder. Still no clearer. Still no good. She started to struggle. He held her.

"Cut it out," he said.

"Eddie, stop."

"Jesus, Cyndi." Less than amused. "Come on. The Mighty Godzilla is waiting for you."

He was on his knees now, sliding up to straddle her almost-naked hips. His fingers went up to the center of his chest, where the zipper to his black jumpsuit began. Over the thudding of the music from below, she heard the gentle ungnashing of metal teeth. "No," she said.

"Yes." The zipper was down to his navel.

"No," she repeated, but it was closer to a whisper. The head of the thing that he called Godzilla had come up for air. It stared at her, cyclopean. The rest followed shortly. There were twelve of it, doing that Ferris wheel spin: a whirling penis bouquet, less than a foot from her mouth.

"Your tongue," he said, "is Tokyo. And the monster is coming."

He aimed and leaned forward.

A screeching of brakes erupted directly outside the window. It might as well have driven a nail into her ass. She was a foot in the air by the time the raucous howling reached her ears. So was Eddie. They let out matching howls of their own. Her forehead, not her tongue, had met the Mighty Godzilla. He fell over backwards. She fell on her back.

"Ow! Ow! *Shit!*" Eddie yelled, cupping the monster's damaged luggage. She considered saying she was sorry, then decided that she wasn't. All that screeching and leaping about had whipped her adrenaline up to a fine fever pitch. The world and her body were still out of control, but her mind cleaved through the murk like a hatchet.

The window was open; its beige curtains danced in the

breeze like suntanned ghosts on a midnight beach. She crawled across the matching sheets to the windowsill, reached the foot and a half across empty space without falling over, caught the sill, hoisted up, and peered over the side.

She didn't recognize the bone-white Cadillac idling outside her front door. Nor, at first, were any of its six passengers familiar: they could have been any of the thirty thousand Scream freaks who'd hit the concert tonight dressed to kill. They could, in fact, have been Eddie.

But they weren't, because Eddie was right behind her, still moaning and holding his nuts. Cyndi struggled with her vision, trying to make the many boil back to one, trying hard to focus. It wasn't easy. The tequila had not gone away.

The words *Who* are *you people?* were halfway out her throat when she realized suddenly that maybe she didn't want to know, not really, not ever.

But by then, of course, it was far too late.

"HEY, CYNDI! HOO, BABY! TONIGHT IS *THE NIGHT!*" The shadow who screamed it was in the backseat, his sunglasses pointed straight up at her face. He looked and sounded vaguely familiar; but the voice had a nasty rasping quality that was utterly *un*familiar, and the face refused to come clear.

"What do you want?" she hollered down.

"I WANT *YOU*, BABY! I WANT YOUR *ASS!! EEYAAOW!*" They all echoed the sentiment. They got out of the car, knives flashing in the moonlight.

That was when she dimly realized that maybe they weren't kidding.

That was when the real party started.

He had no eyes. He didn't need them anymore. They were just two moist relics of his past: always filled up with the bullshit reflections that everybody'd always shined down on him. The wimp. The psycho. The darling baby boy. His holier-than-thou folks'd have him on restriction for the next twenty years if they'd found out that he'd snuck out to hit a Scream concert, and that was all but guaranteed since his so-called fucking friends dumped him there.

He'd caught a glimpse of them, all right. Piling into Eddie's car and laughing, while he fought his way through the riotous, exiting masses. They'd driven off on purpose, laughing. Even Cyndi.

Laughing.

And he'd stood out in the bedlam of overamped kids and cops clashing and bashing it out in the parking lot and fucking cried, for Chrissakes. Just cried, from rage and frustration and the wrath of things beyond his control. Weeping like a little lost lamb.

And that was when the others found him.

It was as if they'd been waiting there all along. Just waiting for him to reach his moment of maximum desperation. He'd stood in the parking lot on the ragged edge of fifteen-year-old doom and watched as the bone-white Caddy slid up. He watched as the door opened, and the long cool hand reached out to take him. . . .

They gave him a ride, but that wasn't all. Not by a long shot. They took a little, yes; but they gave back much, much more. In the backseat, with one cold white hand reaching down to unzip the front of his jeans and another moving up to place sharp white nails on his fluttering lids, they gave. A little bit of pain. A great deal of pleasure.

And the promise of so much more to come . . .

He reached up underneath his shades and touched the still-moist rims of flesh where his baby blues had been. So what if they were history? Fuck 'em. The pain had gone with them, and the loneliness, and that was all very nice. In its place was a new sense of mysterious purpose, a knowledge that everything was indeed running like clockwork, and now he was another happy cog in the Master Plan. Tick tick tick tick.

And as his new friends, his true friends, piled out onto the lawn all around him, he felt a joy and communion and a power the likes of which his short life had never known. He would have what he wanted, both now and forever.

And now was a fine place to start.

Steve was midway into a double gainer—feet over head, spinning backward in midair, the diving board still thrumming behind him—when they came around the side of the house. He caught a microglimpse of shadows under the porch light, moving fast, before the aqua-green underlit water came up to embrace him. It blew his concentration at a critical instant. There wasn't even time to curse.

He hit the water awkwardly, bubbling his frustration. A thin, chlorinated jet rocketed up his nose. He choked and made mad thrashing movements toward the surface. The chlorine-taint burned like a son of a bitch; the pain shifted him into Automatic Panic.

His head broke back up to the air. He coughed, treading water, edging blindly toward the side of the pool. There were noises that confused him. He opened his eyes, but they stung and they couldn't see shit, so he closed them again, putting up with the confusion until the coughing stopped and his hands latched hold of the poolside's cold concrete rib.

And a cold hand latched hold of his hair.

Steve's eyes came open easily then, despite the burning bleariness. The first thing he saw was John Masey, tumbling backward into the pool. Were it not for the blood shooting out of his mouth, he might have been just horsing around.

But the pool was full of screaming people; and when Masey bobbed back up to the surface, he just kept right on bobbing. Steve took a second to digest that before he pivoted on the end of the wrist that held him, turning to see himself darkly reflected in the wafer-thin plastic curve of Perry Dempsey's shades.

Perry was smiling. Steve's reflection was not. Something sharp and shiny and all-too-familiar waved slowly back and forth in the space between their faces.

"Hey, Perry . . ." Steve began. He could feel his flesh goose-bumping. It had nothing to do with the water.

The knife got closer. Perry's smile got broader. His grip on Steve's scalp stayed just the same.

"You'll never make fun of me again, dipshit. Whaddaya think about that?"

The words *I don't think that would be a very good idea* flitted vindictively across Steve's mind, somewhat worse than déjà vu. The point of the knife was getting closer to his throat. Somehow he didn't believe that it was going to stop at the skin this time. He tugged to the left. Perry's grip held.

A shrill, piglike squeal in the same direction made Steve stare wildly out the corners of his eyes. A Screamer he'd never seen before had Betsy Waverly dangling inches above the water. He also had a knife. He was using it to remove Betsy's face. A few more bodies were floating beneath her feet.

This time, when Steve yanked, it was with all the strength in his possession. A handful of long dark locks came loose: the price of freedom. He let out a little triumphant yell as he pushed himself backward, away from the wall.

There was a brilliant flash of silver and aqua-green, brilliantly underlit by the pool. Steve watched it disappear under his chin, felt the snick and tug of it. The pain came a split second later, hot on the heels of the cold steel slice that neatly bisected his Adam's apple.

Then he was up to his nose in the water again, the water that met his new aperture and didn't know which way to go with it. Blood and water shot down to his lungs and spritzed back up his nose, intermingled in the sputtering gash. He tried to scream, got bubbling red and green.

Perry was laughing. Steve wished to God that he couldn't hear it. God didn't appear to be listening. It was the sound that he carried with him as he sank, the sound that greeted him as he surfaced.

And sank. And surfaced. And sank.

And sank.

And sank.

Eddie was pissed when he came down the stairs. His balls hurt, his poontang strategies were blown, and now Perry and a bunch of assholes had crashed the party. The only good news was that it gave him an excuse to hit something. Like a Dempsey, for instance.

There was a lot of noise coming from ol' Dr. Wyler's Wreck Room. The Scream's showpiece tune was building toward its climax, with the chanting and the screaming on the record cranking the speakers way past the blowout point. Then he realized that the damage wasn't confined to the airwaves. Things were actually getting trashed in there. He wondered what kind of rowdy shit the kids were up to now.

The Scream played on; it was the only thing going that didn't piss him off. He paused for a moment, listening to the haunting chorus of the last song on the album, "The Critical Mass" . . .

"When we all come together in blood and bone
In flashing light, in crumbling stone . . ."

"God, this is the shit," he told himself. The music swelled.

"The Father spits on all their fears
The Mother slits the veil of tears . . ."

There was screaming on the album, artfully interwoven with the music, accentuating the black Armageddonal mass that the song was designed to evoke. He could almost see Tara, at the front of the stage, her robe slipping away to reveal more exquisite female flesh than mortal teenage man was ever meant to see, her belly swelling in hideously erotic mock-pregnancy, the gleaming dagger in her hands poised to slide into her navel as the taped voices and the audience chanted . . .

"Magdhim Dios! Satanas Dios!
Asteroth Dios! Ellylldan Dios!"

The bass and drums pounded relentlessly; the voices joined in ecstatically as Tara slid the knife slowly in . . .

"Sancti Dios! Omnitus Dios!
Magisterulus Baalberth Dios!"

It was his concentration on the screams that ripped the vision from his head, brought him back to the living room and the commotion downstairs. He had listened to the album at least a million times.

He was hearing screams . . . real horrorshow screams . . . that weren't on the recording.

Eddie froze; automatically instinct kicked in. Adrenaline chiseled through the drugs and the anger, assumed control. His senses heightened. The dull ache in his nuts oozed up into his vitals. He found himself scoping out every detail of the room, as if it were the most important thing he'd ever seen in his life. Touch assailed. Scent assailed.

Sound assailed.

Somewhere in the house, large expanses of glass exploded: the picture window perhaps, the mirror behind the bar. There was only one way to be sure, and it was entirely out of the question. Thuds and screams and wet tearing sounds came together in terrible, terminal polyrhythms.

People were dying down there. That much was clear. He didn't know who, or how, or why. He wasn't sure that he cared. A curious calm had settled over him, a silencer muffling the report of his fear. The words *YOU CAN STILL GET OUT OF HERE* impressed themselves upon his brain in twenty-four-point banner headlines.

He turned and took a glance down the hallway to the front door. It was open. Curtained oblong windows surrounded it like Roman pillars. He could see split-shots of the Caddy, still idling there. It was his guess that it hadn't been left all alone.

Then he looked at the fireplace.

God only knew what use Dr. Wyler had for a fireplace in California: romance, perhaps, or simple *savoir faire*. Whatever the case, it had all the necessary implements in the stand beside it: poker, tongs, dainty shovel in cast iron and bronze. As he looked at them, the six-inch switchblade in his pocket seemed not nearly long enough.

All he had to do was step fully into view of the Wreck Room stairway, snag the little fuckers, and make his merry way home. By force.

I can't do it, his mind said. *Oh, yes, I can.* Shades of gray argumentativeness erupted between his logic's poles. He needed the weapons; he needed to survive. He was amazed by how succinctly each side of his brain argued its points.

Then the point became moot.

Someone came up the stairs.

It took a moment to recognize Deke Eli, even though they'd been friends since kindergarten. But it was understandable; Deke's face wasn't usually drenched in blood and terror, and his lower lip didn't usually dangle by a thread like a rope of mozzarella in thick red sauce. The moment of unrecognition was a blessing for Eddie; it lent an air of detachment to his perception of the seconds preceding Deke's death.

Eddie stood, frozen, as Deke tripped at the fourth step from the top. The third step caught him at mid-shin, toppled him forward. The top step caught him across the chest, between armpit and nipple. His face slammed into the living room carpet.

He lifted his head. It left a skull-sized splotch. "HELP!" he screamed, his eyes searching Eddie's and finding them, holding them.

Then the Screamer came up the stairs behind Deke. He had one of Dr. Wyler's lovely metal-sculpture lamps raised over his head like a bludgeon, upside-down. For one hysterical moment, it looked as if he were wearing the lampshade on his head.

Then the lamp came down, and Deke's head exploded like a ripe tomato full of brain and bone. It sprayed six feet in every direction, polka-dotting Eddie from forehead to toe. Eddie shrieked. The Screamer howled.

The paralysis shattered. Eddie broke for the fireplace. There was a sofa in the way. He jumped over it, his feet neatly skirting the glass and brass coffee table. The Screamer was not nearly so slick. Both feet went through the glass, from the sound of it, immediately followed by both knees. Eddie sensed this in the moment before his hands closed around the poker's handle. Then he whirled.

The Screamer was framed in the brass and jagged glass. He looked confused. Blood was smeared across his cheeks and chin in a clownish, psychotic oval. Blood covered his gloves. The broken glass had etched fresh gouges in his shins, his thighs, and his biceps, but they didn't appear to be bleeding at all.

Another smell, stronger and richer than the reek of Deke's mashed brains, cut into Eddie's nostrils. A high, sweet smell, of sick things crawling under the porch to die.

Eddie gagged, but his grip on the poker was firm. He brought it back in a Pete Rose stance, his gaze trying to cling steadily to the mirrored black expressionless expanse of the Screamer's sunglasses, as if he could see through to read the intention in the eyes.

"EEYAAOW!" the Screamer howled. Its teeth were black. Its gums were black.

"NO!" Eddie screamed. Even then, he was swinging. The poker made a clean connection with the bridge of the Screamer's nose. The face collapsed inward with alarming ease. The shades, deprived of their center of balance, slid off. Eddie saw what was behind them.

That was when he lost it.

Completely.

"EEYAAOW!" the Screamer persisted, reaching forward.

*   *   *

Perry found Cyndi under some Anne Klein originals on her mommy's closet floor, after everybody else had been dealt their hands. She was dragged out easily. Noisily.

Beautifully.

Then his friends came in, and they held her down on the thick white shag. The music downstairs was still pounding up through the floorboards. The screaming had long since died off. "Gonna be my baby tonight," he said, and then helped himself to a few of the things she would no longer be needing.

Her T-shirt.

Her panties.

Her eyes.

THE JACOB HAMER BAND

Side One

"Musical innovation is full of danger to the State, for when modes of music change, the laws of the State always change with them."
—Plato

"So where's the moral
When people have their
Fingers broken?
To be insulted
By these fascists
Is so degrading;
And it's no game."
—David Bowie

One

THURSDAY, SEPTEMBER 3
NEW YORK CITY

The crowd smelled blood.

Jake Hamer could see it in their eyes, in the subtle flaring of nostrils, in the way they surreptitiously licked at the dry corners of their mouths. It was the high, heady scent of blood just about to spill, simmering in the air beneath the hot stage lights, hanging above the studio audience like a canopy of cannibal musk and expectation.

Thank God, Jake told himself, *this is only a talk show.*

Indeed, today's broadcast of *The Dick Moynihan Show* had a true gladiatorial air about it. People had come to experience a pitched and furious battle—to the death, with any luck— much as the jolly old Romans of yore had hit the coliseums for some viscera and wine. Nobody was armed; at least not visibly. This was lucky for everyone, the Christians in particular.

Though He'd be surprised, Jake continued, somewhat snidely. *His kids are holdin' their own, alrightee. Out of the red sand and into the bleachers.*

Jacob Hamer was no stranger to the arena. You could see it in his dark eyes, which smoldered even when he smiled. You could see it in his barbaric black mane, the ruddy lines of war in his face, the pumped-up muscularity that his Rock-Star-on-Parade garb accentuated. At the age of thirty-three, he had done his share of bleeding: both physical and emotional. Much of the blood had spilled back in early '71, at the tail end of America's adventure in beautiful Southeast Asia; but there had been much since. He had a Purple Heart, a Certificate of Valor, and a platinum album on his wall. He had been a teenage troublemaker, a grunt, and a vet with a dream. Now he was a band leader, a family man, and a spokesman for that dream. The more things changed, the more one thing stayed the same.

He had always been a warrior.

There were five other people on the stage with Jake. One was Pentecostal, one was Fundamentalist, and one was merely Catholic. Jerry, on the other hand, believed in money. Yke (rhymes with *like*) believed in rock 'n' roll.

And I, Jake mused, *believe that it is time to raise some hell*.

That evened the scales, at least in terms of body count: three Christians, three infidels. Nice symmetry for the studio audience and all those millions of viewers at home. *At least no one can say it wasn't a fair fight. . . .*

BAH-DAH DAH *DAH*-DAHHHH . . . The taped theme music swelled. Moynihan stepped into the crowd, which promptly went nuts. It was like the first thunderclap in an electric sky where the storm had been brewing for hours: an awesome sound, a slight release, the knowledge that this was only the beginning.

Dick Moynihan smiled cherubically and just sucked it all in. *He* knew how much power was crackling in this studio, no doubt about it. It was feeding his fire.

Moynihan trod firmly on the trail blazed by Phil Donohue, from the format of his show to the gray of his hair to the roving microphone in his hand. He had just the right combination of boyish charm, wit, intelligence, and good liberal common-manliness to pull this kind of housewife's talk show off in style. Jake had always liked him, found him wonderfully evenhanded. He gave everyone just enough rope without ever quite letting them hang themselves.

But, boy, did he ever love the smell of blood.

The applause was steady and loud. Dick waved his free hand in the air for silence, got it even as his first words eased out through the speakers.

"How many of you," he began, "like to listen to rock music?"

CLAPPITYCLAPPITYCLAP! A vigorous response, unsurprisingly focused in the prorock section of the audience at his far left. He picked out a handful of sympathetic faces—the cute redhead and her smug, lucky bastard of a boyfriend; the bald guy with the enormous handlebar mustache; the executive woman with the bird-of-prey features—and filed their locations away in his mind. *Play to the crowd* was the name of the game. It was a game that he excelled in.

"How many," Moynihan continued, "have *kids* who like to listen to rock music?"

CLAPPITYCLAPPITYCLAPPITYCLAP! Way more than half, this time around, pretty much scattered through the three audience sections. Fewer prorockers seemed to *have* kids than *be* them, but not by all that much. The overwhelming sound came from the middle section: people with kids and no hard, fast opinions.

"And how many of you don't like rock music at all?"

CLAPPITYCLAPPITYCLAP! The prorock forces were just slightly outnumbered by the antirockers, most of whom were gathered in the seats to Jake's right. Awfully crafty of Moynihan to put the speakers and their opposition directly across from each other. Jake noted and filed his adversary of choice, a twitchy little woman in the front row who looked like Aunt Bea from *The Andy Griffith Show*. She looked like she'd be fun to piss off.

"Okay," the talk show host concluded, gesturing again for silence. "I'd like to read you some statistics now, see what you think." He pulled an index card from his pocket, made a subtle issue of scrutinizing it. "It says here that fifty-one percent of our teenagers will have experimented with drugs by the time they're thirteen. Fifty-one percent will be consuming alcohol. Thirty-five percent will be involved in teenage pregnancies, ninety percent of which will wind up as abortions. And thirty-one percent will have attempted suicide by the time they're *fifteen years old*."

Pause for dramatic effect.

"These frightening statistics come to us from Pastor Daniel Furniss, nationally known evangelist and director of Liberty Christian Village, a religious community for teenagers with just the kind of troubles we've mentioned. Pastor Furniss contends that rock music is the *key factor* in the corruption of America's youth.

"Concurring with Pastor Furniss are Joel Wenker, author of *The Knock Rock Handbook*; and Esther Shrake, wife of the esteemed congressman from Vermont and founding member of Morality Over Music. They all feel that rock music must be stopped, before it's too late. And they're prepared to do something about it.

"Pastor Furniss has been making headlines with his Teens for Christ Task Force, which selectively pickets targeted groups, and something he calls the Big Blaze for Jesus, wherein teenagers are invited to bring their rock and roll records, posters, and magazines to Liberty Christian Village every Sunday night, throw them on the big blaze, and hopefully"—Moynihan added just a touch of soft-spoken sarcasm—"see the light." He turned to the audience with a flourish, voice rising.

"And M.O.M. has lobbied to get sweeping restraints in place on record sales, on video broadcasts, and on the airwaves. Congressman Shrake has recently introduced a bill into Congress that would require the rating of albums, much like the rating of films; forbid the sale to minors of albums and concert tickets of acts featuring objectionable references; empower the FCC to ban airplay of any 'adult' material which violates prescribed 'community' standards; and establish a screening board to check music videos for references to sex, violence, drug use, occult practices, or anything that promotes, and I quote"—and Dick raised his eyebrows just a little as he read this—"'disrespect for traditional family-oriented values.'"

He turned toward Esther Shrake, his shoulders shrugging, his face an open question mark. The floor was obviously hers. Mrs. Shrake, a trim, chinless woman with wide blue eyes and neatly tailored hair and suit, cleared her throat. "First of all, Dick," she said, "let me say that this is not a censorship issue."

A titter rose from the heathen element of the audience. Moynihan didn't say anything, though whether this was in agreement or just the playing out of more rope was impossible to say. Esther composed herself and pressed on, enunciating every word as though she were a grade-school teacher driving the point home to a group of particularly slow children.

"We are simply trying to give parents the information they need to make an informed choice! Parents have a right to control the kind of stuff their children are being exposed to. The legislation proposed simply gives them the means to recognize that right."

It was an impassioned appeal, and it drew a mixture of

catcalls and applause from the audience. Jake rolled his eyes dramatically and shook his head in disbelief.

Moynihan turned to address the man three seats to Jake's left. "Pastor, perhaps you'd like to elaborate on that a bit."

"Yes, I would, Dick." Pastor Furniss's rich baritone voice had a hint of hickory-smoked good ol' boy in it, friendly and forceful all at once. He was plump and serge-suited, with a silver-sprayed pompadour and expensive black leather shoes.

"I've got a number of things I'd like to say on the subject, but let me start with this:

"Your kids are in trouble, people. Your families are in trouble. This country's in trouble. And a big part of it is pouring out of your kid's stereo system. When he turns on the latest record by The Slabs or The Scream or Jacob Hamer or what have you, he is leaving himself wide open for a sound that promotes sexual permissiveness, drug abuse, alcoholism, disobedience of parents, rebelliousness, violence, Satan worship, occult practices, abortion, and suicide."

Jake looked over at Yke Dykeburn, the blond-maned giant to his immediate right. Yke was making a goon-face and jabbing his thumb at Furniss as if to say, *Duh, yeah, wut he say.* It would have been difficult not to laugh; and Jake obliged.

"Of course, these gentlemen find it amusing," Furniss continued, unruffled. "They're the ones who are creating the problems, and reaping the benefits. They, and others like them, are directly responsible for the death, debasement, and misery plaguing our youth—"

Boos and applause, in equal frenzied parts, cut him off. He shrugged, grinned, and nodded in a way that dismissed his critics and acknowledged his supporters simultaneously. *You can't say he's not slick*, Jake thought, and then Furniss got another shot in.

"I just pray that America will be strong enough to come to its senses, 'cause we'll be in one heck of a mess if we don't get back on the track, and I do mean pronto." He deferred, then, to the crowd's mixed response and Dick Moynihan's next comment.

"So, on the one hand," Moynihan said, "we've got one group saying that the devil is making our teenagers do it; and whether you believe in the devil or not, you've got to agree that rock music is dangerous in that it promotes destructive and anti-social behavior in our young people.

"And then"—indicating Jake's side of the panel at long last—"we've got these guys over here."

A healthy portion of the audience laughed: for the first time during the show. Moynihan was a master of comedic timing and the subtle release of tension. Even Furniss grinned, giving credit where due. Jake had to do the same, despite the fact that Furniss was the most pernicious rectal grievance in his life at the moment.

"Let's start with Jerry Crane, promoter of the Rock Aid concert being held this Saturday at JFK Stadium in Philadelphia," Moynihan said. Jerry cast a tanned and robust nod to the crowd. He was pushing fifty in style, and it was clear that he knew it; at the same time, the stress he was under was equally clear. "Now, in a generation that has witnessed Band Aid, Live Aid, Farm Aid, Hearing Aid, AIDS Aid, Amnesty Aid, Nature Aid, Space Aid, and even the Florida-based Gator Aid—a benefit to preserve the Everglades from developers—Rock Aid is still something of an anomaly. It is, to the best of my knowledge, the first time that the rock industry has thrown a benefit concert in self-defense. They claim that the proposed legislation is the thin end of the wedge, that it attacks freedom of speech, freedom of the press, the separation of church and state . . ." He let it trail off, hinting that the litany of accusations was nothing new.

"With Mr. Crane are two men whose rock bands will be performing at Rock Aid: Yke Dykeburn, lead singer for the heavy metal group The Slabs, and Jacob Hamer, founder of the aptly named Jacob Hamer Band."

Jake's calculated third of the crowd came through with applause. It was interesting to note that fewer Christians than rockers booed the opposition. He tried to imagine Aunt Bea standing up, raising her fist, and shouting POLITENESS RULES! at the top of her lungs. Somehow, it didn't quite jibe. Maybe that was the difference between the good guys and the bad guys. Or maybe not. Who knew.

"Mr. Hamer," the show host said. "You came to notoriety with your recent hit song, 'TV Ministries.' Not only is it enjoying its seventh week on the Billboard charts, it has also aroused the ire of virtually every evangelical group in the nation."

Jake smiled.

Moynihan smiled back. "We'd like to show a clip from that video, if you don't mind."

"Please do."

There was a pause in the stage monitors, a second or two of video static that the home audience didn't catch . . . and then the last verse of the song kicked in, rock-solid and pumping. Peter Stewart, the Hamer Band's lead guitarist, appeared on the screen in the guise of a gawky and ludicrous nerd, lying on his bed, watching television. His hair was slicked back with sweat and Brylcreem. Enormous horn-rimmed glasses perched on his beaky nose. He was clad in a white pajama shirt, a black pajama tie, black pajama pants, and black and white bunny slippers. A big fuzzy Bible-shaped pillow was clutched to his bosom as he lip-synched to Jake's voice . . .

"I am a sinner,
Yes, I'm lost in sin.
Each night I
Let the holy angels in.
I do exactly
What they want of me;
I give them money
And they set me free."

The nerd scribbles checks furiously and holds them out to the screen as an impossibly long arm reaches out to grab his big fuzzy wallet.

"I have no trouble
When I go to sleep.
I lay me down
The Lord my soul to keep.
I work for Jesus
By the light of day.
We fight abortions
And the E.R.A."

Cut to extreme close-up of Pete, in fish-eye distortion,

stamping big red forbidden symbols on records, tapes, magazine centerfolds, books, newspapers . . .

"They told me
'Blessed are the poor and meek'!
So now I send them
Money every week.
It's so nice
To be e-van-gel-i-cal.
It's been so peaceful
Since they took control!"

Then came the thundering chorus, with the visuals jump-cutting rapidly:

"TEE-VEE MINISTRIES!
TEE-VEE MINISTRIES GOT ME!
TEE-VEE MINISTRIES!"

Cut to the nerd in the straitjacket, clutching his Bible-pillow and howling as he's overwhelmed by a half dozen gorgeous, nearly naked women . . .

"TEE-VEE MINISTRIES!"

Cut to the Jacob Hamer Band in live performance, Jake spinning, guitar in hand, as Hempstead the sax player ground out his lines over Jesse's wall o' synth sound and Bob One and Bob Two thrashed through the beat . . .

"TEE-VEE MINISTRIES GOT ME!"

Cut to a hundred black and white bunny slippers, goose-stepping in unison, then black and white documentary footage of ten thousand lock-stepped Nazi jackboots . . .

"TEE-VEE MINISTRIES!"

And Jimmy Pastor, pounding the pulpit to bring his point home . . .

"MINISTRIES!"

And Adolph Hitler, exhorting the crowd to hysteria . . .

"MINISTRIES, MINISTRIES!"

And brownshirts, burning piles of forbidden books . . .

"MINISTRIES!"

And Pastor Furniss, tossing a pile of records into a blazing pyre . . .

"I think you get the idea," Dick Moynihan said, as the music faded and the screen went blank. He needn't have bothered.

Because the audience was waving its hands and wiggling in its collective seat like an assembly of grade-school kids who all had to pee at once. There was a beehive hum of mutterance, some hoots and hollers from either side of the theological fence. They had gotten the idea, alright; and they all had something to say.

Dick Moynihan moved up the aisle toward the back of the churning throngs. There was no way of saying where he'd stop, who he'd pick, what the chosen would choose to say. All that Jake knew for sure was that the smell of blood in the room was stronger now. Much stronger.

Much closer to the surface.

Let it come, Jake thought. *Let's see your best shot, clowns. I'm ready.*

Dick's mike went down in the next-to-last row. It came up with a steel-eyed matron who looked fit to spit nails. "That was the most insulting thing I've ever seen," she said, staring straight at Jake. "And I'd just like to know who in the world you think you are!"

CLAPPITYCLAPPITYCLAP! Aunt Bea and roughly a hundred other people seemed to agree. Boy, were they pissed. Jake did a spot-check of his people: the redhead and her boyfriend were smiling and shaking their heads; the guy with the mustache was laughing his head off and waving his hand at Dick; the eagle-lady looked as pissed as his opponents. *Good for them,* he thought. *The salt of the earth, the spice of life.*

Then it was time to address the nice lady's statement. The applause was dwindling at last.

"Thank you, thank you," he said, feigning bashfulness. "And I'd especially like to thank *you,* ma'am, for bringing up the word 'insulting,' since I'd put it right at the heart of this debate.

"See, it's like this: everybody's got a different idea as to what they want out of life. Some people like Lawrence Welk, some people like the Dead Kennedys. Some people kiss hot and sloppy, and some people like it with their lips sealed tight. These are largely matters of taste and disposition, from people who have different ways of looking at the world.

"But then you've got your born-again types, and they're a very special group. They've got exclusive dibs on the voice of God, you see. It says so, right in their manual.

"Now, Pastor Furniss and his friends are going to sound very logical and reasonable today, because they're in front of a secular audience. That means us heathen folk.

"But let me just read you this 'Action-Gram' that we intercepted just last week from Liberty Christian Village, and then tell me how reasonable they sound."

Jake glanced over at Furniss as he pulled the letter from an inside jacket pocket and lavishly unfolded it. Furniss was trying hard to conceal his anger and, yes, sudden embarrassment, but it wasn't working all that well. *Ha ha, fucker*, Jake thought, and then began to read in a teary, tremulous voice:

" 'Dear friend of Liberty Christian Village,' " it began. " 'You hold the future of America in your hands. Without a blessed miracle, every teenager in our great land could well find himself facing the roasting fires of Hell!

" 'I'm speaking of the vicious assault on our children's moral fabric that Satan is waging through his insidious Murder Music. We must have a *MILLION-DOLLAR MIRACLE* immediately —or we will lose the fight!' "

The first chuckles began to issue from the prorock crowd. Yke laughed out loud. Pastor Furniss did not.

" 'Satan has hit us like never before since we obeyed God's call to "stand in the gap" for North America's teenagers. Satan has been hurt as we've led the fight against his life-destroying rock music—a fight others have feared. Thousands of teens are finding our blessed Savior through our ministry, and Satan is trying to shut us down before we can reach millions through our TV specials.' "

The laughter was getting louder now. Yke's face was almost as red as Furniss's, for exactly the opposite reason. The furious silence of the Chosen was a palpable, terrible thing.

" 'Please—we must have your help *now*. The guillotine is hanging over our ministry.' " Jake couldn't resist a throat-slitting pantomime. Several unbelievers howled with delight.

" 'Everything hinges on God using *you* to be a part of a million-dollar, ten-day miracle—or Liberty Christian Village, and our entire ministry, will be gone!

" 'We must not lose one precious teenager! God has entrusted us with so many lives! Please help us. Send the largest possible gift you can *TODAY*!' "

"One has to wonder," he concluded, "what kind of massive assault ol' Satan was launching there, and how a million bucks would help; but, Pastor, I'm pleased to see that you survived."

Aunt Bea, the nice lady who'd addressed Jake in the first place, and the other hundred who'd flapped paws against him were unsurprisingly outraged, but there was another hundred or so who seemed to agree with him. The *CLAPPITYCLAPPITYCLAP* of their hands slapping was a source of enormous gratification to Jake as he continued.

"So there you have it, folks: if you disagree with these people, you're not just wrong. You're in league with the devil himself.

"Which brings us back to the word 'insulting.' I think that these pious idiots are the most insulting people I've ever met. They act as if they own morality. They act as if they own God.

"Well, let me tell you something, people. They *don't*. They don't own God, they don't own morality, and they don't own this country. At least not yet. But they will, if we don't start standing up for our rights.

"And I don't know about you, but I don't want to live in the kind of sexless, joyless, brain-dead theme park that they're trying to pawn off as God's will for America!"

That did it. Half the audience broke out in a flurry of ovations. Jake caught flickering glimpses of Moynihan through the craning crowd as the host moved swiftly toward the stage. Dick's face expressed a concentrated excitation, the confidence that he had a winner here, as the creeping theme music went *bah-dah dah dah-dahhhh*, insinuating itself into the dialogue and indicating an impending commercial break.

"OKAY, FOLKS! LET'S ALL JUST CALM DOWN HERE A MINUTE!" Dick's voice boomed through the speakers. He wasn't yelling—there was a lilt in his voice—but the nascent boom of his words plowed through the crowd noise like a strike through tenpins.

Jake panned his gaze back along the semicircular stage seating, locking eyes with Pastor Furniss. Furniss was smiling ever so slightly. Jake nodded. They were opponents of the most severe stripe—they were *adversaries*, with every conflict of flesh and will that the word implied—but they seemed to understand each other like chess players of the very top seed.

They both knew the game. Well enough to understand how very badly they needed each other.

Well enough to understand the next round was only just beginning.

STEWARTSBURG, PENNSYLVANIA

"Oh, la-dies," Pete Stewart insisted through the copy of *Spin* magazine draped over his face. "Let's not get too comfortable, shall we? Break time's almost over, and there's still a half a show left to rehearse."

"Oh, certainly, Mr. Dedication," the Jacob Hamer Band's irascible bass player replied. His real name was Robert Epstein, but everyone called him Bob One. "If we find ourselves slipping," he muttered, "we'll just follow your sterling example." Bob Two, otherwise known as Robert Baker, tapped tedious polyrhythms on every available surface that wasn't his drums.

"Do as I say, not as I do," Pete insisted. "I *am*, after all, de Heap Big Boss Mon 'round heah—"

"Only until Jake gets back," Bob Two sighed, between paradiddles.

"—and I have big plans for Saturday. I think we should

start the set with something special, maybe a nice musical salute to Jim and Tammy Bakker entitled 'She's So Big' . . ."

"Jake!" Bob Two rolled his eyes and called to the ceiling. "Hurry! Please!"

"It's no use," Pete replied. "You're all in me clutches now!" He cackled maniacally, the sound slightly muffled by the magazine.

Pete and his guitar lay sprawled upside-down across the sofa, legs hanging over the back. He wore black and white fuzzy bunny slippers and neon-bright mismatched socks. His baggy black ripstop pantlegs were crossed at the knees. His rainbow suspenders covered a black T-shirt that featured a smiling *Shicklegruber* and the words ADOLF HITLER'S WORLD TOUR 1939-45.

Pete Stewart had two heroes. One was Eddie Van Halen, whose technical virtuosity on the guitar and rampant good cheer onstage were the ongoing inspirations behind his own not inconsiderable style.

The other was the utterly fictional Chris Knight, a character played by an actor named Val Kilmer in the 1985 comedy *Real Genius*. The film promptly died in the theaters and was resuscitated on video, at which point it became Pete's favorite torture device: he insisted that everyone he met watch it with him at least three times, whether they liked it or not. He even looked a little like Val Kilmer: blond, hunkish, with the same winsomely Aryan features that would have been arrogant were it not for the gleam of mischief in his eyes. Pete was a great guitarist and a great showman and was completely out of his mind.

"Oh, Jesse, dear," he said expansively, "whole life forms have evolved and become extinct waiting for you to fix your program. Entire species have gone the way of the wind. . . ."

No response was forthcoming from Jesse's corner. She sat listening to a developing waveform and staring out across the room to the phone table on the far side, near a well-worn Castro convertible that usually lay between her and the main stairs. They'd both been pushed unceremoniously back from their normal positions to free up floor space for more of the rampant techno-sprawl, which clashed against the rough-hewn expanse of the hunting lodge like chrome bumpers on a grizzly bear.

Yeesh, Pete thought. *Better hurry, Jake.*

It was 10:30 A.M., which meant that, barring disaster, their fearless leader would soon be finished playing Joe Public Relations and Doing Lunch and Talking About Important Things, and Slim Jim would be flying his ass back to the mountain.

And not a moment too soon, Pete thought. *Last rehearsal before Rock Aid, and we sound like a goddamned garage band.*

It was true. From a performance standpoint, the last few weeks had swung between half-assed and nothing at all. The band was increasingly uneasy about the growing perception of Jacob Hamer as a one-trick pony, a smart-assed pariah with a trendy cause. It had started out as a good thing, and they had willingly milked it for all it was worth. There was an old saying: *Even bad press is good press, so long as they get your name right.*

And it was true, at first.

The news crews ate it up, of course; especially the local ones. They played heavily on the visual contrast. It made for great TV: the lodge itself, a rustic, rambling turn-of-the-century structure with a spectacular view, peeking out on a southern slope of the Appalachian spine northeast of Harrisburg; the band, riding the crest of the Rock Aid wave, giving the area a claim to fame other than nuclear plant meltdowns.

As stories went, it had all the right elements: national media splash with a scenic local slant. It had good pull. It attracted a lot of attention.

Not all of it favorable, he thought, as the wind shifted slightly and brought a faint trace of the protesters' insipid rally songs wafting up the drive. The lodge itself was not visible from the road and, except for the big stone-and-wrought-iron gate and the sign marked PRIVATE DRIVE, was just another fleeting bit of scenery on Rt. 443.

That is, up until the Moral Majoritroids got wind of it. Now it's practically a mountaintop fortress. A regular citadel of evil, heh heh heh.

And, he thought, *it's under seige. . . .*

That was only one of the irritating side effects of their big hit-fluke, and not the most worrisome at all.

Because worse still was the amount of time that it took Jake away from the band. Pete had been around long enough to know that it could be the critical difference between the #1 slot with a bullet and the cutout bins at K mart. It was clear in the boredom of Bob and Bob, who were beginning to lament having turned down an offer to play with The Del-Rays. It was clear in the lion-in-a-zoo restlessness of Hempstead, the sax player, who was even now roaming the grounds and waiting for them to get their parts together, and in Pete's own increasing reliance on Hawaiian bud, nose candy, and videos for jollies.

But nowhere was it clearer than in Jesse Malloy, who hadn't spoken a nontechnical word all afternoon. It was exceedingly clear that she'd made intimate friends with the end of her rope. There was no talking to her. There was no reaching her at all. She was lost inside her headphones and the sampled waveforms on the synthesizer's computer screen.

Her back was to the rest of them. It seemed broader than usual. *Oh, God,* he thought. *She's even gaining weight.* This was as un-Jesse-like as humanly possible. In the two years he'd known her, she'd never strayed from her picturesque borderline anorexia. It was as if she just *knew* that the next call in would be from *Rolling Stone* or *Playboy,* and they just *needed* her bold, tight little lines for the cover. *O Vanity!* he thought, *where is thy shame?*

Even as he thought the words, Jesse tore the headphones from her ears and slammed them against the rack that held her video monitor.

"Dammit!" she muttered, and the profile she displayed was pale and distracted. Pete smiled winningly.

"Are we having a problem?"

She shot him a glacially cold glance then stormed out of her seat and up the stairs without another syllable. The sound of her door slamming carried all the way down the hall and into Pete's face. It wasn't a general I-want-you-to-be-aloneness; it was a bulletin, aimed right at his head. He could almost see the little picture of himself inside the circle with the slash. NO PETE-ING ZONE.

What did I do this time? he wondered. His relationship with Jesse was a long and convoluted one, full of more than enough ups and downs to go with the ins and outs. It could be anything. It could be his criticism of her string samples in the last song. It could be her period. It could be the fact that he was ten or so behind in the Oral Sex Sweepstakes, according to estimates taken in March. Or maybe all three.

Of course, it's always possible that she might have an actual good reason, he realized. *Maybe I did something I didn't even know I did.* The amount of dope he was smoking these days, it wouldn't surprise him if he were to wake up one morning naked on a straw mat on top of a mountain, with a beard long enough to braid around his lotus-positioned toes.

"This does not look good," Pete said aloud. He flashed a glance at Bob and Bob, finding corroboration there. *Hey, stupid, I wouldn't leave my lover looking that miserable while I lie around with a magazine on my head.*

"Well," Bob One sighed, "what are you waiting for?"

This qualified as incentive. He made a gymnastic leap from prone to upright, put his guitar down, and shrugged.

"Guess we'll be breaking a little longer, after all."

TWO

"Get a load of *those* assholes." Yke jabbed his thumb at the tinted glass of the window on the driver's side. They were stuck at the light for the moment; there was nothing to do but watch.

Across the median strip, on the west side of Broadway and Sixty-sixth, some fifty protesters were shouting and waving signs out front of Tower Records. It was a sight that he was getting used to.

Jake groaned. Jerry moaned. Yke laughed and took a swig off his Amstel Light. His feet were resting on the limousine bar, all 6'4" of him luxuriously sprawled. Jerry Crane Productions was footing the bill for their afternoon wheels, as well as the postdebacle lunch uptown. Yke loved limos, and they were twice the fun when somebody else was forking over the green.

"So they're really camping out in front of your place?" Jerry asked from his place on the passenger side.

"Every day and night," Jake replied wearily. "From seven A.M. to midnight, without fail. Furniss's got his kiddies whipped up into a tizzy, so we can count on anywhere from a dozen to a hundred of 'em outside the gate at any given time."

"Have you thought about calling the cops?"

"Yeah . . ." Jake let the word drag out lackadaisically, donning a wistful little grin. "But, see, it's rained every day for the last week, too. . . ."

Jerry laughed. Yke wasn't really paying attention. He was reading the signs on the picket line and checking for cute young feminine asses. The cute asses were few, but the signs were many. He took another swig and then proceeded to read them aloud.

" 'Jesus Saves! Rock Enslaves!' " he asserted. " 'Sex and Drugs and Rock and Roll Will Damn Your Own Immortal Soul!' " He turned to his fellow passengers and improvised a nifty one on the spot. "Knock Rock! Knock Rock! Jesus Never Had a Cock!"

"The man's insane." Jake laughed. Jerry groaned and rolled his eyes, as though that were the end of it. Not true. Yke was inspired now. His feet swung off the bar and hit the floor, the rest of his body in close pursuit. He had opened the sun roof and stood, poking out through the hole, before the others could so much as grab his legs.

"KNOCK ROCK! KNOCK ROCK! JESUS NEVER HAD A COCK!" Yke screamed at the top of his considerable lungs, hand cupped around his mouth to project the sound straight at the protesters' heads. Several of them turned and gaped.

"FUCK YOU PEOPLE! EAT MY SOCK!" Yke elaborated, flipping them the bird with either hand.

The light turned green. The limo started to roll. So did a small handful of the faithful, who broke away from the mob and started to follow the limo up the opposite side of the street. Evidently they had recognized him. The weed of crime bears bitter fruit.

"THAT'S RIGHT, DIPSHITS! TAKE A WALK!" he concluded, and then they finally managed to drag him back into the car.

"Yke, why did you have to do that?" Jerry looked suddenly dyspeptic, like someone who'd just noticed the green complexion of the hot dog he was eating.

"I'm havin' some fun with the doughwads, man. I think they're fuckin' adorable."

"Well, that's really nice, Yke. Unfortunately, we're only two blocks from the restaurant."

"Oh." This was news.

"This is really what my ulcer needs right now: a side order of screaming assholes," Jerry continued. "Thanks, guys."

"Sorry." Yke, only marginally embarrassed, turned to look out the window again. Four sign-bearing young sphincteroids were pacing them determinedly up Broadway, a textbook case of dogged pursuit. Twice that number were just starting to follow behind. One of the front-runners was an athletic little teenage fellow . . . the Great White Hope, all blond and blue . . . who looked just clever enough to have invented the legend he bore: NO ROCK STAR EVER DIED FOR YOUR SINS. If traffic didn't pick up and let the limo gain some ground, it was a legend that stood to invalidate itself in the very near future.

"Why don't we just take a little detour?" Jake asked the driver directly. "Wouldn't take five minutes."

"Sounds cool to me." The driver said. He was a would-be Tom Selleck with an easy California smile that belied his New York pallor. "Mr. Crane? Take a right at the corner?"

"Alright." It was a sour concession. "If it'll get them off our tails for a minute, fine."

"They're history." The driver wheeled rapidly to the right in front of a Korean cabbie who brake-slammed, grimaced, and leaned heavily on his horn. It was only then that they saw the tail end of the truck poking out of Sixty-fifth Street.

"My heart," Jerry moaned, and he looked as if he meant it. Judging from his skin tone, that half-eaten hot dog was getting greener by the minute.

"It'll be okay," Jake said. The limo was barely squeezing through the yellow light to jut out in the intersection. The front-runners were crossing Broadway, closing in. "We didn't come here to get chewed up by these pissants."

Jake's face looked passionately chill in that moment; it was easy to see the soldier behind the star. "Look at 'em, Jerry. Soft little American kids. Their idea of pain is being denied a second helping of Count Chocula. We're supposed to get palpitations over *them*?

"Come on. At worst they'll be a pain in the ass for the poor people who run the restaurant."

"I eat little fuckers like them for between-meal snacks," Yke added, rallying to the cause.

Jerry shrugged, unmollified, and started sickly scanning the sidewalk for gossip columnists and photographers. Jake turned to look at Yke with a shrug of his own and said, "Here come the lil' darlin's. Should we be nice to Jerry and not kill them?"

Yke grinned. "Won't be easy."

"He's buying lunch."

"I'll make nicey-nice."

"Me, too," Jake said, and then the first protester thudded against the side of the car.

Yke's response was instantaneous. He unlocked and threw open the door in a second, knocking the impactor back and away. The other three front-runners were just converging; their sudden startledness was amusing as all get-out.

"Can I help you?" Yke said, stepping out and up to his full height. Jake stepped silently out behind. The tallest of the protesters was about Jake's height, which meant that he came up to about Yke's chin.

Yke was pleased at the shock effect. It had always been that way for him: even back before there was an Yke Dykeburn, before the fourteen years of shameless hustling in bar bands and women's underwear it had taken for The Slabs to make it big. Back when it was just Vinnie Spaglioni on the streets of Brooklyn Heights, it had been the same deal: little dweebs rising up in packs to smite him, falling back in droves when they realized just how large he actually was.

It was, as always, an extreme pleasure to watch their courage fizzle as they started to back away. Up close, with their little tails suddenly between their legs, they were just homely enough to be paper-trained. He told them so.

"Yeah, well, you can call us anything you want, mister—" the Great White Hope began.

"Oh, really? Great!" Yke cut in.

"—but you're the one who's going to Hell, not us!" the kid concluded. Yke was impressed by the teenage conviction, the firm set of his lips between those chubby little cheeks. He had balls, you had to give him that, even with his face flushed and his voice piping up toward *castrato* range.

"You're gonna burn in Hell for all eternity!" added one of his compatriots, a spotty-faced geek whose eyes bulged with the effort of the words.

"You hang out with this guy?" Yke asked the Great White Hope incredulously.

A crowd was starting to gather on Broadway, and traffic was nowhere close to moving. Eight more of the godly were making their way across the street and toward them. That would make it twelve to two. Twenty more, and Yke might start to worry.

"When the Lord comes back, you'll be sorry!" yelled the guy who first slammed into the limo. He was the one who was as tall as Jake, and he appeared to be their leader. His jet black bangs hung nearly into his eyes, and they were sweated to his forehead as he proclaimed: " 'For none shall enter the Kingdom except through Me—' "

"Who, *you*?" Jake cut in, stepping to Yke's side and immediately in front of Fearless Leader.

"No, *Jesus!*"

"So what have *you* got to do with it?" Jake demanded.

This was a trick question, evidently. By the time the kid thought of a comeback, the limo's horn began to sound and traffic began to move.

"Oh, well," Yke said. "Better luck next life."

"So what is it," Jake asked, a bite-sized forkful of swordfish steak dangling inches from his lips, "that you don't understand?"

"I'm thinking," Jerry said as he idly poked at his spinach salad. The wrinkled green seemed to leave him uninspired. "I just want to phrase this properly."

"Man, I got some suggestions for that, if you wanna hear 'em," Yke added, a mouthful of filet mignon barely impeding the syllables.

"Look," Jake persisted. "We're here to promote Rock Aid, right?"

Jerry nodded sourly.

"And the whole function of the gig is to kick their propaganda machine in the nuts, yes?"

"Wait a minute," Jerry cut in. "I don't want you putting words in my mouth, okay? As far as I'm concerned, that is *not* the function of Rock Aid."

"Then what is?" Jake's chunk of swordfish hovered rapierlike in the air between.

"Rock Aid," Jerry said very deliberately, his own fork brandished, "is a fund-raising enterprise, to provide assistance for bands who are currently under legal assault, and to subsidize the prorock lobby in Washington."

"It's also a consciousness-raising enterprise, am I right?"

Jerry rolled his eyes. This was where the real problem lay, alrightee.

"You've called it a consciousness-raising program from the beginning, Jerry."

"Well, yes, but—"

"Well, so let's raise some fucking *consciousness*, dammit!" Jake slammed his spare fist on the table for emphasis. "Let's talk about where the problem really is! We're not just talking about a series of random attacks on rock 'n roll; we're talking about a calculated assault on our freedom as American citizens, our just plain freedom as human beings!"

"Now, listen—"

"No, *you* listen!" Jake was not about to be stopped. "All my life I've been hearing these people piss and moan. I've listened to them tell me what was right and what was wrong, what I could think about and what I couldn't, which pieces of my anatomy were okay and which ones were filthy in the sight of God. And I had it pounded into me to the point where I started doing some thinking of my own."

"Amen," Yke contributed, through another mouthful of meat.

"And what I came up with," Jake continued, "was that I *do* believe in certain things. I *do* believe in a universal intelligence that underlies all things. I believe in infinity. I believe in love. I even believe in good and evil.

"But I don't believe *those* fuckers for a goddamn second, and you know why? Because they're weasels. They're scared to death of their own bodies, they're scared to death of their own desires, they're absolutely *terrified* by the prospect of thinking for themselves; and so they've copped themselves a nice little belief system that they can hide behind when things get rough.

"And they *lie*, man! They lie their asses off! I mean, look at some of the statistics these guys trotted out today: 'Three point five million disappearing children,' they say, when the FBI only chalked up a grand total of sixty-eight for the whole year! Come on. Is this garbage or what?"

Jerry had gone back to toying with his spinach salad. His head shook sadly back and forth, awaiting its chance to respond.

"I know you've heard all this before, Jerry. I'm sorry to have to bring it up again. It's just that I've been waiting my whole life for the chance to nail these suckers right where they live. And now it's not only a joy unbounded, it's also critically important. We *have* to raise hell, man! It's our sacred duty. It's a moral imperative."

"See, that's the whole problem," Jerry said. "You're right. It *is* important. And that's why it's so important that we don't come off like foaming maniacs—"

"RARRRR!" Yke snarled, leaning suddenly forward and dipping his chin into the full head of his beer mug. He came up looking rabid. "RARRRR!" he repeated emphatically, suds oozing down his chin.

Jerry looked pained and embarrassed. So did Jake, but at least he was enjoying it.

"Oh, Jerry," Yke said, shaking his head sadly as he wiped off his froth. "Jerry, Jerry, Jerry. You're missing the point, man. Of *course* rock is flamboyant, and excessive, and insane. People would be real disappointed in us if we *weren't* crazy, you know it?

"And besides, that's the one thing we really have in common with these bozos. I mean, the only things weirder than rock 'n rollers are TV evangelists and professional wrestling. We're the only ones qualified to fight 'em, 'cause we're the only ones whacked enough to get in the ring in the first place."

"And we *are* being good," Jake added. "Not once on the whole show did Yke or I call Furniss a larcenous sheep-fucker, which is exactly what he is. I think that shows admirable restraint."

Even Jerry laughed, albeit ruefully. Jake finally took the bite of long-suffering swordfish, as if to rest his case.

"Yes, I know," Jerry said. "And don't think I don't appreciate it." He leaned forward, speaking softly, confessionally. "I'm sort of a lunatic myself, you know; I have to be, working with nuts like you."

"Thanks," Yke said. "You're a sweetheart. I love you."

"No, honest to God," Jerry continued, undaunted. "There's a part of me that cheers every time you tear into 'em. Don't get me wrong. The old radical in me loves it. Sometimes I hate him for it, but it's true.

"The problem is, guys, that the old radical isn't the one who's producing and promoting this gig. He's not the one who's responsible for the seventeen million dollars involved. The producer and promoter is the guy who's turning green in front of you, while his brand-new ulcer gnaws away at his old one and his heart wonders if now might not just be the time to seize up forever. He's not having as much fun as the old radical; but then, he can't afford to. You see what I'm saying?"

Jake and Yke sighed in unison. "What, exactly," Jake asked, "are you afraid of?"

"To tell you the truth?"

"That would be nice."

"Violence," Jerry said, the word blunt and emphatic. "I'm afraid that if enough people get pissed off enough, we won't have a concert: we'll have a battleground."

"Oh, man," Yke cut in, mildly exasperated. "What're you talkin' about? The heavenly host, goose-steppin' down the aisles? That ain't gonna happen." He looked at Jake for confirmation of that simple fact, not entirely sure that he got it. Jake looked real sober all of a sudden, too.

"I don't know," Jerry said. "All I know is that I've been having very bad dreams lately, and they all involve this hideous monster called Your Liability Insurance Has Just Been Revoked. It makes King Kong look like Mr. Rogers, I'll tell you that. And it makes Rock Aid look like Custer's last stand."

"Who," Jake said, "are you afraid of? Exactly?"

Jerry said nothing.

"Who are you more afraid of: the born-agains or the rockers?"

Jerry gave it a minute of thought.

"Yes," he said at last, "that is the question."

"Hey, Jerr," Yke said. "Don't be such a wimp. We're not the ones you ought to be worried about."

"How so?" Jerry cocked an eyebrow as he spoke.

"What I mean is, the worst thing you can accuse ol' Jake here of is being a smartass and standin' up for truth, justice, and the American way. The worst thing you can accuse me of is pointing out that authority sucks."

"And wearing women's underwear," Jake added.

"If I were you, man, I'd be lookin' at people like The Scream. That's where the real danger is."

Jerry's mouth opened, closed. Something inside him, already propped up tenuously, sagged a little more. Yke had hit the mark, all right; it wasn't pretty, but it had the advantage of being true.

Because rock music had always been a target, born with a bull's-eye on it. It was confrontational by nature. It was music to get laid by, to take drugs by, to dance to, and question authority by. It demanded your body, your heart, and your soul. It was born to piss parents off.

And that was, to Yke's way of thinking, an extremely positive thing.

But The Scream were a different story entirely.

"What do you know about them, man?" Jake asked.

"About as much as anyone," Yke replied. "Which means hardly anything at all. I mean, nobody even knows what their real names are! Tara Payne? Rod and Alex Royale? Oh, sure!

"And that's just the beginning.

"I mean, we spent six weeks on the road with them; and in all that time, I never exchanged so much as a howdy-do with anybody in the band. The only time you ever saw 'em was on their way to the stage, on their way back from it, or on their way in or out of the limo."

"Friendly people." Jake laughed.

"Fuckin' *weird* people, if the truth be known." Yke rolled his eyes and made an uncharacteristically sour face, remembering. "It wasn't just that they were private. It was more like you were watching a secret society, you know? Like they were up to something heavy, and they'd have to sacrifice you to Kali if you found out too much or something.

"And that's just it." He leaned forward, strangely adrenalated by the topic. "They were *scary*. You know the kind of shit they sing about—demon worship, sacrifices, fucking the devil, and all that crap?

"Well, I've seen a lot of metal bands. They're my contemporaries, right? And a lot of them bring that shit into their shows. But when you're watching it, you know it's an act. It's like watching Vincent Price on the late late show. You know, sinister laughter and all that." He let out a wide-eyed BLOOO-HAH-HAH-HAH! that made the waitress look over and Jerry wince, then continued.

"But The Scream are different, man. You get the feeling that *they really believe it*.

"And anyone who really believes in that shit is not well in the head.

"They're twisted."

"What about Tara?" Jake asked, unable to restrain a sophomoric leer.

"Oh, Jesus, she's a case," Yke went on. "Have you ever seen her act?"

"Just some pictures and videos."

"I've seen her," Jerry cut in. He was leering, too, albeit sickly.

"Well, anything you've ever heard about her is true," Yke said. "She could give a dead man a boner just by walking past the graveyard."

Everybody laughed, but that wasn't the end of it.

"I'm serious!"

"We believe you."

"Yeah, but it's *scary*." Yke made a point of emphasizing the word. "It really is. Because it's not a healthy thing. It's almost supernatural, you know?

"I mean, being on the road with that chick was the weirdest six weeks of my life, without a doubt. But I couldn't get anywheres *near* her; and I'm not so sure I'm sorry. There's something really truly *dangerous* about her. Like a fucking black widow. You know what I mean?"

"They eat their mates."

"Yeah. Exactly. Like, if I let her blow me, I'd count the inches as they came out of her mouth, just to make sure they were all there.

"But if she offered to, there's no way in hell I'd be able to refuse her, even thinking what I think. If she wanted me, I'd be hers, and she could do whatever the fuck she wanted."

"That *is* scary, now that you mention it," Jake said.

"You're goddamn right," Yke asserted. "And the worst

thing was the effect that it had on the kids. I mean, we had fucking *riots* sometimes: all these sexually frustrated fifteen-year-old dudes going nuts on each other, and you just *knew* it was because of that chick and that group."

"And, of course," Jerry moaned, "some asshole had to line them up for Rock Aid."

"Which asshole was that?" Yke inquired, slowly grinning.

"It wasn't me, I guarantee you. If it was up to me, they wouldn't even be able to get a deal. They do, they honestly *do* scare me. I don't trust them at all. They give the industry a bad name. They're like the Khmer Rouge of rock and roll."

The conversation paused, uneasily. Yke and Jerry looked at each other, as if to confirm where the vibes had taken them.

Then they looked at Jake.

He did not look good at all.

"Jake?" Jerry said, and Jake snapped back from the abyss into which he had been staring. "What is it? You look bad."

Which was true. Jake had picked up a little pallor to go with his grim expression. Yke expended a good second thinking about it before Jake spoke.

"I was just thinking about the Khmer Rouge."

"The who?" Yke asked.

"The Khmer Rouge." He blinked, as if kicking an image back into his head, then swept an articulate gaze from Jerry to Yke. "A guy named Pol Pot led them through Cambodia, round about the time that Saigon fell. They declared Year Zero, the new beginning of time. And then they implemented a purge that was pure slaughter.

"We don't even know how many people they killed, but we're talking easy seven-figure genocide. Couple of million people got stabbed, shot, gutted, clubbed, or starved to death in less than a year."

"That's a charming story," Yke said. "But what's the point?"

"I was just thinking"—Jake stared straight in Yke's eyes—"that the average age of the Khmer Rouge was fourteen. It was an army of teenagers, man. Fucking kids.

"And the deadliest army you'd ever hope to see. . . ."

Los Angeles, California. A long-standing gang war erupts at a concert held by a thrash-metal band called

Suburbicide. Seven die. Twelve more are hospitalized. It is the worst in a long chain of L.A. concert riots that have killed eighteen and injured hundreds so far this summer.

Passaic, New Jersey. The naked, mutilated body of fifteen-year-old Cheryl Davis is found in a vacant lot near her home. She has been stabbed over thirty times. Authorities arrest five members of the "Satanic coven" to which she had belonged. They confess to the killing and to a slew of animal sacrifices, as "blood gifts for Satan." They also admit to the use of PCP and "lots of loud heavy metal" in their rituals. All are between the ages of fifteen and seventeen.

Lawrence, Kansas. Sixteen-year-old Denise May Smith bludgeons her stepmother to death after being forbidden to attend a Scream concert in Kansas City.

Milwaukee, Wisconsin. Thirteen-year-old Scott Wizotski sticks the barrel of his father's .45 into the mouth of schoolmate Thomas Granger, also thirteen, and blows off the back of Granger's head. Wizotski claims that Granger stole $130 worth of crack and over a dozen albums from him at a recent party and refused to give them back.

Diamond Bar, California. Fifteen teenagers are brutally murdered at a party at the home of Dr. Lawrence Wyler. Dr. Wyler's daughter, Cyndi, who is believed to have thrown the party in her parents' absence, is not found among the victims. . . .

The tip of the paintbrush dipped daintily into the burnt orange on the palette, came up with a fleck of color, and dabbed it onto the flaming circle taking final shape below. It augmented the billowing black outlines, the brilliant smoky red at the core, lending stormy nightmare texture to the holocaust image.

"This," Chris Konopliski said, "is pure genius, man. I hope you appreciate that."

"I'd appreciate it even more," Ted replied, "if you'd let me see the goddamn thing."

"Nuh-uh. Not till it's done. Bad juju." Chris dabbed more orange onto the cloud: refractions of light, making it reflect more of the sky surrounding it. "Why don't you just roll another joint and get off my back?"

"Because I wanna see this masterpiece."

"Not good enough."

"Because I can't roll for shit, and you know it."

"Better. But still no excuse for laziness."

"Because I'm not apt to magically become a better joint-roller than you are in the next sixty seconds, no matter how hard I try. Because I want to see what you're doing to my damn jacket. And because I'll kick your farm boy ass. How's that for three good reasons?"

Chris yawned theatrically.

The needle on the Sansui belt-drive had just dragged its way through the last of the latest from The Slabs, fevered metal ax-grinding and drum-barrage giving way to the dull rumble that signaled the end of the album. It was three-thirty in the afternoon on the last Thursday before the meat grinder known as public school resumed for another agonizing year. Outside, it was raining again, hard enough to steam the windows and make an ephemeral gray-green mosaic of the trees outside. Nice day for a funeral.

Nice day, Ted thought, *to stay inside and get stoned.*

It was a good room to stay inside and get stoned in, as well. Ted had made it his own, stuffed it with the accoutrements to his teenage wild life. Posters of rock bands, movie monsters and scantily-clad women smothered the walls. Stacks of albums, comics and *Fangoria* magazines covered the floor. Lunatic doodads were everywhere: Japanese robots, Don Post masks, Ooze-Its, Ick-Men, Head-Popping Action Figures, fart machines, eyeball glasses, chattering teeth, Garbage Pail Kids, and Flesh-Colored Muscular He-Men of the Universe. If it was weird, stupid or potentially disturbing, he had three of it.

It was more than a behavioral problem.

It was a way of life.

Ted Adams-Hamer was a tall, skinny sixteen-year-old,

with long dark curly hair shaved down to sidewalls an inch above the ears, and with a coppery skin tone all around that had little to do with the sun. In the gene war between his mother and the father he'd never met, the Invisible Dad had won by a clear margin. Ted looked more like Jake than he did like Mom; and he and Jake were only related by common-law marriage.

But that was enough to scuttle me down to this godforsaken pisshole, Ted noted glumly. This was not an original thought. He bitched about it every time things got boring, or gloomy, or drearily hot or cold or wet, for well over a year now.

Ever since, in fact, the moment Jake and Mom sealed his fate that night at the ironically named Old Homestead Steak House on Ninth Avenue, on the upper lip of the meat district in good ol' NYC. . . .

"Hey," he'd said, dropping his fork onto his plate. The biggest, best filet mignon he'd ever tasted lay before him. Too bad his goddamn appetite was gone; the flavor of bile overwhelmed it. "Thanks a lot, man," he continued. "I'm really glad you guys bothered to ask me first."

"We're asking you now—"

"You're not asking me anything, Mom!" He slammed his fist on the table, once, hard, making the silverware bounce and spilling a dollop of Coke Classic onto the white tablecloth. "You're telling me!"

"Come on, honey—"

"No, he's right," Jake cut in. "It sucks, but he's right." Then to Ted he said, "We have pretty much made up our minds."

"Well, that's just great!" Ted stormed. "It's good to be a real contributing member of the decision-making process! 'Hey, Ted! Guess what! You're gonna have a little baby somethin'-or-other!' 'Hey, Ted! Guess what! We're packing you off to Pennsylvania!' "

"Oh, lord," Mom lamented, her own steak looking lonesome now.

But Big Bad Jake was strong; and evidently, Ted had just hit a nerve. "Listen," he said. "I know how you feel—"

"Oh, do you, now!"

"Yes, I do. You're not the first person in this world who was ever packed off to someplace he didn't want to go. If I were you, I'd be ticked off too. It's not fair. And we should

*have talked to you earlier. But I'll tell you right now, sport,
life gets like that sometimes. You know?"*

Ted was incredulous. Rage had made a bug-eyed rictus
of his face. He stared down at the fist that had lingered
at the end of his right arm, tried his damnedest not to cry.
He managed to stop the tears. But there was no way to
stop the words. *"Well, that's real fuckin' easy for you to say,
isn't it?"*

"TED!" Mom cried. She was not a big fan of foul language, and she was pretty torqued out by the whole scene
already. Somehow, that made him feel better. Share the pain.

"No, it isn't." Jake stared straight into Ted's eyes. *"Not
at all, man. Not at all. This whole thing is jerking me
around, too. If it was just me, things would be a whole lot
simpler. Believe it. But it isn't just me anymore, or you, or
your mother. It's all of us."*

Jake had then proceeded, in excruciating detail, to describe just why they all had to move to the armpit of the
universe. The litany was impressive: money, privacy, space,
consolidation, money, fresh air, nature, money, true love,
safety, the end of struggle, money, the future, the baby,
money, his career, the band, the family, and money.

"Besides," Mom said gingerly, *"you're always complaining about how much you hate your room, the lack of privacy, the lack of space, the crowds . . ."*

And Rachel began to do her Mom-thing, dredging up
every petty crank and bitch of big-city life that Ted had
ever mouthed off about. She was good at this; raising Ted
had long been the focal point of her life, and when she
needed to he swore she could remember every lunch she'd
packed for him since first grade. It made him wish he'd
kept his mouth shut more often.

And he hated to admit it, but an eensy-weensy part of
him had been thinking that maybe it wouldn't be the End of
Life as He Knew It to bug out of the big city at this tender
age.

Because the bottom line was that Ted was no fool, and
Ted knew that the crowd he ran with was by and large
destined to do hard time. Jimmy was stabbed in the bathroom at school just last Tuesday, Jules was busted, Elmo
and Carl had been packed off to Rikers Island for some bullshit joyride through Queens that the cops called grand theft
auto and which he had come this close to being in on, and

he was beginning to feel a little like one of the faceless drones in Pink Floyd's "The Wall," marching lock-step down the conveyor belt, then face-first into the meat grinder. . . .

Ted looked across the table at Mom and Jake, who were trying so hard to make nice. Hell, maybe having Jake as a surrogate father-type wouldn't be so bad. Mom would be happier. He was light-years past any of the other guys she had brought home over the years, most of whom were real dicks. He was famous; and that meant free records and free concert tickets and hobnobbing with Robin Leach and stuff. Maybe Ted could pick up some farm girls in fame's afterglow. Maybe he'd get laid more often. And they'd have a lot more money on Jake's meal ticket.

And besides, they looked so guilty. . . .

He'd sat there, wearing a mask of sullen silence that was more stubbornness than artifice, until Mom had said the magic words. "Honey, c'mon. Don't you think you'll like having a whole mountain in Pennsylvania?"

He had smiled then, begrudgingly sly.

"I'd like it better on a motorcycle."

There was, at this moment, a big black Harley down in the garage. Hell of a guy, that Jake. Mom, too. They were a peach of a pair. Two best slave drivers you could ever hope to meet. And generous, too. The Harley was beautiful, and a dream to ride.

But he wasn't quite sure if it made up for the indignities of exile in Cowtown.

Especially given the people he had to work with.

"Oh, come on, man," Ted bitched. "Don't be an asshole. Let me see it."

"Okay, okay." Chris sighed and set down his paintbrush. "But only because you're such a little weenie and I need to get stoned. Throw me the smoke."

Ted took the rolled-up baggie out of his back pocket and tossed it onto the bed, then moved to Chris's side. The artwork in progress on the back of his jean jacket lay before him, unveiled at last.

"Oh, wow," he said. "That's really beautiful stuff, man. Sincerely. You're an artist."

"Oh, wow," Chris mocked him. "As if I didn't know that."

But that was just the kind of guy Chris was.

* * *

Ted had met Chris on his first day at Northern Lebanon High, just five days short of a year ago. It had been a day just like this one in fact, capping off a miserable Memorial Day weekend; in the thirty-second run from the car to the door, Ted's clothes had adhered completely to his skin. He found himself cold, wet, disoriented, and nervous as hell. Life had never sucked quite so badly.

The hallowed halls of Northern Lebanon didn't help. Everybody was so goddamn straight there. Compared to the New York City schools, it was like fucking Pippi Longstocking High. Droves of clean-cut boys and girls roved past, eyeing him with frank disdain even though he was downright conservatively dressed by his own standards: clean straight-leg jeans and two-tone gray denim jacket, white shirt, the boots without the chains. He'd even forgone the silver skull earring, opting for a simple dot of gold.

No dice. For the first time he caught a whiff of what it might be like to be a black dude surrounded by whites who ask, "So, hey, how's it feel to be a nigger?"

And then, in the depths of his despair, an apparition had rounded the corner to appear before him: a beefy guy with scraggly brown hair in a black leather jacket and mangled jeans, being led down the hall by a pair of Joe Fridays in suits. He didn't appear to be struggling . . . in fact he was grinning . . . but they had him by either arm anyway.

"Had to start the year out right, didn't you, Konopliski?" said the Joe Friday on the right.

"Yes, sir, Mr. Smith," the kid replied. "Nothin' like a gestapo escort to get my motor runnin'."

"Shut up," said the Joe Friday on the left with an unfriendly jostle.

Ted had frozen fast in the corridor, watching the procession, which was almost upon him. He was surprised to find himself locking eyeballs with the happy captive: a gaze momentarily broken for a wicked little wink.

"I must be the luckiest boy in the world," the kid said in a passable Pee Wee Herman imitation. "First day of my tenth-grade year, and already I got two dates for the senior prom!"

Ted laughed. Joe Fridays One and Two cast a quartet of baleful eyes toward him. "Cutest girls in the school, too," the prisoner incanted, and then they were past him, reced-

ing down the hall. But there was no mistaking the instant camaraderie that their introductory gaze had signaled.

Later that day Ted discovered the nature of the heinous crime that had sent Chris Konopliski perforce to the principal's office. When Chris's homeroom teacher, a wretched old bat named Miss Renquist, had inquired as to the scholastic appropriateness of his black leather jacket, he had said, *"Why, I'm just modeling the new Miss Renquist line of lingerie."*

It was nice to have found a friend.

Ted studied the painting on the back panel of his jacket. It was a staggeringly good reproduction of the Scream album cover. The superimposed images of the band in the foreground, semitransparent and shimmering. The tortured sky. The burning lake.

Best of all was the mouth, subtle but unmistakable, that spanned the length of the sky.

Its subtle, unmistakable smile.

God, he's talented, Ted told himself. No way he was gonna say it out loud again, but lordy, weren't it the troof. In New York or California . . . in any halfway civilized place . . . Chris would be rakin' in the bucks with a talent like that.

But here, way out in West Buttfuck, nobody gave a shit. It was like the whole town had already decided that Chris was no good, that he'd never amount to anything, that he and his whole deadbeat Polack family were completely beneath their contempt.

If Chris is ever gonna get anywhere, Ted concluded, *he's gonna have to get the hell out of this town first. Go somewhere where people's taste isn't lodged in their ass.*

Somewhere where nobody knows his name.

Then he looked at the jacket again. From where he stood, it looked damn near perfect. It made him want to look at the cover and compare. Unfortunately, Chris had opened it up and was using it to clean the pot. He leaned over Chris's shoulder to check the readiness, and wound up looking at the inside painting instead.

It was an uppergrandstand view of an enormous indoor coliseum. The oval floor was ringed with a wall of brilliant flames. Within it was a pool of what appeared to be molten lava, in the shape of a five-pointed star. There were contorted tidbits of human anatomy at every point within the pool: clawing arms, straining torsos, screaming faces. They sizzled and smoked in what seemed phenomenal anguish.

In the heart of the pool, something huge and terrible was beginning to emerge from beneath that steaming gumbo of body parts and souls. A misshapen claw.

The crest of the head.

And surrounding the pentagram on all sides was the crowd: filling the seats, the aisles, every bit of available space. They were all young. They were all hip. They were all dead.

And though their bodies were extended in wild gestures of supplication, they all appeared to be screaming. . . .

"You know," Chris said, as he folded the E-Z Wider and began to load it with clean green, "I wonder about these guys sometimes."

"Well, you can wonder out loud to your little heart's content at the concert on Monday."

"I mean it," Chris reasserted, lighting up and taking a deep lungful off the joint for emphasis. "These guys are extreme."

"So what are you saying?" Ted took the doob for him.

"*I'm . . . just . . . saying. . . ,*" Chris began, then his lungs exploded in a racking cough. Ted laughed. Chris was roughly twelve times more stoned by the time he finished. "I'm just saying I *wonder* about them, sometimes."

"I'm sure they wonder about you, too. You're such a dork."

"No, but really. Think about it. All this 'Critical Mass' shit: it's like they really *want* the world to blow up, you know it?"

"Well, hell"—Ted laughed—"who doesn't?"

In the living room, nearly three minutes of blessed near-silence had passed. Those minutes were over. The heavy-metal thunder from above had resumed.

"Bang, crash, boom," Rachel Adams said, rolling her eyes in time with the music. A lock of her long red hair fell over said eyes; she brushed it away without losing a beat. She was scarcely an inch over five feet tall; her faded denim dress clung to the voluptuous padding that pregnancy had draped over her frame over a year ago and that still clung tenaciously on. Among those who knew and loved her, it was unanimous that she was one of the ten cutest people ever born.

Rachel didn't feel especially cute right now. She was on her knees on the hardwood floor, chunks of a mangled turkey frank in one hand and a sopping sheet of phone bill in the other. All around her was debris of the most terrifying sort. Directly in front of her was the cause.

"D-dah-dah-dah," little Natalie informed her. "Dah-dah-dah PFTHHH!"

"That's charming," Rachel assured her. "That's what I think of Daddy, too."

"PFTHHHH!" Tiny pink tongue abubble, slipping past pursed lips and toothless gums to waggle in the breeze. "PFTHHH! PFTHHH!" The state of the art in nine-month-old communication.

"C'mon," Rachel provoked, sliding closer. "Can you say 'antidisestablishmentarianism'? Of course you can." The hand with the savaged shreds of wienie gestured encouragingly.

"Dah-dah-dah," Natalie insisted, and then began to chew on the remote control unit for the VCR. Natalie was like that: the mouth was the doorway of perception. *She must have learned that from Jake and me*, Rachel thought, and then beamed at her baby daughter.

At nine months, Natalie Guinevere Adams-Hamer was fourteen pounds and twenty-three inches of miniature human beauty, even in baggy disposable diapers. Her eyes were huge and grayish-blue, like her mother's; her fingers were long and delicate, like her father's; her body, not quite grown into proportion with her head, was petite and cuddle-demanding. She was one of those babies for whom laughter comes as easily as tears: she had a great sense of humor, also inherited from both her parents, that made the joy of being around her transcend the obvious pain-in-the-butt qualities.

"Oh, boobie-boobie-boobie," Rachel cooed, dropping the damp phone bill and sliding closer. "Gimme that. And come here." She pulled the remote control out of Natalie's hands and mouth—not the world's easiest task, as the kid had a powerful grip—and hoisted the midget to her no-longer-lactating breasts for a deep and abiding hug.

It had not been an easy birth; comparatively, Ted had been a piece of cake. Thirty-four and a half hours of labor do not a picnic make, especially when you throw in three rejections from the hospital (you're not dilated enough, the rooms are full, don't come back until you're ready), coupled with a one-boy history of cesarean delivery and the fact that she was thirty-seven years old.

Lots of fear.

Twelve times as much pain.

But the worst was the waiting, the seeming eternity of it. Nine months and four days had evidently not been long enough. God and Mother Nature were clearly taking some cues from Hitchcock, masterfully dragging out the suspense without ever once letting it get close to boring. All the questions she and Jake had been nursing since conception— boy or girl, dark or pale, bright or retarded, and so on— flared brighter than ever in the moments between contractions, when what passed for rational thought was, if barely, even possible.

And then, on the thirty-first hour, when the seconds between the screaming pain had all but evaporated, Beth Israel Hospital had finally opened up one of their puke-green rooms to her. They had stripped her, enrobed her, slapped her on the comfortless bed, drugged her, greased her up, and strapped on the monitors: one for the baby and one for her. They had turned on the machines, transformed the heartbeats of mother and child into shimmering waveforms that looked as if they belonged on Jesse's keyboard oscilloscope.

Then the three more hours of waiting for the doctor to arrive, with Jake nearly collapsing from lack of sleep, and the nurses saying Don't push, Don't push in direct contradiction to everything her own body was telling her. . .

. . . and then the doctor arriving, looking freshly golfed (though she knew it wasn't true, it just felt nicely cruel to think so in those fleeting seconds of sanity now allowed between contractions), checking out the elastic sprawl of her distending vaginal lips and going Mmm-hmmm, we've got ten centimeters as Jake and a nurse spread her numb legs wide . . .

. . . and then the long gurney-roll down the corridor, the crash through the double doors into what Monty Python had so aptly named the "fetus-frightening room," the hefting up onto the bed . . .

. . . and then there had been no more room for thought at all, just the Push and the Push and the pain and the

*Push and the prick of the needle and the slash of the scal-
pel and the Push and the Push and the Push . . .*

"And there you were," Rachel hissed, back-datedly triumphant. "And even though you were covered with slime, you
were perfect, baby. Perfect."

Natalie grabbed a handful of her mother's red tresses and
yanked. Mommy went "YOW!" and wrenched the tiny hand
free, pulling the baby to arm's length. Through the thin skin on
the baby's face, every trace of emotion from surprise to terror
flickered with staggering clarity in the instant and a half before
Natalie began to cry.

"Oh, boobie! I'm sorry I scared you!"

"WAH!"

"I just don't like having my hair pulled, that's all!"

"WAH!!!!"

"Oh, no. You're getting sleepy, aren't you, sweetheart?"

"WAHHH!!!"

"I'll take that as a yes."

"WAHHHH!!!"

It was pretty clear where this conversation was going, so
Rachel gave up her end of it, resigning herself to coddling
Screamo for a minute and surveying the wreckage. It was
considerable. The rest of the poor mutilated turkey frank, a
half dozen remnants of crackers past, a toy chainsaw, and an
Ugly Ball shaped like a leering skull (Ted's warped sense of
humor), seven brightly colored concentric rings and the stick-
stand to ring them on, a Busy Box full of ringing bells and dials
to twiddle, a mangled *TV Guide*, the rest of the phone bill, one
well-soiled diaper, and a couple of wipes were among the
visible casualties. This was not to mention the well-known
cacophony and ferment to be found inside the playpen. God
only knew what lurked behind the sofa, lay furtive in the
unseen corners of the room.

This was the curse of life: eternal vigilance. The minute
you finished one thing, twelve other things caved in. This was
especially true of motherhood. There was never any end to the
detritis that needed to be picked up, cleaned, put away, and
then slid through the cycle again.

But it's my house, she thought, and the truth of those
words made all the difference in the world. *Jake and I own the
thing: lock, stock, barrel, and twenty-year, variable-rate mortgage.*

The house was old-style big; Pete's grandparents had been fairly well-to-do for their time, and their living quarters had reflected it. Most of the original furnishings remained, though she'd solicited brother Cody's help in stripping and refinishing them, and she'd reupholstered them herself. Lots of solid oak and mahogany to go with Jake's beloved burnished brass. Above all, tons and tons of *space*, the likes of which she couldn't have achieved in New York City for less than the gross national product itself.

It was hard to believe sometimes; even now, with almost a year in the house behind her. It was hard to believe how lucky she was, how close to ideal her life had actually become. She had a man she loved: more important, a man she trusted with her life, who would be with her till the end and maybe even after. She had the baby she'd been dreaming of and the economic freedom to stay home with that baby. She had gotten Ted out of the city, whether he liked it or not. She had gotten out herself.

But most of all, she was *centered*, at long last and hopefully forever; and, God, what an amazing feeling that was! What a weight off the shoulders and the soul! There was an incredible sense of completion, of all the threads running through her life finally having come together into something coherent and beautiful. Something she could show for all the years of struggle, the years of mistakes and shortcomings and failure, the years of making do and making peace with imperfection.

This was what life was supposed to be like.

This was her dream, come true.

And that was the scary thing about it, the tiny terror that struck her occasionally, unexpectedly, like walking face-first through a spiderweb in the dark: the idea of just how fragile it was, how delicately balanced the pieces of her joy. What if anything were to happen to Natalie? To Ted? To Jake? What would happen to them if anything happened to her. . . ?

"WAHHH!!!" Natalie remarked. Her face was a Kabuki mask of misery.

"I think it's nappytime for you, kiddo. Give Mom a little bit of time for herself and her art, whaddaya say?"

"WAHHH!!! PFTHHH!!!"

"Well, that's a start, anyway."

They turned, Natalie helplessly, toward the staircase. It was an elegant old affair, wide enough for three fat people abreast, winding slowly to the right and upwards at the fifth to fifteenth steps. Like so much of the rest of her life these days, it was a gorgeous thing.

Even with the crazed music pouring down from its summit, courtesy of good ol' Deadbeat Konopliski and her own ever-lovin' son. In a minute she would be telling them to turn it down so that Natalie could manage a nap. They would be grumpy about it, and no doubt stoned again. God, life was tough.

But even Ted's music was pretty good these days. It was nice to see him graduate from the angry young no-talents to more sophisticated fare, even if they *were* still singing about demons and gang bangs and all that charming smarm.

Take this group, for instance. The Scream. There was real depth there, real sonic texture. Even Jesse had to agree. Whatever else you might say about it, the music was powerful; you could almost believe, engulfed in that sound, that hell wasn't such a bad place after all. . . .

"PFTHHH!!!" Natalie said.

"Yes," Rachel agreed. "Then again, there's always that."

Four

Jesse was waiting for the phone to ring.

She sat watching the silently replicating waveforms on the monitor before her. The amber screen flickered and glowed. On it, pirated dulcet tones of the entire New York Philharmonic string section silently reinterpreted themselves as a series of sharply etched peaks and valleys, cascading forward like the topography of an alien planet.

The light pen sat limply in one hand, its fiber-optic tip staring blankly back like a tiny, glowing eye. Watching, impassively. Waiting patiently, like everything else in the great hall, for her to make a move.

Waiting, for the phone to ring.

And the bottom to drop out.

She looked up, past the high-tech sprawl of cables, keyboards and consoles that covered well over three quarters of the room. She was alone at present, the amps and mike stands that marked the positions of the other band members pointing only toward empty space.

Normally she'd be thrilled. Solitude was an all-too fleeting phenomenon in the hyperpace of the last five months, with its concert preps and news clips and round-the-clock rehearsal/recording/production/promotion sessions. Normally she'd be seizing on the chance to diddle, undisturbed, with the vast array of digital samples that were her specialty and the textural trademark of the Jacob Hamer Band's muscular sound. Normally, the animated patterns on the screen would mean something.

Not today. Nothing today would be normal.

Not until the telephone rang.

And maybe not even then . . .

On the screen, the patterns had ceased cycling. One—it looked like a pizzicato violin sample, but she wasn't really paying attention—had frozen in mid-strike. It was an eerie metaphor for the immediate future, like a cheap videotape stuck indefinitely on pause, static bands of white noise blotting out any hope of concentration.

Jesse reached over and laid the light pen to rest. Her breasts ached, full and heavy. Bad sign. Even the slightest brush of fabric against her nipples was becoming almost unbearable.

And you know what that means, don't you?

Down the hill, the voices came together in ragged, homegrown harmony:

"Holy, ho-lee,
Holy, ho-lee,
Holy, ho-lee,
Lord God Almigh-tee"

Shut up.

Jesse winced. If she heard their spirited off-key rendition once more, she would explode. The likelihood was high: that was the twelfth tuneless time today, and they showed no sign of stopping. Once an hour, every hour. A dawn-to-dusk, daily vigil of prayer, song, and righteous wrongheadedness.

Ordinarily she'd find it amusing to sharpen her wit, and her claws, on the pious blockheads who power-jockeyed for God and country and five-figure love-gifts on cable affiliates nationwide. Lately, though, they had been hitting a little too close to home.

Today particularly, she simply wasn't in the mood.

Down the hill, the voices swelled, majestically akilter. Probably a fresh news team had arrived. The protesters started in on the rousing third verse:

"Father, fa-ther,
Father, fa-ther,
Father, fa-ther,
Lord God Almigh-tee"

"Shit."

Jesse brought a nimble, articulate hand up to rake through her cropped auburn hair. Then she stood and stretched. It was a purely symbolic act, relieving absolutely nothing. The cramps were gone, but what did that prove?

Her first time, she had thought she had the flu. The second, there were no symptoms whatsoever beyond a little swelling and tenderness.

And the third?

She made her way across the room, heading for the open window. She didn't want to think about it.

She couldn't think of anything *but* . . .

The three mike stands were spaced in an arcing parabola, dividing the room into irregular pie-slice quadrants. It was the preferred rehearsal arrangement of late, as it left everyone facing inward and hence able to communicate better.

"But not as good as New York," she said to herself, thinking back to the cavernous, forty-eight-hundred-dollar-a-month converted dance loft into which she'd built the separate light-and-sound booth and the floor-to-ceiling mirrors that let them see *exactly* how they'd look on stage. That had been her dream and her domain: a huge work area with a kitchen and a sleeping loft, a weight room and even a little niche where she could escape to meditate, though even that had become a luxury in the months before they'd left.

Pennsylvania had seemed intriguing at the time—positively *idyllic* if one bought Pete's heartfelt schmooze, which she did more often than she wished. She could kick herself for just letting go of the place, for not hedging her bet and going through the myriad hassles of subletting. Another fool for love learns the hard way. She should have known better.

Too late now.

Shut up.

It had seemed like a good idea, then: Pete's dad had died, and his grandmother was in danger of losing the whole mountain. Jake and Rachel were anxious to get their newborn out of the funky confines of Manhattan's Chelsea section, and the appeal of a farmhouse on a mountain in Pete's old stomping grounds, yet still within an afternoon's drive of the Apple, had proved irresistible. The inevitable tinge of urban burnout was beginning to reach even through her carefully cultivated patina of fast-lane fever.

Eventually, the country called. Bigger work space, lower cost of living, scenic splendor, quaint and friendly locals . . .

Outside, a bullhorn blared and fed back in howling counterpoint to her train of thought. She reached the window and shut it abruptly, mercifully muting the harangue. Something about homosexuals; she couldn't tell. The following ripple of cheers didn't make it through either.

"Shut up," she said, out loud this time. Another bad sign. Stress.

There was definitely trouble in paradise. The first six months had been great, like a protracted working vacation. The hotel was long defunct; they leased it and began fixing it up. The combined monies had allowed Pete's grandmother to keep the family property from being parceled out to pay ongoing taxes. She and Pete and the rest of the Jacob Hamer contingent had a twenty-six-room hideaway to live and work in. The potential was staggering. In theory, anyway. In theory, they should all be one big, happy family.

Except . . .

Except that she hated sharing the kitchen. And the bathrooms. And the clutter of sixteen wildly different souls, and the homey chore sheet that no one but her ever seemed to take seriously, and a thousand other niggling little domestic details that marked the loss of autonomy.

Mostly, though, was the simple fact that the old studio had been—when all was said and done—hers, and hers alone. One person with the bottom-line say-so. One name on the lease.

And she liked it that way. She'd always been nothing but generous with regard to its access, even from the early, hungry days. She dearly loved the group and was as dedicated as anyone, perhaps more so. But she'd had a decent career as a hired studio-gun before this gig, and she always considered the loft, which facilitated that success, her ultimate safety net. Her ace in the hole should things, God forbid, ever go wrong.

Hamer band or no Hamer band, Jesse Malloy's butt was covered in New York.

But this place . . .

This one was theirs.

And that was a difference she'd spent the better part of the last five months trying to pretend she hadn't noticed. It was getting harder and harder to do: the renovation process, which had been massive and unanimous at first, had gradually tapered off with the increased workload that the Rock Aid gig had brought on.

It was pretty much in an everyone-for-themselves status lately. The contractors were unreliable and expensive, especially with the lack of session money coming in and royalties not due in for another couple of months. The crew had their rooms in varying states of disrepair. Pete had helped her a little, but somehow his latest efforts to put the finishing touches on his own private writing room had superceded any commitment to helping her with the carpentry work she needed to get hers going. And so on and so on.

It was selfish, to her way of thinking. The same self-absorbed quality that had so recently emerged in other areas of their lives. Like the bedroom.

It wasn't that she was helpless, even though carpentry was not her cup of tea. It wasn't just that she was so damned busy, even though major portions of her day were consumed in programming data for the new album as well as integrating the special effects and video sequences for the ever-so-important

Rock Aid gig on Saturday, their big fifteen minutes for the history books.

She just needed some time to herself, in an utterly private space.

Especially now. Her second home test had conflicted with the results of the first, at which point the instructions on the box cheerfully suggested that you purchase yet another to be sure. Yeah, right. There was only one way to be absolutely certain, and she had already gone and done it, yesterday afternoon.

And now she sat, trying not to think about it, unable to avoid it. Waiting for the results.

She looked down at the phone, which sat in squat black antiquated silence on the end table. Its dimwit Radio Shack companion sat next to it: an old-style, boxy answering machine in fake-wood tones that ate more messages than it ever relayed.

"C'mon, Jaws, cough it up."

She stared at the little green running light, hoping that the red incoming light would magically light. Nothing. The green light winked balefully back.

Her guts throbbed from the tension. She couldn't stand it anymore.

"Ring, damn you," she said to the phone, half-convinced she could psychically *will* a response. She waited a beat. *"Ring."*

It did.

She gasped, feeling as though a garrote had suddenly tightened around her throat. Faraway sounds of trapdoors swinging open echoed in her inner ear.

The phone rang again.

She did nothing. The throbbing need to take charge just froze up inside her. A distant, more dispassionate voice informed her that she should pick up, that Jaws would do it on the third ring if she didn't. She debated the wisdom of letting it. She debated the wisdom of a lot of things.

But she caught it, halfway through the third ring.

Too late.

Jaws cut on, red incoming light glowing dutifully. She put the phone to her ears. A howl of feedback instantly started up. She slapped down on the volume, muting the speaker. The howling evaporated. Jaws looked utterly indifferent and continued recording for its allotted three minutes maximum. She would play the tape back another dozen times before ultimately erasing it.

"Hello? Yes?" *Be calm*, she thought.

The voice on the other end was crisp and female and professionally compassionate. *"May I speak to a Miss Jessica Malloy, please?"*

"This is Ms. Malloy."

"Miss Malloy, this is Lenore Kleinkind at the Susquehanna Women's Services Center."

"Yes." Small voice, sounds of throat clearing. "I've been expecting your call." She paused. "So . . . what's the verdict?"

"Miss Malloy, your blood test results are positive."

Silence. Oppressive. Muted bullhorn in the background, wailing something about saving children from—

"Miss Malloy? Are you there? I said—"

"Yes, I heard you. The test results are positive."

"Yes."

The remainder was brief and to the point. Miss Kleinkind, pointing out, in accordance with recent federal regulations, she was obligated to point out the many services available. Further, suggesting that Miss Malloy come in for a consultation. Ms. Malloy agreeing to come in the next morning and informing her that there was only one service she currently required, and that she required it immediately. Miss Kleinkind saying very well and arranging for a time.

As Jesse listened and cried, she thought back to the other times in her life she'd marched down this very same road. Once, when she was seventeen and stupid and a little too fertile to ride bareback. Her parents had paid for it, thinking they were sending her on a weekend skiing trip. It had passed like a very bad dream into the closet of her soul, and hardly rattled at all.

The next time was four years later and a whole world wiser. She had quite literally fucked up, putting a little too much faith in the glowing advertising claims of a certain brand of contraceptive sponge. She fell into the unlucky twentieth percentile, who were almost certain to never appear on the box looking happy and carefree.

She'd refused to allow herself to view it as anything other than an invasion of her autonomy, and further refused to submit to the biological conscription at a time when her career looked so promising.

All the same, she had done it with a little more penitent awareness that time: bargain-shopping through the Village Voice classifieds for the best price, ultimately opting for a local anesthetic. It was cheaper, and besides, that way she saw exactly what was going on from start to finish.

Sounded good at the time, anyway. The procedure was performed by a petite Korean physician at a service on East Thirty-seventh Street, who was very concise and competent. As they prepared the local, the matronly nurse advised her to "hold my hand." She wondered why.

She found out soon enough. The procedure was competent and expedient and modestly professional.

And, to no one's real surprise, excruciatingly painful.

That was okay, though. That was to be expected. And seeing it had helped, somehow, to accept the responsibility. She needed to see it and hear it and feel it, as the suction pump pulled and pulled and . . .

She became very cautious from then on: multiple methods, more caring selection as to partners. A lot of introspection. She was resolved that that would be the last time.

Which was exactly what was so unfair. She had been cautious. A little overathletic, maybe, but still . . .

The rubber had broken. It happens. The sperm were heroically inclined. Unfortunate, but to be expected, knowing Pete.

But the cap . . .

Her cervical cap had come dislodged. It shouldn't have. It was new and a perfect fit right down to the centimeter. The odds were astronomically in their favor against that's ever happening.

But it went and happened, just the same.

And now, as the late summer afternoon peaked and the unfairness of it all became moot, Jesse savored the flat taste of bile that accompanied the title of the only service she would be requiring tomorrow afternoon. A strangely brutal word, with harshly backlit consonants that raked against her insides like a rusty coat hanger.

Outside, the chorus was dying down.

"Holy, ho-lee,
Holy, ho-leee . . ."

Jesse cried.

Five

Mark Schimmel was just pulling the last trash barrel into position when the jet-black van screamed into the BP Gas 'N Go. It was 5:56 in York, Pennsylvania, which was checkout time for the second shift, and Mark had no intention of wearing his goddamn green regulation grease monkey jumpsuit for one second past six o'clock. In this kind of heat, it was a goddamn pressure cooker. It was insane. It ran against every civilized notion of human decency.

Unfortunately, however, Big Joe Glandular was there, and Big Joe was district supervisor. He was also a complete bastard, but that did nothing to mitigate his authority. Enhanced it, in fact. He had proven that by firing Sally, docking Alan back to beginner's wages after nearly ten years of dedicated service, and single-handedly turning the lives of all who worked there upside-down.

Not to mention zeroing in on the mysterious cash shortages that had plagued the station for the last four months.

Which was not good news for Mark Schimmel: he of the skinny build and bold beak nose and twenty years of age. Oh, no. Not when he'd been generating an extra three hundred dollars a month that was entirely off the books. The odds against getting caught were great (he was very careful, making a point of visiting everybody's shift every day and—trusted buddy that he was—only pilfering five to fifteen bucks per shift from the cashbox in the back). It wasn't fear of reprisal at all.

It was just that he'd come to rely on the extra income. Rather heavily, in fact.

So, with Big Joe on the premises, it was important to be cool. Everything by the book. Hence, the keeping-on of his miserable BP uniform. Hence, the orderly blocking-off of the islands on his side of the station. Let them get gas on poor old scapegoat Alan's side for the next four minutes.

But did the black van get the hint? Hell, no. It howled in off Queen Street from the direction of I-83, neatly circumvented the trash barrel in the center of the outside lane, and screeched to a halt in front of the #3 Regular pump, engine idling high and heavy, stereo blaring.

"Oh, nice," Schimmel bitched to himself. "Thanks a lot, guys. Real bright." He thought of yelling at them, then thought instantly better. Big Joe would like that a lot, you bet. *Time to play Politeness Man*, he told himself, and sauntered over to the driver's side.

"Fill it up. Regular." The driver said. He was an intense-looking guy in his late thirties, early forties, with a thick brush of red beard and very little hair up top. His voice was soft, but it cut surprisingly well through the noise of the van. His eyes were hidden behind black shades.

"Sorry," Mark said. "This side is closed. If you want—"

"Fill it up," the driver repeated. It wasn't as if he hadn't heard.

"You don't understand," Mark began, and then the smell socked into his nostrils. A ripe and rotten smell, made dizzying by the heat.

It was coming from the van.

"No, *you* don't understand," the driver said, and Mark could feel the cold gaze from behind those sunglasses with alarming clarity. "Fill it up or I'll blow your little nuts off. And I do mean now."

From inside the van, several voices made an identical sound:

"EEYAAOW!"

It was time to reconsider, Mark realized. Perhaps it would be a good idea to serve this guy after all. Bravery was not his long suit; and besides, he liked his nuts right where they were.

"Fill 'er up," he said with obedient pleasantry, and nearly gagged on the words. The smell was that bad. It made the reek of petrol almost heavenly by comparison. A rush of nausea gripped him as he took the nozzle out of #3 pump, flipped the handle down, and walked over to where the van's chrome gas cap hung gleaming in the evening sun.

"You wanna cut the engine?" he called out as he twisted off the cap and inserted the nozzle.

No response.

"I can't fill it up if you don't cut the engine!" he announced, and then he heard shouting, followed by the sliding-open of the side door on the passenger side. More impassioned shouting followed: some of it from the driver, none of it directed at Mark. He decided to leave well enough alone on that particular subject, set the nozzle on the second notch, and moved toward the bucket where his squeegee lay waiting.

That was when the Screamer came around the back of the van.

"*Hey*, dude! EEYAAOW!" the guy hollered. "How's the gas-pumpin' bizniz?" His voice was thick, and his gate was stumbling, as if he didn't really have control over his body. Drugs, most likely: downs, or booze, or both together.

But that wasn't the worst of it.

No, not by a long shot.

Because the guy's skin was all wrong: so wrong that it was painful to look at. It was puffy and pale and greenish, mottled, as if there were some rank disease just waiting for its chance to burst through the surface. And it was *slick*, in a way that made Mark's own flesh crawl.

It didn't sweat the way skin sweats.

It sweated like *cheese . . .*

"Oh, Jesus," Mark said, involuntarily backing away. He felt the kick of his double Wendyburger with onions, pickles, and extra cheese, reminding him that they weren't quite digested yet, they could come kicking back at him in a highly acidic and lumpy state at any moment. It did not give him happy feets. He wavered, belched a rancid bubble, and backed away some more.

"Hey, man!" the Screamer continued, grinning. His gums, Mark saw, were black as the wraparound shades that mercifully shielded his eyes from view. "You dig The Scream?"

"Uh . . . yeah." There was a lump in Mark's throat that was easily the size of his prominent Adam's apple, and it tasted very bad. There was no hiding the revulsion that grimaced across his face; but there was still the voice in his head, and it said *be cool, be cool* . . .

"Yeah, well, we're goin' ta see 'em tomorrow night, man," the Screamer enthused. "Up in Philly. Gonna be fuckin' great. EEYAAOW!" He threw his head back as he howled the last, coyotelike. The flesh between his chin and his shoulder blades pulled strangely taut.

As if it were threatening to snap . . .

"Oh," Mark said. It was in response to his stomach, which said that it was, yes, ready to kick into reverse. He clutched his belly and stepped backward off the island, stumbling as he landed one step down.

"And you know what's really cool, man?" the Screamer persisted. "They got this backup band called Cleaver, man, and they're really fuckin' great. You ever hear 'em?"

Mark shook his head no, less in answer to the question than in denial of the truth that shambled toward him now. He shot a quick glance back at the office, saw Big Joe still bawling out the new station manager, both of their backs toward him. Suddenly, the great outdoors as seen from the top of the Queen Street hill seemed monstrously claustrophobic, all that dark blue sky and rolling countryside closing in like the walls in one of those 1940s Universal Pictures torture chamber scenes.

"They got this great fuckin' song, man. It's called 'Saigon Lullaby,' and the lead singer sets himself on fire an' shit when they do it. It's really wild, man. EEYAAOW! You know?"

Mark didn't know anything but the sudden pain in his ankle as he slipped, the slowly dawning realization that things were going to get worse, much worse, in a matter of seconds.

The Screamer was reaching for the #5 Premium No Lead nozzle. "GET THE HELL AWAY FROM THERE!" the driver hollered, but the Screamer just smiled and kept on reaching.

"He just goes like this," the Screamer said, and then the nozzle was in his hand, and the lever went down, and the nozzle was over his head, pointing downward like the finger of God.

"No," Mark whispered.

The Screamer pulled the trigger.

*   *   *

In the next ten seconds too many things happened. Mark Schimmel saw them all, saw them all too clearly.

He saw the fierce Premium No Lead jet stream plow into the crown of the Screamer's head, spitting spray in the air, sending curtains of sheer and combustible fluid down the face and either side. He saw the Screamer's mouth open wide to emit another animal "EEYAAOW!"—garbled and gurgling this time . . .

. . . as Mark found himself thinking, Why doesn't he scream, I got gas in my eyes once, I screamed for a half hour . . .

. . . and the Screamer's sunglasses washed off his face in the high-octane torrent, revealing sockets black with emptiness and stunted, lingering decomposition . . .

. . . and pools of tiny worm-things oozed, gleaming red, from out of those sockets and onto the Screamer's cheeks, then flopped like squirming confetti down to the pavement below . . .

. . . and the back tires of the van began to squeal as the driver yelled, I CAN'T DEAL WITH THIS! and kicked into gear, peeling away with the #3 nozzle still attached . . .

. . . and the hose ripped away, a literal geyser of gasoline spewing out to puddle then pool an area that was ten feet, twenty feet, thirty feet wide . . .

. . . and the numbers on the gas pump spun . . .

. . . and the severed hose caught, and the nozzle yanked out, and the cold steel clattered to the pavement . . .

. . . and the numbers spun . . .

. . . and the worm-things fell blindly off the curb . . .

. . . and the numbers spun . . .

. . . and the Screamer pulled a Bic lighter from his pocket, held it aloft with jittering fingers . . .

. . . the ring finger of which was missing . . .

And Mark Schimmel began to run then, even though his left ankle was screaming pain and his mind was completely fried. He didn't run toward the tiny little BP office building, because he knew that it was already too late to throw the emergency cutoff switch, much less the circuit breakers in the back. He could see gawky Big Joe Glandular and the new manager staring slack-jawed, inches from the switches. They would not get to them in time either.

There simply was no time.

He ran, instead, toward Queen Street. There was a steep embankment on the other side. It would shield him, he knew, from the explosion to come.

And the explosion was coming, oh yes, without a doubt. He didn't need to see the Bic flick, see the Screamer come alight with bright gyrating frenzy. He didn't need to see the spilled gas catch, then spread its flaming tongues of death back to the pumps . . .

. . . then down into the tanks . . .

. . . the subterranean tanks that supplied the thousands of gallons that supplied the hundreds of satisfied customers each day . . .

He was still running when the #5 tank blew, setting off the inevitable chain reaction. The exploding sound muffled the rasp of his breathing as he reached the center of the northbound side of Queen Street, paused, and stared straight into the blank headlights of the Mack truck roaring toward him.

And then the station and the parking lot and the houses behind it, the north and southbound lanes of Queen Street, the truck, every other car chain-reacting in the intersection, and Mark Schimmel, all joined together in that cleansing white light. . . .

"Hello, friends in Jesus," Furniss began as the canned music started up, "And welcome to *Triumph Tonight*. I'm Pastor "Daniel Furniss, your host, and today we'll be sharing the Good News of our blessed Savior, as we continue our discussion on the effect of rock music on our young people."

It felt good to be back on his own set, minus adversaries and a volatile studio audience, many of whom numbered amongst the godless. He knew Bobby, Kelly, and Clarence, the three guys behind the cameras. He knew Daryl, the sound man. He knew Stacey, the gal who ran the lights. He was on his own plush executive chair, behind his own sturdy desk, asserting his own control, with his own fake plants surrounding the seats that *he* provided for *his* guests, and not the other way around.

And, best of all, he had an array of the least-challenging guests that a man could ask for: a handful of the kids from Liberty Christian Village. Every one of them well-behaved, not a one of them contrary in the tiniest way, the boys in their crisp haircuts and shirts and ties next to the girls in their demure skirts and blouses. It was a gravy show, absolutely free of conflict.

It was exactly what he needed after this morning's encounter.

"As you know," he continued, "this program's focus over the last few weeks has been Satan's desperate grab for the souls of our teenagers through the device of rock music—or more accurately, *murder* music. In the past weeks we've had authorities like Joel Wenker and Jacob Aranza; we've had concerned parents like Esther Shrake of Morality Over Music and Muriel Slate from the PMRC. We've had a veritable outpouring of people, from all walks of life, come on and witness before us about the terrible dangers that rock music, with its emphasis on absolutely the *worst*, most foul kinds of sin, have posed for decent Christian parents and their young.

"We'll also be going up to Brother Paul Weissman in the parking lot, where we're going to be burning some more filth— that's just a little later on in the show—and we'll be taking calls from our listeners and answering questions, *and* we'll be having our altar call for some of our newer members here at Liberty Christian, but right *now* I'd like to speak with some of the youngsters themselves. Specifically, some of the fine young men and women that our beloved Saviour the Lord *Jeezus* Christ has delivered to us here at Liberty Christian Village. Let me tell you, they have suffered every kind of temptation that the Devil has to offer: from drugs to occultism to sexual promiscuity, they've done it all. They really know the score. And they're here to tell you the truth about rock music, and Satan's very real plan to steal the souls of our youth."

They were all clumped together on his right: the three girls spaced evenly across the couch, the boys (except for Dwight) cross-legged at their feet. Dwight, of course, had the chair next to the desk; it was the stage manager's idea of a funny har-har.

That's right, Dwight, Furniss found himself thinking. *Drool a little for the camera*. And though he chastized himself instantly before God for the thought, a whiff of the sentiment lingered on. Dwight was, after all, not quite as clever as a clothespin.

"Let's start with this young fella right here on my right," Furniss began aloud. "Dwight's been with us since the very beginning of Liberty Christian Village . . . that's been, uh, six years, hasn't it?"

"Yessir," Dwight said. He had a Dudley Do-Right chin and an overbite to his narrow puckered slash of a mouth. His eyes were tiny and set back in his head, as close to the brain as possible. His Adam's apple bobbed and jutted like a fat man on a trampoline above the compulsory stricture of white shirt and black tie. Furniss often wondered what God had been thinking when He invented Dwight; but the phrase *there but for the grace of* . . . often came chillingly to mind.

"We've done everything we can . . . leaving him by the side of the road and what have you . . . but he keeps finding his way back somehow, God bless his heart." Surely God wouldn't object to a little gentle teasing. "Isn't that right?"

"Yessir." No hint of understanding glimmered in those deep-set eyes.

"But seriously, folks, Dwight's a good kid, and we're jus' tickled pink to have him here at the Village." He turned to the boy, who had just last week turned twenty, and addressed him fully. "Now, you say you were raised in a Christian home, right?"

"Yessir."

"And your parents went to church every Sunday?"

"Yessir. They did."

"But still there was something missing spiritually from your household, isn't that right?"

"Yessir. There was. I mean, um . . . they would always make us, um . . . taking us to church and, uh, they would say their prayers and, um . . . well, like they said that they

believed in God, but then, um, like, my daddy, he would, uh
. . . drink alcohol, and there would, um, using curse words,
and . . ."

"And you said that often your parents would allow you to
listen to rock music on the radio, is that right?"

"Yessir."

"And your mother herself would sometimes put it on when
she was doing housework?"

"Yessir."

"So it wasn't really a Christian home, then, was it?"

"Nossir."

"I should say not," Furniss concluded, rather hurriedly.
"And then, moving right along, we have these three lovely
ladies on the sofa here. That's Cathy on the end there, looking
so pretty in her new fall dress."

Cathy smiled. She didn't look all that pretty, if one wanted
to be honest: she was chunky as a side of beef, her teeth were
painfully crooked, her hair was bland, her skin was pale and
troubled, and her horn-rimmed glasses made her eyes look
hardball-huge. But at least she could speak in coherent
sentences.

"Now, *you*, Cathy, you could pretty much read us the riot
act in terms of your life before the Lord led you to Liberty
Christian Village. Disobedience to parents, rebelliousness at
school, drugs, sexual permissiveness, and an actual attempt at
suicide: you pretty much ran the gamut. Can you tell us—and
it's hard for me to imagine, viewers—but can you tell us what
happened, where your life went wrong?"

"Well," Cathy began, a slight blush rising to pinken her
mushroom pallor, "it was the kids at school, mostly. You
know, they said that you were square unless you got high and
messed around—"

"By that you mean sexual promiscuity."

"Yes." Cathy blushed more deeply. Furniss suppressed a
sudden image of what it might be like to have known Cathy in
the biblical sense; it was easily dispatched to the hell where it
belonged. "And the thing was, everything was set up to make
me believe that it was the right thing to do. I mean, all the
songs said that it was beautiful, it was cool, it was where it's
at—"

"You're referring to the rock music you listened to."

"Yes." Cathy's conviction was strong; that much was clear. It lent her a kind of beauty that her body didn't have. "And that was the problem. I guess I had a real low self-esteem at that point. I didn't know that Jesus loved me. So I guess I just went along 'cause I hoped that people would love me if I did all the cool stuff."

"Okay." Somehow, that kind of testimony always got to him. No matter how many times he heard it—and it surely numbered into the thousands by now—the terrible vulnerability of youth found a way to slice through the callousness that his own age and experience had necessitated. Here was a girl who had suffered, suffered grievously, before finding Christ. Here was a girl who stood a fine chance of being a good Christian, a good wife, a good mother to her children; and she had been polluted, swept into corruption by Satan and his worldly minions. Now all she wanted in her life was to be forgiven.

And lo, the Lord had led her unto to him.

"Thank you, Cathy." Only a second of pause had passed. "*Jeezus* be praised, your life has been turned around completely, hasn't it, thanks to God's mercy and Liberty Christian Village."

"Yes, Pastor. It has." Cathy's smile was uninhibited now, free of shame. "I know now that Jesus is my personal savior, and I have no need to fear. I'm so grateful to the prayers and donations of the people who have given to Pastor's ministry. A lot of times I think that if it weren't for coming here to the Village, I'd already be dead."

"And you're how old, Cathy?"

"Fifteen."

Furniss snorted, smiled, and shook his head ruefully on behalf of the folks at home. "Shocking, isn't it? I'll tell you, people. Some of the stories these kids come in with are enough to curl your hair. Every day, more and more young people from all over the country tell me about the traps that Satan has laid for them, and most of them have barely escaped with their lives."

He glanced at the girl to Cathy's left: the new girl, with her straight blond hair and her angular good looks and her terrible haunted eyes. She was the saddest case Furniss had seen in many a moon; and looking at her now, raveling into herself like an unwound tape, he wasn't at all sure that he wanted to drag her story out of her again. Not just yet.

"And this cute little fella here is Tommy." He pointed instead to the dark-haired young whippersnapper at Cathy's feet. "He's four foot ten and full of beans, and I'll tell ya, Tommy has known more suffering at the hands of some of these so-called *cult* he-roes than any right-thinking person could imagine."

Tommy grinned shyly, while the cameraman focused in on him with camera three. Furniss took the moment to sneak one more furtive glance at the new girl . . . what was her name?

Mary.

Mary Hatch . . .

In the black space behind her eyes it was happening again. The pastor's words had triggered it, ground it back into her skull like a drill. She was back in the hedges, staring through the branches and the white gnarls of her hands at the fogbanked slaughter, with the howls of the dead and the dying in her ears.

And it was so hard not to scream, not to betray the terror that sizzled blue-white through her filament nerves. It was so hard to hang on, to remain hidden from the horror, to strangle down the screams so that nothing but the tiniest high-pitched whines escaped. She kept thinking about the electric fence behind her. She kept thinking about her nakedness. She kept thinking about the stuffed animals in her cozy bed and how unlikely it was that she would ever see them again.

And she couldn't see. She couldn't see. That was the most horrid, and the saving grace. Spared, on the one hand, from intimate clips of the size of the gash; like an ostrich with its head in the sand, on the other, hoping to God above that because she couldn't see them, they couldn't see her. . . .

". . . hard to believe," the pastor was saying, "that this little fella could have heard a song that told him to stab a schoolmate when he was only twelve years old . . ."

Again the words jolted her: back to the studio, with the lights in her eyes and the safety of Christian fellowship surrounding her. It was jarring, slamming her squarely back into her place: on the sofa, between Cathy and Lorraine, the former drug-crazed runaway. Close to Furniss, almost close enough to touch.

She met Lorraine's gaze . . . sympathetic, sad . . . and knew that she was being seen now. Seen in her torment, her struggle with the face of the demon.

It was not an exchange that she could hold. The outside was too threatening, the inside too compelling. The vision had been triggered, and it would not be denied.

Not until she had seen it through.

Not until the end . . .

And then the carnage had moved inside, the screams fainter and the killing motion no longer even suggested by the fog. There was a voice in her head that kept saying, Get out of here, get out of here now, but she couldn't obey, there was paralysis in her limbs, paralysis born of wisdom and absolute terror.

And the moments ticked on and on and on. And the screams grew fewer, farther away, while the goose bumps lingered under their sheen of hot/cold drying sweat. And she found it harder and harder to disobey the voice, the voice that said, run, the voice that said, it's safe now.

But there was another voice, separate from the paralysis or the urge to bolt, and the voice said, wait. The voice said, you will know when it's time. It was not her voice. It was not a voice she knew. It was a voice that contained a calm she was incapable of, an inner clarity that she would never know with the world outside.

You will know when it's time, the other voice repeated. As the seconds ticked past.

As the last of the screams, like the lives they bade hearty farewell to, gave way to a silent unknown. . . .

". . . and these kids are the living proof," the pastor continued. Mary could see the intensity with which he directed it at camera one. "Satan is alive, and there's nothing that makes him happier than the corruption and death of somebody's son or daughter. When another young woman dies on the abortionist's table, or when another young man strings the noose in his bedroom and climbs up on that chair, when another teenager goes to a rock concert and hears the message that hell is some kind of great party where all the cool people are, and it doesn't sound so bad as the pastor says, well, you can bet the rent that Satan will be *laughing*!

"But why put your money on a losing bet? Pick a winner, people. Jesus Christ is the winner. Jesus Christ is the way. Jesus Christ is the only one to put your money on!"

The camera zoomed in on a full-screen close-up of Furniss's intense features as he stood and walked away from his desk. "Jesus Christ is the only security you need. Make an investment in eternity, people.

"Invest in Jesus!

"When the Lord held up a denarius, much like this one"—Furniss brandished an obviously ersatz gold-foiled coin—"he asked, 'Whose inscription is on this?' and when they told him it was Caesar's, well, he said, 'Render unto Caesar what is Caesar's, and *render unto God what is God's*.' " He paused for effect, then held up a mint-condition silver dollar. "Bobby, can I get a close-up on this?"

He certainly could. "So whose name do you see on this?" he said, softly luring. "What does it say in big, bold letters right on the face?

"IN GOD WE TRUST!" he exploded. "In GOD we trust! Not 'In ROD we trust'! Not 'In JAKE we trust'! Not 'In MICK or HUEY or YKE we trust'!! There's no trashy rock star's name emblazoned boldly upon the currency of this great nation, am I right?"

Silence from the peanut gallery. They missed the cue en masse. Little bastards couldn't do anything right.

"Right!?"

Timid nods of acquiesence. They were all terrified; everyone knew that messing up on the show was inevitably good for twenty-four hours in the Quiet Room. Oh, well. Furniss didn't need 'em now anyway; he was on a roll.

"So stop givin' 'em your *money*, people! Stop givin' 'em your souls! Stop buying their records and going to their shows and believin' their wickedness and their lies. Stop bankrolling Satan, before it's too late." His voice decrescendoed back down to a reasonable level again. He could feel that big old studio audience in the sky, bitin' down collectively on the show's first hook. It was time to start reelin' 'em in. His voice became pure as silk and honey.

"Give your money to God, instead."

"There's a number I want you to call that will put you in touch with one of our Prayer Pals. They're here to help you write a letter to God, beggin' his forgiveness and askin' him to come into your life and save you from yourself, and while they're doing that I believe we have some young people who want to commit themselves over to Christ right now . . ."

. . . and yes, she could still hear that laughter, even as the car doors slammed and the wheels peeled out on the Wyler driveway. She could still hear the laughter as the monsters disappeared down the hill. It was in her ears now, ringing, forever intermingled with the music and the screams.

Inside, the album played over and over, slicing time into neat twenty-two-minute cycles. It made a nightmare loop of the hours dragging past her shock-scoured consciousness. It was the only thing that changed. It was the only thing that moved.

And still the voice did not return. The comforting voice. The one that knew when it was time. She waited, muscles cramping in terrible stasis, for the word. Her body needed to pee again; it was entirely out of the question. One of the killers might still be there; the slightest movement might betray her.

And she did not want to die.

Not like that.

So she waited, while the music played on and on, and the moon made its way ever so slowly across the ink-black sky.. . . .

". . . for God so loved us that he sent his only begotten son to pay the blood price for your sins. That's his promise, people! And the Lord never went back on a promise, for He is the source of all truth and light and beauty. Just when you think that it's all over, and there's nowhere left to turn, Jesus will be there for ya. If you ask him into your heart, He will never fail you . . ."

The first hint of gray dawn had begun to soften the heavens when the convulsions began. They came in an explosive one-two shot of matching charley horses, sent her crashing to her knees in panic and pain. The terror, so rig-

idly held for so long, forgot itself for a moment. When it regained its poise, it was already too late.

"NO!" *she heard herself scream.* "OH, GOD, NO, PLEASE!" *She toppled over on her naked back in the dew-damp grass, clutching the anguished chunks of rock that her calf muscles had become. She tried to massage the blood back into them, screaming all the while, trying to listen through her own cries and thrashing for the sound of approaching footsteps, the war hoots and laughter of the mad. . .*

. . . and she thought she heard something, so she started to scramble on hands and elbows and useless knees: away from the hedges, out into the open expanse of the lawn. Every dragging foot forward brought its own wail of agony; her eyes, already piss-poor, were utterly blinded by tears. She didn't see the pool until she was nearly in it.

She had Betsy Waverly's body to thank for that.

Mary's left hand came down in something cold, wet, and scabby; she didn't guess what it was until the thumb found an empty socket and fell inside. By then, her right was pressed against Betsy's cold and naked breasts. Her vision cleared enough to confirm the horror.

She came up screaming, both hands caked in gore, and fell frantically back. Her head hit the concrete of the pool deck hard, forced bright stars from her forehead and eyes. Something raw and clawlike scraped against her shoulder: maybe Betsy's, maybe not. It didn't matter. That was the end of the line for Mary's sanity.

And she whirled, blind, away from the dead weight smorgasbord bobbing on the surface of the pool, away from her hiding place and deeper into the charnel house yard. She tried to get her oxygen-starved legs to support her. It didn't work. She screamed and fell again, this time face-first. Another body broke her fall.

And she screamed, and she screamed, the slick horror thick in her eyes and nose and mouth now, choking and gagging and blinding her completely. And she crawled over the body, past the head that rolled away at her touch like a bearded volleyball, past the wet fetal curl of another aborted life. Her fingers curled around a blood-drenched bikini top, dragging it along before her.

Until she came upon the foot.

Felt the neat hole in its center.

Dragged her gaze up the pale leg standing before her.

And in the moment before her mind's dark implosion to limbo, found herself staring up into the face of Love . . .

". . . and that's the whole point," Pastor Furniss concluded. "Once you've seen that face, how can you help but love it in return?

"And how can you help but obey?"

"Holy, Ho-lee
Holy, Ho-lee
Holy, Ho-lee
Lord God Almigh-tee . . ."

There must have been twenty or thirty of them: gathered around the bonfire across the road from the gate, swaying to the endless thrum-dee-dum of a half dozen badly tuned acoustic guitars.

"As we lift our hearts
Be-fore you
As a token
Of our love . . ."

They were, without exception, clean-cut white kids between the ages of thirteen and twenty-five. *Even the black ones,* Hempstead silently noted. *Of which there are three.* In the flickering light of the three-foot flames, their eye sockets were pockets of shifting shadow. It made their heads look hollow as dinosaur skulls, which Hempstead felt was strangely appropriate.

"Holy, Ho-lee
Holy, Ho-lee . . ."

"Holy moley," Hempstead muttered, fingering his sax and watching them as he stood at the top of the long driveway. They were about to start the second verse, and he wasn't sure if he could stand it. In the week since Pastor Furniss's vigil had begun, he had heard that song and a dozen just like it at least five million times. And though the guitarists had pretty well mastered their C and G chords, that pesky ol' F major was still giving some of them major problems.

"Father, Fa-ther
Father, Fa-ther
Father, Fa-ther
Lord God Almigh-tee . . ."

Aaron Hempstead took a long drag off his Camel, exhaled it through clenched teeth, and scratched an itch that the heat had placed beneath one corner of his meticulous goatee. He was a large black man at the tail end of his thirties, with not a discernable ounce of flab upon him. His neatly mohawked head glistened faintly in the bonfire light, as did the arms of corded muscle his sleeveless shirt exposed. He moved with a tiger's fluid power and grace, a predator's deadly precision.

He was a musician, first and foremost. But he was also a warrior.

And a damned scary one at that.

It was 10:45 p.m., and the crowd outside the perimeter had shrunk to less than half. He estimated the number of born-agains at thirty-five, forty max. During the peak hours, there might have been as many as a hundred: waving signs, burning records, making speeches, praying, faith-healing, speaking in tongues, and singing those goddamn songs on behalf of God, Country, and Media Exposure.

"As we lift our hearts
Be-fore you . . ."

Because this was the Big Time, no question about it. Jake had, at long last, gone the full nine yards: from media celebrity to cultural crusader.

And all the way up to Antichrist. He grinned, shook his head, dragged some more smoke in and out of his lungs. *Shoot, man. An' I thought that your* guitar-playing *was impressive. . . .*

"As a to-ken
Of our love . . ."

The bulk of the news media was gone, their daily reports long filed. The only ones left were stringers, independents hot on the trail of the story: videotaping the bonfire, interviewing the geeks, waiting for something dramatic to happen.

Burning witches at the stake, perhaps.

Feeding pagans to the lions.

Or maybe just a nice bright explosion . . .

"Jake, man, this has gone too far," he muttered, looking away from the bonfire and up into the starlit Pennsylvania sky. There were no answers there.

But there were no questions, either, and that was the nice part. There were no morons laying claim to intimate knowledge of the method underlying all this madness. Just darkness, occasionally punctuated by pinpoints of light: as fine a metaphor for the full scope of human understanding as anyone was liable to make.

It was not, however, an opinion that anyone was liable to voice. On either side of the fence. Not these days.

Not when there was a war going on.

Hempstead forgot about their lame vocalizations. His concentration was on the heavens, the subtle *phut-phut-phut* of a vehicle so far away that its presence could be little more than intuited.

But he knew it was there. Oh, yeah. No question. One could not spend so much time at the mercy of those big whirling blades and not feel it in his bones.

Somewhere . . . probably just over the next peak . . . a black dragonfly was casting its moonlit shadow over the green green Pennsylvania mountaintops. He could close his eyes and see it clearly: all the beauty and horror, the brutality and grace, the desperation and hope that the image had come to embody for him.

The tenor sax hung flush against his chest. He took another drag of smoke, blew it out, clutched the instrument closer. It had stuck with him through the bright hell and tragic heaven that was Vietnam, given voice to the pain and joy within when words could not even come close.

And it felt like singing now. That much was clear.

Hempstead grinned, then brought the mouthpiece to his lips. They were still *plinka-plink-plink*ing away at the bottom of the hill, still in the key of C. It was an enormous musical challenge, but Hempstead thought he'd take a crack at it. What the hell.

"Holy, Ho-lee
Holy, Ho-lee . . ."

A blistering assault of gravel-edged blues fired out of the saxophone's throat. It took the words right out of half the singers' mouths, ran a quick 220 volts through the entire bonfire battalion. *Don't you fret none*, Hempstead thought. *It's just dem ol' wild coyotes up on Debbil's Peak.*

Lord knows they're everywhere these days.

The bone-white Cadillac sped east along the rolling midnight hills just south of Pittsburgh. The turnpike was desolate at this hour, the darkness broken only by an occasional passing semi throwing long beams down the westbound lanes as it howled toward Ohio.

The top was down. The music was up. Steel City itself was rapidly receding into the background, the afterglow of the evening's melee at the Civic Arena already melding with fractured images of the riots in Cleveland, and Detroit before that, and Chicago before that, and on through the Midwest and the Plains States and the Southwest and . . .

"Eyaoww!" cried the Screamer in the front, little Dempsey Whatsisface. He had one arm out the window, hand pounding the door panel arhythmically. He looked decidedly green, even in the meager instrument lights. "Turn it *up! Eyaoww!*" His head bounced and bobbed like a cheap dashboard ornament.

The driver, whose name was Kyle, obliged him, cranking the music to the blasting point. Tara's voice poured out of the speakers. You couldn't hear the words. It didn't matter.

"*Eayowww!*" screeched Dempsey, fists pounding the door in whacked-out syncopation. His free hand pulled a Budweiser free from the warming six-pack on the floor, tabbed it open; he tipped his head back, tried to shotgun the entire twelve ounces. Gold carbonation poured into his mouth, only to bubble back and dribble down his chin and onto his ratty garb.

The others spasmed and snickered as the can crunched and pinged back into the slipstream. Dempsey didn't appear to notice. He passed the other cans back and shook his head like a dog after dinner, liquid flecking from the corners of his jaws. He was completely mad. Completely burnt.

Little fucker won't last much longer, Kyle thought. *Walker was right.*

They never do . . .

The endless joyride rolled on and on, as the Caddy's ever-changing occupants followed the tour. Outside every coliseum, every arena where the music had played, the finned silhouette had waited—poised, engine warmed and purring—after each show, for the pressing throngs and the thrash of fresh flesh.

Every time, they found another stray. Sometimes two. In Kansas City they'd even found twins: fifteen-year-old bimbettes with high little titties and the combined I.Q. of a pair of lead bookends. They squealed like piglets for damned near three hundred miles; and what was left of them eventually got dumped on First Avenue in St. Paul, where Prince first learned to steal Jimi's licks.

To further spread the Word.

Sometimes it was girls, sometimes boys. Always, they were young, drugged, and semidisplaced. The actual technique itself varied only slightly, depending on things like gender, geography, and individual style. But every time, the end result was the same.

It was a marking, like the *tickticktricktick* of meshing teeth on a gear, of the Passage.

Tonight was to be no exception.

There were five of them in the Caddy. Four were veterans of past incursions. Three were full-fledged Screamers. Two were almost spent: too far gone or unstable to rely upon anymore, too dangerous to keep around.

Only one was a neophyte, this evening's sacrificial lamb, plucked from the abundant flock pounding out of the Civic Arena not two hours past. He seemed, from all outward appearances, to fit right in: the hair was right—all starched up to look like black and purple cycle spokes. The clothes were right: all spandex-leather-stud-strapped stupidity. The attitude was right.

He's cocky, thought the driver of the Cadillac. *And wasted. He's perfect.* The shy ones usually flamed out, and the straight ones couldn't handle the Passage.

Kyle should know by now: he'd chauffered enough of them. Dozens, over the course of this tour. Of the speeding car's five occupants, he was the only one who'd been there from the first. Which was, of course, exactly as it should be. The entire operation was running more or less as planned; the end of this particular phase was rapidly drawing near.

He greatly looked forward to it.

Kyle's thoughts turned back over the span of the last three months. Many little spuds planted. Much ground covered, as the Caddy chewed up the night miles. He gunned the engine up past seventy; the V-8 guzzler responded with a smooth thrusting rush of power.

The highway hummed beneath them.

He looked into the rearview mirror. The little Wyler bitch wasn't looking too good these days, either. He wasn't surprised; from the moment they'd dragged her limp, shapely buns out of her house in Diamond Bar, he'd had his doubts. *Too stupid to live*, he thought, turning a grim smile inward. *Even* after *death*.

If that was, in fact, what it was. He'd seen an awful lot of death in his time and had personally administered more than his fair share. But this . . .

This was different.

He wasn't entirely sure exactly what happened to them *during* the Passage, but he was all too familiar with what happened to them afterwards. They were *all* bad; but this bitch, in particular, was starting to get under his skin. As her baby fat had dried up and her features had grown more gaunt and parched, she'd begun to remind him of the way a girl he'd once knocked up looked after she came out of the body shop:

like something had been sucked right out of her, and her body hadn't quite caught on yet.

Kyle thumbed in the cigarette lighter and pinched a Winston between his lips. They were lean and bloodless, like the rest of him; on the whole he bore a marked resemblance to a zombie Keith Richards, resuscitated by voodoo for MTV.

Strictly an illusion. Kyle wouldn't be caught dead on MTV, and was one of the only two beings in that car who could reasonably be called living.

And, most certainly, the only one apt to remain that way.

The lighter popped out. He lit the butt and drew smoke in deeply, expelling it back out into the rushing night air. He didn't like this job.

Screw it. He white-knuckled the steering wheel into submission. *Life's a bitch, and then you die. Kill 'em all, let God sort 'em out.* The dime store philosophy of Kyle Weatherman could be contained on the T-shirts offered in the back pages of *Soldier of Fortune* magazine: the very same source that had run the classified that had called him to serve his destiny.

It was a starkly simple ad: six words and a P.O. box number. They spoke of worlds past, and debts unpaid.

MOMMA SAYS: TIME TO PAY UP.

He knew instantly that it was true. The throbbing knuckle-scar of his missing finger told him so, like a bunion predicting a coming storm. His dreams told him so, every single night until his reply arrived. His sanity told him so, for its own sake.

He answered the ad, all right. Any choice in the matter was long since forfeit.

It brought them all back. People like Logan: spreading the Word randomly in his black van, cruising death and deliberately avoiding the tour path, to further throw off the scent. It brought Kyle: to this night, in this speeding car, to serve as strange an act as The Scream and their even-stranger manager, Walker. And strangest of all, to serve their fans.

Momma's own little kamikazes.

The Screamers.

Tara's voice husked something unintelligible through the speakers. Something moved in the rearview mirror. The tiny hairs on the back of Kyle's neck stood up as if trying to work their way around front, accompanied by an almost involuntary surge of bile as he contemplated what the stud in the back was about to quite literally get himself into. Kyle shuddered slightly. *Jesus, couldn't he smell it?*

Guess not. The stud rustled around and said something that sounded like "Ooh, baby." On the passenger side, the Dempsey-thing twitched spastically and delivered another clipped *"Eayoww!"*. That was starting to get on Kyle's nerves.

It was their common expletive, after the transformation; and it seemed that, the further along they went, the more that became the most cogent sentiment the little fuckers could voice. It increased in tandem with their instability.

Screamers, bottom line, really were rock 'n' roll kamikazes, with their engines on fire and the conning tower in sight. And the only things they were good for were making trouble.

And making more Screamers.

Cyndi Wyler sat in the back seatwell, hair whipping around her face in a medusan swirl of Rasta-clumped, ropey tendrils. Not bathing for extended periods will do that. Her clothes were similarly ripe with the smell of stale funk, stale beer, stale sweat.

Her head lolled dreamily. The Mylar Band-Its reflected stray oncoming lights of passing traffic, giving the appearance of glowing, shifting eyes. Strictly an illusion. The eyes were the windows to the soul, after all.

She was possessed of neither anymore.

She'd also lost her tan, fourteen pounds, and major portions of her frontal lobes. But she still had her girlish figure, much to the joy of the geek sitting beside her. *What was his name?* She couldn't recall. He leaned closer, smelling of Stiff Stuff, smoke, and poor oral hygiene. It hardly mattered. There had been so many like him: in parking lots and beer bashes, in woods and under bleachers.

It was always the same. They'd drug her, she'd take them. They'd prong her, she'd let them. Grunt and thrust, grunt and thrust. She'd take it. And only then, when they were lost, deep inside, would they meet her Maker.

That alone felt good.

The rest she felt as if from a great distance. There was very little of her left to feel *anything* anymore: decaying shreds hung in the space where her soul had been, ruptured synapses trying vainly to comprehend the full scope of what was going on.

No use. She wasn't in control. She *had* no control. Her body was a bootleg far-removed from the master tape, endlessly churning out fourth-generation dupes as it hurtled toward a blood-red blackness that throbbed in perfect syncopation with the speakers behind her head. She could vaguely discern voices, howling like a pack of joyriding banshees as they pressed her ruined relays to overload. The sound pounding into the back of her skull was the only thing she could seem to key in on; it filled her many empty spaces, gave her the only sense of direction in an otherwise reeling void.

She felt the insistent, brutish probe. Her body responded in kind, heat and moisture pooling up deep within her belly. Something was moving down there; she couldn't say exactly what. It was like trying to decipher stray signals bleeding in from another bandwidth, one that was forever beyond her grasp.

Understanding wasn't important, however.

It was time to spread the Word.

"Give it to me, baby.
Wanna feel you fill the hole.
You gotta giveitomee, bay-bayee . . ."

Stiff Stuff tugged at her jeans.

"C'mon, baby, like the song says," he slurred, *"giveitto-mee* . . ." She moaned, low in her throat.

Stiff Stuff took this as a positive sign and pressed on. Unbuttoning the last fly-notch on her 501's. Hiking out her paisley bigshirt-tails. Moving in for the kill. He'd never done it in the back of a moving car before, but hey. The chick was a pig, fer sure; but she was *into* it, man, and he wasn't about to argue.

His pants slid down to his knees in record time; hers came off entirely. He shoved one thick-knuckled hand under the rim of her rancid panties, groping her breasts with the other. Her body felt chill and goose-pimply in the whipping breeze, but he liked it that way. Made her nipples nice and stiff.

She groaned a little louder and writhed beneath his touch.

Nobody else seemed to be paying the slightest attention. It was a dream come true.

The music wailed.

The voices grew louder: *"Give it to me, bay-bayee!"*

Stiff Stuff made full contact, pushing deep inside her.

Cyndi pushed back. Something inside her went *snap!*

Blood started to well in her crotch; Stiff Stuff realized that something was amiss. He tried to pull away; Cyndi held him tight.

Snap snap.

And the real screaming started.

Nine

ate summer. Darkness.

And Jake was back again.

Thick scent of exhaust wafting up from the LZ as the choppers finished their drop and made for the relative safety of the bigger base to the south. Jake limped up the hill to his sandbagged bunker, unhitched his rucksack, and heaved his tired self down. He picked up his two warm cans of Bud: today's big treat. His reward for survival.

Yahoo.

In his left hand, gripped by its dusty, sweat-tracked neck, was the battered black market acoustic guitar he'd picked up in Saigon on his last in-country R&R. It was a tiny thing, a Silvertone, with a cheap plate tailpiece and a skinny little string-strap and a Day-Glo sunburst finish that he knew would last about a week back in the bush, and nothing at all like the vintage Strat he'd left back in the World. So what. It was something to hold on to that gave back anything but heat and pain and hurt, and it was his friend. He'd spent the rest of that R&R wacked on Jack Daniel's and Thai stick, singing his

Saigon lullaby to the whores, orphans, and cyclo-boys who littered the hot, stinking alleys in the Paris of the Orient.

For three whole days, nobody died.

That was a million years ago, give or take a millennium. Jake was back again. The guitar was dinged and cracked and ugly as ol' buddy Duncan's specks, but it was still here, dammit. It was his friend, the only one he had left.

Much safer that way. It didn't pay to get too close to anything that could draw fire. Duncan taught him that much. *Don't bunch up, Doc. Don't get too close*. Good advice, when you could follow it.

Pity it didn't always work that way.

Jake felt the back of his throat choking up. Too much dust, swirling up in the choppers' wakes. Too many friends going home; too many of them in pieces. When he closed his eyes he could practically see the black rubber sacks that would fill the bellies of the freedom birds, day after day after day. It got to the point where they hardly seemed real anymore; just tag 'em, bag 'em, load 'em up, and move 'em out. *Next . . . Next . . .*

Zip, zip. Snap, snap.

Next.

It was a factory, a big assembly line of death. It was utterly amoral: progress measured daily in gross tonnage of dead flesh. Every pound counted. Head. Chest. Arms, legs, eyes, balls; alone or in pairs. It was currency, the only one that counted. A hundred times a day. On brush-clogged trails and both sides of the endless miles of can-strung concertina wire. In hooches and hamlets. Buy now, pay later.

And pay.

And pay . . .

He drained the first beer in three gulps and crushed the can, very slowly, in his fist. He was amazed at how calm he was, how strange it felt to *be* back. As if he'd never left at all. He looked out over the darkening fire base, a littered mass of canvas and burlap, steel and tin, and vast, sweating humanity that sprawled across the denuded hillside and flanged out toward the jungle like the hand of Doom. Gun emplacements like thick knuckles, daring anyone to come closer.

They hardly ever did; in person, anyway.

They much preferred for us to come to them.

Twenty klicks north, a detachment of Skyraiders from the 172nd Airborne was doing just that, busily pounding the Ho Bo woods into mulch. He could feel the shock waves running into his ass and all the way up his spine, like God and the devil going one-on-one in the Cosmic Badass playoffs.

At the moment he wasn't exactly sure who was winning.

One thing was certain: he wasn't.

There was nothing *to* win out here, beyond another sixty seconds of surrealistic survival. This was an alternate universe, unto itself. The future didn't exist. The past had never happened. There was only one elongated, screaming present, now and forever, amen.

Besides, the forces moving through this world didn't care whether you understood; they didn't even appear to fully understand themselves. So what.

Understanding wasn't mandatory.

Participation was.

So you played the game: endless cycles of mines and booby traps and spider holes that held opponents who nine out of ten times you never even fucking saw. Not that it mattered. The opponents were young and old, men and women, little kids and babies. The faces changed, but the name was always the same.

Victor Charley.

And he was a crafty little fucker. Believe it.

He made you play on his turf, by his rules. In the jungle, mostly: wired and tired and permanently strung-out. He'd turn your own body against you, forcing you to live for months with your skin rashing in the heat and your feet rotting in your boots and the ringworm and lice and fire ants and scorpions and snakes all around and over you and in you. He's snipe at you by day and lob mortar rounds on you at night. He'd send his own fucking kids to beg for candy and cigmo with grenades taped to their bellies. Or maybe he'd just blow your pecker off when you paused on the trail to take a leak.

And always, after the tripwire or the ambush that left half your team splattered and dying before you could bind 'em tight enough to be Medevacked the hell outathere, he'd fall back. To the one place you'd never ever want to follow.

Straight into the bowels of the mother herself.
Into the jungle. Into the tunnels.

Jake popped the other can, fired up some Buddha grass, and leaned back on his pack. The gauze-packed pressure bandages made for a nice cushion. Comfy-cozy. He sipped and toked, watching the smoke rise up to mingle with the distant smoke lofting off the horizon. The Skyraiders had gone bye-bye, having shot their collective wad; a Spooky gunship was now cruising the trails, long tongues of flame licking out its side as its belly guns belched death. Munch munch. Winning hearts and minds.

In the funny papers, maybe.

In the bush it was another story. It was way too easy to die out there. Duncan had taught him that. Big, gawky guy with X-ray specs, King Nerd turned tough. Legally blind. It was Duncan who had taken Jake under his wing during his first-days in-country, when Jake was still a shavehead FNG.

Fucking New Guys were routinely scorned. They were always cut less slack than anybody, and Jake had geared himself up for his fair share of abuse.

Then Duncan came along.

Maybe he just felt sorry for him, maybe this was kar-mic payback; Jake never really knew or asked. Like or dislike happened instantly in the bush: it was a real pure kind of thing. Duncan took to him, showing him the ropes and keeping him from getting his butt shot off, until Jake could fend for himself. Even got him the corpsman posi-tion on his squad.

Hell, it was Duncan who pointed out the Silvertone on that long-gone R&R; at dusk, after a day of booney-humping, he'd liked to perch up on the sandbags, grinning and squinting as Jake pounded out the changes to every-thing from Creedence Clearwater to "Purple Haze."

And when Jake had first heard the distant wail of an alto sax answering back one night, it was Duncan who knew who it came from.

"Hempstead." He drew out the syllable in his native Lou-isiana coonass till it came out "Heyamp-staid."

Jake looked up at him: hunched over on the bunker like that, Duncan looked like a bird of prey in a Warner Broth-

ers cartoon. His glasses caught a ray of waning sunlight, flashing amber in the shadow of his face.

"Say what?" Jake asked without breaking his rhythm.

"Hempstead, boy. Big black dude. Door gunner with the hundred and twentieth. Carries that horn with him absolutely everywhere. Plays it in the clouds on the way out. You ain't met him yet?"

Jake shook his head, still playing. The sax faded away.

"You will." Duncan nodded sagely and lit a joint. "Shoot, Doc, I b'lieve you are the only person in the entire world could get feedback outta a 'coustic guitar." He jumped down and held the doob up to Jake's lips.

"You gonna be a star, boy. Ol' Doc Rock. Yup, yup, yup . . ."

Jake laughed, erupting smoke. He'd had to stop playing. When Duncan wanted to he could seem like the stupidest person ever born.

Nobody ever fucked with him, though; it was a luxury he had earned. Because Duncan could just as easily run and hip-fire an M60 like most guys could shoulder-fire an M16 standing, all while carrying enough ammo to qualify as his own assistant. Could blow the titties off a field mouse at five hundred yards. He also had a knack for sniffing out booby traps and set-ups.

Duncan was a squad leader, scout, and one-man fire support team, all rolled up in one. His patrols had a higher survival rate, and that made him very very popular. He took care of his people. No one really seemed interested in winning, not anymore. The good guys were pulling out, the party was over. It was only a matter of time before the gears of the big green death machine ground all the way down.

And no one, but no one, wanted to get pinched in the last few turns . . .

Jake looked out into the darkness; the gunship was moving south. Fire-tongues licked the distant ground, going *brrrraaaaaaaaatttttt* like big neon raspberries from hell. He snuffed the joint and leaned back, stoned again. The buzz was almost as strong as the fatigue that nailed his bones to the bunker. He wished he still had some morphine ampules, but he'd used them all up this afternoon. He watched the gunship till the darkness swallowed it completely.

When he looked back to the bunker, Duncan was gone. Of course. Jake wasn't really surprised; he was just back. He closed his hollow eyes and clutched the guitar to his chest like a dead puppy.

No one ever wants to get caught in the last few turns, he thought.

But someone always does . . .

It should have been another routine, nine-to-five search-and-destroy on some suspected VC cadres operating supply routes out of some butthole dinville near Chu Ci: chopper out, win the hearts and minds of the locals, burn down a hooch or two, and split. Snap snap.

Except . . .

Except that the lieutenant, that fucking brown-bar ROTC idiot no more than three days in-country, had to tag along for the ride. Which would have been tolerable, had he stayed out of the way.

But no; he had to go and pick up the fucking kid. Never pick up the kids. Especially near an unsearched ville, especially the ones that run up to meet you at the edge of the trail. Never. It was like a rule.

But he did it, a big shit-eating grin on his pink-cheeked, all-American face. They had barely spaced their line, coming off the trail. Brown bar had no idea of reality, was heavy into the hearts-and-minds trip, as if he really believed it. The kid was maybe five, maybe six. Mama-san nowhere in sight. Little high-pitched, reedy voice calling out Pidgin English, going "Numba One, GI! Candee, GI!" Couldn't even tell if it was a boy or a girl.

Didn't matter.

It blew up, just the same.

The lieutenant and the kid died instantly. So did the top-six and five grunts: Sanchez, Claiborne, Ricechex, Gomer, and Natch, the radio operator. Natch's radio was ripped right off his back, went flying ass-over-teakettle some thirty feet into the air and landed with a tube-crunching whump! The squad's remnants flattened into the earth in a split second.

Just as the automatic weapons opened up . . .

Jake cried out, as the fabric of time itself again went all

rubbery and strange: too short here, too long there, stopped altogether in manic frozen-flashes of nightmare replay. . . .

Three more hit at once. Half the squad gone, stone-dead. Two still twitching in the undergrowth, desperately trying not to attract fire. The rest of the team falling back onto the trail, capping wildly on a ragged azimuth to the ville. Duncan and his A-gunner laying down clipped, suppressing fire. Jake tried to inch over to the wounded. No go. Answering rounds cut through the jungle canopy like a swarm of hot metal bees, whizzing inches overhead or pinging clumps of sod out of the packed earth of the trail. The wounded started screaming. Duncan's A-gunner, big black guy from Philadelphia named Willie, had to lift up a little to get one of the hundred-round bandoliers over his shoulder.

Willie from Philly took two rounds in the face: boom boom.

The A-gunner's brains blew all over him. His squad was getting greased.

And Duncan just freaked.

He opened up with the M60, rocking and rolling and screaming incomprehensibly, and just wilted the place. Answering fire from the ville momentarily halted in the onslaught of it; the rest of the squad seized the opportunity to let loose with M79's, willy petes, M16's, absolutely everything they had.

The fire cut a swath of destruction across the entire face of the hamlet, shooting up huts, animals, anything and everything that moved, stood still, bled or blew up. Judgment Day in dinville, and God was pissed.

Only trouble was, He couldn't seem to decide which side He was on.

Because the enemy had already disappeared in the confusion. Retreating back into their hooch-holes and tunnels, giving up the hamlet as lost.

But not before they found the big, bad M60.

Not before they found Duncan.

It came like a parting shot, tracking in slo-mo: a well-placed farewell lofting out of the smoke and burning debris of the huts and arcing toward the one thing they particularly did not want pursuing them. Jake saw it coming, tried to holler: his mouth complied, but flesh could not possibly *move fast enough to meet his needs. He wheeled, like a man dipped in a vat of molasses, toward Duncan.*

Duncan stood, hip-firing, a weird shadow playing across his gore-flecked face, unaware of the long, smoky fingers singling him out for doom. At the last possible second, he turned to meet Jake's cry.

And the rounds caught him square in the chest.

Jake screamed. And he kept right on screaming long after Duncan fell. He screamed as he stared at his dead friend's face, the glasses bent and blasted and shattered. He screamed as he hunkered over him, ripping open the pressure bandages that would never, ever stop all that blood coming out of all those holes.

But he wasn't screaming at that anymore. His hands worked by rote as his attention remained transfixed on the burning huts of the ville. He was screaming at the smoke, which rose in greasy plumes to curl and mingle with the canopy of foliage, to flicker and shift as Jake's screams melded with those of the incinerating villagers ahead, to form what looked very much like an enormous mouth.

And then the mouth suddenly split open to reveal teeth in light and smoke and shadow, which flickered, and glistened, and grew.

And grinned, like a giant Cheshire cat.

The firing broke off, ordnance-echo ringing his ears like cathedral bells. The jungle grew very still for a split second.

And then the shelling walked in.

One-twenty mike-mikes started dropping through the trees, covering Charley's retreat, going boom boom boom boom like some invisible giant throwing the world's biggest temper tantrum. There was no way to call in their own fire-support; the radio had been blown clear to shit. The squad had, too. The shells came down in waves, blowing rocks and earth and trees into ten billion spinning splinters.

And there was no time.

To do anything.

But run.

And scream.

And run . . .

Ten

And then he was in the room, in the clutch of the cool dark air, with nothing but dim shape and shadow to see and nothing but his own scream in his ears.

He stopped screaming, and the pieces fell together. He was sitting bolt-upright in the bed, covered with sweat, heart thudding from his toes to his temples. He caught a hitched breath, drowned for a moment in the silence that followed it, and then Rachel was beside him, sitting up and staring into his eyes.

"Jake?" she said, her voice a croaking whisper. He couldn't see her eyes, lost as well in pools of shadow, but he could feel the terror behind them.

Yes, he tried to say, but again his flesh betrayed him. His mouth closed, opened, let out another razor breath. He realized that his whole body was shaking, and that his heart and left armpit were throbbing in unison.

"Oh, God." The words came out of his mouth before he knew it. His teeth began to chatter, and a rush of nerves-gone-haywire rippled through him. It was the dream, the fucking dream, come back again to rake him and destroy him if it could.

Rachel touched him, and he wanted to recoil, but his body was not his own. It ran itself, and it had programmed itself for another spasm, which came. "Nuh," he said. It was meant to be *no*.

Rachel pulled her hand away, and he sensed her click into focus. God, she was great. She was the best. She knew instinctively just what to do.

He tried to think about how great she was when the next spasm seared through him with jiggling hot hooks. It was called *anxiety attack* in polite circles; he preferred the term *nervous breakdown*. His kind thoughts about her gave him something to do while his body lost control again and his teeth continued to chatter.

Another breath rasped in. It was shallow and utterly unfulfilling. Another followed. And another. He might as well have not been breathing at all. *I could die right now*, said a voice in his brain. It was a rational voice. It was more terrifying than the pain. His heart let out a surge of agony and sorrow. His voice began to moan.

"Breathe," Rachel said. It was not a request. "Breathe deep and relax."

He tried to laugh. He tried to say the word *relax*. It didn't work. He tried to breathe and did a marginal job. Another tremor ran through him, volcanic. "Ah," he said. Tears began to well in his eyes.

And his chest, his chest was caught in a constricting steel claw, his heart a muscle within a network of muscles that squeezed and squeezed and squeezed, the *mectoralis major* is connected to the rib bone, an' hear da word of da Lord. He tried to think about Rachel again, how beautiful she was, the words she was saying. He breathed again, a bit deeper this time.

"Hold it in," Rachel said. "Count to ten. One, two . . ."
Another rush of pain.
". . . three, four . . ."
He held the air inside.
". . . five, six . . ."
He thought of beautiful things.
". . . seven, eight . . ."
He couldn't name one to save his life.
". . . nine, ten." And he exhaled. The pain was still there. His teeth jackhammered together.

"Again," she said, taking hold of his right hand. "Breathe in." She squeezed. He squeezed back and inhaled.
"One, two . . ."
The room was dark, but he could see the details now.
". . . three, four . . ."
It was his bedroom. The one that they shared.
". . . five, six . . ."
I'm going to die, the voice said. *Fuck off*, he told it.

". . . seven, eight . . ."

His breath wheezed out of him.

"Let's try it again." Her voice calm, rational. "Breathe in."

Another rush. Electric spasm pain.

"I said breathe in."

"Ih . . . it's easier seh . . ."

"Don't fight me, baby." No change in the tone.

"Said than done," he completed. The pain was enormous. He tried to smile, heard the words *heart attack. Stroke.*

"Take a big deep breath."

"Uh," he said, and breathed in. Not too deep.

"One, two . . ."

He breathed out.

"Okay. Breathe in."

He couldn't.

"Breathe in."

"Ah cahn . . ."

The terror was complete now, stunning in its depth. The words *Yes, I am really going to die now* tried to articulate themselves, couldn't, left him to deal with the feeling they expressed.

"Yes, you can. Breathe in. Start counting."

He tried.

It worked.

"One, two . . ."

She needs me, he thought.

". . . three, four . . ."

She and Natalie.

". . . five, six . . ."

There's no way I'm gonna let this kill me.

". . . seven, eight . . ."

The pain locked into a sudden stasis: there but not active. He held his breath.

". . . nine, ten."

He exhaled, felt a little bit better.

"Again."

He breathed in. It was easier this time. His mind had room to roam as he listened to her count. He was not looking at her, but he could see her in his mind; the image was sharper, clearer, than the dim light would have afforded his eyes.

And as the numbers ticked past and he breathed on command, he got a flash of role-reversing perfection: of Rachel on the bed, breathing deep as he counted out the contraction times in approved Lamaze fashion. Giving birth, preserving life.

"Ease the tension out of your shoulders," she said. "Down to your feet and right outta your body."

He concentrated on his shoulders. Yes, unspeakable tension there. They were hunched almost up to his jawline, like a bag lady huddled against the cold. Funny, perverse: the more you hunched, the colder you got. He wondered why the exact wrong reaction was the most automatic, what the hell God had had in mind, as he concentrated on letting the wire-tightness seep down and out.

"Breathe again," Rachel said, then paused and added, "How are you doing?"

"I'll live." He took another shot at smiling. This time, it worked.

"Breathe in." She was smiling, too.

Fifteen minutes later, he could start to think about it. The pain had receded to a low drone, a wash of background color. If Anheuser-Busch still knew their stuff, even that would start to vanish in the next twenty minutes or so.

He was down in the living room, which gleamed faintly blue in the light from the TV screen. The volume was kept low, in deference to those members of the household who hadn't just been dragged to hell in their sleep.

His underwear and robe were damp with sweat, like the dark locks that were pasted and had been pulled away and pasted again to his forehead and neck. The bottle of Bud in his hand was damp with sweat as well. Most of it was down the tubes; the backup was already on the table beside him. He was not a heavy drinker . . . had not been for several years . . . but the old craving for sedation would never ever completely go away.

How could it? Pain was pain. Pain was no fun at all. Pain was something to be alleviated immediately, or at least as fast as possible. You could sit and philosophize about it all you wanted to, talk about the vital function it performed . . . *no pain, no gain*, and all that . . . but when it had you by the screaming vital mortal organic tissue, you wanted only one thing, and that was for the pain to please please Jesus God just go away.

Blue static pulsed on the TV screen, anticipating the unreeling of the tape in the VCR. It was Cody's edited-down version of the best of today's news and views, culled from every available network and slapped onto VHS cassette. Jake had mandated this video accounting of the world several months before, when Rock Aid became official and mandated that he know what the hell was going on. Good ol' Cody Adams had risen to the occasion, as Jake had known he would: scouring the *TV Guide*, recording up to five stations at once if need be in pursuit of the up-to-the-minute broad-band perspective.

The remote control was on the table, next to the lamp and the extra beer. Jake picked it up, pressed it into service. A click. A whir. A glitch in the signal.

"Make me feel better," he said. "Har har har."

The world, ever-perverse, denied and satisfied.

Fighting in Nicaragua. Fighting in El Salvador. Central America in a tight-cogged military grip. Billions of U.S. dollars already sunk into offensive defensive posturing. Torture, disappearance, assassination. State of terror. State of siege.

That was a comforting comparison: Central America in the late eighties, Southeast Asia in the early sixties. Jake got a clear picture of his little buddy Ted, watching the teeth of flame smile up at him from a dead and burning Panamanian village. It didn't seem too soon for full-scale U.S. involvement, did it? Not really, no.

His chest twanged discomfort. He finished his beer.

The next story came on.

Evangelical wars, growing ever more sordid, as this minister accused that minister of the next most depraved indiscretion, and the televised Kingdom of Heaven teetered on the increasingly rickety scaffold that held it aloft.

There was no end to it. At least none in sight. The media and the government were coming down on Godscam feet first—it was clear that they'd been waiting a long time for this, were having a field day, in fact—and every time they landed, a little more spew came up. Lot of skeletons in the closets of the Kingdom, it seemed. Rattling louder all the time.

I don't know, Jake mused. *But if I had a multi-million-*

*dollar tax-free empire, with $600,000-a-year "special assis-
tants" working for me, I think I might just send some of those
skeletons down to the briny deep. Tie up the loose ends, so to
speak.* He wondered, for every $254,000 tail-piece, how many
other indiscretions had wound up on the pay end of the food
chain. Lot cheaper that way. Less noisy, too.

He wondered, briefly, what kind of bones his ol' pal
Furniss clutched, hidden, in the dark.

"One thing for sure, ol' buddy," he said, talking to Furniss
as he talked to himself. "You play your cards right on this
Murder Music shit, everybody will want to know *all about you*,
real soon."

The amazing thing was that the faithful kept coming back.
Like Nam, like Iranscam, like every other fucking thing on
the news, it came and it danced and it went out again. After
all the allegations of Hahn-humping and ho-moing came and
went, and the Jim-bone connected to the Jerry-bone, and
heah da word ob de Lawd!—after all that, the faithful still
believed.

They needed so desperately to believe . . .

The next story came on.

*Controversy, digging ever deeper into an already controver-
sial administration. Hirings, firings, guns-for-money, or drugs-
for-guns, the entire cast spinning like an enormous wheel of
fortune that loses, not because they don't know the answer, but
because they lie about it.*

No surprises there. He'd already called that tune with the
band's follow-up to "TV Ministries," a touching ballad called
"Just Like Richard Nixon." Another hit, fer sure. Duplicity
forever: past, present, and doubtless future. To expect anything
else was to gum the ring pacifier of unheeded history. Santayana
be sadly damned; those who learn from the past were doomed
to repeat it anyway, just because of all the other dumb fucks
who hadn't.

Jake opened the second beer.

The next story came on.

He tried to watch it. He couldn't. He got the vaguest hint
that it was about a crackdown at the Mexican border, but that
only helped to drive him back into himself. The thought of
guns and helmets and perimeters held was the last brick in the
wall . . .

. . . and then he was back in the dirt, with Duncan's susurrating chest pressed like a seashell to his ear . . .

. . . and the words *Why are you doing this?* took shape in his mind: more than a prayer, any answer from God more than welcome. It didn't make sense that the dreams should be back. There was no reason, no reason to freak out at all.

Unless the dreams were more than just spooky subtexts, more than psychoanalytically significant phantoms. Unless the dreams themselves were some kind of messages, scrawled on the bulletin board of the collective unconscious.

Unless something's coming.

The words caught him off-guard, sent him ass-backward into the ice-water portion of the soul. Everything looked different: focus intensified, diamond-edged in perfection and precision of cut. It put a thin red line around everything he loved.

It reminded him of just how easily those things could be sliced from his life.

And then it showed him Rock Aid, with Jerry's foreboding words afloat in the air around him. *Violence*, it said. *All I know is that I've been having these very bad dreams lately . . .*

. . . and the next clip came up: a video, one that Cody must have picked up off the satellite dish, some obscure program that featured the promos that never made it through MTV's homogenous muzzle-filter.

It was vintage Scream: their first hit, "Stick It In": brutal, chillingly precise, compelling as hell even with the sound down low . . .

. . . because the images themselves were so frentic, opening up with some kick-ass animation: of a sunglassed face, skin purpled as night-flesh, turning to meet the camera as flames burning twin holes through the dripping lenses gave way to glowing, smoking pits and the mouth stretched impossibly wide, as though no orifice could adequately shape the force of what was coming . . .

. . . and Jake found himself inexorably sucked in, as the camera's point-of-view zoomed closer, closer, then completely inside that horrible stratching mouth and on, down a moist and winding esophageal roller coaster . . .

. . . and the Scream was there, alive and kicking on stage: artfully lip-synching and gesticulating to one of their songs as a

spread-eagled and bound nymphet offered herself on a flaming stage, a squirming sacrificial slaughter of the innocent . . .

. . . and Jake stared into the glowing screen, until the rest of the room, the rest of the world, was reduced to background noise nattering in the wings . . .

. . . *as the angles changed, and changed: Tara Payne, stalking the stage, extorting the crowd to madness; Alex Royale, imperious and remote behind his wall of keyboards; Rod Royale, whirling around the nymphet with a guitar that was all sharp edges and angles . . .*

. . . *then ramming the point of its neck straight through her heart, skewering the girl like a puppet on a pencil, punching clear through the back. The shock of the impact was repeated in hitching, hyper blips, getting closer and closer until you could practically feel the blood running down the neck to spatter Rod Royale's still-moving fingers . . .*

. . . and then he jerked himself back to the living room, where Cody's editing finesse cut to an up-to-the-minute report, pertaining to another riot at another Scream concert in yet another city, this time Pittsburgh . . .

While Jake sat there, thrumming terror.

Fully aware that, if he was right, the dreams were not the only things likely to worsen.

Eleven

Pittsburgh. Six a.m. No trace of sunlight in the sky. Walker lay in the darkness of his hotel room, unable to sleep, listening to the silence breathe and watching previews of the apocalypse in his mind.

It would be soon: that much he knew. All the signs were there. *Too* soon, perhaps, the end.

And then?

"I don't know," he mumbled into the gloom. The sound of his own voice surprised him; he was not the sort of man who often talked to empty rooms.

Usually, the empty rooms spoke to him first.

Down the hall, outside his door, the ice machine clattered. Another frozen payload delivered. Walker had reserved one whole floor for The Scream and another for the crew; shortly after five, it had finally fallen still, given way to stuporous sleep.

The whore was gone, as well; paid for and all but forgotten, just another wet spot on the endlessly changing bed. He lay beside the moist souvenir of her visit, nickel and diming his fifth of Finlandia to death and chain-smoking Lucky Strikes.

While his mind spun off reel after reel of doom for the back of his eyes to see.

Walker had always smoked unfiltered Luckies. Maybe it was the name. Maybe it was the fact that, if any cigarette could finally nail his coffin shut for good, where so many men had failed, Luckies would have to be the ones. He was, like all good soldiers, superstitious in the extreme.

Especially now.

Especially now that he knew.

Walker had one choice coffin nail ablaze in his fingertips, nearly singeing the skin; its tip was the only light upon him. It flared as he dragged on it, setting his gaunt forty-six-year-old face off in stark jack-o'-lantern relief. There was no looseness to his features, no smile; all his angles were jagged and tight as the sheets on a boot-camp bunk. The glint in his eyes fell back to black-lagoon stillness when he exhaled and the light receded.

And that, of course, was when Alex began to scream.

Walker jumped, at first; then his brain kicked in. *You little asshole*, he thought. *Why can't you just hold out a little longer?* He already knew the answer; unfortunately, that did nothing to solve the problem.

Alex screamed again. It was the genuine article: agonized, terrified, in full view of death. It was a sound that Walker'd come to know intimately, had hoped against hope that he'd never hear again. Not for the first time, he thought about how nice it would be if they could just leave the little fucker behind.

But no. Like it or not, the crip was critical to the plan.

Momma had made that plain. *Without our boy genius, there is no Scream.*

Something black as oil and heart-blood in the tone: a sarcasm born of dread. *Even Momma is nervous now,* Walker noted with an inward grin.

The question is: Why aren't I?

"Listen," Walker said. "Tonight is Philly. Saturday is Rock Aid. Monday is Labor Day. Tick tick tick. We take over the Spectrum in eighty-eight hours. That's not very long in the scheme of things, is it?"

"It only takes a second to die."

"He won't die."

"I wasn't speaking of him. *I've tried this before."*

Touché, Walker thought, taking a moment to focus.

"Yes," he countered. "But now you have me."

Momma chuckled. Schizophrenia: darkly divine.

"Yes," it said. *"Now we have each other."*

Alex screamed again, but this time it was muffled. Walker turned and surreptitiously scoured the room with his gaze. The only light in the room crept through the slit beneath the door, laying an ornately corrugated slab of brilliance across the thick pile carpet.

The light distended, grew long and wide.

It smiled at him.

"You say he's fine," it said. *"I'm sure you're right.*

"But go check, all the same."

The light had teeth.

"You got it," Walker said. He didn't bother with shoes. There were still things to be feared, even this close to the end.

If there are no guarantees, he thought, *then the end might just as well be the beginning. . . .*

He moved toward the door.

Carefully side-stepping the mouth of his master.

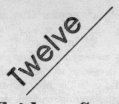

Twelve

Friday, September 4

Morning on the mountain came up picture-perfect: sunny and bright, with broad hints that the rest of the day would follow suit. The temperature was gently warm and inviting, the humidity unseasonably low. Birds' songs riffled through the lush greenery of the mountain. A cool western breeze swished the overhanging branches, the last hints of the darkness receding from the insistent press of day. If you strained an ear toward the southern lee, you could hear the faint burble of the stream that spilled down the falls on its way to hook up first with the Swatara creek, and ultimately the Susquehanna itself.

Slim Jim loved that. He was a city-turned-nature boy, his very name an anomalous holdover from younger, leaner days. A lot had changed since then: he'd traded in a big green Huey Bell for a fleet of sleek, black Engstrom turbos, and his clientele had switched from scarred armies of teenagers to well-heeled, traveling businessmen. *Like rock stars, for example.*

He'd also traded in his bean pole physique for a barrel chest and a full head of cropped black hair for a half head that culminated in a piratical ponytail. But James Edgar Willis had managed to keep a few things intact over the years, in spite of it all. His smile, which was still wide and genuine and easily invoked. His friendship with Hempstead, door gunner/saxman supreme, which had ebbed and flowed over time, but invariably returned to its source. His love for the sticks of hickory-flavored beef by-products that forever graced the right-hand corner of his mouth.

And his love for the morning. The morning was always his favorite time of day, the absolute finest for flying. The air seemed clearer, somehow, and the still-sleeping world appeared an incrementally more peaceful place. It was an illusion that had proved itself wrong more than once. But it was one that he held on to, nonetheless.

Especially here; in a lot of ways he preferred an overnight stopover on the mountain to just about anywhere in the world. He munched on a doughnut as he did a little impromptu inspection tour around the parking apron/landing pad to the rear of the lodge.

Not that he really needed to or anything—he always tucked his bird in nice and tight at night, making sure the rotor blades were anchored and everything stowed right. He just liked the excuse to get out and appreciate the silence.

Besides, he had a relatively low tolerance level for zealots of any stripe, and he didn't want one of the righteous to help the wrath of the Almighty along any. By dinking with the helicopter's clutch, say, or loosening the bolts on the tail rotor. The idea of losing power and crash-landing on these piney rocks appealed to him not in the slightest.

And who knew? The way Hempstead was talking, these clowns were probably harmless. But it wouldn't hurt to take a little sunrise stroll around the perimeter. Just in case.

So he walked, munching his doughnut. And he checked.

And when the twig snapped behind him, he whirled like a two-hundred-pound ballerina and brought the .38 out of his belt clip with a deft and practiced grace that belied his bulk.

It was head-level and cocked in a second.

"Sloppy, very sloppy," Jim said, smiling.

"If I was tryin', you'd be dead," Hempstead replied. "And a pleasant good morning to you, too."

"In your dreams, homeboy," Jim said sarcastically, uncocking the pistol and slipping it back under his shirttail. He turned his attention back to the sleeping whirlybird. "Out communing with nature, are we?"

" 'Bout half."

"Know what ya mean. How is the dear girl?"

"She fine, but she wish you'd quit scaring the wildlife with this bug of yours." Hempstead smiled and gestured to the Engstrom.

Slim Jim nodded. "Be scarier with your ugly ass on board, squatting behind a .50-calibre. We could buzz the bozos."

"Just like *DIE HIGH*." Hempstead grinned nostalgically,

and both men broke up. *DIE HIGH* was the name they'd given to their Lucky Bird, the only chopper in the entire wing of their Airborne Brigade that had made it through the entire tour. It was the source of their bond and helped explain why Spectra Helicopters, Jim's Jersey-based transport operation, had landed the bid for the fairly lucrative Rock Aid gig.

"Any idea when we're heading for Philly?" Jim asked.

Hempstead shrugged and checked his watch: oh-seven-thirty. Most of the system was already taken care of by the concert promoters; the particular specialty items that the Hamer Band required were broken down and loaded into the truck the night before. They weren't due at JFK Stadium until early afternoon. Everything appeared to be right on schedule. "I dunno; we prob'ly ought to head out around ten or so."

"Who's going with me?"

"Jake, Pete, the Bobs, and me."

"What about Jess?"

Hempstead looked back to the lodge. "She riding in later," he said, his tone veiled. "Said she got some last-minute shit to take care of."

"Problems?"

"I dunno. She say she can handle it."

They both caught the hollow clunk of a car door slamming around front at the same time. They walked around the building in time to see Jesse's red Suzuki 4 × 4 disappearing down the drive, kicking back a trail of tiny gravel projectiles in its wake.

"Well, she's sure's shit gettin' the jump on it, whatever it is." Jim said.

"Yeah," Hempstead sighed. "Or vice versa."

Thirteen

There was no one at the gate.

Thank God, Jesse sighed, although she somehow doubted that He had anything to do with it. Certainly, if the Pastor Furniss was to be believed, the heavens should go black and great fiery holes should open up in the macadam to swallow her, carnal sins and all. At the very least, a gaggle of finger-waggling tongue-cluckers should appear in white raiment, beseeching her to *Please, please, stop before it's too late!*

But there wasn't, and they didn't. The sky stayed clear and blue. The road wound on, unbroken.

And the good Lord was mercifully keeping His opinion to Himself.

So much the better.

After all, He isn't the one who'll be on His back with His legs spread wide, is He? The thought blurted out; instantly regretted, if not retracted. She was just feeling a little bit crabby, and torn.

It helped that she hadn't gotten more than one hour's sleep in the past thirty: she'd lain in bed last night, alone—a fact which thrilled Pete no end and precipitated yet *another* stressed-out confrontation—writhing helplessly as the demons of guilt and self-doubt crawled up to torment her. *Was it right to do this—again? Could she go through with it with the same kind of laissez-faire ambivalence with which it was noted in her Pocket Planner?*

She looked at the purse on the passenger seat beside her. The notebook lay within it like a bug in a Venus flytrap, its finely ruled pages serving as a repository for the endless onslaught of notes, expenses, appointments, and detritus that packed her days. The log for *Friday: Things to Do* was as abbreviated as it was chilling:

9 A.M.—Big Z Music, get MIDI disks, Maxell digital tapes.

9:30—Computerland, get extra cables for DIOS.

10 A.M.—Women's Clinic. Get it over with.

She wished it were that cut and dried.

It certainly looked that way yesterday. After the fight. Before bed.

But actually *lying* there, with the music down low and the covers up high and the lights turned out, was another story entirely. It was suddenly lonely and complicated and terrifying, the only choices available either brutal or suffocating.

Maybe it was the fact that nocturnal fantasizing always brought out vestigial traces of the other child within her, the little girl lurking within the adult. Maybe it was purely hormonal, the biological sense of pride in her ability to reproduce colliding head-on with the adrenaline fear-rush of the unexpected.

And maybe it was the music.

Just about anything would have been better, she knew: from Lawrence Welk's greatest hits to The Scream, for Chrissakes. *Anything* but the music she ended up picking.

Anything but *her* music . . .

Not the band's. Not Jacob Hamer's. Hers. Her private stock, the stuff she'd been working on in the stray spare moments of the last year. The music that allowed Jessica Malloy to flash a glimpse of her inner self to the world outside herself.

It was Jesse's song of life, her symphony: ethereally esoteric soundscapes that she cultivated and tended for no one but herself. The music was as a garden in her mind, the place to which she could always turn for solace and solitude. Her love was there, and her pain, and her joy and frustration; all sculpted in shimmering chords and textured, rhythmic underpinnings. It grew as she grew, and she wasn't nearly done yet.

The second, slightly more complicated rationale, involved the technological infancy of it all. She had wanted to go further, to use her music as an expression of the deepest reaches of her soul, the places beyond her ear's ability to hear. And she needed something to lure it out and capture it.

Five years before it wouldn't have been possible. Or even two.

But that was then. This was now.

And now there was DIOS.

The Digital Interface Operating System: a black box translator that had hit the booming musical firmware market in the last year or so. It was designed to make the burgeoning world of MIDI—Musical Instrument Digital Interface—a less confusing mishmash for the musicians who employed it

It did this primarily by making it possible for virtually any computer-controlled musical system to "talk" to any other system. With DIOS one digital microprocessor-controlled synthesizer could understand another's programming and use it at will. It made the working musician's world a breeze: one controller could now run whole banks of different keyboards. DIOS, the master translator, had deciphered the digital Tower of Babel.

Jesse simply put it to another use. One the designers had never really considered.

It was common knowledge, by the mid nineteen eighties, that synthesizers could be used to simulate almost any sound found on the planet, and quite a few which harkened to whole other worlds. With the microchip revolution came the development of digital wave sampling, and the ability to not just simulate but recreate the essence of any sound and reproduce it, at will. It added yet another dimension of clarity and control to the fundamental concept that sonic energy could be translated from one form to another, simply by converting it into upwards of fifty thousand cycling slices of reality per second.

Jesse had seen this wave coming and ridden the crest. And it had dawned on her: Why stop with just sampling sounds? DIOS made it possible to translate and transfer digital information. And if DIOS could allow her synthesizer to understand virtually any input from another system, why couldn't it allow her to "hear" anything else that could be digitally graphed? Things like muscle contractions. Magnetic fields.

Brainwaves . . .

That was the ticket. Brainwaves: EEGs, EMGs, MEGs, her brain's myriad natural electrical impulses, amplified

a millionfold and turned into neat little squiggles on a computer screen.

Squiggles that ofttimes looked an awful lot like the waveforms that were her stock in trade.

So she did it: scoring some secondhand med-tech equipment, reaching up and tapping in. Most of the readings were too random to register as anything but noise; and even some of that was usable, at least as a filtering agent.

And then, a few of them . . .

A few of the readings were periodic. They ran in discernable cycles. They could be looped. And once looped, she could use them . . .

She experimented on herself at first, sampling and blending, shaping the sounds of her life. Her brain waves, awake and asleep and even meditated into as pure an alpha state as she could attain. Her day-to-day emotions. Joy. Anger. Anxiety. Excitement.

She collected these readings and replicated the waveforms. And from there she began to weave it all into the growing tapestry of her music.

The results were surprising, and surprisingly beautiful; the melding of the various timbres of her being into hybrid instruments. The effect was subtle and deep, like the presence an underground stream exerts upon the world above it.

The symphony grew over the months, until about eight weeks ago, when she decided that the symphony was missing something. She was almost finished with the first movement; she needed an accomplice for the second. She wanted to capture Love. She needed help.

And she had found it. In Pete.

He was certainly willing enough; that was for sure. He didn't even mind the many electrodes stuck to their naked bodies; he thought they were kinky and made several characteristically crude references about their being "wired for love."

"Save it for the meters," she replied dryly, pressing him back onto the bed and powering up. She loaded a disk into the sampler's drive and then worked him over like a professional, with tongue and hands and lips, alternately tending the needs of the flesh and the patchwork jumble of sensors

that connected to their scalps and ran down their spines
until the heat and the motion of the sweat ultimately broke
the connections to the higher points and left only enough
concentration to hold on to the lower ones, as their priori-
ties shifted and he pressed deeper and deeper and—

She considered the experiment a major failure at the time, but neither of them cared. It wasn't until sometime afterward that Jesse discovered the true extent of the failure.

And the success.

Because she discovered, in the aftermath, that they had tapped some very usable stuff indeed. In fact, the traces were like nothing she had seen before. Curiously powerful: particularly the signal she recorded at the moment of orgasm.

On the screen, it read like a spike with a long, ghosting trail; through the speakers, with a little tinkering, it sounded like a clear steel bell. She'd gone on to use it repetitively in the weeks that followed, in the second movement. For emphasis.

In the solitude of her bed last night, she suddenly realized what that little spike of energy might just be. Maybe more than a bell. Maybe more than she could handle.

Maybe the *spark* itself: the exact moment of miracle.

And disaster.

Which was why she was in the car right now, pulling into the northern edge of downtown Harrisburg, knowing damned well where she'd be stopping first and foremost. Just as she knew that she probably shouldn't have played that tape last night.

Things were hard enough as they stood, and she already knew what she had to do. She didn't need to be reminded.

She just needed to get it over with.

The Susquehanna Women's Services clinic was a storefront operation situated in a quaint little red-brick, three-story building on Second Street near the Taylor Bridge. Parking wasn't too tough—Jesse hooked around the block and found a space for the Suzuki on one of the narrow cross-streets that offered a view of the flat, rocky river beyond. The morning rush hour crowd was bustling in that small-city way—but hell, after New York, just about everything seemed quaint. Even a crowd.

One of the more pleasant aspects of culture shock. She

realized it had been a long time since she'd been in any urban environment whatsoever; even the comparatively low buzz of Harrisburg was a welcome jolt of energy. Maybe she'd even have a little lunch afterward. If she wasn't too wiped out.

The clinic was dead ahead.

She walked up to the lace-curtained door. Took a deep breath.

Get on with it.

And stepped inside.

The place smelled of air-conditioning, pine-fresh disinfectant, and lilac-scented stick-ups. After the fresh air and real smells of the mountain, it was nauseating. She looked around: tile floors, imitation-walnut paneling, the kind of solid pine living room suites regularly proffered in *Parade* magazine with a free black and white TV thrown in. Lumpy 3-D pictures of cute little puppies and kittens adorned the walls.

There were two other women in the waiting room, paging nervously through a stack of well-worn magazines. Jesse sighed deeply and stepped up to the receptionist's window.

"May I help you?" the receptionist inquired with a voice reeking of purely professional courtesy.

"Yes, I have an appointment."

"Name?"

"Jessica Malloy."

The receptionist checked the logbook, nodding perfunctorily. "You're early," she noted, then added, "but that's okay. Just fill out these forms and bring them back, and someone will see to you shortly."

Jesse took the forms over to one of the tacky chairs and sat down. The inner door opened and a nurse emerged, inviting the older of the two already-waiting women to come inside. The remaining one looked all of about nineteen and scared shitless. Jesse looked at her and offered her best pillar-of-strength smile; it was pretty clear that this was her first time.

"Don't worry. It really isn't the end of the world."

"Yeah," the girl whispered nervously. "It just feels like it."

Jesse nodded and looked back at her forms. *Name. Address. Date of birth. Medical history. Maternal history. Single or Married?*

She'd been through all of this before. She was already projecting through the rest of the process. . . .

After the forms, the ritual flash of cash. She'd been in too big a hurry yesterday to even ask them how much and had brought two hundred along just to be safe.

Then came the blood test/urine sample, the tour through the procedure in all its stainless-steel, rubber-tubed glory, the final okay, and onward to the Undressing Room to be outfitted in the latest in bare-assed hospital chic. Another half hour in the inner waiting room, shivering with more old magazines as you waited for your number to come up.

And eventually . . . sometime later this century by the feel of it . . .

Next!

You wake up in the recovery room, feeling dazed and grogged and Roto-Rootered to hell and back. You get up. You get dressed.

You get the hell out of there.

Of course, some women seemed to take it all in stride; sit around scarfing the juice and cookies and trading horror stories like veterans at a VFW post. Others broke down for a while, quietly wringing out their inevitable sense of loss and regret.

Jesse preferred to do her crying later.

At home.

Alone.

Which was why this should work out just fine: everyone would be cleared out when she got back. The drive to Philly would give her plenty of time to shake it off.

Plenty of time.

She stood with her forms, crossed the tiny room, and handed them through the window to the receptionist, who perused them expressionlessly. Finally she looked up, smiling that thoroughly professional smile, and said, "Thank you. Someone will see you shortly."

Jesse was ready to fork over the cash, but no request was made. The receptionist turned back to her busy busy book.

Hmmph. she thought. *In New York they'd probably be turning me upside-down and shaking me by now.* More culture shock. This was Pennsylvania, after all; she figured they just must do things differently here.

She returned to her seat just as the younger girl was ushered in. *And then there was one* . . .

Another fifteen excruciating minutes crawled by. She frittered the time away, looking at back issues of *Time* and the *National Enquirer*. She picked up one issue and a card fell out into her lap. Probably a subscription renewal insert or such. She held it up, and was momentarily stunned by the three words emblazoned in bold red strokes on the front.

Abortion Is Murder.

Jesse stared at the card hard before balling it up. *Bastards.* She'd known about antiabortionists' tactics for a long time, but had never actually gotten kidney-punched by them before.

This was a favored trick. There were others. She'd known friends who had breached their picket lines, gotten blood thrown on them; friends who'd been assaulted, psychologically and otherwise, by pious, impassioned do-gooders who behaved as though the decision to go through with it were some sort of callous romp. The stupid motherf—

"Miss Malloy?"

Jesse looked up; the nurse was standing at the door, waiting. Jesse nodded. The nurse nodded back, unsmiling.

"Miss Malloy, please, come in."

This is it, she told herself. There was nothing else to say.

Then she stood.

And she followed.

"Your record states that this is not your first time." *The corridor was long and low-ceilinged: more tile, more paneling.*

"Yes; there were two others."

"*Mmm-hmmm.*" *Make a little check. Turn right. Into a room with a short row of lockers and a short, low bench. Table with a vase of plastic flowers.* "Please get into this." *A powder-blue paper smock thrust in her face. One size fits none. An accompanying plastic wristlet, her name typed on it.*

Strange: no briefing, no show-and-tell, no tour through the shiny tools of the trade. Oh, well. They do it different here. She knows you know the paces. She leaves, you stay.

Pull off T-shirt. Kick off boots. Pull down jeans. Slip out of panties. Belly barely bulges. Good. It'll flatten right out.

*Into the johnnie. Hate the fuckers: waxen-feeling, stiff.
Butt hangs out as you swish swish swish into the next room.
Next room itself: dim lit, empty. Pine-fresh scent. More paneling, more magazines. A battered Zenith and a VCR on a
stand: odd. Silently playing an "I Dream of Jeannie" rerun
off some insipid cable station. Whatever.*

*Sit down. Cold: cold plastic bucket seat, too much air-
conditioning. Sounds of someone crying softly in another
room. Major Healey is watching Jeannie blink Master back
to his space capsule. Wait for the blood test, and the fresh
urine sample.*

Wait: for your turn.

Next . . .

The door opened.

A tall, softly imposing woman came in. She looked at
Jesse and smiled: it was genuine smile, and slightly sad. She
was fortyish, dressed in a very nice summer linen suit with a
tasteful scarf at her throat and a tasteful gold pin on her lapel.
She had Jesse's file in one hand. She walked up and held out
the other.

"Miss Malloy, I'm Lenore Kleinkind, the director of this
facility. It's a pleasure to meet you. I'm a big admirer of
yours."

"Thank you." Jesse felt extremely awkward, stripped naked in the face of fandom. *Can we get on with this please?* She
smiled and shifted in the cold plastic bucket.

Lenore sat down beside her, hands folding neatly over her
file. She stared at Jesse intensely: brow knitted, consternation
playing across her features. *What's the deal? Let's go already. . .*

"Jessica—may I call you Jessica?—we have a problem."
Her face leaned close: a kind face. Intense. Concerned. "Your
medical history indicates that you've already had two abortions.
Is this correct?"

Jesse nodded. Lenore shook her head.

"Jessica, frankly we're very concerned." Pause. *What is
she talking about?*

"Jessica, there's something very important that I think you
should be aware of. With two prior pregnancies under your
belt, so to speak, another abortion may well risk sending your

body mixed signals: in effect, you may be inadvertently *training* yourself to spontaneously miscarry."

Jesse stared at her as if she'd just fallen off the back of a truck. "What the hell are you talking about? That was *five years* ago."

"That's hardly the point, Miss Malloy," Lenore said flatly, unequivocally. "We're talking about another *life* here."

"What?"

Lenore Kleinkind reached into her jacket pocket, producing a small silver remote control. She pointed it at the VCR and punched a button. The VCR whirred dutifully, engaging a tape already cued up.

"You're a very influential woman, Jessica. A visible woman. A lot of young women look up to you as a role model."

The tape cut in with the sound turned down, showing a pair of anonymous, gloved hands wielding a long rubber hose.

Jesse's stomach curled up into a tight little fist.

On the screen: an anonymous pair of hairless legs, spread wide in the shallow steel troughs.

On the screen: a jar, filling in hitching gulps with red red goo.

On the screen: a jumble of red, spongy matter on a white white background, shiny spattered forceps pushing it this way and that.

"You have a responsibility, Jessica. To your audience."

On the screen: tiny tattered arms and legs.

"To our children."

Tiny hands.

"To *your* child."

Tiny feet.

Jesse stared blankly, eyes swimming. She refused to look at the video. She felt nauseous. *Where are my clothes?* Her eyes rolled around, searching for anything to key in on.

Lenore leaned forward earnestly. Her lapel pin sparkled in the dim light of the room. Jesse saw it clearly, recognized it at once as a symbol of allegiance. Like a cross. Or a swastika.

Or a pair of tiny, golden feet . . .

"Where are my clothes?" she hissed.

"Jessica, please—"

"Fuck you. Where are my goddamned *clothes?*"

Jesse stood bolt upright, the paper smock rustling violently around her. Her ass had goose-pimpled from chill and weirdness. Lenore grabbed her shoulder. Jesse wrenched away.

"We want to help you!"

"GET *AWAY* FROM ME!"

"Jessica, *please!* It has a *right* to live!"

"Fuck off!"

"Jesse, I *understand*—"

"You understand NOTHING!"

Jesse pulled away and stormed toward the outer door. The monitor showed a woman crying and clutching her stomach. Jesse grabbed the cart and flung it as hard as she could across the room. It careened sideways for five feet before tipping to dump its load in an explosion of sparks and glass.

She slammed into the undressing room, yanked open the locker door, and pulled her clothes out in a heap: dressing frantically, sobbing with rage and frustration. If she didn't get out of there in the next twenty seconds, she was going to kill somebody. It was that simple.

The nurse heard the commotion and started in from the outer room. Jesse roared and grabbed the vase of fake flowers, heaving it straight at her head. It missed by half an inch, smashing against the door jamb. The nurse fled, screeching, but not before Jesse picked up the glint of gold on her breast.

It's like Invasion of The Body Snatchers! she thought hysterically, half expecting to burst into a room full of pod people chewing through their sacs. She fought back the pounding in her temples, the urge to just pass out on the spot. An involuntary cramp racked her, the fist in her belly squeezing tight, too tight. She needed to get out of there, she needed air, she needed her purse, *where was her fucking PURSE!*

She spotted it, squashed down onto the bottom of the locker. She leaned over to grab it . . .

. . . and in the last seconds before she blacked out, she saw the contorted opening of the bag twist: as if the leather had reanimated, becoming skin again.

Changing.

Into a gaping, toothless grin . . .

It only lasted a couple of seconds; a fleeting moment of unguarded oblivion and black black space. But it was enough. Time enough to comb through the chaos, to find the

seed. Time enough to plant it deep in the soft folds of her
brain. A thought. A tiny cry.
It has a right to live!
It has a right . . .

Jesse awoke with a start. She was slumped awkwardly in
the space between the locker door and the wall. Her left leg
was entangled in the wreckage of the table that had so recently
held the vase.

Lenore Kleinkind and the ersatz nurse were hovering at a
safe distance, like a bomb squad stalking a piece of unex-
ploded ordnance. Visions of lawsuits danced in their heads.
When they saw her eyelids fluttering open, they leaned in
slightly, looks of vast relief washing over their faces.

"Just lie still, dear," Lenore said, speaking in slow, loud
syllables. "The ambulance will be here in a moment." She
smiled and stepped, eggshell-light, a little closer.

Jesse looked at them with an unveiled disgust. Their
compassion was self-serving and as two-dimensional as the
puppies on the waiting room walls.

She sat up and saw her purse lying where she'd dropped
it: harmless, inert. The Pocket Planner was sticking out, half
on the floor. Jesse scooped it all up, grabbed her boots, and
pushed past the mock-nurse, who whooofed air like a ten-cent
squeeze toy.

"Miss Malloy! Jessica! Please!"

Jesse walked faster, shaking her head. The opaque glass
of the waiting room door was two steps away. One step.

"Jessica!"

Jesse burst through the door, scaring the hell out of the
women that were waiting. Two of them were teenagers; one
looked to be Jesse's age. "This place is a lie," she spat. "They
don't do abortions here, they trick you and try to talk you out of
them!"

They all stared at her, dumbstruck. One of the younger
ones' eyes opened wide with recognition.

"Did you hear what I just SAID? This place *lies* to you!"

The door opened again; Lenore Kleinkind stood there,
huffing and puffing. "No," she said. "This place gives you the
truth."

"You wouldn't know the truth if it smacked you in the face!" Jesse shrieked.

Then she was out the door, running, the sunlight blinding as it burned into her eyes, and the eyes of the world upon her. . .

Fourteen

". . . and the next day's headline read, 'ARTIE CHOKES THREE FOR A DOLLAR AT SAFEWAY'!"

Hempstead beamed, all too pleased with his lame joke. Everyone else in the cockpit groaned: Jake pausing over his lapload of papers to shake his head remorsefully; Junior, the road manager, smiling against his better judgment; Bob and Bob making loud retching noises in the back.

Even Jim cracked a grin, though the bulk of the joke failed to make it past the muffled throb of the rotors and the garbled barks of static-tinged information blaring through his headset. Didn't matter. He'd heard it before. In fact, he'd probably heard *all* of Hempstead's jokes at some point or another and was probably destined to hear them all again. And again.

Still, he enjoyed it. And everyone else seemed to as well. With one possible exception.

"Yo, Space Shot," Hempstead said, nudging Pete. "Whas-samattah? You seem less than your usual bundle o' joyous self today." Pete remained oblivious, staring, nose semismushed into the window glass, out at the rolling terrain. The outskirts of Philly were looming on the horizon. The mountain lay far behind.

The concert was dead ahead.

And Pete was elsewhere entirely.

"Yo! Earth to Pee Wee!" Hempstead nudged him again, harder. "Earth to Pee Wee!"

"Wha . . . oh. Sorry." Pete shrugged and sniffled, looking chagrined, and his attention drifted right back to the window. "I'm just a little out of it, that's all."

"You don't look 'out of it,' " Hempstead offered. "You look *dead*."

"Lay off him," Bob One said. "He's emotionally distraught."

"Yeah, I'll say," Bob Two interjected. "Somebody was up late last night, fighting tooth and nail with somebody who is noticeably absent."

"That's none of your business," Pete muttered. The words scraped out like a line drawn in playground dust. "I was up working on a new tune, is all."

"Ye-e-eah," Hempstead said expansively, chiding him. "It's called 'Gotta Hose Up My Nose.' Been hearin' a lot of it lately."

"Piss on you," Pete tossed back a little too quickly, as though the customary acid-tinged pregig banter were anything but expected. Everybody knew it was S.O.P. It was practically tradition, a way of pumping up for the ego-rush of being scrutinized by thousands of people, when every tick and twitch of your personality could either work for or against you. It usually did the trick.

Usually.

Not today. Jesse wasn't here, and Jake might as well not be, and Pete's dourness was a little out of character. The balance was thrown off; in some vaguely perceptible way, the delicate sense of fraternity was disrupted.

And that was not good.

Not good at all.

"C'mon, Petey, what's up?" Hempstead asked. A big black hand clomped on Pete's shoulder. "You been kinda lumpy all mornin'—"

"Hey, just fuck off, okay?" Pete spun around in his seat, shoulder harness pinching into his side.

Telling Hempstead to fuck off was not the act of a rational man. Neither was the sudden physical gesture. The chopper lurched with the unexpected motion. Jake looked up, startled. So did everyone else. The guitarist remained in his defiant, awkward twist, locked in an eyeball war with the sax player.

Then Hempstead smiled, a tactical move. "Whoa, blood," he said, not moving his hand. "Just chill out a second—"

"I don't want to chill out. I want your hand off my fucking shoulder, okay?"

"Hey, Petey, we just playin'."

"Yeah, well, it's no *game*," he hissed, jerking out from under the grasp. The chopper lurched again.

"Oh, *chil*-dren!" Slim Jim called over his shoulder. "This bird is quite hard enough to fly as it is, without all the creative weight redistribution. PIA is less than twenty minutes away. Can we hold off on the festivities until our scheduled ETA, or would you like me to crash us into the Haverford State Mental Hospital?"

"Might not be a bad idea," Jake said.

He had been hip-deep in data the whole way in: Cody's news updates, Junior's revised lighting schemata, a million other piddling details that needed his attention, *now*. Things were wired enough without this shit.

And judging from the pile of papers in his lap and the document in his hands, there were plenty worse things to be worried about . . .

. . . *like the fact that the latest articles in* Time *and* Rolling Stone *showed that people were pretty much burned out on compassion, fresh out of helping hands to lend. Jake wasn't terribly surprised: the mood of the whole damned country had turned volatile and snappish of late, like a household pet with its legs in a steel trap. What with the Age of Reagan sputtering out and the inheritors of the legacy making over the nation in their own image, everybody was starting to feel the hurt.*

Besides, a concert to benefit poor little rich and famous rock stars wasn't worth its weight in noble sentiments like the myriad This, That, and the Other Aids that had sprung up in the wake of the original. Never mind if over half of the "rich and famous" stars in question made less than your average computer hacker per annum; never mind that many of those involved in the show were under either Congressional scrutiny, actual litigation, or both. And never mind the fact that the juggernaut of Right-thinking Decency was chugging full speed ahead.

Never mind all that.

People wanted to see the blood on the sands. People wanted their bread and circuses. They wanted heroes.

And even more, they wanted scapegoats.
And if you couldn't be the one . . .

Jake stared back and forth, from Junior to Pete to Hempstead to Bob to Bob to Pete to Junior, who just shrugged and riffled his lighting charts. They stared back: all but Pete, who sniffled and slumped back down in his seat.

Jake sighed and shook his head.

A bark of static sounded from the cockpit; final clearance for landing from the PIA control tower. They were nearing the airfield, which lay just to the other side of the I-76 bridge and the industry-clogged banks of the Schuylkill River.

The chopper banked to the south.

And JFK Stadium was directly below.

"Do a lap around it, wouldja?" Jake asked.

Jim nodded affirmatively. "Check it out, kiddies."

The arena sprawled beneath them like a gargantuan, multi-tiered concrete horseshoe, the stage sealing off the mouth in a labyrinthine mass of plywood platforming, electrical cables, and steel scaffolding. Twin towers of heavy-duty sound reinforcement bristled on either side, as well as a pair of huge, multifaceted Diamondvision screens that would broadcast close-up images to the unfortunate thousands seated at the very back of the amphitheater. The dozen-odd trucks and vans on hand for sound, video, and satellite uplink were scattered across the neatly carpeted sod of the football field like a jumbo toddler's Matchbox toys.

There were maybe fifty people visible in a space that tomorrow would hold upwards of fifty thousand; from the copter's-eye view, they looked like ants. Another swarm milled outside the gates and in the car-, camper-, and minibus-speckled parking lots. Some of them held aloft placards that looked like specks of confetti . . .

. . . then the chopper was out of range, floating over the gracefully arcing Schuylkill bridge. Everyone had grown suddenly quiet in the realization of the enormity of what they were about to face.

"I only want to say this once, people," Jake began quietly. "So listen up.

"In a very few minutes we will be touching down. A limo will be waiting to pick us up and take us, one and all, to the hotel. On the way we'll pass back by the stadium, where you'll get a close-up view of the crowds. Most of them are just waiting on line and trying to have a good time.

"But let us not forget that there are also protesters there, and rumor has it that the two camps don't much care for each other. The temperature is inching toward ninety-three, and the humidity is high, and it's apt to stay that way. The long odds are saying that there might be violence this weekend. A lot of people are very nervous. They should be.

"And so," he added, "should we.

"So when you step out of this bird, I really hope that you leave whatever's going on here behind." His attention was leveled at Pete and Hempstead. "Cause if we fuck up out there, they might just eat us alive."

The portent hung uncomfortably in the air for a few moments, then sank like a stone. Bob and Bob just rolled their eyes. *Oh, boy, more threats*. Hempstead gave him a very cool, cryptic nod. Junior sighed and went about his business.

Pete stared purposefully at his shoes; a man caught red-handed at being an asshole and yet completely unable to let it go. His anger was like that, Jake knew: it could never roll over, it could only recede.

But, and Jake knew this equally well, *a lot of damage could be done in the waiting*.

The airfield was directly below. Slim Jim spoke into his headset and then tilted the cyclic imperceptibly; the helicopter responded in a smooth, steepening spiral.

"Hang on, boys and girls," he called back, grinning. " 'Cause we be goin' down."

By three-fifteen, Jake and Hempstead were sweating like pigs in the sleek new chromed and mirrored expanse of the Hilton's Holiday Spa. They were three quarters of the way through a practiced, killer workout; running, abs, jump rope, and a full three times around the Universal weights, followed by a slow bake in the sauna.

Another tradition. Their contract rider always included a gym-access clause, as well as the requisite food and drink demands (like Pete's bizarre insistence on six-packs of Yoo-Hoo and grapefruit-flavored seltzer in the dressing room, with which he made a vile concoction he called a Florida Yoo-Hoo spritzer).

Perspiration slicked their hair and left stains like Rorschach-blots tracking down their unfashionable sweats. Bland disco music blared through speakers flush-mounted in the ceiling; a smattering of guests in carefully coordinated togs moved through the circuit, trying very hard not to make a mess.

Hempstead leaned over to adjust the set pin on the bench press. "God, I hate this music," he muttered into the towel draped around his neck. "Whatchoo want this on, anyway?"

Jake huffed, staring at the ceiling. His T-shirt (emblazoned with a college logo that read *CATATONIC STATE*) stuck to his heaving chest, the light gray color gone charcoal in the dousing. He took another deep breath and tightened his gloved grip on the press bar.

"Two-forty."

"Two-*forty*!" Hempstead looked down at him, a bead of sweat dangling on the end of his nose. "Man, you crazy. You never lifted that much in your *life*."

"Yeah, well, I'm going to now."

"What, d'you have an extra helping of Wheaties today or somethin'?"

"I'm a masochist. Set it up, already."

"Seems like an awful lot of trouble, sometimes, just to stave off decrepitude." Hempstead grinned.

"Yeah, yeah, yeah. Just set it up, wouldja?"

"Okay," he shrugged, "it's your hernia."

He pushed the pin into the rack of black iron blocks and watched as Jake started to suck air, going *whoof whoof whoof* like a derailing steam engine. On the third *whoof* he pushed, and pushed . . .

. . . and the weights rose up, faltered, rose a little more. . .

. . . and Jake pushed, pushed some more, his face beet-red, the veins in his forehead bulging as he let out a roar and gave it every last ounce of strength he had . . .

. . . and still, it wasn't enough.

He released his grip and let them clatter back down on their guides; they *ker-chunked* into place with brute finality. "*Damn,*" he gasped.

"So you ain't Superman." Hempstead smiled. "You still sing pretty. Where d'you learn to breathe like that, anyway?"

"Lamaze classes with Rachel," Jake moaned, lifting himself painfully off the bench. "Owwww . . . I'm gettin' too old for this shit."

"Bullshee-it." Hempstead handed him the towel and slid into place on the bench. "You jus' gettin' raggedy around the edges, is all." He took a huge lungful of air, expelled it, shook the sweat out of his eyes. "Got your perimeter spread too thin, muh man." He sucked in another gust, exhaled, and pistoned the bar straight up.

"You been runnin' yo'self like a fool: takin' on the world, eatin' and sleepin' like shit, gettin' all stressed out over this thing . . ."

He levered it smoothly back down, repeated the motion—up, down, up, down—going through a full set of ten in the time it took Jake to fail once, threw in one for good measure, lowered the bar back into place with a dull *thump*, then sat up and took the towel.

". . . all kinds of weird shit can happen," he concluded.

"Yeah, so tell me something I *don't* know."

Hempstead rolled his eyes and said nothing.

"What? Are you holding out on me?" Jake waited for more, but nothing seemed forthcoming. "Would you mind filling me in already," he pressed, "or should I hold an envelope to my head to get the answer?"

"Dunno." Hempstead shrugged and shook his head. "Lotta seeds of discontent been sown in your con-*side*rable absence. Jesse's got some kind of problem she won't talk about; Petey's been getting wasted every fuckin' night; the Bobs are restless—with you gone most the time, it all kinda flies apart."

Jake just looked at him.

"You know, Petey runs a good rehearsal," Hempstead continued, "but he ain't the leader. *You* the glue that holds this thing together, Jake, and I think everybody's gettin' a lil' bit tired of the holy war."

Jake squirmed under his best friend's appraisal and tried to shrug it off. "Comes with the territory, I guess."

"A *lotta* things come with the territory, man, and sometimes there's more than one road to go by. Best to keep that in mind."

"So what are you telling me?" Jake insisted. "That I should give it up? I can't do that. Not now."

"I ain't even sayin' that you should. But be advised: we players, first and foremost. *Not* politicians; and for sure, not saviors."

"Oh, come on, man—"

"No, Jake. You wanted to hear this, so now you will." Jake humphed and tried to keep his fists from clenching. Hempstead's voice was steady and low as he continued. "Ever since 'TV Ministries' hit it big, we been less of a band and more of a circus sideshow; an' ever since this whole Rock Aid thing started, you been gettin' further an' further away from what it is you're all about. Talk shows an' shit are fine, but the best hype in the world is still just hype.

"Talk is cheap, bro'. It's the action that counts."

"This isn't just talk!" Jake was hopping mad now. People stared nervously in their direction. "God damn it. Out of everybody, I thought at least *you* understood! These people didn't stop with warning labels; you give them an inch and they take a continent! They *have* to be stopped, or the whole game is over, and you can't do that by sitting around at the studio—"

"No, you do it by sittin' around on the Moynihan show—"

"You do it by raising money to *fight* them, God damn it! In Congress! In the courts! You do it by *matching* them, blow for blow—"

"Can we do this at a lower decibel level, please?"

"Yeah, right," Jake hissed, but his volume dropped. "I just love all the fucking support I'm getting. Makes me wonder what I'm even doing it for."

"Hate to break this to you, babe, but lots of people been wonderin' the very same thing."

"Oh, great." Jake was red-faced and miserable looking. "So what's that supposed to mean?"

"Let me put it to you simple. How many people go out an' buy Bob Geldof's solo albums, you think? As opposed to the Boomtown Rats?"

"That's not fair."

"You'll have this. Next question: When was the last time you sat in on rehearsal? Three weeks, at least? Almost a month before that?"

"Oh, Jesus . . ."

"Bottom line, Jake. Once this show is history, you're gonna have to make a decision: Do you want a band or not? I mean, you got to consider: you got a bunch of professional musicians who picked up their lives and *moved* them, from New York City to Pennsylvania, just for the chance to keep working with you. Now they sittin' around like bored little wifeys with nothing to do but watch TV till the hubby comes home."

"You want me to bring you flowers, is that it?"

"Not funny, bro'. You keep this up, they maybe start to thinkin' they made a mistake."

"Oh, man." Jake had his head in his hands now. "This sucks. I really don't need this."

"Well, you got it."

Silence dropped like a gauntlet between them. Hempstead felt he'd said enough; he waited for Jake to pick it up. The silence had allowed the hated chintzy disco pap from the speakers to intrude on their lives again.

"God, I hate this shit," Jake muttered.

"Me, too."

"You know, if Furniss has his way, *all* music will be as lame as this crap. No, worse. Even *this* is immoral, to his way of thinking. That jungle rhythm, don't you know."

Hempstead said nothing, but he smiled a little.

"I didn't choose this battle," Jake continued. "This battle chose me. I think you can appreciate the difference. If I felt like I had any choice in the matter, I'd just play with you guys every day.

"But they're trying to take that away from me, man. They're fucking with our tribal music: our freedom to play it, to be who we are. They want to take our whole stake in the culture and drive it back underground.

"Can you live with that? I know I can't."

"I hear you."

"Okay. But freedom isn't something that God doles down. It's something you fight for, if you want it bad enough. If you don't, then the people who want to control you just haul its ass away, and you're left with whatever they decide to give you.

"And it's a bitch, because *freedom* is a bitch. But what other choice do you have?"

Hempstead shrugged, remained in silence. It was clear

that Jake had a psychic boil to lance. Best he get it over with, soon as possible.

"But you know what the worst of it is? I'm not even sure what side I'm on half the time. I mean, on the one hand, we've got Pastor Furniss and Esther Shrake trying to legislate morality and make the world safe for stupidity. That's easy: I know they're my enemy. We can smell each other a mile away.

"But then you get to what's supposed to be *our* side, and we've got crazy bastards like The Scream, causing riots in concert parking lots and telling people to fuck the devil and raising hell every which way and otherwise telling us that maybe the assholes on the other side of the fence were right in the first place!"

"That's 'cause you're not on anybody's side. The fact is, you're on your own. You just have to go with what you believe."

"That's what I'm doing. For all the fucking good it does me."

"That's people, Jake. They don't give a shit. They just want to go along their merry way, do whatever the hell they want. They want to have opinions, so long as they don't have to back 'em up. They want to be left alone.

Now you come in here all pissed off, and you say, 'Let my people rock 'n' roll!'; and that's cool, so long as you know that everybody doin' the same dance here. We don't want equality. We want to be on top. And because there's so many of us, and we all disagree, ain't nobody ever goin' to really win this game."

"But you have to try."

"Oh, yeah." Hempstead smiled. "Otherwise, what's the point of even playin'?"

Fifteen

"Ah, mundanity," Rachel sighed. "How sweet it is."

She was at the kitchen counter, scrawling her grocery list on the back of a used envelope from Jake's nut file; these days, his mailbag averaged about fifty true fruitcakes a week. This one was from a Mrs. Clarence Rorbaugh of Glen Rock, Pa. It was spread out before her as she jotted down funzies like light bulbs and diapers:

> Dear sir:
> My friend Lois and I saw your rock music vidial, and we just want to say that you are sick. There should be a place for people like you and there already is. Its called the Loony Bin and thats where you belong.
> In case you dont know mister, this is a Christian nation. People who are in leege with Satan shouldnt be alowed to spread there filth. We rote to MTV but they wont listen because they belong to Satan too.
> We will pray for you but it wont do any good if you dont repent. God loves the sinner but hates the sin and if you dont wise up and ask Jesus to forgive you, you will be damned to Hell with no one but yourself to blame.
> Think about it Mister Hammer, because its your Immortal Soul your talking about. Don't be a fool. Give up your evil ways. Apoligise to God. Beg His forgiveness. Then you can now the true love that Jesus has for His disipels.
> Jesus loves YOU!!!
> Thats all I have to say. Think hard Mister Hammer

or you will suffer the fires of Hell forever. Its your choice. You seem like a smart man so use some smarts. "For God so loved the world that . . ."

"Don't tell me," Rachel muttered. "Let me guess." There was more—three more pages, in fact—but she really didn't have time to waste on it. She'd read a thousand clones of the sentiments therein, dispatched by a thousand identical clowns; the odds were pretty good that she was missing nothing new if she passed on the remainder of the text.

The ones that really concerned her were somewhat fewer and farther between. The most recent came last week, in fact: so brief and succinct that she could still picture every gnarled pencil stroke of its being . . .

> Dear Scum!
>   You will die. Your family will die. You won't know when. You won't know why. God has spoken. Say good-bye.
>   Love,
>   A Friend in Jesus

Now *that* was a goddamn chilling piece of stuff to find in your mailbox. It was one of those rare times that Jake actually sent the thing off to the FBI, in fact: check the handwriting, check the style, check the Shreveport, Louisiana postmark and date. Nothing had come up, of course, and probably nothing would.

That only made it all the worse.

The most terrifying thing about it was the sense of cool control: this person, whoever it was, knew exactly what they were saying. It had the embalming fluid reek of deadly professionalism, minus none of the psychosis to be found in lesser fruitcake fare. This person, whoever it was, knew that flying to and from Harrisburg International was a matter of maybe twelve hours and three, four hundred dollars.

If he was even from Shreveport at all.

You won't know when.

You won't know why . . .

At her feet, Natalie was making ominous overtures toward the trash receptacle. "No, baby. Don't eat the garbage. No."

Natalie paused and looked at her: the beginnings of moral inquiry. She wore a pair of purple bloomers over her last Ultra

Pamper, tiny silver Reeboks, and a white tanktop T-shirt that read *I Know You Are, But What Am I?* Her wide eyes swarmed with infant guile.

"No," Rachel repeated, engaging those baby blues.

Natalie let out a toothless grin. "Nah-nah PFTHHHH!"

Rachel smiled. "You're beautiful."

Natalie, appeased, turned back to the trash.

"Natalie, NO!" Rachel yelled, and that was the end of Funtime. The Midget from Beyond Her Loins switched masks, from comedy to tragedy, in the space of a second. The wailing began. Rachel thought again of Jake's promised vasectomy, and smiled.

Toilet paper. Scott towels. It was time to wrap the list, get going. For some reason, the rug rat's screams were perfect sound track music for the task. *Mr. Clean. Uncle Ben's.* She penned it, assessed it, vowed she'd fill in the blanks when she got to the store.

"Okay." She folded the envelope and jammed it in the back pocket of her jeans. She stooped and ensnared her ululating offspring, kissed one moist pink cheek, and strode into the living room. "TED! CHRIS! IT'S TIME TO GO!" she bellowed up the stairs against the heavy metal thunder.

No response. No enormous surprise. Even if they heard, there was no rush to respond. God knows they *lived* for the opportunity to hit the grocery store with Mom.

"C'MON, GUYS! LET'S ROLL! IF I HAVE TO COME UP AFTER YOU, I'M GOING TO BE UNPLEASANT!"

She moved to the foot of the stairs, paused, and counted the tappings of her foot. She had gotten to twelve when the bedroom door opened and Ted shuffle-footed to the stairway's head.

"Can we just finish listening to the album?"

"It's time to go."

"There's only one more song. It's three minutes and twenty-one seconds long."

"That'll give you time to change your shirt and maybe brush your hair. It's been two days since you changed clothes, hasn't it?"

Ted made an ugly face. Shades of Natalie, still a-whimper in her arms. The more things change, and blah-dee-blah.

"Come on," she said. "Get Chris, if he's coming."

Ted turned away, mumbling something. She was tempted to demand to know what it was, then thought better of it. *Yeah,* she thought. *It's a universal law. Nobody wants to do what they don't want to do.*

But the fact of the matter was that she needed him to go. It was too crazy out there. She couldn't take Natalie out alone. Her brother Cody had too much work to do, Pete's gramma was eighty-six years old, and everybody else was either in or nearing Philly. There were fifty brainwashed teenagers at the gate and God only knew how many more beyond. Ol' Friend in Jesus might be anywhere; maddening as it was to think about at all, it was madness to ignore.

"And so it goes," she said to Natalie. "Try to remember this, if you can. We didn't make the rules. God did. We just have to live by them."

Natalie sniffled and stared, listening to the sound if not the words.

"We just try to live up to the chores God sets up for us and do the best we can with what we're given. If it gets difficult sometimes, that's just the way it is. If it gets scary sometimes, that's just the way it is.

"That's why we're going to the store. Not because we want to. Because we have to. Okay?"

The thin flesh over Natalie's face did nothing to conceal the concentration that the muscles beneath denoted. No poker face, she: every ripple of thought played open as the sun addressing the morn. Sodium pentothal should have it so good. She was *listening.* That much was clear.

How much she actually understood remained to be seen.

Somehow, it didn't stop the tiny tears from welling in her own.

On the other side of the gate, Mary Hatch was suddenly equally unable to keep the slightly larger tears from welling in her eyes.

It had been, to use the vernacular of the Dead, a long, strange trip. And in the last two months it had taken more turns than the rest of her young life combined. She had seen, albeit dimly, the leering essence of Evil.

Now she was being treated, albeit grimly, to the lobotomized leer of Good.

And as she stood on the far side of the Jacob Hamer barricade, with her JESUS IS LORD placard held tightly in her hand, her mind had no choice but to roll back over the madness that had led her to this time and this place . . .

The first two weeks were spent reeling. No chance to make sense of the horror or the revelation: just an endless succession of flashing cameras and jutting mikes, loaded questions in no way prepared for the only answers she had.

Did she know who the killers were? No, she did not. Was there any possible motive for the slayings: drug wars, gang rivalries, a chance encounter at the concert with some homicidal fringe group? No, she insisted. She didn't know.

Did she know how she had managed to survive? they asked, and she had only one thing to say.

Jesus saved me.

After that, they had tons of questions, but the tone of them changed entirely. No longer were they concerned with receiving hard evidence; now they just wanted to know about the little wacko chick. Had she had previous religious experiences? Did she have a history of active church-going or was this something new? Exactly how many hits of acid was she on, anyway?

The quality of journalists changed, also, as time dragged on. She stopped getting visits from the L.A. Times and started seeing much more of the Weekly World News. Mary often had the feeling that her poor parents, God love them, were going to lose their minds.

They were already quite sure that she had.

Because the Hatch family had no real religious background whatsoever. Dad had been a Catholic till the age of six, at which point his father stopped going to church and the papist patriarchy of home caved in for good. Mom's blond-haired Jewish upbringing was orthodox as a chocolate-covered pork sandwich, which is to say that Jehovah rarely came up in conversation. Between them, they had steered the developing Mary clear of divine dogma in any way/ shape/form.

And so it was still. Thank God, Mom would say, that it's summer. Can you imagine what going to school would do to her? And Dad would pace around the living room, muttering, Jesus Christ, when will those assholes leave her alone?

But that was pretty much the extent of the supernatural cre-
dence they lent to the situation.

Bottom line: the girl was on acid. She went to a god-
damned party, and she witnessed something horrible, and
the totality of the experience had fried her out. This was not
the first time someone had flipped out and seen God in
California. The sixties had been full of that shit, and God
knew that neither one of her parents had stood on the side-
lines through that infamous Summer of Love.

But there was more, with no way around it. There was
the fact that she had grieved them sorely, and that the
resulting emotions were confused at best. They were pissed
at her, in a terrible but incontrovertible way that was very
hard to deal with. She had been found—drugged and na-
ked and covered with blood—at the scene of the worst ur-
ban California massacre since Chucklin' Charlie Manson and
his pals descended on Tate and the LaBiancas. She had
turned their lives into a three-ring circus, full of predator-
geeks with no handle whatsoever on how deeply this whole thing
had savaged their lives. She had found Jesus, fercrissakes!—a
belief that ran absolutely counter to their worldview.

And it made them furious. And they couldn't help it. And
the emotion ran so counter to all they held dear that, yes,
it really might just make them crazy.

Because . . . at the deepest, most bottom line . . . they
loved her more than anything in the world.

Because she was their daughter. Because, out of their
three incipient impregnations, hers was the one that they'd
decided to bring to term.

Because they had brought her, through the juncture of
egg and sperm and the screaming agony of passage, into
this world.

Because it didn't matter how independent she got, how
fully her life became her own, how strong or weak or wise
or stupid or cool or lame she turned out to be.

It didn't matter.

She would always be their baby.

And there was baby Mary: sole survivor of the Dia-
mond Bar Holocaust, sole survivor of her parents' own per-
sonal life-or-death decisions. There was baby Mary, at the
center of the cyclone, while Dr. Wyler and his wife searched
panic-strickenly for their own baby girl, and the parents of
the deceased went rightfully berserk over the loss of their

own precious children. The pressure at home had become insurmountable.

There was only one thing to do.

Mary's dad had a sister in Pennsylvania who lived a life of quiet seclusion and was an absolute sweetheart besides. So at the end of those crazed two weeks, Mary was surreptitiously sent off to stay with Aunt Elaine. It was a good decision: far from the crowds and the scene of the crime, in a peaceful place where she could begin to heal, if not make sense of what had happened.

And then, while watching the tube one day, she happened across Pastor Furniss's program, and there was something going on there that reached out to her. His association of rock and demonic forces, Jesus and salvation, set a buzzer off within her. It was clear that, if she was to understand her own very tangible salvation, she would need to learn more about Jesus. She would need to study Him in an atmosphere completely devoted to His name.

Within the hour, she had phoned her parents.

Within the week, she had been enrolled in the summer session at Liberty Christian Village.

Mary would never forget the last conversation she had with Aunt Elaine, on the eve of her departure. They were in the kitchen, brewing up some Celestial Seasonings Wild Forest Blackberry tea—Elaine was an herb tea fanatic, with at least a dozen varieties on hand at any given time— and they were both feeling things pretty profoundly. But that just made the encounter that much sweeter.

"Honey," Aunt Elaine began, "you're a very smart girl. Your folks have a lot of faith in you. That's why they're letting you do this, you know."

Mary nodded, not looking up. She was watching the hot water deepen in color, watching the tea bags steep.

"But they don't believe in Jesus, and they definitely don't believe in the people you're going to see. In all honesty, I can't say that I do, either.

"But I will say this: I believe in your experience. I believe that a higher being came to you that night, and I believe that it saved you. It must have had a reason; and I admire you for trying to find out what it is."

Mary stood over the teapot, watching its contents darken, watching the teardrop plummet from her cheek to stir the steaming surface.

"Just remember," Aunt Elaine continued, "that these people only have part of the truth, no matter how hard they try to convince you otherwise. Their view of God is extremely limited, and they can only tell you so much.

"But they have the Bible, and you can study that. Listen to how they interpret it; then make up your own mind as to whether you agree. Remember: you had a personal experience, not them; and nobody can tell you more about it than you can.

"Once you get their message, it's time to leave.

"And move on to the next step."

Mary wanted to look up then. She couldn't. Not quite yet. Elaine was moving closer to her, enfolding her with her arms, holding her tight, and she could do nothing. Couldn't hug back. Couldn't anything.

But let the tears roll.

"Oh, honey," her aunt continued, the voice and the hug so warm. "You'll be fine. I swear you will." She gave an extra squeeze for emphasis, then continued, "Now I want you to sit down and drink your tea.

"I want to give you something."

Elaine let go, and Mary moved obediently to the kitchen table and sat. A cup was set in front of her. She brought it to her lips, blew gingerly, waited.

A book was set in front of her.

Mary looked at the cover. The Gnostic Gospels by Elaine Pagels. Meanwhile, her Aunt Elaine sat across from her, blew at her own tea. Mary looked up for the first time, startled, found the power of speech at last.

"Did you write this?"

"Oh, no," her aunt responded, almost laughing. "I wish I had, but no such luck. It's just a book that I admire, and that I want you to think about.

"You see, it's been nearly two thousand years since Jesus was crucified, and that's a long time; but in certain ways nothing has changed. We're still fighting over what's right and what's wrong. We always have. We always will.

"Back then, even the apostles were fighting over who understood Jesus the best. It was a fight that lasted over two hundred years. That's how long it took to put together the Bible.

"In the end the orthodox Christians won; and that's the Bible that you'll get to read when you go to the Village. But there was a whole 'nother group—the Gnostic Christians—who had a whole 'nother view of it."

"And that's what's in this book?"

"Well, they talk about it. And they've got quotes from it. Mostly, they just talk about the difference between the groups and the politics that went down. But this is the important thing, the thing I want you to remember.

"The Gnostics dealt with personal experience. They said that the kingdom of heaven was within you, and that God spoke personally to you. That means that if God comes to you in a vision, you listen, even if it contradicts everything you know or believe in. Even if it contradicts the church.

"I'm going to make you a bet now. I'm going to bet that they take this book away from you. They won't want you to read it. They won't want you to know what it has to say.

"If they do that, then remember what I've said.

"And when you've learned all you can from them, you have a place to stay. You know that.

"I love you."

Mary agreed that, yes, she knew that, then cried a little more.

The next day she arrived at Liberty Christian Village. The first thing they did, after assigning her her room and uniform, was to confiscate her copy of The Gnostic Gospels. . . .

There was a hand on her shoulder, a hand that, in a short time, she had come to equate with all the hate and jealousy that seemed to have so successfully subverted the word of Christ. She tensed at its touch, sent out a silent prayer.

"Let's go," said the voice from behind her.

Five minutes later, the shopping party were on their way: the gate having opened and closed behind them, the crowd having parted, the road winding outward and beyond. Ted, still pissy, sat in the back beside Natalie and her safety chair. Chris sat beside Rachel in the front of the Jeep, fiddling with the tone controls on the dashboard cassette ("You gotta hear this group, Mrs. Hamer. They're incredible. Really.") and telling some of the bawdiest jokes she'd heard in years. It was understood by all that Chris had a thing for Rachel—one hundred percent teenage, somewhere between "a crush" and "the hots," very similar to the way she figured Ted felt for Jesse—but she liked him anyway and was more than happy to let his good cheer cut through the bad vibes Ted transmitted from the back.

None of them were in any position to notice the carload of Liberty Christian villagers that piled in and took off behind.

It was a five mile drive to Grossinger's, on the outskirts of Jonestown. They were too far in the boonies for an actual supermarket, so Rachel opted once a week to hit the fairly well-stocked counters of Arnie Grossinger over the homespun minit-marts festooning the miles between. He took the time to order what she wanted, distribution permitting; his produce was fresh and his attitude refreshing.

In fact, ol' Arn was making headlines when Jake and company first arrived on the mountain. It was a couple of years back, when the big radical fundamentalist craze was boycotting stores that sold *Playboy* and *Penthouse*. He had surprised them all by saying, "Fine. Don't shop here. I was sick of you people anyhow. You want someone to tell you what you can or can't read, go to the goddamned Soviet Union. This is America."

At the time, Liberty Christian Village had been his largest customer, so the move took major balls. But he was a crusty, self-reliant old coot, and he didn't much take to that kind of pressure. He was pleasantly surprised to discover that business held steady, with a bunch of new faces who told him they were proud to do business with him. So much for godly retribution.

To this day, he refused to do business with Pastor Furniss and his clan.

Rachel wheeled her Wagoneer into the Grossinger parking lot at 12:15. It was largely old macadam and potholes; the recent rain had whipped up some mean mud puddles. They parked on an island between two large ones and carefully disembarked, Ted handing off Natalie to his mom without a word, his gaze wandering sullenly off toward the stores that flanked Grossinger's left.

"You can hit the video store if you want, honey," Rachel said. "Just meet me inside in ten minutes."

"Okay." Ted wouldn't look at her, but it was clear that his armor was cracking.

"Do you need some money?"

"Yeah."

"Okay. Hold Boobie for a second." Rachel handed the munchkin back to Ted. Natalie gave her brother a broad and toothless grin. He smiled despite himself.

"Just three films, okay?" Rachel said. "And give me back the change."

"Okay." Ted traded Natalie for a ten-spot. "I guess this is what you call white slavery," he said. Rachel laughed, and he tossed her a smile. End of conflict.

For now.

"So everybody knows what to do, right?" Paul Weissman said. "No questions from the peanut gallery?"

A rumble of silent assent wafted up from the backseat. Paul assessed it through the rearview mirror. To his right, in the passenger seat, Mary Hatch expressed no feelings whatsoever. She never did. He was getting tired of waiting for Jesus to jump-start her; he had a feeling that he wasn't leaning on her nearly hard enough.

By the age of twenty-three, Paul Weissman had grown to become Pastor Furniss's right-hand man. He was in charge of the boys' dorms, which he ran with an iron fist; he edited the monthly newspaper, *LCV Times*, which included ghostwriting Pastor's column; in the last year he had been blessed with the duty of organizing and leading the antirock protests, from the record burnings to the crowd at Hamer's gate to tomorrow's Rock Aid insurrection.

And more than once, he had tidied up the loose threads in the pastor's affairs. Sometimes, tightly; even more than Pastor himself imagined or would necessarily approve. Pastor was in many ways a weak man, Paul realized; at least, a weaker man than Paul. Too New Testament for one thing, too forgiving. And all too often given toward the weakness of the flesh.

Paul's savior was made of much sterner stuff. And he realized that, while his father's house contained many mansions, those mansions contained many closets, in which there rattled many, many skeletons. A given percentage of which sometimes rattled a wee bit too noisily, at which point they needed a thorough cleaning. Cleanliness was next to godliness, after all, and Paul was just the man to do it.

All of which was fairly auspicious for a curly-headed

jewboy from Long Island. He had come a long way from the liberal politics and literary aspirations of his college days, when he was certain that he would be the great social critic and intellectual beacon of his generation. It didn't take more than a dozen rejections for him to realize that the literati were fools; that the scope of their critical faculties were microscopic compared to his own; and that they rejected him out of jealousy and sheer blind ignorance.

Quite naturally, the revelation had left him bitter. Quite inevitably, that bitterness had led to his split with academia, the decline of his health, his descent into substance abuse and perverse, self-destructive sexuality.

And then, somewhere near Wall Street, when it seemed that all was lost . . .

He was *saved*.

And with that he found, indeed, all things were possible. Redemption for his own sins, retribution for the sins of the wicked. He knew the power and the glory, amen. He knew now that he would be on hand for that final Day of Judgment—that he would watch from the heavens as the souls of the fallen were consigned to a just and fiery Hell.

For the time being, however, the power and the righteousness of the Kingdom of God rested right where it belonged. Within him, praise Jesus.

And power was such a wonderful thing.

Paul Weissman pulled the station wagon to a halt right beside the empty Wagoneer. That set them squarely in the middle of a muddy pool, but God works in mysterious ways.

"Okay," he said, throwing it into park and cutting the engine. "Let's go."

"But . . ." Cathy began, eyeing the slop outside her window with dismay.

"No buts," he countered sternly. "O ye of little faith. Consider the lilies of the field in Matthew six before complaining to me about your silly shoes."

Mary threw him a glance that didn't seem entirely Christian. He thought about chastising her, decided to wait. *When we're alone*, he concluded. *In the Quiet Room*.

Then he was out the door, leaping heavily to the perimeter of the mudhole, his left heel sploshing heavily and very nearly causing him to slip. *"Damn!"* he cursed, under his breath, and then turned and waited for the flock to follow.

"Hey, Ted!" Chris yelled with high good humor. "Check it out! It's *Attack of the Gumbies!*"

"Where?" Ted laughed. He was looking at tapes in the Video Shack horror section—a section he knew well—and the closest thing he saw to it was *Return of the Alien's Deadly Spawn*.

"No, no, man. Outside." Chris pointed to the window. Ted turned and looked. So did the guy behind the counter.

Six of Pastor Furniss's shlock troopers were getting their feet wet in the parking lot. With temperatures in the nineties and their ties tight around their button-down collars and all, it looked to Ted as if it might have been something of a relief. But, no. They were complaining.

"Mercy me," Ted said, and repressed a stoned giggle. "Think they need a lifeguard?"

"If one of 'em starts sinking, we'll throw 'em a rope."

They thought this was funny. They were young and on drugs. "Whoo-EEE!" Chris continued. "Check out the legs on *that* babe!"

A young, well-formed blonde was getting ready to jump from the driver's side, her plain gray culottes hiked up to mid-thigh.

"You know," Ted said thoughtfully, "she'd be awfully cute if she didn't dress like a dweeb."

"And if she had any tits."

"Jesse's got small tits. I *like* small tits."

"You're a homo. That's why."

"That's why you always wanna crash at my house."

"It's your mother I want."

"Dream on," Ted said, and then the connection struck. "Wait a minute. What the fuck are they doing here?"

"It's a free country," Chris said.

"Yeah, but Grossinger's won't sell to 'em. He says they're a pain in the ass."

"No shit."

"So why are they here?" He turned to the guy behind the counter. "Do they ever rent videos from you guys?"

"Not ever."

"How about Thrift Drugs?"

"I haven't seen those assholes here in over a year. Believe me, I've been counting the days."

"This is not good," Chris said.

"Oh, yeah," Ted replied. "You know what tapes you want?"

"*My Bloody Valentine*—the first all-Polack splatter movie."

"Okay. And?"

"I could get into some *Return of the Living Dead*. Now, *that* chick has a set of world-class knockers! Whatsername? Lynia Quigley?"

"Mmm hmmm." Ted grinned at the thought. "That leaves us with one more. How about . . . ummm . . . how 'bout *Invasion of the Blood Farmers*?"

"Apropos," Chris said, staring out the window. "Real apropos."

Rachel had the shopping cart optimistically half-full when the first white-shirts came through the door and headed right for her. The irritating fat kid was in front, not surprisingly. The rest of them looked embarrassed to be there.

"Oh, boy," she muttered, then took a deep breath and a jar of Clausen's Kosher Dills off the shelf. *It was bound to happen, sooner or later*, she told herself. *Might as well get it over with now.*

I wonder where Ted and Chris are?

Natalie, in the seat of the cart, turned to grapple with the jar of pickles. "No, baby." Rachel substituted a shatterproof bottle of Herbal Essence shampoo. "Not unless you're going to throw it at them."

And then they were upon her.

"Hello," she said with what she hoped was a disarming grin. It fell upon the thick flat lenses of Paul Weissman's glasses and died there.

"Hello, Mrs. Hamer. I've—"

"Adams. My last name is Adams."

His eyebrows raised, and his mouth began to smile unpleasantly. "You're not married?"

"I kept my own name."

"Ah, I see. Well, I've been meaning to speak with you for some time, Mrs. Adams—"

"*Ms*. Adams. About what?"

"About the *world*"—a bit exasperated—"that you're bringing your children into."

"Okay. Speak. But if you don't mind, I'll be shopping while you talk. Excuse me a second." She pushed forward a little, forcing back the throng, and snagged a jar of Dijon mustard.

Then Paul Weissman put his hand on the front of the cart and said, "Stop."

Rachel paused, feeling her spine turn suddenly cool. The calm before the storm. "What are you doing?" she inquired pointedly.

"I'm making you listen."

"You're making me mad. Let go of the cart."

"Will you listen to me?"

"Not if you don't let go of the cart."

"Okay." He pulled his hand away, making an entirely bogus gesture of hand-raised apology. "Is that better?"

Rachel took a minute for a few deep breaths and a good look at Natalie. Her little girl was staring at Weissman, much as she'd appraise a spoonful of food that she really didn't want to eat: not crying yet, but fully prepared to. *Make her cry, I'll roast your butt*, Rachel thought, then deferred it for the moment. A poker face was better.

"Speak."

Paul Weissman smiled then. His eyes were like chunks of gray slush, gray and intensely cold. He was, in that moment and for the first time, frightening. His mouth, when he spoke, seemed too wide and had too many teeth.

"The world is in serious trouble, *Ms*. Adams. It's an ugly world. Full of wickedness, corruption, and sin. You, of course, already know that."

Rachel said nothing. She was fascinated. It wasn't every day that you met someone who could say that with conviction.

"But are you familiar with the word of God, *Ms*. Adams?" He was obviously enjoying the emphasis, now that he'd turned it around. "And are you aware of how it reflects upon a life-style such as yours?"

"Yes."

"Yes to which question, *Ms*. Adams?"

"Yes to both questions, *Mr*. Whatsyername."

"Paul Weissman."

"Mr. Weissman. Okay. So what's your point?"

"The *point*, Ms. Adams, is that your husband is a danger-ous man. Don't you ever think about the moral consequences of raising a child with a man who espouses the . . . er . . . *principles* that he seems to represent? I mean—"

"Do you have any children, Mr. Weissman?"

"Umm . . ." Perplexity flashed across his features. The question had caught him clearly out of the blue.

"If you had any children, what values would you hope to give them?"

"I . . . I would, of course, raise them with the Bible."

"With emphasis on which parts?" She felt any fear she might have had slip away. It was not the kind of question Jesus freaks had an easy time with. His muddled expression said it all.

"Why . . . with the book in its entirety, of course. There is no legitimate separation . . . that is to say, no way of breaking down the word of God and saying this part is valid, and this part isn't—"

"Well, maybe there is, and maybe there isn't," she cut in, advancing upon him now. "That isn't the question. The ques-tion is, Where do you put your emphasis? Old Testament or New Testament? Luke or John or Paul? Do you lean toward the word of Jesus, the word of people who came before Jesus, or the word of people who came after?"

"Umm . . ."

"It's a big book, buddy. There's plenty of room for favor-ites. What's your favorite story? What's your favorite quote?"

Paul Weissman couldn't answer. Apparently he was bright enough to realize that he'd just been put on the spot. Rachel diverted her gaze to the five little Liberty Christian Villagers behind them. They were there, no doubt, to learn about the ins and outs of converting the Whore of Babylon. They had spoken not a word, and she doubted that they would. Theirs was not to reason why . . .

"You are changing the subject," he said at last. He was, to say the least, piqued.

"No. I'm focusing the subject."

"No doubt," he sneered, "you'll say that the Bible is a matter of interpretation."

"I won't make it that easy on you," she sneered back. "Believe it or not, I spent a year or two doing just what you're doing: assaulting people, insulting people, using the Bible to bully people into bending to my will. And if there's one thing I learned, it's how easily you can twist the Scriptures to back up any position you want to take."

"So you know your Bible, do you? Well, then, perhaps you can tell me what you make of First Corinthians fourteen, verses thirty-four through thirty-five—"

"Oh, piss off!" Yes, Rachel was angry now. "Of course you'd like that one. You're so predictable."

"You know what it is."

"Are you kidding?"

"Recite it."

"No. But I'll tell you what. How about if we just skip ahead a few lines, to verse thirty-eight? It's one that applies very nicely to you."

Paul Weissman winced.

"That's right. 'But if anyone is ignorant, let him be ignorant.' " She grinned fiercely. "And while we're at it, why don't *you* recite Matthew seven, verses one through six? That might be refreshing."

Paul Weissman glared at her, prepared to say something scathing.

It didn't happen.

A third voice, soft yet unwavering, spoke from behind him first.

"Judge not, that you be not judged. For with what judgment you judge, you will be judged; and with the same measure you use, it will be measured back at you."

"Be quiet!" Weissman snapped, turning to the blond girl with the strange, sad eyes. She did not listen, but only stared back and continued.

" 'And why do you look at the speck that is in your brother's eye, but do not consider the plank that is in your own eye?' "

"Shut up, I said!"

" 'Or how can you say to your brother, "Let me take the speck out of your eye"; and look, a plank is in your own eye.' "

" 'You hypocrite!' " Rachel cut in gleefully, still quoting Matthew seven. " 'First remove the plank from your own eye, and then you will see clearly to take the speck out of your brother's eye.' "

" 'Do not give what is holy to the dogs,' " Paul Weissman growled, his cheeks flushed red. " 'Nor cast your pearls before swine—' "

" '—lest they trample them under their feet,' " Rachel concluded, " 'and turn and tear you to pieces.' "

Paul Weissman's stare was poison. She met it evenly, eye for eye.

And that, of course, was when Ted and Chris and old Arn Grossinger arrived to save their damsel in distress.

Sixteen

It was 6:35 when Jesse finally showed up at the Penn Towers Hotel. Pete was almost positive, because Mickey's big hand was pointing at the seven and his little hand was just a weensy hair below it. That, Pete felt, pretty well nailed it down in terms of the time.

Whether it was Jesse or not was a different and more difficult matter. It required that he be able to see straight at a distance of nearly seven yards. This did not currently seem possible. Pete found that he could still read the dial on his watch if he leaned real close and concentrated real hard for a couple of seconds.

After all those drinks, in fact, the only things holding him upright were the coke and his own keen frustration. The latter had lingered through last night and today; the former had to be administered every fifteen minutes or so. In the little rocker's room. With the stall-door locked securely.

"Wait a minute." He wasn't above speaking aloud to himself right now. "I can't talk to her like this. I am more than sedated. I'm toast. This is madness."

For a few wobbling seconds he almost had himself convinced. Then he went ahead and started chasing her anyway. Even if it wasn't Jesse, it might be fun.

Especially if it wasn't Jesse.

"Be right back!" he yelled at the bartender as he stumbled from his seat; with any luck, it would save his spot at the bar and his peach schnapps till the debacle was over. He'd been warming that seat in the hotel lounge for just over three hours. He couldn't quit now. It was a moral imperative.

The bartender nodded acknowledgment, or at least he seemed to. Again, at this distance, it was hard to tell. Pete felt confident enough to leave a five-spot next to his drink, laying odds that it would still be there when he got back.

The Thing That Might Be Jesse barreled past the entrance to the Penn Fields Lounge, leaving vapor trails behind. He staggered after, cursing his fried state, wishing that he'd hit the hopper for a toot a bit more recently. He was fading, he could feel himself fading, most of all he could feel his mind rambling and rambling about how much he could feel himself fading.

Nice drug, cocaine, he told himself. *A real friend of a friend of intelligent thought.* A second voice in his head—the voice of the drug—tried to echo the sentiment, and wound up tripping over itself. *Oh, yeah,* he went on. *And the booze helps, too.*

He rounded the corner, proceeding down the burnt-orange and blue striped carpet to the front desk. The colors were too severe: they pulsed and vibrated like video feedback, burnt into his eyes like the sun. "Ai yi yi," he muttered under his breath, then felt himself weaving to the left and put all his concentration behind achieving stability.

Before him, the woman who looked like Jesse was approaching the registration desk. At this point, he was virtually certain it was her. Nobody else could possibly move like that, dress like that, have an ass quite so delectable. He was half inclined to sneak up behind her and squeeze it; but the sliver of rational thought still able to squeeze through the drugs pointed out that it might not be Jesse and would he ever be embarrassed.

Worse yet, it might *be* Jesse, in which case she would probably smack him.

Because Jesse was going through some weird shit just

now. She wouldn't tell him what it was, and he was so far unable to guess, but it must be awfully goddamn bad, because it had her so worked up that she was gaining weight and cutting out of practice and turning very cold to him indeed. . . .

By this point, he was within five feet of her. She was leaning against the desk, a suitcase at her feet, checking in. He wavered there, his doubts reprising, his throat inadvertently clearing.

She turned and faced him.

"Pete," she said with uncharacteristic softness. "Not now, okay?"

It was Jesse, all right. But it was not a Jesse he'd ever seen before. Her features looked as if they'd all been lowered at least an eighth of an inch; she'd been crying, that much was for sure; her whole face was sagging as a result, a subtle sort of hillside erosion.

A glimmer of intelligence, faint and fleeting, sparked somewhere deep in the folds of his brain. He felt an important revelation tickle the tip of his tongue, then vanish. "Shit," he muttered in frustration, stumbling closer.

He wanted to understand what was wrong with her, what he could do to help. He wanted to take a stab at empathy, see if there were any way to get inside her experience.

He couldn't.

The coke wouldn't let him.

And that's the great thing about Ye Olde Peruvian Marching Powder, he went on. *It's like psychic Saran Wrap: it locks in freshness so well that you can't even feel your own soul ticking, much less anyone else's.*

The voice of the drug echoed the sentiment into oblivion. And then said, *Do another line. It'll clear you up.*

"Jess, I gotta talk with ya," he slurred.

Her sunken features hardened, set that way. "You don't listen very well, do you?"

"No. But I hear real good."

"Don't play word games with me."

"Don't play head games with me."

She paused, and that gave him a second. He felt that he was doing fairly well, all things considered. "You won't tell me what's wrong," he continued. "And I don't think that's fair. I'm your friend—"

Jesse snorted out a snatch of abrasive laughter. It hurt.

"An' I'm your lover—"

"*Oh*, yeah." Her lips curled into a pain-filled sneer. It hurt even worse.

"And I'm on your side, dammit! I'm on your goddamn team! You think I don't wanna know what's hurting you? You think I don't care? Come on! If I did anything to hurt you, I wanna know what it is."

"Will that make you happy?"

"Yes."

"I'm pregnant."

"I . . ." he began, and then froze.

"There." She smiled, bitter. Her face was a mask. "Are you happy now?"

"I . . ." There were no words, no words he could say. He felt his strength, his wit, his everything spiral down and away like turds in a flushing toilet. Balance deserted him; he staggered back, grabbing for a wall when none was there and barely held himself up.

"I wasn't going to tell you." The mask began to redden. "You didn't need to know, you know. I would have just taken care of it, and . . ." It was her turn to lose the words.

"You would have what?" His voice was a croak, and his eyes were wide. Like hers, they were filling with tears.

"Oh, Pete. Do I have to spell it out for you?" The first lines of clear saline dribbled down her cheeks. "Are you that fucking stupid?"

"Hey . . ."

"Hey what?" She was crying, yes, but she would not weaken. "Are you gonna try to tell me that you're ready to be a father? You're not even ready to be a real *boy*friend! You're not ready to commit to anything! You're twenty-six years old and you're a little goddamn *kid*, Pete!"

The lobby of the hotel was spinning now; he felt himself losing control. When the anger flared, irrational though it was, there was no way he could stop it. "And you're all grown up, is that right?"

"No, I'm not," she shot back. "And that's the point. I'm not ready, either—"

He moved forward then, and took her by the shoulders.

"God*dammit*, Jesse," he said, voice quavering. "This is different. This is our *child* we're talking about."

"No, it isn't." Her eyes were dripping fire. "This is a *mistake*. And it's not gonna happen."

He shook her roughly then, and the words blurted out.

"How can you *say* that?"

"Read my LIPS!" she hissed.

He pushed her back violently. "THIS IS A LIFE!" he began.

"No shit," she growled, pulling away. "In fact, it's *three* lives. And I refuse to fuck up any of them."

"No, you're just going to *kill* one!"

And that was when she slapped him. Hard.

"Get away from me."

Pete just stood there, the left side of his face on fire, his eyes stinging almost as badly. He watched her push past him, her suitcase in hand, and move to the elevators. The one on the far left was open and waiting. She closed in on it rapidly, resolutely, leaving trails of ghostly motion behind.

It wasn't until she was inside and the door started closing that he began to move toward her.

But doors, like opportunities, are funny that way.

They open.

And then they close.

Seventeen

At seven-thirty, the ramp rats were gathered in force around the loading dock at the back of the Spectrum Sports Arena, banners and beer bottles in hand, spandex clinging tight. They had come in the ludicrous hope that, when The Scream's limo came rolling in, they would somehow be chosen from the flock: to come backstage and party with the band, to do quality drugs, to get balled by a star.

Walker's main man, Hook, paused by the police-style barricades, watching them dispassionately. It was a sight that he was more than used to; at this point, bored contempt was the best that he could whip up.

"Vermin." He muttered the nickname sarcastically. "Even if the band wasn't here already, what do you think the odds would really be?"

Ramp rats and vermin were always there, of course, at every show, in every town. They were staples of the heavy metal scene. They swarmed over the parking lot in denim-and-leather-jacketed droves, hooting and howling and shattering glass, scenting the air with thick sweet smoke and exhaust, partying till they puked or passed out.

In their faces, Hook saw an alarming continuity, a numbing repetitiveness of attitude grafted to features. There was the lumphead, the rock slut, the would-be tramp; there was the handsome young rebel and his tag-along idiot friend, and the hopeless fat feeb in the too-new leather. There were the three good buddies who gawked and guffawed; there was the fat chick with the sad eyes lined in thick black Maybelline.

They were the vermin, the scuttling hordes.

They were the teenaged dispossessed.

They were the life blood of The Scream.

They were the Chosen Ones.

Hook watched them, dragging one finger idly across the unshaved stubble at his chin. He was short and stocky, powerful-looking. His long, dark, thin and thinning hair was pasted to his head. His legs were thick and stiff at the knees, where decades-old masses of scar tissue lay over the joints like wax drippings on a candlestick. They were forever hidden in the baggy green cargo pants that he wore, as always, with his battered, blasted field jacket. Its sleeves and left breast-pocket bristled with insignia and the awards he'd earned in the days before his return to The World. The back was painstakingly embroidered with The Scream's logo: a bright red slit-eyed baby in a flaming pentagram, with a banner that read, *Your Mother Should Know*. He had done it himself: fingers dancing with needle and thread, making something both fearsome and wondrous. Hook's fingers were magic.

All five of them.

His second most prominent features were his oddly bulging eyes. They were pale blue and watery, and they gave him a look somewhere between Peter Lorre and an ill-tempered mackerel. One could not help but be drawn, albeit reluctantly, to those eyes.

Until one noticed his missing left hand.

Tonight, he was wearing the prosthetic claw; it was, to beg the pun, the *handiest* of the twenty-odd appliances he'd designed to adorn his otherwise-useless stump. It was stronger than the real thing, with a grip that rivaled a pit bull's jaws in pounds of pressure per square inch.

It could crush a man's skull.

It had done so before. It would do so again.

With any luck at all.

He was proud of it, proud to have made it reality. He was proud, most of all, to Serve: to have his talents, at long last, put to their proper use.

And Tuesday night would be the pièce de résistance. Tuesday night, the world would learn just exactly how brilliant he actually was.

And there would be no more pissing on that bum John Hook.

Not ever again.

A lone figure moved through the ramp rat cotillion, emerged on the near side, and strolled up to the barricades. He had on a nominal Screamer uniform—black leather pants, black canvas duster, black cycle gloves, and shiny Mylar Band-Its—but his T-shirt brightly proclaimed I ♡ TOXIC WASTE. He was a little taller than Hook, maybe 5'9", and his blond good looks were more than vaguely familiar. One thing was for certain: he was not your basic ramp rat. He carried a leather shoulder bag that marked him as either press—which were practically crawling out of the woodwork on account of the big gig assembling just across the boulevard—or a freelancer trying to weasel in for some behind-the-scenes dope on the band.

Which was strictly. Strictly.

Forbidden.

Who is this guy? Hook heard himself wonder. *Where do I know him from?*

And what does he think he's doing?

The guy walked over to Lloyd, the asshole Spectrum security guard. To Hook's surprise, they shook hands with annoying enthusiasm. Evidently they were buddies; Lloyd had not seemed to be a friendly type. But there they were, talking. Hook couldn't hear the words, but it had the tenor of a long-time-no-see rap.

A bad feeling swept over Hook. A very bad feeling. It came as a knot of coarse terror in his belly and a seering phantom twinge in his absent left hand that predicted trouble like a bunion foretold the weather.

Oh, shit, he thought, clutching his prosthetic limb instinctively, as if he could massage away the pain. *Lloyd's gonna let him in,* his mind said, and his mind was just telling the truth.

He started moving toward them, just as the guy swatted Lloyd on the back and started moving down the ramp.

Hook muttered "Damn" and shifted to intercept course, cursing his knees, cursing the fact that they made him move so goddamn slow. There was no way that he could keep pace; there was no way that he could even achieve it. The guy was ahead of him already, and gaining ground.

"Hey!" he yelled.

The guy ignored him.

"Asshole!"

The guy looked back.

"Where the fuck do you think you're going?"

"Inside!" the guy yelled back. "What does it look like?"

"You just hold it right there!"

"Oh, Jesus," the guy muttered, but he stayed where he was. It gave Hook a couple of seconds to catch up, which he did, despite the fact that it made his knees ache like crazy.

"You can't go back there," he asserted, standing now face-to-face.

"You're with the road crew?"

"That's right."

"Hi." He smiled and extended his hand. He looked half-fried. "I'm Pete Stewart. I play lead guitar with the Jacob Hamer Band, and—"

Hook ignored the hand, stared straight into Stewart's black shades. "I don't care who you are. You're not going back there."

"Why not?"

"It's closed."

"Hey"—Stewart looked perplexed—"I'm not John Q. Public, okay? I'm not after autographs. I just want to cut through to the press box."

"So go through the front."

"I don't like crowds."

"That's not my problem."

Stewart laughed. "It's not my problem, either, Jack, cuz I'm going through the back here. Why don't you just relax a little?"

"You don't understand." Hook could feel, aside from his burgeoning anger, the phantom pain in his prosthesis. "Nobody goes backstage."

"What, you afraid I'm gonna steal your trade secrets or something? We don't even do a show like yours. I'm just going to the press—"

Hook grabbed him by the shoulder with his claw-hand, exerting just enough pressure to hurt. "You ain't going anywhere—"

"HEY!" Stewart hollered, yanking free and stepping back rapidly. His breath came out in voluminous huffs, and he pointed a wrathful finger. "You are a rude motherfucker, you know that? I *know* people here! I play this place at least once a year! I don't have to answer to pissants like you!"

"Like hell you don't!" Hook took a giant step forward.

"BACK OFF!" Stewart yelled, and jogged back out of claw-hold range. "Just try and stop me, asshole! In fact, you'd better move, cuz I might just have your job by the time you hit backstage!"

"HEY!" Hook hollered, but it was too late; Stewart was already striding rapidly downward and away. The knot in his stomach was growing by leaps and bounds, but he was too slow, and the interloper would no longer listen.

"Oh, God," he muttered as he staggered behind, but that was not what he meant. He was asking for guidance and mercy and strength.

But not from God.

Not exactly.

*   *   *

Pete was hissing steam by the time he hit the hallway that led backstage. The fresh air had mown through his intoxication; the fury had taken care of the rest. If there were any more douchebags like that last guy in the Scream entourage, they had best beware; he was liable to gnaw his way through them.

The craziness with Jesse wasn't bad enough, it seemed. No, evidently the fun was just beginning. *Who knows?* he silently fumed. *Maybe we could drive a threshing machine through the crowd, just to round things out.* His anger kept him from noticing his surroundings until he was nearly halfway down the hall.

Then he stopped.

And stared.

Astounded.

The backstage corridor was long and high and wide, but The Scream had it very nearly packed with Anvil cases of every conceivable size and description. Pete had heard about The Scream's stage setup—fourteen tractor trailers' worth, requiring over two hundred thousand watts to power, and costing over three quarters of a cool million to build and run. Reputedly, it was the most elaborate and expensive road show in rock 'n roll history. Staring at its luggage, he could well believe it.

We take up a third of this space, he mused. *Packed loose. You couldn't fit a greased weasel through the holes in these stacks.* It was outrageous. He whistled appreciatively as he wormed around them.

Two roadies approached from the opposite direction, carrying something large and heavy. The guy whose back wasn't to him thought to say something, then merely grunted. *Good,* Pete hissed internally. *I'm not feelin' that cheerful.*

And then he reached the end of the corridor, and it was clear that there was one hell of a lot of business going down onstage, so he automatically veered to the right. A quick jaunt past the humming generator room, the closed doors to The Scream's dressing rooms, and then cut through the hospitality room to the stairs leading up to the press box mezzanine, and—

"Hold it right there, scumbag," said a cold voice to his right. He froze, just long enough for the voice's owner to appear beside him and latch hold of his arm.

"Get your fucking paws OFF me!" Pete shouted. He

whipped violently free and spun to meet his aggressor, right hand pulling back as if balling up for a blow.

The chance never came. Too swiftly, the palm of the tall man's hand slammed into his solar plexus. He felt all the air in his lungs *whoof* out of him, pulling his attention away from the buckling of his knees and the pull of gravity until his ass landed hard on the concrete floor. The back of his head followed in short order. Then came the dancing neon stars.

The world was still spinning when he opened his eyes a split second later. The man who had hit him was saying something vicious and incomprehensible. Pete shook his head, got only pain for his efforts. Clarity availed him not.

Then there were several people around him, and they were all saying something, but the only one he understood was saying, *Leave him alone, what's the matter with you?* Perhaps he understood it because he identified with the sentiment, perhaps because he recognized the voice, perhaps because the lips were right next to his ear. Someone was hoisting him up.

"Frank?" Pete wheezed. It was the best he could do. His consciousness was coming back, but so were the drugs and alcohol. The scrappling sound of flailing limbs and shoe-soles on concrete were supernaturally loud as he awkwardly regained his footing.

"Yeah," said the man who'd helped him out: a wiry little black security guard with salt-and-pepper hair. "Look, Mr. Walker. You're out of line here."

"This man has no business backstage." Mr. Walker's manner was incalculably cold.

"Maybe so, but he's not gonna hurt anything!" Frank said, exasperated. "I know him. He's with the Jacob Hamer Band, for Chrissakes!"

"Yeah, what *is* it with you people, anyway?" Pete said with some effort. "I just came to see your damn show, man! It's not like I came to assassinate the president or something!"

Walker was about to say something else when a door behind him opened. Pete thought he noticed a flicker of apprehension on the man's icy face. Then he, too, turned to look.

As Tara Payne stepped into the hallway.

Suddenly, his eyes were focusing perfectly. It was still not enough to fully appreciate the sight.

Rock music had always had its share of breathtaking

women; be it Kate Bush, Annie Lennox, Sheena Easton, Whitney Houston, Pat Benatar, Madonna, or a host of others, unique and exotic females were well within the rock 'n' roll tradition. Pete had met a great many of them in his time and was continually awed by the strength of their allure.

But there had never been a woman quite like Tara Payne.

She moved, and the air around her shuddered as if she had just thrown the switch on some carnal Van de Graaff generator. She moved again, closer, and Pete felt the tiny hairs on his skin sway in her direction. There wasn't a man in the corridor who didn't appear similarly affected.

But she wasn't looking at every man in the corridor.

She was looking at Pete.

And he found himself lost in the dark depths of those almond eyes, lost in the abandon they so insistently imposed. He felt the rearing of *kundalini*'s spinal serpent of fire, felt his heart palpitate wildly in his chest.

She looked at him, and he was hers.

It was as simple as that.

She moved closer. She moved closer. She moved right to Walker's side. Pete found himself staring at her lips, which were soft and full and painted a ripe berry-red. They stopped an inch from Walker's ear and parted, revealing perfect white teeth and a small glistening tongue.

"Leave him be," she said very softly. The words resonated in Pete's ear as if she were leaning into *him*. His ear flamed as if sunburned. He stared at Walker.

And Walker *shuddered*. There was no getting around the fact. There was an element of pain in the way the ice floes of his face gave way that was perfectly understandable. It was evident that he suffered her proximity quite a bit; given the way Pete felt, it was only human for his discomfort to be nigh unto unbearable. She whispered something else that Pete *couldn't* hear; a trickle of sweat ran down the back of his neck. She whispered something else. Walker nodded and grimaced and produced a bright yellow backstage pass. He handed it to her. She took it, whispered something else.

And all the while, she was staring at Pete: a trained and searching gaze that made his every nerve ending feel scrutinized and aflame. *Omigod*, a voice in his head informed him. *Omigod*.

Tara smiled then, as if she knew precisely what effect she was having.

She left Walker's side.

Moving. Toward him.

And he could feel the crackling tension mount as the space between them diminished. It made all the short hairs on his body want to leap straight out of their follicles; it was as if she were a Tesla coil, an electromagnet supreme, with the most perfect body on this or any other planet. He tried to swallow; it was like trying to turn over an engine that had been out of oil for years.

He tried to think of Jesse.

His mind said, *Jesse who?*

And then she was upon him, an inch from his face. He was vaguely aware of Frank's moving back—of all of them, in general, retreating. He was vaguely aware of his own pounding heart. Her smell was what overpowered him now; he could almost see the pheromones, sweet and musky heart-shaped molecules that touched his soul with satin lips.

"I want to see your eyes," she said.

"You do," he barely managed.

"Yes." She smiled. "I want to see them now."

His hands hung, helplessly trembling, at his sides. He did not seem to have the strength to lift them. A warm paralysis, snake-venom intense, had gripped both his body and his conscious will.

But something else was there: a serpent's guile, a reptilian charm from the oldest and most powerful part of his brain. It was enough to force his mouth to work, force his lungs to give voice.

"Help yourself," he croaked.

Her hands were small and long-nailed and articulately-boned and absolutely perfect. She brought them up to either side of his head, gently pulled the sunglasses away from his ears and his face.

The world went instantly brighter.

And her eyes . . .

. . . *her eyes* . . .

"Ah, yes." Her smile was absolutely radiant. "I thought so."

Confusion let off a dim and insignificant flare in the back of his head. He was staring into her eyes.

And her eyes were everything.

"You thought what?" he heard himself ask.

"You know that the eyes are the mirrors of the soul."

"Yes."

"I've been looking for a soul. And I think that I just found it."

"You are incredible." At last his lips did his bidding.

"So are you. In fact, you are perfect.

"Let me feel your heart."

His skin was quite damp now. The slick wet heat of it only stirred him more deeply, intensified the tremors that racked him as she brought those delicate hands to rest against his chest.

And his heart, his heart was going mad, his heart was a lunatic Edgar Varese percussion ensemble that rumbled and thudded and clattered against his breastbone, sending black-red heartblood and adrenaline pulsing from crown of skull to sole of shoe and back again. If there was a bottom-line message to be found in his being, it was pounding out now, perfect braille for the discerning.

Tara had her hands upon his breast.

She read him.

Loud and clear.

"I will want to see you tonight," she said, handing him the pass. "When the show is over. You will still be here?"

The laugh he managed was not under his control.

"This is a trick question?" he gurgled.

She smiled again. "No, it's not."

"Well, it should be."

"Which means?"

"Which means yes." He said it with all sincerity. "Yes, I will be here."

She came closer then, which seemed barely possible. The lips that had been driving him crazy brushed up against his earlobe as she spoke. The tongue touched briefly, hot and feather-light. Then withdrew. Touched perfect teeth. And whispered.

Three words.

"I need you."

Then she turned away, and he staggered back, and the rest of the world clicked back into gear. He looked at Walker, whose face had set back to stone; he looked at Frank, whose eyes were bugging out, almost as wide as those of Hook, who had finally caught up to the scenario. Their paralyses were less-than-aptly mirrored by his own. They stood. And they watched.

As her perfect body vanished through the doorway from whence it had come. Her breath, still ringing in his ears, second only to the last words she'd spoken.

I need you . . .

Fifteen minutes later his brain began to work again.

He was sitting in the front row of the otherwise-empty press box, overlooking the already-massing throngs below. It was early yet, with another forty-five minutes or so till showtime. To his left and down was the massive stage setup, concealed from the masses by a matrix of black, flowing curtains. From his vantage point he could make out the frantically scrambling crew hastening through their last-minute preparations: Hook was visible stage left, gesticulating to a pair of roadies beside a blinking wall of massive power amps. Looking across, he could see the scaffold crew at Pete's-eye level, crawling along the L-shaped catwalk to the front spotlights. An enormous-scale replica of a Cobra gunship hung wobbling in the wings. All told, there must have been a good sixty people at work getting the Scream-machine ready to rock and roll.

"Jesus," Pete whispered. "What a setup."

Above, at the center of the theater, an enormous two-ton, six-sided video module called ArenaVision dangled. ArenaVision was Spectrum's baby, Pete knew: a prototype system that allowed up to six cameras to give everyone a jumbo front-row view. Pete also knew RJ, the amiable young guy who ran the system, from previous gigs. He laughed as he thought of a conversation he'd had about RJ's preshow rationale: "How else do you keep an arena full of stoned kiddies quiet?

"Turn on the giant TV."

Right now it was showing a series of vintage Warner Brothers cartoons, which at this moment entailed showing the classic *Duck Amok*. Daffy had just endured the indignity of having his entire body erased by an enormous pencil, only to be replaced as a polka-dotted, four-footed, flower-headed freak. Stoned giggles wafted up from below.

Ordinarily, Pete would have been similarly absorbed in the grim travails befalling Daffy; it was, after all, one of Pete's favorites, and he'd never seen it on quite so colossal a screen. But tonight was different.

To say the least. Tonight was shaping itself up to be the screwiest and most convoluted night of his life.

There were two voices speaking in his head right now, neither of them his own, both pulling in separate directions. The first one was Jesse's, full of anger and dread and woe. *Oh, Pete. Do I have to spell it out for you?* it said. *Are you that fucking stupid?*

It was the voice that he was running from.

The other one, of course, had something much nicer to say.

—*I need you*—

"But that's not the point," he told himself, cross. "She's pregnant. She needs you . . ."

—*This is a mistake*—

". . . whether she wants to admit it or not," he continued, but there wasn't much juice behind it. Pete was big-time confused. He could scarcely believe the words that blurted

—*THIS IS A LIFE!*—

out of his mouth. He never really realized that he felt that way, was barely sure now that he really agreed. He was trying to whip up some righteousness

—*you're just going to KILL one!*—

get behind the thing that he knew he ought to be doing.

But he couldn't figure out quite what that was.

Jesse was right. That was the bottom line. He *did* act like a little kid, and he *wasn't* ready for the responsibilities of fatherhood, not to mention just treating his lover right. He knew it. He'd always known it.

But he didn't like to have it rubbed in his face like this.

Because it made him wonder what was the matter with him. It begged the question *why*. He was twenty-six years old, for God's sake. Wasn't that old enough to start getting his act together? *I mean, here you are, Mr. Rock Star, waving your dick at anything with tits, not really worrying about it, having a good time . . .*

And the next thing you know, you've knocked up one of your best friends, one of the people you love the most.

You put her through all kinds of personal anguish that she won't even tell you about.

And she won't have the baby. Zygote X eats the big one.

Cuz you're a fucking little kid.

Yeah, that was nice. That was a swell bit of self-realization. His ego withered like a slug with salt poured on it. Pete slammed his fist down on the press box counter, simultaneously bruising his hand and spilling a dollop of his beer. "*Ah!*" he yipped as the pain hit home. It only brightened the futility of the gesture.

He did it three more times in rapid succession.

It was still not nearly enough.

Suddenly the vacant expanse of the press box seemed too confining. This wasn't why he came here. He didn't come here to think about his problems. He came here to get *away* from them. And maybe, just maybe, get in touch with something far more fundamental. He wanted to party. He wanted to forget.

He wanted to *rock*.

And that's just what he was going to do.

Pete looked around in mock-caution, pulled out his vial, and laid out two jumbo lines on the shiny black surface of the press box ledge: a good quarter gram in one mega-toot. *Two for the road*. He sucked them up, donned his shades, stashed his bag under the counter, and headed out. To mingle.

He had just hit the mezzanine when the first soundcheck power-chord slammed out from behind the curtain. The crowd roared. The Merry Melodies theme receded into the concentric cartoon hole from whence it came, and the ArenaVision screens went momentarily blank.

The concert was still a ways off, but the effect was unmistakable.

"EEAYOW!" The cry rose up from the hordes amassed around the front of the stage, rang out from the surrounding seated throngs. A bass drum thudded: *boom boom BOOM*. With each successive *BOOM* more hands jerked up in the classic two-fingered metal sign: index and pinkie fingers erect on a raised fist. It was like some sort of Pavlovian response. It was thunderous and fervent and exhilarating as all get-out. It yanked Pete out of his self-abasement and pulled him into the maelstrom of mad teenage enthusiasm.

He bopped down the stairs, hit the main floor, and looked around. Hand-painted banners made from pilfered bed sheets fluttered from the balconies. *METAL RULES. PHILLY LOVES TARA.*

WE LOVE THE SCREAM.

This kind of response didn't happen at a Jacob Hamer concert. The audiences were older, more restrained, too damned tight-assed. He couldn't remember the last time an audience had hollered, "HA-MER! HA-MER!" or spray-painted his name into perma-pressed infamy.

It was too cool. The air buzzed with the excited abandon of people temporarily cut loose from the cubicled constraints of parents and principals and preachers and everyone else who ever tried to make them knuckle under to the wisdom of their elders and betters, who held the absolute answers to absolutely fucking everything. Here they were a tribe, they had *power*, they were loose in a far wilder world than the old farts ever dared to admit. You could see it in the wary stance of security people, who really only wanted to get them in and out with a minimum of mayhem. It was mysterious and exciting. It was a blast. It reminded him of his own rebellious teenhood, catching groups like Alice Cooper and Aerosmith, Led Zeppelin, The Who, The Stones, Black Sabbath.

So now it was Ozzy or Iron Maiden or AC/DC, Van Halen or Twisted Sister or The Slabs or The Scream. *Plus ça change*, dude. The more it changed, the more it boiled down to the same damned thing: getting pumped up, caught up and lost in the frenzy of twenty thousand screaming lunatics who had come to catch fire in the realm of the forbidden. Hard Rock or Heavy Metal. These kids weren't here for scholarly edification or hairsplitting subdivisions, any more than they were here to sell their souls to the devil.

They were here to rock out, God bless 'em.

Every fucking one.

Then the lights went down, and the howling began in earnest, and the curtains parted, and the power quad called Cleaver head-banged their way into the cranial spotlight.

*   *   *

A power-slam from the rhythm section, a howl from the vocalist, a blistering lead from the guitarist, and they were off and running. The whole thing was orchestrated at peak break-neck pace. They were the warm-up band, and they were bloody well going to warm things up.

It did the trick: the guitarist was an absolute maniac. Pete could feel his own fingers itching for that kind of license to excess as Cleaver propelled itself into the first verse of its opening tune.

The singer sang about the Mark of The Beast and the number 666 and a few other cultural totems. No big deal. Pure comic-book, bone-thudding, head-banging Fun. From where Pete stood, it was pretty clear that these guys were approaching the whole issue of good and evil from a neo-Wagnerian, muscle-flexing type of stance. It was about as dangerous as a *Conan the Barbarian* strip. Hard to see the harm in that. Boneheaded adolescent oversimplification has its place, after all, in the scheme of things.

Its place took up the next forty-five minutes of smoke and thunder. He watched it all from the floor. By the end of that time, the kids were stoked, and Pete felt almost sober. He stood there screaming with the rest of them over Cleaver's showpiece finale, "Saigon Lullaby." *Oh, well,* he thought. *Nam chic is all the rage these days. Especially for those who've never been there. It's like they missed out on something big, and they want like hell to recreate it.* And damned if the singer *didn't* come out dressed like a mutant Buddhist in a head-to-toe skintight asbestos bodysuit, goggles, and saffron robes, douse himself with what certainly *looked* like gas from what certainly *looked* like an army gas can and Zippo the whole shebang.

WHOOOOOSH!

There was a blast of flames, flashpot-smoke, and blinding strobelight, and the band was gone.

The audience flipped. They were stoked, alrightee. And Pete could scarcely remember having had such a good time. The eternal fifteen-year-old in his brain was firmly in residence, with an added plus.

The eternal fifteen-year-old still had half a vial of blow in his pocket.

And it was high time to have it.

There was the obligatory intermission as the crew ripped

down the Cleaver set and stowed it to the side. A hardcore contingent of Cleaveroids stomped at the foot of the stage, chanting, "CLEA-VER! CLEA-VER!" Their call would, alas, go unanswered.

Cleaver was gone.

And Scream-time was near.

Intermission ran nearly forty-five minutes. Pete left the sprawling floor of the arena and decided to cruise the drafty promenade for a bit. He was more than a little disappointed that the beer concessions were closed—it was a kiddie-fest, after all—but what the hell. He could always breeze backstage later. Right now he was digging the energy of the Cock Walk, as Jesse had so neatly pegged it: thousands of kids cruising the outer perimeter in their best leather 'n' spikes *Strut dey stuff! EEAYOW!* He was half-tempted to go ahead and *scream*, thought better of it, changed his mind yet again, and—

"EEYAOW!"

—nobody seemed to mind. He did it again, louder, going:

"EEEEYAAOW!!"

Damn, that felt good! His scream just went up and out and mingled with the thrum of the crowd. "EEEEEEEYAAOOW!!!"

More than a few answered back; a staggered chain of echoes through the promenade, the common call of the tribe. It was a blast. Pete smiled and nodded to a passing couple; a lion-maned guy in leopard-spotted spandex and a fringed leather jacket and his petite and extremely cute girlfriend in a torn suede miniskirt. They smiled back and moved on, not seeming to recognize him at all. Pete felt only the tiniest twinge of jealousy; he was sure if Rod Royale trotted out here he'd be mobbed.

But fuckit; invisibility had its own advantages, and tomorrow he'd be onstage again, if only for the nineteen politically correct minutes that scheduling permitted each act. Tonight he could hang out and dig the show with the rest of the crowd.

And afterwards, well . . .

—You're perfect—

Well, the world was just full of possibilities.

Pete was so wrapped up in contemplation that he bumped

right into another fun-loving couple. "Excuse me . . ." he started to say. And then he stopped.

Because for one thing, he didn't think they'd noticed. And for another, he didn't think that they noticed much of *anything*. The guy was a hyper little runt in filthy denim and shiny shiny Bandits. And the *girl* . . .

The girl was wasted. *Correction*, he amended, *the girl was* beyond *wasted. The girl was to wasted what chum is to Mrs. Paul's fish sticks*. No drugs of Pete's considerable acquaintance could wreak this degree of havoc.

She stank like old road-kill; nothing fresh and heady, just a deep-set taint of steady steady decay. Her hair was matted and the color of stable straw; her skin dry and brittle as the Dead Sea scrolls. At one point in very ancient history she might have been a looker. No more. Her Scream T-shirt was tattered in a dozen places, but what it revealed no one would ever want to see. And her eyes . . .

—the windows to the soul, you know—

Her eyes were obscured by cracked Ferrari shades. Pete felt strangely grateful; he very much doubted that he would care to peek through her windows and see whatever had taken up residence there.

The girl looked up to him blankly. Then she smiled a split-lip expression of dimmest cognizance and said, "I know youuuuuu. . . ."

Pete was horrified and dearly hoped she wasn't speaking in the biblical sense. "I'm sorry—" he began.

He was just about to ask what she meant when the first bass drum thudded, and the crowds began to roar.

"C'mon, Cyndi," the runt said, "we're gonna missummm—"

"Wait, I *know* himmmmm."

The bass drum thudded again. "Cyndeee, c'monnnnn . . ." The runt pulled weakly toward the sound like a rummy smelling a bottle. Cyndi acquiesced, and the two stumbled away from him and toward the stairs.

"Jesus," Pete muttered, "whiners from hell." He continued on until he saw the small blue PRESS ONLY sign, flashed his pass, and toddled on in.

In the half hour or so remaining, Pete amused himself by yakking it up with the reporters from the music mags and the local papers, as well as what appeared to be a *60 Minutes* news crew, who were getting some press-box footage to intercut in an upcoming segment. He got his picture taken with some district reps from The Scream's own Bedlam Records and Liza Robins of *Hard Rock Ragazine*, who was busy sucking up to anyone even remotely schmoozworthy.

In the course of it, he learned an interesting thing or two. For starters, tonight's gig was special: the last in a nonstop blitzkrieg 270-day tour for The Scream (another twinge of jealousy: it had been damned near a *year* since the last JHB tour).

More astounding still, though, was the fact (conveniently leaked by Derrick Swillman, of Bedlam) that they would be turning around and launching an all-new, mammoth show, right here in the Spectrum, in a mere three days. Absolutely guaranteed to blow absolutely everyone clear off the map.

"All this time," Swillman insisted, "we've been threatening to let Momma out of the bag. But this Monday night— Labor Day, that is"—and he paused to let the journalists groan—"The Scream guarantees it!"

"If you miss out now," he concluded dramatically, "you'll never know what it is to really raise hell!"

Pete envied them. It was all over his face. And he was just about to say so out loud, when the intro kicked in.

And the show began.

A decibel-crunching blast of brass, drums, and guitar pounded out the intro as the Cobra gunship swooped like some great deadly insect, perilously close to the press box and the throngs of fans below. Spotlights tracked it as a low-frequency synth sequence insinuated itself into the beat. The Cobra arced gracefully and headed out toward the center of the arena, turned, and hovered just beneath the ArenaVision module. Pete did another toot and then hooted with the best of them: he couldn't figure *how* they got that thing airborne, no less controlled. Radio maybe, or Voodoo; he sure didn't see any guide wires in evidence. The Cobra's cockpit lit from within: a hologram of Tara's helmeted face was clearly in evidence, underlit from the control panel like a B-movie psycho. She turned it back toward the stage. Angled down.

And started to fire.

It was a strafing run, straight toward centerstage. The screen backdrop projected aerial footage of tropical foliage reeling under the rapidly expanding concentric shock waves of a hundred bombs. The band pumped in sync as twin lasers in the minigun pods splattered the audience with harmlessly devastating blood-red light. The crowd howled appreciatively. The band wailed back, electric guitar screaming in billion-note-per-second synchronicity. The Cobra dove toward the stage, still firing: flashpot-flak exploded in perfectly synchronized ersatz mayhem.

The Cobra dove . . .

And dove . . .

And just as it seemed that it would smash into the backdrop screen, it veered off . . .

. . . and the backdrop exploded into a napalm wall of fire and smoke, smoke and fire that roiled and split into a hideous, leering horned Death's head grinnn . . .

. . . and the Cobra was gone, and Tara appeared, as the film disappeared and the flak-smoke cleared and the Death's head reared . . .

And the entire band came to with stop-on-a-dime tightness. Switched gears. And started into the first mega-chords of their opening number, "Filet of Soul."

"*Ohmigod,*" Pete whispered in awe. No one heard him; he couldn't even hear himself. It didn't matter. Tara was strutting up to the microphone with a presence that all the fan fotos and video clips in the world would never come close to conveying. Her costume was mercenary dominatrix perfection: thigh-high strapped boots and leather gauntlets over a sheer black bodysuit that accentuated every ripple of muscle in her taut feline form, with enough chains to anchor the *Intrepid.* She brandished a very real looking samurai sword, tossed a long rope of ebony hair back over her left shoulder, and started right in:

> "I want your body
> no bones about it"
> Want you to know that
> I can't live without it."

She drew the blade casually across a bare forearm: a shimmer of very real looking blood rolled down smooth smooth skin.

> "Got to possess you
> got to control you

You've got to know that
I bought and sold you."

Pete glanced up at the giant ArenaVision screens: Tara seemed to be staring right at him. Correction: right *through* him. It was a wonder the vidicon tubes didn't melt down right in their portapaks from the sheer intensity of her gaze; Pete wondered vaguely if any—or every—one else staring into those dark eyes saw it.

He wondered. But he didn't care. His heart pounded with excitement and anticipation. *If this is the intro,* he thought, *I may not survive the encore.*

Tara smiled.

And the show rolled on.

Eighteen

Jake was afraid to open his eyes.

He had lain down to play on cool white sheets, with his Strat in his hands, a wicked buzz from too many beers in his head and the moist *shhhhhhh* of the air conditioner filling the room. Now the sheets were gone, the buzz was gone, and the hiss of climate-controlled comfort had been replaced by something far more sinister.

And Jake was afraid.

Because he was once again locked in the dream's dark embrace. He tried to shut it out, wanting not to breathe even for fear of what information each new lungful would bring. He tried to think of Rachel, desperately murmuring her name there in the eye-clenching darkness.

But he could not, for the life of him, remember her face.

That figured, in its own mad way. The dreams were pulling him back: to rob him of any life that stretched beyond their tight confines. To steal his future right out from under him. To get what he owed them. With each passing second Jake sank deeper and deeper into a black hole from which he might not this time have the strength to return.

You're not really here, his mind whispered, heart pounding out his throat as he scrabbled through the blackness. *You're going to open your eyes and be in your tacky double suite in downtown Phila-fucking-delphia. There's a beer on the bedside table and a gorgeous gloss-black Strat lying on your chest!* He clutched at it in confirmation.

The guitar slipped through his grasp like sand through a fist.

And Jake opened his eyes.

The village was gone.

That much was fairly certain on their retreat, even more evident upon their return. There weren't any *villagers*, either: no crispy critters curled amongst the smoldering thatch, limbs bent back like blackened matchsticks.

But that wasn't all.

Someone had come back in the night and tidied up, just hauled the carnage away. The dead were gone, every last scrap.

It happened, everybody knew it happened. Fucking dinks. They knew that Marines always brought back their dead. Always. They knew it messed up their heads, and their body counts.

So they took 'em, he thought bitterly. *Sanchez and Natch and Clairborne and Ricechex and Willy from Philly they took my fucking friends they took Duncan they took—*

Jake clamped down, hard. They were gone. Probably for good.

But that wouldn't stop him from looking.

The squad moved up the shallow rise toward the ville, cautious from fear and habit. The new guys looked wired to the max. The air was hot and tainted with the stench of burnt things; Jake expected as much, as they topped the rise.

What he hadn't expected, somehow, was company.

Lurps.

A Long Range Reconnaissance Patrol was already there: members of the deadly cliques who found their niche on the darker edges of an already murky world. They were the chosen

ones in the Nam, the few who excelled in arts that most merely
endured.

Jake had actually seen them occasionally in his tour, and
he'd heard plenty: outrageous accounts that were routinely
guaranteed to beat out the top-this category in the nightly
bullshit sweepstakes. Stories of Cambodia, of missions that
never happened, executed by men who didn't exist. Lurps
sometimes seemed elevated to mythic status; certainly by the
pogues in the rear, often by those in the bush. But myth or no,
there was no doubt: Lurps played the game by another set of
rules entirely.

These guys were no exception.

There were seven of them, clustered around one of the
blackened tunnel entrances. Nothing about them seemed even
remotely regulation, from their fetish-festooned tiger-stripes to
their some-braided, some-mohawked hair. Maybe their ordnance, but even that was customized *in extremis*. They carried
Bowie knives and *seppuku* blades, AKs and ARs and shotguns
and greaseguns and seven NVA-issue nine-millimeters; hell, in
a lot of ways they more closely resembled renegade Montagnard
tribesmen or the CIDG or the fucking Pirates of Penzance than
they did anything that was weaned on Wonder bread. They
were specialists in a war of general practitioners; they were
beyond reproach, and they knew it. Everything about them said
so.

Especially their attitude: coldly professional, uniformly
brutal. There was an air about them that made Jake's scrotum
retract; they had that look. Men who killed without compunc-
tion, without hesitation, absolutely without remorse. They re-
garded the squad's approach with disdain, as if they were
crashers at a very private party. They were busy.

It wasn't until Jake came abreast of them that he saw what
they were busy *with* . . .

It was V.C., and it was still alive, more or less. It took
Jake a few seconds to realize why he'd not recognized it
immediately.

They'd questioned it, presumably. Then they'd peeled it.

Like a moist, shiny grape.

From head to toe.

One of the Lurps, a tall, rangy man with one side of his
head shaved and a long black braid draped across the other

shoulder, was casually tacking the strips of flesh to a bit of still-standing fence like little banners to dry.

Jake didn't scream, didn't say a word; familiarity bred contempt, and he had plenty of that. Instead, he turned his attention toward their leader.

The man wore no insignia that denoted his position, but they knew beyond doubt that he was the one. Something beyond his appearance or demeanor, though both set him apart as being older—and appreciably more military—than the others. His hair was clipped and slicked with sweat and grime, and he was the only one in the group that wasn't wearing a necklace of dried, shriveled ears. A black patch ran over a puckered scar that traversed his left eye.

Even so, it was something *else* that said it. Something in his face.

Something in his other eye.

"What are you men doing here?" His voice slipped out low like a snake through saw grass. Jake felt that eye, black as coal tar, scrutinizing the squad.

"That's a damn good question," Jake said. "What are *you* doing here?"

The rest of the Lurps glanced up at Jake in what could only be described as pure amazement, like senior fraternity members hazing a cheeky freshman. Their leader, though, only seemed amused. He took new stock of him; smiling thinly, one eye narrowing to a feline slit, he raised the index finger of his left hand to those sly, humorless lips. *"Shhhhhh . . ."*

It was a gesture. Sinister. Mocking.

And all the more shocking for the missing joints—the upper two on the ring finger—that it emphasized.

"Shhhhhhhhhhh . . ."

In another world Jake shivered on the bed, his clothing sweat-soaked in the freon-chilled air, his face twisted into a mask of grotesque fury. His guitar had slid from its resting place on his chest and clattered to the floor, unheeded. His hands reached down to feel crisp white cloth, came up with tiny clods of dirt.

Noooo. His mind vainly fought.

NOOOOOO . . .

* * *

He said he was a captain. He said that his team's presence in the sector was classified. He invoked the sovereign immunity of military intelligence. Jake didn't really feel like confirming or contesting it; in fact, he didn't give a flying fuck one way or the other. He felt dead inside; just too cold and too old and bone-stick-stone tired of scary shadowfuckers doing their ghost-in-the-machine shtick. Intelligence. Mission. Whatever.

Captain Classified told him further that he still had a man in the tunnel, and that there was an arms cache down there that they were fixing to blow, and that there was a suspected regiment of ordnance-hungry NVA humping across from the Cambodian border to this very spot, very soon. The information was fresh from the human grape, who had popped out of a spider hole shortly after the Captain Classified's man, Vasquez, had gone in to set the charges. Jake looked over: the grape had mostly stopped moving. Blank eyes stared in horror out of the stripped raw musclemeat of his face. Flies buzzed in the hot morning sun.

And Vasquez was still below.

Oh, well. There was nothing much to do about it, he figured: the whole place would be DX'd soon enough, and this dude and his whole lunatic contingent were more than welcome to it. In fact, Jake was just about ready to order the squad out of there . . .

When he heard the screams.

Definitely plural: a burst of raw shrieking terror followed by the muffled *pop!pop!pop!pop!pop!pop!pop!* of small-arms fire. A whole clip emptied at once. And then, silence.

Deathly. Still.

Silence.

Jake felt that split-second *glitch* again, as if someone had accidently hit the record button and blanked part of the world's sound track. Something *pinged* in him, and a cold twinge of déjà-vu spiked down his backbone as he turned toward the head Lurp, who was standing tensed with his weapon up and his head cocked at an odd, quizzical angle. He was staring off at the hole worriedly, lips murmuring the tiniest bit, saying something over and over and over.

"Haul him up!" Jake said. The Lurps stared at the hole like a display of heavily armed cigar store Indians, refusing to comply; his own squad stood as if in deference to the other's inaction. "What the fuck's wrong with you people?" Jake said, louder now. "Haul him UP!"

"*No.*"

Again that serpentine voice, low and flat and deadly. Jake looked at the man. "What do you mean *no*?" he shouted. "Are you out of your fucking *mind*?!"

"It's too late. He's gone." Captain Classified looked at his men. The first flicker of what could be called fear passed between them. "That's it," he said, turning. "We're gonna blow it in place."

"You can't do that with a man down there."

"There's nobody down there," he spat, then said softer, "not anymore."

"*Bull*shit." Jake reached over and grabbed the nylon tether that led down to Vasquez and pulled and pulled and pulled . . .

It came up readily enough. There was no resistance whatsoever. Jake reeled in the slack. The end came out.

It was bloody.

"MotherFUCKER!" Jake shouted.

He held the end up. It looked chewed.

"NO!!"

He dropped the rope and started stripping off his gear. He held on to his AWOL bag, which was packed with extra medgear, and grabbed a flashlight from the new meat.

"What do you think you're doing?" the captain asked.

"I'm going down there." He could scarcely believe he was saying that. He had claustrophobia, taphephobia, any and every kind of phobia that steered one clear of dark, confining spaces.

But those terrors had seemingly evaporated in the heat and rage of the moment. More accurately, it had been *displaced*, shunted aside by something far more disturbing. Maybe it was guilt, or the fear of standing by and doing nothing. Maybe it was because of Duncan and everybody else who'd died before him. Maybe it was because he was sick of the endless bullshit, because he realized then that that's what *they* counted on: that you'd just get so tired and numb and jaded and betrayed that absolutely none of it mattered anymore, no matter how pointless, no matter how vile or repulsive or insane.

Maybe that was it. Not that it made the slightest bit of difference.

"I wouldn't do that if I were you," Captain Classified warned him.

"Thanks for the advice," Jake hissed.

"I mean it. Don't go down there."

"Go to hell." Jake started to turn toward the hole.

That mutilated left hand landed squarely on Jake's chest, stopping him. Captain Classified smiled his humorless, sly grin. Then he dropped his hand. And he backed off.

"You first," he said.

He couldn't really see the walls. But he could feel them. Oh, yes.

All around him in the damp, smothering blackness, in some places only an inch or two above his head. He could feel the hard-packed laterite clay pressing down; it stank of sweat and darkness and death. He reached forward blindly, dragging fresh rope behind him, feeling gingerly along the trail of intertwined det cord that led to Vasquez. The darkness swallowed the puny light from his flash as he crept closer. He could hear things scuttling all around him. He tried to say "Hang on, I'm coming," but when he opened his mouth, no words would come.

Only air. Hot. Stale. Rank.

He sucked it back in, panting like a lungfish, breath raggedly amplified in the dark till it filled his head. His heart felt as if it would explode, his mind threatened to scream and scream and never stop. But he bit down and pressed on; crawling, probing for booby traps, yard by excruciating yard.

Until he found the head of the wounded man.

"It's OK, buddy, I'm here," he whispered, lightly braille-probing the extent of the injuries. He could clearly discern the ragged, bubbling wheeze of a sucking chest wound. Vasquez was hurt bad, and Jake could tell by the sound that he was in danger of drowning in his own blood.

Jake holstered his weapon, ripped open a pressure bandage, and tried to position the flash so he could see just how bad it was. It was hard; the light threw shadows and distorted contours. He scanned the soaked, shredded cloth across Vasquez's chest. It looked wrong somehow, a series of lacerated punctures that peppered his torso from clavicle to crotch, not like gunshot or shrapnel wounds at all. Strange.

"We're gonna get you outta here, man, just hang on . . ."

He slipped the rope under and around Vasquez's shoulders and clipped the halyard. Vasquez moaned weakly; Jake gave the rope two sharp tugs, signaling the team above to hoist their asses the hell out of there. The rope tightened, and they began inching slowly backward out of the hole.

They hadn't gotten more than a yard when Vasquez screamed. The rope kept pulling.

And something started pulling back.

Vasquez screamed again: a sound unholy in its intensity, all the worse for the piteous, hollow burbling that was all he could manage. There was a wet sliding sound, and the overpowering stench of suppurated flesh. Jake spun the flash around to face Vasquez and the tunnel depths . . .

. . . and he saw the unwinding coil of small intestine, snicking out and out of the hole in Vasquez's belly like a soft pink-veined rope, sliding out and away into the dark, dank depths of the tunnel. He felt Vasquez go tight in his hands, the howl of his voice a hysterical sucking wind that never seemed to run out of air. He pulled frantically, trying to get him out of there, gripped in an insane tug-of-war with some unseen force, as the coil fed endlessly on and Vasquez shrieked and reached up and grabbed on to him with surprising force, and the pink, wet rope kept on pulling, running out of the smaller and starting with the larger, with its attendant flop and rip and tear; Vasquez shrieked and Jacob joined him, because now he wouldn't let go and his grip dug into Jake with unbelievable desperation, and Jake felt the both of them being pulled now back into the black, stinking depths, and he suddenly wanted more than anything to just get away, get this guy off, get him OFF!

He jerked free of his grasp, felt Vasquez go sucking back into the tunnel, felt the rope spinning back. At the last minute he grabbed hold of it and braced himself against the wall of the tunnel . . .

. . . and the rope spun through his grip, friction-burning raw the skin of his palm as it went taut, then tight, tighter still until it whined from the tension like a guitar string tuned too high. Jake screamed, a high, keening "NOOOOOOOO" . . .

. . . and the rope snapped, and the too-sudden release
sent him plummeting backward, through the buckling tun-
nel wall behind him.

And he fell, screaming.

And he fell . . .

She began with his toes and the soles of his feet; with
tongue and finger, she stroked and probed them. Sweet.
So sweet. Nerve endings in glee. He could feel them
leap as she ministered to them.

He was stripped and strewn across the length of
the bed. She was nakedly coiled at its foot, with his. Every
taut-fleshed inch of her shimmered in the dim light of the
monitors. He wanted to reach out and touch her.

He couldn't.

Because Tara was thorough in every respect, from her
mouth's technique to the electrodes on his skull to the knotted
silk that bound and spread-eagled his extremities. The only
limb not tied down was his cock, which lay hard and long and
flat across his belly. There was little chance of its untying him.
It twitched helplessly.

He twitched helplessly.

Twice in two months, Pete had been bound up and wired
for response. He was beginning to wonder if this was a trend.
He could almost see the cover on next month's issue of *Penthouse:*
"Those Power Hungry Techno-Sluts of Rock 'n Roll."

Featuring a picture of Tara.

And Jesse . . .

"No, no," he muttered, pulling his attention back to his
feet. What was happening there was too good to despoil with

guilt. It was over with Jesse. It was best that they move on. It was best . . .

Oh, Jesus. Bottom line. It was the best toe-sucking he had ever received; and that, more than anything, decided him. There wasn't a nerve in his body that didn't culminate there, at the base of his physical being. Every kiss and caress made him aware of his heart, his lungs, his nipples, the short hairs surrounding them. Every flick of tongue ached languidly in every fluid speck of marrow in his bones.

And it was magnificent. Oh, yes, it was. He could barely lift his head, what with the drugs and the bondage and all; but the glimpses he caught were enough.

Almost too much.

And then her mouth and hands began to track their way up his legs, with her own body dragging luxuriously behind. He could feel perfect breasts glide along his inner thighs as her lips reached and suckled on his slender pelvic bones, the flesh surrounding them, could feel her maddeningly steering clear of his focused desire.

Please stop, he moaned internally. *Please stay.* But she could not hear him, and she did not obey. When her tongue burrowed into his navel, his desire disregarded its previous demand. Her breasts pressed together, enfolding and kneading him like unbaked Italian bread. His spine coursed with neon light.

"Let me know," she whispered, "when you're ready."

"Right now," he answered, voice husky and harsh as her own.

She pulled up and away from him then; and for the first time since she'd secured him in place, he met her darkly blazing gaze.

"Then you won't mind waiting for me to catch up." Then she smiled, and he marveled at how brightly her teeth gleamed: bright as the monitors that graphed his brain waves and illuminated the back of the tour bus. Almost *too* bright, in fact—as if they were a light source of their own.

Pete felt an angel-hair tickle of dread stroke his soul. It wasn't the first time that had happened tonight. From the moment he'd walked into Tara's private tour bus/playground, there had been glimmers of something amiss.

Like, for starters, her black lace, four-poster canopy bed. It was beautiful, yes, but only in a perversely antivirginal way. High kink indeed, with a very dark slant. And God only knew what weirdness lurked behind those reams of dangling curtain. The Phantom, perhaps. Dr. Caligari.

And then there was the twelve-foot mirror: adjacent to the monitors, overlooking the bed. Though she swore otherwise, it was hard to believe that it wasn't a two-way, and that somebody wasn't sitting there watching them now.

This groundless paranoia was abetted somewhat by the electrodes she had taped to his skull. He'd laughed when she'd brought it up, asked if this wasn't some sinister zombifying technique in disguise. Now he wasn't quite so reassured by the fact that she'd smiled and said *yes*.

And then, of course, there was the fact that she'd tied him down.

"Why did I let you do this to me?" he asked out loud. A rhetorical question, with a lump in its throat. She answered anyway, still hovering above him, face swallowed in darkness.

"Because you were chosen."

"Ah, right." He chuckled softly. "I *thought* that free will was just an illusion."

"And you were right." She placed her hands, very softly, on his chest. "Like a heart. It doesn't beat on a whim. It beats because that is its reason for being."

He smiled. "And I was born to make love with you."

Her grinning teeth shone out of the darkness above.

"Something like that."

Then she lowered herself upon him, straddling his belly, leaning into his ardent kiss.

And in that moment, he could almost believe it was true.

There would be no more talking now. He no longer thought in words. It was the shared vocabulary of passion and sensation that spoke through him now, spoke in goose bump braille and illiterate moan. His heart was pounding beneath her touch, and his tongue danced mute and madly with her own.

And he ached, God he ached, at the root of his being, to be inside her.

Inside her.

Before it was too late . . .

But then she rose again, sliding up instead of down him, and he was helpless to do anything but whatever she willed. That was the crazy thing about bondage games. Dominance. Submission. He had abandoned his power to act independently when he let her tie him down. He had abandoned himself to her and to his own desire. Now she could take anything she wanted from him.

And he would gladly give her everything he had.

"*Your soul,*" she whispered. Gutteral. Animal.

Then she took his temples gently but firmly in hand and lowered herself onto his face.

His tongue came out to greet her, to taste her heady womanfolds. And her taste was succulent primal madness. Intoxicating. Overwhelming. He lapped at the nectar that was its form. She ground herself against him, arched and tensing.

A massive tremor erupted in her belly; he sensed it seismographically. *Can she really be coming that fast?* he wondered, making a strategic drive for her clitoris. She wouldn't allow it, only ground in deeper and let out a desperate moan.

The tip of his tongue touched something hard.

A question mark formed in the grooves of his brain. The word *hymen* appeared before it. It sent such a shock wave of doubt and confusion and sudden inexplicable resurgent dread through him that his tongue, for a moment, forgot to move.

"Ah!" she cried, grinding harder, almost painfully. His eyes shot open, found themselves staring up at her perfect belly. Staring with suddenly perfect horror.

Something was pulsating under her flesh.

And it was moving lower.

He tried to pull away then; of course it was impossible. For the first time he realized how strong her grip on his head was. No longer gentle, her hands held him in place.

"AH!" she screamed, pushing down nearly hard enough to snap his jaw . . .

. . . *and then the secret membrane snapped within her, and the vileness began to gush down his open throat. He tried to scream. It was muffled and throttled. He felt his soul begin to lurch, tear free of its moorings with a sickening rending sound that meshed perfectly with the blinding seering horror of his final moments, the vomitcumshitslime abomination that sluiced in and infested his skull.*

Then Tara screamed, letting go entirely, and his soul went out shrieking to nestle like an egg in her poisoned womb.

As she buried her thumbs in his eyes.

And the Passage began.

Side Two

ROCK AID

"Somehow, someday,
We need just one victory
And we're on our way.
Praying for it all day,
Fightin' for it all night,
Give us just one victory
It'll be all right."
—Todd Rundgren

"If it takes a bloodbath,
let's get it over with."
—Ronald Reagan

SATURDAY, SEPTEMBER 5
JFK STADIUM
10:00 A.M.

The bone-white Cadillac found its own personal space on the far horizon of the JFK parking lot. An hour and a half before showtime, and the place was already all but jammed to capacity.

The top of the Caddy was down, of course and thank God; when they were in motion, Kyle barely smelled his passengers at all. But the motion was over, and the morning air already held ninety swollen degrees of humid heat.

"Alright," he said, careful not to breathe through his nose. "Here's your tickets, boys and girls. Have a nice fucking time. And remember: be fruitful."

"And multiply."

10:17 A.M.

Outside the little groundkeeper shack that sat on the south side of the mountain—roughly halfway between the house and the lodge—there sat an enormous white satellite dish. It squatted on its cinder block base, blunt snoot pointing skyward through a niche in the trees, looking altogether imposing enough as to suggest some nefarious Stavro-Blofeldian missile base, replete with underground armies and a fake volcano opening at the top of the mountain.

Cody Adams liked to entertain the notion, even though he knew darned well that (a) the mountain was not hollow, and (b) the antenna sent its signal to the tier upon tier of audio/video gear that packed the interior of the shed. On one monitor, James Bond—not Roger whatsisname, but Sean Connery, the *real* Bond—was busy fly-walking his suction-cupped way across the set of *You Only Live Twice*. Cody chuckled and took another hit off his first joint of the day, pleased that the film was appearing on Showtime. His mind was elsewhere, even while his fingers were busy.

But then, that was Cody. He was a drifter and a dreamer; always had been, probably always would. That was just fine by him; to Cody, what other people invariably mistook for a lack of ambition was merely a radically different set of priorities. Cody Adams had been, at various times in his thirty-nine years, a carpenter, technician, electrician, pro surfer, truck driver, acid head, cemetery groundkeeper, pizza chef, warehouse worker, and war protester. He had left each in its turn, not because he couldn't handle the task, but rather because he had gotten out of it exactly what he required to continue on.

It was a trait that drove his parents crazy, right up to the day they died. Cody suspected that to the end they held out that their fair-haired eldest would any minute wise up and pack off to medical school—or more likely Tuscon Community College—get a job in something boring and stable, find a nice girl, and settle down to spawn. It never happened. But they never got over hoping.

Even his baby sister, Rachel, who was always the responsible one, seemed honor-bound to continue the tradition as best she could. She settled for talking Jake into offering him a job as caretaker/babysitter/bodyguard. Cody didn't mind. He liked it here on the mountain. It was peaceful here.

Sort of.

He ran one big-knuckled, tanned hand through his wheat-colored shock of hair, brushing it out of his face. He had the look of the perennial beach bum: lean, muscular build that showed very little of its nearly four decades wear and tear, strong, nimble fingers, a craggy, open face that usually sported a three-week growth of sandy beard, ice-blue eyes, and a hairline that receded so gracefully as to be a blessing. He and Rachel hailed from opposite ends of the parental gene pool in just about everything, from looks to temperament to political orientation.

But there were some things they held in common. A deep, abiding love: for each other, for Mother Nature, for good ol' rock 'n' roll.

And for magic on the big screen.

Which was exactly why Cody was putting the finishing touches on his pièce de résistance. It was one thing to stay up all night rigging twenty VCRs to tape the entire twelve-hour run of Rock Aid on as many networks, another to edit them into a cohesive whole after the fact. But *this* . . .

This was gonna be something special.

Baby Sis had judged that a sweltering concert was no place for a nine-month-old and had reluctantly stayed home. Ted and Chris had cycled down on Ted's new scoot. Baby Sis had resigned herself to watching it all on the tube and had invited up a few girlfriends to do it with her.

Cody twisted the last hex nut on the last coaxial cable into place and squeezed around the clutter to seat himself on his throne: a pneumatic swivel chair in front of a battered Apple computer, a budget video mixer, and his little switcher box. Baby Sis was bummed.

Not for long.

With this setup he could simultaneously record uninterrupted and play mix-n-match on the homefront with any of the one hundred and seventy-eight channels that the dish pulled in. A video camera on a tripod was aimed squarely at the chair: Cody turned around, focused the camera, stuck a joint between his lips, and grinned into Monitor One.

"So who needs to be there," he said. His finger poised on the switch that would fire it all up.

Here goes nothin', he thought. *It'll work, or it'll blow every circuit in the building. What's life without risk?*

Cody took one last hit. James Bond blew the missile base.

And Cody pushed the button.

Inside the house, Rachel and Natalie were strolling through the Twilight Zone, a dining hall that had been converted into a sort of community fun house for the group. It was an airy, spacious room with large windows, Ping-Pong and pool tables, and a central seating area dominated by a Toshiba rear-projection TV with matching bootleg videotape library. Rachel had just breezed through with her squirming armload and a bowl of dip when the set fired up and a voice boomed out, *"This is COH-DEE TEE VEE . . ."*

Rachel looked up in shock.

". . . bringing you the finest in on-the-spot coverage of the Rock Aid concert broadcasting and other choice bits of video wizardry."

The face on the screen donned shades and turned grim, forty inches of flat, deadpan delivery. *"I know what you're thinking,"* it hissed. *"You're thinking, 'Do I feel lucky?' "* Then he smiled.

Rachel stared, agog.

"Well, you should. Because even though you can't be there, even though you're feeling like the chains of motherhood are keeping you from the event of the decade, there's no need to be sad and blue.

"Because you, Sister dear, are in for the media blitz of a lifetime. You will soon take your rightful place in the global village, thanks to none other than that Modern Day Pirate of the Air Waves, Commander Cody Adams!"

Rachel giggled and sat down on the one of the leather sofa modules that ringed the tube. Natalie turned in her arms, bracing herself delicately with one hand on Rachel's cheek, and gazed at the screen. "Dahh," she chimed. "Dahh-bah-dah-bah-PFHHHT!" Rachel smiled and kissed her.

"Well, boobie," she said, "this might not be such a bad day, after all."

"You're darned tootin', it won't!"

Rachel was startled. "You . . . you can *hear* me?"

"Yup." Cody beamed. *"See you, too. Look on the mantel."* He pointed offscreen. Rachel looked: a handicam stood perched above the fireplace, red eye winking dutifully. "When did you *do* all this?" she asked incredulously.

"In the dead of the night, my dear. I told you, I'm a genius."

"I guess . . ."

"I'm also starving. Could you make me a sandwich?"

Rachel laughed. "What? You didn't wire the kitchen, too?"

"Only for reception. Bring me something yummy, okay?"

"You got it. Watch the midget, okay?" Rachel got up and deposited Natalie into the playpen at the corner of the sofa.

Natalie looked momentarily as though she were contemplating turning on the waterworks, when Cody came to the rescue.

"Hey, Swee'pea! Yo!" Natalie looked up at the screen, confused. *"Hey, don't cry! It's Pee-wee time!"*

Back in the shed, Cody flipped over to CBS. A full-color, forty-inch Jhombi was busy granting Pee-wee his wish for the week. He looked on Monitor Four: Natalie stared in wobbly awe at the image.

Then she smiled.

Yup, he thought. *This is gonna be great.*

10:50 A.M.

Click

Black-and-white clip of a young Mickey Rooney as Puck in A Midsummer Night's Dream, *hopping about to the sound of the pipes as a Burgess Meredith-like voice-over solemnly intoned:*

"Music censorship is nothing new. Aristotle said that 'the flute is not an instrument that has a good moral effect; it is too exciting.' "

Cut to silent film footage of stiffly swirling men and women in black tie and ball gowns.

"And the waltz, in its time, was loudly pronounced to be 'disgustingly immodest,' and 'will-corrupting.' "

Cut to herky-jerky film clips of happy Negros in straw hats and summer dresses, dancing the cakewalk.

"Ragtime was rife with lewd gestures and obscene posturings,"

Cut to "Elvis the Pelvis" on the Ed Sullivan Show:

"and Elvis Presley's first television appearance could only be broadcast from the waist up . . ."

Fade to black. ROCK AID logo bleeds up in bright white letters, along with the toll-free number.

"Rock Aid.

"Because some people *never* give up . . ."

Click

Medium shot of Bernard Javits, in sweltering suit and tie, sweaty CNN microphone in hand.

"I'm standing in front of JFK Stadium in Philadelphia," he began, "where an estimated ninety-six thousand people are gathered for today's Rock Aid festival. Despite a storm of controversy and protests from various factions of the radical right, both the concert's promoters and the crowd seem confident that this will be a great day in the history of rock 'n' roll."

Cut to a pair of too-cute teenyboppers, Carol and Cheryl, with matching streaked-and-moussed explosions of hair.

"I think it's disgusting, what these people say about rock music," said the one on the right. "Rock is the greatest! If they think they can take it away from us, they're crazy . . ."

Click

Cut to a throng of sign-waving protesters some fifty strong marching around and around. Note the 700 Club logo in the lower right-hand corner of the screen. Focus on the stationary form electronically identified as REV. WALTER PAISELY, his big sweaty frame dominating the screen as the marchers maintained their spiraling orbit.

"They say that they aren't anti-Christian. They say that they're just standing up for their civil rights. Well, if you believe that, I got this nice bridge in Brooklyn that I'd just love to sell ya.

"The fact of the matter is: No matter what they say, this concert is a slap in the face of God Almighty; and in all honesty, it wouldn't surprise me too much if the Lord took a mind to smite everyone involved . . ."

Click

Cut to electric-blue Independent Network news background, hosting a litany of statistics that jibed with the words being quoted by the anonymous voice-over.

"Though a number of sponsors have backed out on Rock Aid, the list remains impressive. It includes Pepsi-Cola, Lee Jeans, Miller Beer, Swatch, Vidal Sassoon, Clearasil, Nissan, Toshiba, JBL, Panasonic, TWA, and Frito-Lay. All of them can safely be said to hold a vested interest in the youth culture: a culture that clearly feels threatened by attacks from . . ."

Click

Cut to lunatic clay-mation MTV logo, then to the smiling face of VeeJay Alan Belsen.

"Hello again. We're backstage here at JFK, talking to some of the stars that have made Rock Aid possible . . ."

10:55 A.M.

This was Al's lucky day. He had dragged his intrepid roving crew through media hell to get this close, but it was worth it. It was a bitch getting out of 'the corral,' as the journalists had nicknamed the holding area behind the eastern sprawl of the stage, and over toward the snow-white dome of the practice field that had become the inner sanctum of the stars. *Live Aid was twice as big,* he mused, *and half as complex.* But, that was then; a lot of things were different. Backstage had been a jumbled cluster of trailers, a crazed promenade, and access had been much easier.

Earlier today, the bulbous monstrosity that divided and conquered the lion's share of the already limited space had thrown a very real barrier between Al Belsen and the people he needed desperately to talk to. The place was a zoo. All of the floor teams of the networks were jostling for the best angle. Twenty-minute clips of scrambling ambience would simply never do. He needed *in*, and fast.

So he greased the burly security personnel (decked out in their bright orange RockAid Staff T-shirts like refugees from the Anita Bryant Memorial Crisco Bar), and he got in ahead of everyone. It was worth the Andrew Jacksons folded in each hearty handshake. It was worth almost anything.

Because now Al had his cross hairs lined up on *the* perfect pair for his kickoff newsblast. The honchos in the press box had made it very clear that they were tired of being tagged as the bubble-babble network and wanted their big-time coverage of today's festivities to be filled with *content*, dammit. Content.

Well, Big Al Belsen would give 'em content, all right. Big

Al Belsen had a plan. He turned back to the cyclopean eye that focused at him shiny and black as Carrara marble and got the okeydoke from his cameraman. He was going to capture all sides of this little war.

And he had just the right people to fire the first shot.

"Jake, Jerry, you're certainly two of the main men of today's big event." Al smiled his best preppie surf-bum smile. "How does it look to be shaping up out here?"

Jacob Hamer looked tired and distracted; he took a deep breath as if about to say something of earth-shaking significance. But before he could speak, Jerry jumped in.

"Al, I think it's gonna be just great. It's a beautiful day, everybody's psyched, we've got so many great acts lined up— Iron Maiden, U2, Genesis, Mr. Mister, Joni Mitchell, Amy Grant, Frank Zappa, Jackson Browne, Pat Benatar, David Bowie, Peter Gabriel, Ozzy Osbourne, Suburbicide, The Slabs, The Scream, even this dude here"—he nudged Jake, who smiled as Jerry proceeded to throw a brotherly arm around his shoulders—"but most importantly, we're doing something for a good cause.

"All these people here today are here because they believe in something." Al nodded sagely. Jake smiled and shook his head as Jerry puffed up for his "America" rap. Al was hoping this would happen.

"They believe in America, Al, American freedom and American diversity and the American right to rock and roll. And we're standing up for that right."

Al smiled and nodded some more. *Good, good, good,* he thought, turning a brief glance toward the press box and watching the imaginary ratings needle in his head start to bounce off the dial. "And how 'bout you, Jake? How do you feel? Are you ready to rock?"

Again, that strange, tired smile.

"Al," he said, "I'm just ready to kick some ass."

10:59 A.M.

The tent door flapped open as Jake edged in. Jesse continued sipping Veryfine apple juice out of a bottle and staring at the nine-inch monitor perched on a folding table. "You were just on. Very diplomatic."

He shrugged and picked up his guitar. "Hey, call me Mr. Charm."

Jesse continued staring at the TV. A commercial for Pepsi came and went, as did another squiggly MTV logo, and Al Belsen was back, cornering Sting and David Bowie. "Hey," Jake said, "you okay?"

Jesse nodded, just a little too quickly.

"Yeah, well, you look like hell."

"Thanks, boss. You look pretty spiff yourself."

"Get much sleep?"

Shrug. "You?"

Shrug.

Silence: awkward, halting. Finally:

"Have you seen Pete?"

"Not since last night. We sort of had it out."

"Anything you want to tell me about?"

"Just . . . personal," she said. "But it's weird. I felt bad afterwards about some of the things I said, and I paged his room about midnight."

"And?"

"He wasn't in. I tried again at one and at two and"—her voice cracked the tiniest bit—"shit. He was gone all night."

Jake said nothing; it was hard to avoid the obvious. *Maybe he was busy. Maybe he found somebody else.* He shrugged. "You try this morning?"

"Nothing. Zip. Nada," she said haltingly. "It's like he just disappeared."

Jake didn't like the sound of this. Not at all. "We can't very well go on without him."

"I know."

They looked at each other then, the same thoughts etched

across their features in mirror-imaged relief. *So where in the hell is Pete?*

And the same answer.

Good question.

11:25 A.M.

They were pouring through the gates now, slowly at first, then faster and faster as security found itself overwhelmed by hordes beyond number and coolers beyond counting. Can five dozen people thoroughly search ninety-six thousand? Past a certain point, it made more sense to just pack 'em in and then contain 'em from there. A riot in the parking lot did no good for anyone.

And a riot there could easily be. Disregarding the protesters entirely, there was ample potential for havoc from the crowd itself. It was Whitman's multitude made flesh, culled from every conceivable rock 'n' roll stripe: metal heads, Dead heads, punk and folk and heads *à la moderne*. That some of them loved Judas Priest and hated Jackson Browne was clear. Ditto with the inverse. Ditto for the ones who hated both, but couldn't wait for Madonna or Zappa or Wang Chung to hit the stage.

And then there were the anomalies: the ones who bore no icons on their T-shirts, no small round totems pinned to their denim lapels. The ones who looked more like someone's mom or someone's mutant cousin than a bona fide lover of rock 'n' roll.

Like the rather severe-looking woman from the Susquehanna Women's Clinic, with her informational pamphlets on teenage pregnancy and the little red Igloo chest that she claimed to be her "survival kit" . . .

11:30 A.M.

"EEYOW!" Chris Konopliski hollered, fists waggling triumphant in the air. "This is too cool, man! I can't believe it!"

"*Shhh*," Ted cautioned. "Keep it down, okay? Relax."

Chris stared at him, grinning but astounded. "Relax? You want me to relax? I just saw fuckin' *Madonna*, man! And you want me to relax? Hah! EEYOW!" He leaped two feet in the air, did a little dance in short-lived defiance of gravity. Several passersby—roadies, security folk—sent him cautionary glances that zipped right past him.

"If you don't chill out, they're gonna take your goddamn backstage pass, and then you can scream and jump up and down all you want in the fucking audience with the rest of the bozos. Okay?"

Feet squarely back on terra firma, Chris turned to his friend and let an exasperated snort. "What's *with* you, man? Why are you being such a drag?"

"It's just that you don't understand what backstage is all about."

"Oh! Well, why don't you just tip me off then, Mr. Big Time."

"Hey, come on—"

"No, *you* come on! What, I'm not supposed to have a good time?" Chris was suddenly, clearly, pissed. "Why did you even bring me then? To sit on my goddamn thumb? Christ!"

"It's called protocol, kid." A new voice, deep and low, from behind him. Not kidding. Large hands, suddenly upon his shoulders. "The thing to remember is that these are famous people, and they put up with a lot of shit from total strangers, and backstage is one of the only places where the crowds can't get to 'em. If you're cool, you'll get along fine with everyone. If you act like a geek, they'll throw you out. Simple as that. Okay?"

Ted looked up at the wild-maned rock star towering over Chris. His eyes went wide, all stoned droopiness banished. The dude was huge, maybe bigger than Hempstead. Chris turned, too, as the grip released. His lower jaw dropped, attempting to match altitudes with his cast iron belt buckle.

"You're Jake's kid, right?" Yke Dykeburn said, turning to Ted now.

"Um. His stepson. Yeah."

"I thought so. Ted?"

"Um, yeah."

"Pleased to meet you." He extended his massive right hand. Ted met it with his own smaller version. They shook. Yke grinned and looked over at Chris. "And who are you, man?"

"Chris Konofuckingpliski." Nothing to prompt a speedy recovery like the presence of another rock 'n' roll hero.

"Well!" Yke laughed, reaching out with his left. "Pleased to meet you, too, Mr. Konofuckingpliski." The three-way handshake went on for several seconds, then split. "So. Are you guys ready to rock?"

"*Oh*, yeah!" Chris enthused.

"You can handle bein' cool, can't you?" Yke's head cocked, mock-paternal.

"Piece of cake," Chris asserted. Ted nodded easy agreement.

"Good. Because you know that this is it, right? This is where the path splits in two. We can either take the high road, or we go right off the cliff.

"And if we take the wrong turn, boys, the music goes with us . . ."

11:45 A.M.

Pastor Furniss paused in prayer momentarily to catch up on Reverend Jimmy's latest installment of "America, You've Gone Too Far." The Smurfs—those little blue minions of Satan— had just finished wreaking their insidious havoc on the tender flanks of yet another Saturday morning audience; Lord, how clear need it be? *They have eyes, yet still they do not see.* Teaching innocent kids that sorcery is an acceptable, even desirable, way of dealing with the trials and tribulations the Lord saw fit to mete out. Where would it all end?

A rhetorical question. Daniel Furniss had no doubt at all

exactly where it would end. In Rapture for some, a heavenly ascent into the arms of a loving Shepherd. For others, though . . .

Daniel didn't want to think about that. Not now. There was still time, thank God; even in the face of the assault the Enemy was fomenting this very morning, there was still hope for those lost sheep. He was already doing almost everything he could, with people in the field and tomorrow's show setting up to be a doozy; right now what he needed was a spiritual jump-start, a little prayer pit stop as it were, to keep things on the money.

So to speak.

Which was exactly why Jimmy's show was such a blessing, praise God. Daniel had long admired Jimmy: his passion, his vitality, his depth in the Spirit, the sheer magnitude of his ministry and how many lost sheep he was able to bring back into the fold.

This latest series was a prime example: Jimmy didn't mince words. Nossiree; he went right out and grabbed Lucifer by the short 'n curlies and made that Serpent *bend* to the Will of the Lord.

Amen.

". . . I want you to *hear* what I'm saying: there's a movement afoot—brought to bear by the same people who want to hand out pro-phylactics to *babies*, who want to teach your children that we descended from *monkeys*—a movement that wants to padlock every church in America, burn every Bible in America, and make it *illegal for every American to worship the Lord Jesus Christ* . . ."

You tell 'em, Jimmy. Daniel felt a surge of deep Christian love at the thrust of his words; a little overstated, perhaps, but nonetheless true. ". . . and today, *this very day*, this country is drowning, lit'rilly DROW-NING, in a sea of sexshial sensialty, *hummu*sexshialty, drug abuse, sec-ular humanism and communism and Every Kind of Vile Filth and ROT from the Bowels of Hell itself . . ."

Daniel watched in shameless admiration of the man's style: Jimmy was wicked with style. He strutted across the stage: every hair in place, not a crease in his sleek serge suit, his tie pin and the ring finger on his left hand blazing with diamonds and gold. No doubt about it: Jimmy had the Word.

Jimmy had the touch. Jimmy had satellite uplink and special effects generators.

". . . or better I should say, this *ROCK* from the bowels of Hell."

Jimmy smiled ever so slightly, pleased at the masterful turn of phrase. Daniel could forgive the occasional touch of understandable pride; he was sure the Lord could, too.

"Today, in Philadelphia, and across the nation, there's an army marching to a brimstone beat. Call it what you will: Hard Rock, Soft Rock, Porn Rock Punk Rock Acid Rock, even the so-called *Christian* Rock that a lot of so-called ministries are falling prey to . . . it's there. The rock of DEATH, people. Not the rock of AGES. Not the rock of LIFE."

Murder Music, Furniss amended. *Amen.*

Pastor Furniss was hopeful. He had sent copies of the Village newsletter, had hoped that maybe Jimmy's Outreach people had heard of the good fight being fought up here, what with the Enemy so close and what have you, and that perhaps he was going to lend him some moral support. Perhaps pass on his regrettably non-toll-free number.

"I've prepared a book that I feel every concerned Christian ought to have . . ."

He could understand it, of course. They did, after all, serve the Lord from slightly different vantage points. Liberty Christian Village was small and seemingly continually under demonic attack in the guise of hefty interest rates and lagging cash flow and secular humanist network scheduling. Still . . .

". . for your love-gift of twenty dollars or more . . ."

Daniel felt a need to somehow make his presence known. He prayed for a miracle. He knew that, somehow, the Lord would come through.

". . . with a free set of lapel pins . . ."

The Lord, he knew, sometimes worked in strange and mysterious ways.

Some times, stranger than others.

". . . And who—aside from the puny efforts of this ministry and some attempts by Christian Congressmen's wives and a few other right-thinking, God-fearing people—*who* is standing up to it?"

Daniel knew.

"I'll tell you who . . ."
Daniel waited.
"Nobody."

12:00 P.M.

A cheer went up as the imposing figure strode across the sprawling lip of the stage. The chant started almost immediately, a mounting, thrumming cadence.

"WE LYKE YKE!
WE LYKE YKE!"

Yke Dykeburn smiled wide, showing spectacularly uneven teeth, and held his arms skyward in beaming supplication. The rest of the Slabs were already in place, waiting for their point man to finish holding court. It was A-Okay by them; nobody lubed a crowd quite like Yke.

"Whoa, yeah!" he cried. "Welcome to Rock Aid! Hope you're comfy out there, 'cause we got a big, big day ahead. Are you ready to rock?"

Cheers.

"I can't *hear* you!"

Louder.

"What are you, *sick* or something?!" Yke leered. "I said, ARE YOU *READY*??!"

Louder still.

Yke nodded. "I was hoping you'd say that."

And The Slabs kicked in.

1:50 P.M.

A buzzing in the hive-mind: calling out to the faithful, making the many One. A subterranean rumbling from the tunnel blackness below.

A seemingly infinite patience, winding down to its end.

A word to be spread.

A job to be done.

A time to begin.

The time was now.

2:04 P.M.

"Hey," the fat chick named Andrea whined. It was obvious she wasn't used to moving this fast. It was obvious she wasn't used to moving much at all. "How far do we have to go?"

Dickie grinned. These days, that was getting harder to do. His jaw just plain seized up sometimes. Six months on the other side will do that, even to a Prime.

"You wanna be alone with me, right?" he said.

"Well, *yeah*, but . . ." Her cow-eyes fluttered.

"Yeah but nothin'. Come on."

He was pulling her through the sardine-packed crowd that sprawled like the plastic covering the JFK playing field. Not an easy task in itself. Nobody wanted to budge an inch; there wasn't a spare inch to budge to. This would change, a little later, but now was not the time.

Right now, he just needed to get this heifer down into the darkness beneath the stands. When the signal came, she would come in handy.

Besides, he couldn't wait to pop those baby blues.

Dickie was grateful that he was still strong and lucid. He was grateful to Tara for that. He'd seen too many second-, third-, and fourth-generation Screamers not to be pleased that he was Prime. Motor control and an operative brain made things ever so much easier; he gave thanks as he pushed his way through the unyielding mass, big Andrea in tow.

It was almost like being alive.

And maybe even better.

3:15 P.M.

Halfway through a rousing set by The Pretenders, a ripple passed through the crowd, and at least eighty thousand people turned their gaze skyward to see the tiny silver speck course over the stadium, smoke-jets belching in synchronous rhythm, forming letters of smoke like the world's biggest dot-matrix printer.

R . . . E . . . P . . . For some it took awhile. *E . . . N . . . T . . .* Others caught on right away. Within moments the basic message was clear. *REPENT . . .*

Hardly anyone would admit to being surprised, even when the skywritten coda took shape.

O . . . R . . . . . D . . . I . . . E

4:22 P.M.

Squarely between Mr. Mister and Madonna, the big screen flashed the RockAid logo (toll-free number superimposed conspicuously), and it was breaktime. After an average of thirty-six thousand hours of viewing experience, the rhythm of commercial interruption was firmly ingrained in the subconscious of everyone present: they knew this would be a big block, maybe eight or nine minutes. Plenty of time to pee or make a sandwich or sit around and bullshit.

At Hamerville, they did all three. Rachel was having a really good time; not being there actually had its advantages. It was a heckuva lot more comfy here, good sound system, no crowds, and she got to kick back with her friends in the big airy room and glom the glamorous side of having a bonafide famous hubby. Nancy and Lauren took it in stride, but Sheri and Madeline seemed to regard it as a big deal; Rachel had to concede that it probably looked that way from a comfortable distance. They hooted every time Jake's face came up, which was often, given that Cody insisted on dissolving between channels every time any network mentioned him.

At least he's good at it, she thought. And Jake looked great, considering the pressure he was under. It eased her anxiety factor down a couple of points to see that he wasn't a basket case. Not yet, anyway. Nothing she couldn't fix.

Right now nothing much appeared to be happening, as evidenced by the Warner Brothers cartoon that was running. She'd seen it—at the moment Daffy was singing to the Tasmanian Devil—so she bopped off to the kitchen to refill the munchie bowls and brew some more iced tea.

She found Gram in the kitchen and a fresh pitcher already steeping. She swore sometimes that Pete's grandmother had radar. She was a tiny thing who was on the far side of eighty, but she got on just fine. She did all her own cooking and gardening, put up her own preserves, and generally behaved with the sort of stolid self-reliance that Rachel supposed a turn-of-the-century Midwest upbringing just bred into you.

They hadn't ever really spoken much, but Rachel cared about her quite a bit. In the midst of her bouyant mood, it dawned on her that she had yet to ask Gram for word one about how she felt regarding all of this. Now seemed as good a time as any.

So she did.

"Ohhhh . . . I don't knowwww," Gram replied in her flat Minnesotan twange. "I sup*pose* they have to *do* what they have to do. When you get to be my age, you don't *worry* about things like that."

Rachel paused to consider that Gram probably greeted every morning as though it were her last, and that one day too soon it actually would be. Her gaze flitted to the tiny set on the kitchen counter. The plug had just been pulled on Daffy's radio. The Devil was getting nasty.

"Do you ever wonder, Gram? About what *they* say, you know, about Heaven and Hell and God and the Last Days and all?" Rachel could scarcely believe she was actually asking Gram stuff like this. She was even more struck by Gram's answer.

"Oh, I don't knowwww." Her ancient fingers moved deftly over the surface of the green beans she'd picked herself. "*They*'ve been saying the world was gonna *end* my whole life, ever since I was a little girl. And they're *still* saying it.

"I be*lieve* in God. But not like *they* say."

The rinsed green beans went *snap, snap* in the collander. Gram continued working, small and frail and immutable as the sky or the mountain itself. She only looked up once, but it was enough.

Rachel saw the spark. Dim, yes. But there. Definitely there.

Gram, any Heaven that wouldn't take you wouldn't be worth going to.

This she knew.

And as she thought of the Furnisses of the world, who would have you believe that Gram would roast on a spit in Hell for all eternity for refusing to scrape at the feet of their pious constraints, she knew something else.

Like who was truly filled with the Spirit.

And who was filled with something altogether different.

4:26 P.M.

Click

Red as flame, the heavens. Angry clouds, racing blackly past. Lancing beams of brilliance from a tiny, distant, muted sun too far away to warm the lunatic wind that cursed the camera eye.

Panning down, then. And down. And down.

Until the face of the suffering man was revealed in tight close-up: dark eyes filled with pain, creased brow distorting the trails of blood that tracked down from his thorny crown, long hair whipping violently around the harsh wooden beam behind his head.

A slow pan back and away, revealing more and more details of the all-but-naked man, the large wooden cross to which he was affixed, the bleeding wounds, the primitive nails that produced them.

As the voice-over began, cutting deep and low through the banshee wail of the wind.

"His name was Jesus Christ."

The camera, sliding backward and down a steepening hill. Bringing into focus, from either side, a pair of seamy-looking men in the same agonizing predicament.

"He was crucified as a criminal, a heretic and a rebel, for crimes against both church and state. He was hung between a pair of thieves and left to die slowly in a cruel, humiliating public display.

"The events of that day have changed the course of human history.

"But the crucifixions had only begun."

The camera eye, pulling back now steadily. That ol' Rugged Cross of Calvary, neatly centered beneath the raging sky: the vanishing point from which row upon row of suffering men and women seemed to emanate, each with their own bleeding cross, radiating outward in a tight V-shaped sweep of crimson martyrdom.

"Because there were always more heretics. More deviants from the norm.

"There were the troublemakers, the radicals, and revolutionaries."

Panning back.

"There were the fornicators, the pornographers, and the adulterers."

Over row after row . . .

"There were the whores and the homosexuals."

. . . after row after row . . .

"There were the drug abusers and the dabblers in the occult."

. . . as Christ receded farther and farther into the distance . . .

"There were the godless Communists and the secular humanists."

. . . until you could barely even see him at all . . .

"And those who followed the demon beast called rock 'n' roll."

. . . and then a sudden, lurching reversal: the camera

zooming back the way it had come, racing past the row upon row upon row . . .

. . . and zeroing in to a tight close-up.

On the long-suffering eyes.

Of the Man.

"Hard to believe," the voice-over concluded, *"that it all comes back to Jesus Christ.*

"Isn't it?"

Cut to solid black background, over which the letters read:

ROCK AID
BECAUSE IT REALLY DOES MATTER

As the 1-800 number flashed.

6:02 P.M.

Judas Priest had just cranked up their powerhouse set when Jake found Jerry by the door of the stage manager's trailer. He was busy telling six people what to do and how to do it: they nodded and scurried off in six different directions. Jerry wheeled around.

"How's it going?" Jake yelled over the booming volume.

Oh, just ducky." Jerry sighed. He looked fried. "AT&T estimates the calls at somewhere around four hundred fifty thousand and counting. At an average ten bucks a pop, we'll probably clear a couple of million in pledges, but it's too early to tell. The sun's going down and it's cooling off, so I think we're over the hump. We made it through the afternoon without a riot, there're ten more acts to go—including yours, which is up next—and barring any major catastrophe it looks like I might just make it through the day without having a heart attack."

"We have a major catastrophe."

"Oh, great." Jerry laughed. Then he stopped, because it looked like Jake wasn't kidding. "What's the matter?"

"Missing guitar player."

"What do you mean, 'missing'? Is he lost? What do you mean? What?"

"I mean he's *missing*. As in 'disappeared.' "

"For how long?"

"Since last night."

"Since last *night* you know this and you wait till now to tell me? Are you *kidding*?! Here"—Jerry made a stabbing motion at his chest—"why don't you just stick it in and twist it?"

"Sorry."

"Sorry! *Jesus!*" Jerry shook his head, flinging little beads of sweat, and grabbed the clipboard off the trailer door. "All right, all right. We'll deal with it. Can you go on without him?"

"I'd rather not. Can you bump us?"

"I'd rather not. But I will." Jerry sighed then and scratched out something, wrote in something else. "You owe me, *meshuggener* . . ."

"Thanks, Jer."

"Yeah, yeah." He waved it off, then turned like a kosher whirlwind and snagged his stage manager. "Walter! Set changes." He flashed the clipboard. "Bump the Hamer Band to seven-thirty." He looked over to Jake. "I trust that's long enough?" Jake nodded. "Okay." Then back to Walter. "Switch them with Suburbicide."

"We can't." The stage manager shook his head. "The lead singer's throwing up."

"*Shit!* Well, *some*body's gotta fill the hole." Jerry scanned the chart frantically. Then he nodded.

"Okay, Okay . . . The Scream's up at seven. Put Zipperhead up next."

"I don't know if they're ready."

"Fuck 'em. It's done."

"Jerry—"

"DO IT!"

Walter nodded and headed off toward the other side of the stage. Jerry turned back to Jake.

"Thanks," Jake said again. Jerry smiled wearily and waved it off.

"You owe me . . ."

6:10 P.M.

JFK Stadium was an arena primarily designed for the playing and viewing of football, with two massive tiers of stands overlooking a spacious and meticulously tended field. Plenty of room for a crowd of ninety thousand, not to mention the performers in question.

There was no real need for anyone, player or fan, to go beneath the stands.

There was no reason why they'd want to.

What lay there was a cavernous no-man's-land, a vast concrete catacomb of rubble, trash, the cast-off detritus of days gone by. Musty rooms whose purpose evaded the memory of anyone currently employed, now repositories for rat poison and stage fronts and off-season Astroturf. Long-dead locker rooms. Black, pitted culs-de-sac.

It was a feeding ground for all forms of lower life: rats, bats, stray cats, wild dogs, and wasted vagrants. Junkies jettisoned their trashed works there, and every so often some dispossessed and infirm denizens of the lower hells would choose to quietly o.d. or even hang themselves, down where no one would see or care. The chill tang of old death sat, heavy and unsettling, on the psychic palette.

But today there was new death.

Today, it was a breeding ground.

For the new death.

In the underworld beneath the stands of JFK Stadium, light waged frail and hopeless war against the shadows. Earlier in the day, with the sun at its strongest, hope had almost been an option.

But the sun was going down.

6:23 P.M.

Rock Aid rolled inexorably on, powered by the crowd and the groups that propelled them. Multiplicity be praised: band for band, the show kicked ass. The temperature had dropped to a comparatively pleasant eighty degrees. And as the sun dipped over the western rim of the stadium, the message was clear.

The message *was* the medium.

The message was rock.

It didn't matter what style they played: how loud, how fast, how clean, how sweet. Even the lyrical content was secondary. Jackson Browne could fiercely depict the image of U.S. troops in Central America, the battleground of the nineties; Amy Grant could passionately invoke the spirit of a living, loving God; Zappa's Mothers of Prevention could gleefully trash the rhetoric of tiny thinkers; AC/DC could burn straight down the highway to Hell.

It didn't matter. It still came together.

Because, at root, it was *tribal music*. It spoke from the heart. It spoke from the glands. It spoke from the visions and aspirations of an often clashing cultural milieu nearly two thousand years removed from the murder of the man called Christ.

It was speaking now . . .

6:57 P.M.

"Listen up, people."

A spotlight flashed, arced, and came to rest on Jake Hamer standing center stage. A cheer went through the crowd. "I've got some news for you."

"As of six P.M. Eastern Standard Time, the pledge count hit five hundred thousand. Counting everybody here"—and another cheer crested and broke—"over one half million people took a stand today. The money raised here today is not unimportant"—scattered laughter—"as ninety percent of it goes into our lobbying efforts and the Rock Aid defense fund for the artists and labels currently under attack." Another wave of applause crested and fell.

"But the money is not the most important thing raised here today. The money is only the fruit of this labor.

"What is most important is the labor itself. The music. And the message.

"Music reaches people in ways that nothing else on this earth can. It reaches right into people's hearts, right into their souls, and it touches things that nothing else can reach. Music can work miracles. Music is one of the most powerful vehicles for change that the world has ever known. And one of the most dangerous.

"Because just as sure as it can build things up, it can tear 'em down again. But that's the beauty of it. Music is what dreams are made of, as well as nightmares. You know it.

"And *they* know it, too. That's why they want to control it. They want to own your dreams, people.

"That's why we're up here today, and I hope to God that's why you're out there. We've got a message to send out, loud and clear. The message that says we are *not* going to knuckle under to the power-jockeys, the philistines, the congressmen's wives, or any other self-appointed, gumball guardians of righteousness. The message that says that this—right here, right now—this is *not* gonna go away! This is AMERICA, dammit!"

Cheers went up.

"Land of the FREE! Home of the CRAZED!"

More cheers.

"Don't care WHAT the neighbors say!"

Still more cheers.

"ROCK 'N' ROLL IS HERE TO STAY!"

The audience flipped, hooting and howling. The applause roared.

Jake stood there, riding the crest of the deafening energy. Between the twin Rock Aid icons, enormous neon universal forbidden signs with guitars bursting through the center crossbars, glowing in the dusk air. It was a moment that he had been afraid to even hope for. It nurtured his soul. It was a good thing, genuine and real.

And like all good things, must come to an end.

"Okay," he said, "the show's not over yet. There's been a slight schedule bump. The Jacob Hamer Band won't be up next."

A few boos and groans spattered within immediate earshot; Jake grinned. "Don't worry, it's just a . . . technical problem." He looked over to Walter, the stage manager, who gave him the thumbs-up sign.

"In the meantime, coming up next is a band that's really raised some hell in the last year.

"Ladies and gents, please welcome . . . THE SCREAM!"

6:59 P.M.

There was a single bright moment of illuminated terror that struck Mary Hatch in the moments before The Scream began to play. She stopped in the mouth of the tunnel leading from the second tier near gate number 6 and stiffened as if she'd just grabbed hold of a high-voltage cable.

Paul Weissman continued on for a few pudgy paces before he realized that she was no longer in tow. He had deemed it more important to go back out on the promenade where the Word could actually be heard over the insidious din of devilry within. Now the girl was actually *watching*; her shallowness in the Spirit was as plain as her horsey face. It more than concerned him; it just plain peed him off. He turned back in annoyance.

"Mary!"

She stood, all trembly and moon-faced, ignoring him.

"Mary Hatch!"

She turned then, startled; the eyes that stared back at him were swimming in near hysteria. She said something he couldn't quite make out over the roar of the crowd, something like *Can't you* feel *it?*

It was much clearer a moment later.

When the screaming started.

7:01 P.M.

It hit the fan before the stage had even turned all the way round.

There was a swell of thunderous applause, a blistering boom of megawattage, and there was no turning back.

Talk about a band that hits the ground running. Jake paused to marvel from the wings. *They don't even wait for the platform to lock.* All prior speculation that The Scream were really wimps who relied on lavish special effects and technoflash incinerated in an instant.

Jake was slightly stunned by the sheer spectacle of it all. It was different from the videos: lean, vicious, stripped down to the bone. The Scream pumped out the first changes of their first tune like a juggernaut. The beat was rock-solid, a classic R&B groove reasserted at maximum overdrive slaughterhouse intensity like some heavy metal hambone. The guitar chugged in, a hyperthyroid harbinger of doom. And when the synthesizers started to wail, Jake felt the pit of his stomach drop like an elevator car with its cables cut.

Jesus God, he thought, *where on earth did they get a sound like that?*

It seemed louder somehow, louder than anything else he'd heard today. It was as if they had tapped some source above and beyond the available power, a source manifested in not just more volume, but more sheer *presence*. The dusky fabric of the air itself seemed coarser, grainier, like low-light images in a photographic blowup. He felt suddenly exhilarated and fatigued, as though the sound were stealing energy from him.

Only to feed it back. Slightly, irrevocably, altered.

Jake felt a dizzying rush. *And I'm just on the sidelines*, he thought.

I wonder what it's like out front . . .

7:02 P.M.

Out front, it was madness.

From an aerial view, or the slightly more rarified view of the press box, the floor of the arena was filled with literal waves of humanity, pressing back and forth insistently until even the most stalwart pockets of resistance were overrun. The images being captured and transmitted nationwide from the outer rim of the arena had a savagely hypnotic beauty: thousands upon thousands, vibrating to the rhythm and the beat like sand crystals in a Chladni figure.

Down in the throngs, it wasn't quite so poetic.

In fact, it was goddamned uncomfortable. It was quite literally thousands *upon* thousands, from Brenda and Carl Felscher's point of view, with the former largely comprised of a bunch of asshole metalheads who had pushed their way up front, stomping on cooler chests and blankets and other pieces of queen-sized territory carved out earlier on by the Felschers and a host of others. Carl had stretched his good-natured tolerance to the limits by not hauling off and belting one of them, but it was getting tough.

The metalheads were just too much. Carl and Brenda both agreed with the spirit of the day and all; hell, Carl even supported the fight to keep bands like the Dead Kennedys from getting the shaft, and he liked them about as much as he liked *these* guys.

But their asshole fans were another story. Principles, *schminciples:* Brenda almost got another elbow in the face, and he swore the next goddamned arm that knocked him was going to goddamned well go home broken. He looked at his watch. Goddamn. Carl hoped he could hold his temper until Jacob Hamer came on. Maybe then they'd calm down. Or go away, even.

Though he wouldn't stake his life on it or anything.

7:03:10 P.M.

Rod Royale was pleased. He could feel the Presence mounting steadily, felt masterful in the face of it. Seventy seconds in and his guitar was a demon in his hands, kept in check only by the fluid click of fingertips on steel. It howled with the barely contained abandon of the damned, defiant in the face of Creation. He was in awe of the Presence. It was sweet, so sweet. It was exactly as it should be.

And what's more, it was a mere taste.

Of what awaited.

Rod strode up to the very lip of the stage for his first solo, leaned back and thrust his hips suggestively at the throng. The throng responded. He swayed back and forth with the rhythm; the crowd rocked back and forth in a surging motion that was half slam dance, half Saint Vitus' dance. The motion spread. It looked like quite a few people were in danger of being crushed out there.

Rod Royale smiled. Tara hadn't even opened her luscious mouth yet, and already It was there. This pleased him greatly. It served to confirm several key things.

Like Its imminence.

And her ultimate disposability.

The first song raged on. Tara was working the other side of the stage, getting ready to sing. Rod glanced back at Alex only once, saw the frail form hunkering behind the massive racks of synthesizers like the high priest of high tech. Periodically Alex would spasm and throw his head back, colored light glinting off the mirrored shades that wrapped so tightly around his skull. Not for the first time, Rod wished that his brother could see the crowd.

Or *anything*, for that matter . . .

7:03:49 P.M.

No question about it, Jesse was upset. She had already run the emotional gamut from concerned to annoyed to agitated to a state of quiet panic, and the only thing that kept her circuit breakers from shutting down completely was the analytically frantic chore of getting the show ready to go on.

"*If* it goes on," she muttered.

"Did you say something?" Hempstead asked. He looked concerned. The stress was showing on everyone in the band.

Jesse tried to fake a genuine smile, failed miserably. "Never mind," she said, "I'm just tired, is all. The tension must be really getting to me."

Hempstead nodded in sympathy. "I hear dat. Did Petey show up?"

Jesse shook her head, barely holding back tears. His guitar and effects were being laid out in position, ready to go. Seeing them there gave her the willies. What if he didn't show at all? What then? Go on anyway? Bag it?

It was impossible to even consider. Where the hell was he? Her mind reeled with grim possibilities. Her head ached. Her skin ached. The music from the stage seemed to be penetrating, vibrating in the pit of her stomach, in her very bones. *Jesus,* she thought, *did they have to play so fucking LOUD?*

Stupid question. Of course they did. That was half the point: they pumped out sound waves like a sonic blanket, completely enveloping anyone within vibratory earshot. It wasn't supposed to be mellow or contained or even civilized. It was supposed to rock, shock, shake, rattle, and roll.

Still, this was different. There was something *else* present in the sound, something underneath it or inside it or around it that was making Jesse's belly twist into tight little fists. Her skin felt flushed and goose-bumped. She looked through the translucent backdrop that separated the two halves of the stage, saw the glittering blur that was the band working the masses filling the huge concrete crater beyond.

And Jesse felt afraid.

As the music itself seemed filled with things . . .

7:04:13 P.M.

Walker and Hook exchanged conspiratorial nods of approval. From the insular nest of the master sound board the effect was crystal clear: they were surrounded by a sea of ululating flesh. The Scream's first song, "Rip the Veil," was nearing its climatic wall of white-hot noise. Hook's finger rested delicately on the sub mixer, right over the slider for channel twenty-three. He looked at Walker. Walker nodded.

The slider went up. A tiny, tiny bit. But enough.

For the moment.

You couldn't hear even the result, but you sure as hell could see it. A ripple passed through the thrashing waves of humanity; a shudder, almost. Hook smiled.

They were primed.

7:04:39 P.M.

Kyle and Logan stood at the rim of ramp SC, smack-dab in the middle of the arena shell. Just two more guys in rumpled black field jackets and shades, faceless in the massmind of the crowd. The shiny yellow backstage passes, their purpose fulfilled, had been summarily jettisoned into the nearest trash can.

A pity, Kyle thought. He could easily have parlayed those passes into a blowjob with some succulent ramp rat in the back of Logan's van. Maybe doubles, go around the world in stereo.

But no. Business before pleasure. No time for that now. Way too busy.

And far too dangerous. The passes were for one thing and one thing only: to get them by security. Beyond that, anonymity was the ticket. Besides, there'd be plenty of pleasure later. That, and much, much more.

Or so they were promised.

Kyle surveyed the sprawling panorama before him and felt

the tiniest twinge of regret. It was nothing personal; he bore ninety-nine percent of these people no ill will at all. He liked the music just fine, and he thought the politics of it all were naive, though heartfelt.

But that was all neither here nor there. There was a job to be done, and these poor, unwitting motherfuckers had their own part to play in it, each and every one. Just as Logan had his.

And Kyle had his.

And as he reached inside his jacket to touch the cool steel case of what nestled there, he felt reasonably sure about which part would last longer.

And which couldn't end nearly soon enough.

7:04:50 P.M.

Tara's voice cut through the between-song roar of the crowd like a siren in the eye of a hurricane.

"DO YOU WANT IT?"

Applause.

"I said, DO YOU *WANT* IT??"

BAM! The rhythmic section hit a power chord to underscore the emphatic appeal. The audience went nuts; they wanted it, all right. Tara looked back toward Rod and Alex wickedly. Alex was very busy, making microsecond adjustments. Tara turned back to the crowd to ask the critical question.

"Yeah, well . . . WHAT DO YOU WANT TO *DO* WITH IT?"

The answer came back ragged. *Stick it in.*

"SAY *WHAT?*"

Again, stronger. *STICK IT IN.*

Tara looked back; Alex nodded. He got it.

"And once you got it in, babies. Once you got . . . it . . . in . . .

"WHAT DO YOU DO *THEN*???"

Got it. The Answer.

Loud and clear.

7:05:00 P.M.

The band on the TV screen kicked full tilt no sooner than the words had left their lips. "Stick It In" was always a big crowd pleaser, replete with its follow-the-bouncing-bloody-ball chorus. Alex Royale had captured the audience response on one of his digital samplers, Cody explained, and he boosted it and fed it back into the mix every time Tara sang the fateful chorus.

The band overdrived through the first verse . . .

"Cold steel, hot slice
feel the edge of my
my strange device"

Tara drew a dagger from the slit suede folds of her waistlet and traced it suggestively up her inner thigh.

"It's real, it's right
it's gonna be
my baby tonight"

Blood tracked in close-up on the screen, shiny rivulets down to the muscular curve of her calf.

"Holy shit!" Madeline cried. "How does she *do* that?"

"Special effects," Rachel said. "Cody told me it's rigged with a hollow handle that has a squeeze-bulb filled with stage blood. Isn't that right, Cody?"

"*Yipper*," barked the little speaker over the set. "*That blade prob'ly couldn't cut Cheese Whiz.*"

"It's certainly realistic," Sheri said.

"It's disgusting," Lauren added.

On screen, Tara sang:

"When you lay down
on my wedding bed
we won't get it up
till the night runs red
and you
STICK IT IN!
(*TWIST IT!!*)
STICK IT IN!!

(*TWIST IT!!*)
STICK IT IN!!!
(*TWIST IT!!*)"

"Gak," Madeline sputtered.

Disgusting," Lauren sneered. And they all laughed. It was strangely funny.

For about another thirty seconds.

7:05:29 P.M.

Now. Walker sensed it in the way the shadows shifted, in the way a child senses the advances of a funny uncle. The song had reached its big crowd-call breakdown; time to get over to the Eastern parking apron, to the makeshift heliport.

To get things warmed up.

"STICK IT IN!!!"
(*TWIST IT!!*)

He cast one last glance at Hook; one micro-flicker of optic musculature that said it all.

Crank it.

Hook beamed.

And did as he was told.

7:05:58 P.M.

In the hive-mind: a spark, burgeoning to overglow. The perfect pitch, accomplished. The fuse, ignited.

The moment.

At hand.

7:06:00 P.M.

It was a six-inch blade with a bone-white pearlite handle, and it flicked open easy as pie. Dickie dug it out of his right engineer boot and brought it to glistening life in a second. *Ker-snick*. A whisking arc of stainless steel perfection.

There was a pudgy guy in a white T-shirt in front of him. Dickie picked a spot just below the ribs and maybe an inch to the right of the spine. The point of the blade slid in smoothly, sunk as deep as the hilt would permit, then withdrew. The guy started to sink. His scream was drowned in the sound.

"EEYAAOW!" Dickie howled. All over the stadium, he knew, the same thing was going on. Fifty, maybe sixty of the Faithful, stickin' it in.

And twisting.

It was like a dream. So easy. So cool. Wolves among sheep, doffing the wool and letting it fly. *Snap snap*. Heave ho. As Pudgo collapsed, Dickie moved to the next in line. She was a tiny chick, maybe 5'3", and she went down silently when he slit her windpipe and sunk a boot into the backside of her knees.

And the blade was red. And the moment was hot. Two dripping dumbfucks down, and nobody had any idea what was going on. They were all facing forward, engrossed in the spectacle. They had no idea what was coming up behind or around them.

The next guy was huge, maybe six foot six. Dickie brought his hand up and buried his switch in the soft spot at the base of his skull, prying Heaven's Gate wide open. The dweeb beside him saw Goliath fall as the blade came out, half-turning in recognition that something had gone woefully amiss. No biggee.

Dickie stuck it in his eye.

Withdrew it

And then turned.

He had a neat little swath behind him, and nobody even seemed to fucking notice. It was beautiful. So beautiful. It was just like the Plan had said it would be . . .

7:06:23 P.M.

. . . and the music raged . . .

7:06:24 P.M.

. . . as an MTV cameraman named Robert Harmon, in the midst of a crowd shot, found himself staring through his lens at the murder of a man named Carl Felscher and then broadcasting it live into millions of homes . . .

7:06:26 P.M.

. . . and the music howled . . .

7:06:27 P.M.

. . . and in the last fifteen seconds of Chris Konopliski's life, time careened out of control: stopping entirely, speeding crazily ahead, slowing to a terrible, terminal crawl.

It began the moment that the knife punched in through the shirt on his back, the back of his skin, the latissimus dorsi muscle and soft bowels beyond. It was a swift, sudden, and startling violation that was four inches long, one eighth of an inch high, and three quarters of an inch thick at its widest point. It came from out of nowhere. And it hurt like a motherfucker.

Chris had been in the process of letting out a whoop. It turned instantly into something worse and far more deeply felt. When the blade began to twist within him, he lurched forward and away and let out a squeal that rivaled the three octaves above middle C that Rod Royale's guitar was violently proclaiming in that moment.

At that point the endorphins kicked in: the body's own natural opiates, racing in response to the suddenly savaged area, numbing the slit and severed nerves, trying desperately to bring the pain under control. He felt the blade start to slide out of him, but not the way he'd felt it slide in. It was God's way of buying him retaliation time, if he had it within him to act.

He did. In fact, he was amazed by the force of his own outrage. *IN THE BACK!* screamed a voice in his mind. *IN THE FUCKING BACK!* He whirled then, and the motion slid the invading steel out of him clean as you please. He barely even felt the lifeblood spritzing out through his brand-new hole as he turned to face his assailant.

But five of his life's last fifteen seconds were already over.

The guy who had stabbed him was a little weenie who was dressed like a Screamer, but that wasn't the only thing wrong about him. This was not a person who admired the fine points of rock 'n' roll; this was a person who was rotting from the inside. In those last dying seconds, his night vision was acute.

The guy who had stabbed him was no longer a person at all.

It was at that point that life began to drastically slow down: current experience and memory mingled. It was unfortunate, because it muddied his ability to deal with the last few seconds he had. Some candy he had stolen as a fifth-grader impinged on his awareness of the grasp that he laid on the face of the bastard who was killing him, fingers curling around the wafer-thin Mylar shades . . .

. . . and he felt his hand yanking downward, but it was weirdly abstracted by the face of his mother . . .

. . . and as the Screamer's left ear sliced off and fell, he felt the blade plunge into his heart, and there were not enough endorphins in the world to muzzle that pain, so he screamed and yanked harder on the flesh and Mylar Band-Its in his hand . . .

. . . as a notch in the ridged cartilage of the Screamer's nose gave way, removing the knob at the tip as the Band-Its dropped beneath the chin . . .

. . . and the red wormy emptiness of the Screamer's sockets came clearly into view . . .

. . . and there were less than five seconds left, his heart having exploded in a burst of steel, and it was hard to believe that he was still aware of anything at all. But he glanced to the right and saw his friend Ted's screaming face, found no comfort there, felt himself helplessly vomit blood in its direction.

Then his gaze returned to the death-grip he had on the face of his murderer. His hand was yanking downward, and the flesh was giving way: peeling back like thick wet indoor/outdoor carpeting, revealing the rancid meat and muscle beneath, exposing the greasy skull.

"EEYAAOW!" screamed the late, great Perry Dempsey.

Then time ran out for both of them, and they fell . . .

7:06:45 P.M.

. . . and the music shrieked . . .

7:06:46 P.M.

. . . as Kyle and Logan exchanged nodding glances, pulled the pins, and heaved their willie peters into opposite sections of the crowd. There was a five-second delay before the white phosphorus grenades exploded outward in a shower of thick white flaming tendrils; plenty of time for them to retreat down the ramp and blend into the masses cruising the promenade. The screams of incinerating agony blended very nicely with the general reverie . . .

7:06:50 P.M.

. . . *and The Scream wailed on* . . .

7:06:51 P.M.

. . . as Jake paused in mid-harangue to stare, dumbstruck with horror, at the chaos blooming at the back of the arena. All shout-fests with Jesse, all thoughts of Pete, all concern for the welfare of the band and the doomed next set were rendered suddenly, pointlessly, academic.

All that registered was the dawning, acrid memory of scorched earth, seared flesh and white-hot fire that wouldn't, *couldn't* be put out. Not until it had run its terrible, chemical course.

"*Jesus, no,*" he whispered. "*No* . . ." It was too much to consider, that some lunatic had lobbed willie peters into a crowd of people. But there it was, sending out tentacles of blistering death in a dozen different directions. It was sheer insanity. It was happening. Jake felt his heart leap straight into his throat . . .

7:06:52 P.M.

. . . *and on* . . .

7:06:53 P.M.

. . . as Carol Macon screamed like a baby, her moussed and streaked blond hair a mass of wafting cinders, her pouty lips stretching in agony and running like tallow as the incendiary shrapnel etched charcoal fissures into the soft flesh of her face on its way to the bone. She ran blindly, clawing and stumbling up the steps, sucking in air and getting smoke and flame until the tiny air pockets deep in her lungs collapsed. And she mercifully fainted from oxygen deprivation and shock, a microsecond before her blazing corpse hit the concrete railing that marked the topmost edge of the stairs . . .

7:06:54 P.M.

. . . *and on* . . .

7:06:55 P.M.

. . . as Brother Paisley turned from his up-to-the-minute newscast to behold the sight of prophecies fulfilled, praise God, as there came a great weeping and gnashing of teeth and some poor sinner was quite literally cast into the lake of fire, just a little ahead of schedule . . .

7:06:56 P.M.

. . . and on . . .

7:06:57 P.M.

. . . as Rod Royale felt a sense of absolute elation, transported in the power and the passion of the moment. People were *rioting* before him: visibly, tangibly at each other's throats. It was glorious.

Right up to the moment that Alex keeled over.

He leaned back in his signature Ray-Charles-from-Hell stance, just like he did a hundred times a night. Only this time he just kept going.

Ker-splat.

It was a first. Rod was stymied. The keyboards dropped out immediately, leaving a gaping hole through which the amassed power of the preceding moments seemed to drain. The impact was gone; the band deflated like the *Hindenburg* aflame.

The audience didn't appear to notice; they seemed hellbound on a momentum all their own. Rod watched as a fat chick down in front smacked another kid in the head with a bit of lead pipe; two security types leapt into the fray.

Rod cast around in the escalating confusion, searching both sides of the stage for some type of visual cue as to what the hell was going on here. On the one side of the stage he saw Jacob Hamer and his sax player, arguing with one another. Hamer was pointing at the rising trails of smoke from the back of the arena, where moments ago Rod had seen the flashpot-bright arcs of light go off.

Hempstead was shaking his head and pointing at the other side of the stage. Rod looked.

Walker was there. Making a swift slicing motion across his throat. Repeatedly.

Kill it.

Rod nodded and brought the song down as quickly and gracefully as possible. Which wasn't very.

The music stopped. The screaming went on.

And they were already carrying Alex off . . .

7:06:59 P.M.

All the while, Lenore Kleinkind had suffered quietly as the jostling mob of misguided youngsters careened to and fro. Her ears were packed with two Pamprin bottles' worth of cotton, and still the pounding had gotten through.

Not to worry, though; she was willing to endure even greater indignities, if need be, to ensure that her cause— correction, not her cause, *God's* cause—was clearly heard. *Not my will, but Thine, be done.* Amen. She'd said fourteen Hail Marys, twenty-two Our Fathers, and a novena in preparation for this and felt her loins to be sufficiently girded to breach any barrier to this, her coming out.

But now, things were getting entirely out of hand; several fights had broken out, and the music—if you could call it that—had only seemed to make things worse. Now even that was disrupted; the band had stopped playing, and one of the youngsters appeared to have actually fainted. Lenore was starting to have serious fears that her purpose might be thwarted. She was frightened.

Still, there was hope. And God's will.

And where's there's a will . . .

Lenore started edging her way to the far, far corner of the stage, where the privileged ones were allowed access to the back. She clutched her little red Igloo closely, lest she spill a single drop. And she prayed.

And when another fight broke out before her, this time between a pair of broken-bottle-wielding thugs and the strapping security men guarding the gate, it appeared that her prayers were truly answered.

Knock, and it shall be opened unto thee . . .
Amen.

7:07:00 P.M.

Rachel, Lauren, Sheri, and Madeline were all staring in wide-eyed shock at the melee playing across the screen. Things had degenerated in rapid succession. Cameras that had only moments before been blending one slick stage angle after another were now scrambling to lend some sense of visual coherence to what looked like Beirut on a bad night. Lurching friezes of frantic, blurred action bleeding into screaming sirens, screaming feedback and just plain screaming.

"Ohmigod," Rachel whispered. "CODY!!" Natalie looked up at her mother, face screwing up with a contact rush of dimly comprehended terror, and started to mewl.

"CODY!!! What's going on?!!"

"I dunno! Hang on a sec—"

The screen blipped harsh static between channels as Cody scanned the dial, looking for something solid, and . . .

CLICK

. . . an ambulance screamed by on its way to Gate Six, as NBC correspondent Glenn Javits interrupted the evening news to hunker into a mike and shout something about "a massacre," and . . .

CLICK

. . . a prerecorded telecast of the Ol' Time Gospel Hour o' Power Ministries showed a red-faced Reverend Jimmy howling into his lapel mike about the ravages of Rock Music upon the Youth of Today, and . . .

CLICK

. . . a Channel Four SkyEye copter banked into a sweeping shot of the JFK playing field, with a distorted voiceover barking about the blazing pyre at one end and the sweeping stage at the other and the stampeding dots of humanity in between, and . . .

CLICK

. . . roving MTV correspondent Big Al Belsen tucked his neck into his Banana Republic safari vest and scuttled away from the departing whirlybird, having found The Scream utterly unresponsive to him. He and his crew were trying gamely to keep a handle on the situation. They collared the very next people they saw, and . . .

"Oh, no," Rachel cried, very nearly bolting out of her seat to touch the screen. Natalie started to bawl. The images that filled the camera's eye were simultaneously familiar and utterly alien.

"Jake, Jesse," Big Al hollered, "is it true that Jerry Crane has just suffered a heart attack in the wake of the Rock Aid Riot?"

Jake paused to glare at him, and for a microsecond it appeared that he might bash in Big Al's bridgework. Instead he wheeled and pushed his way through the scrambling crews. The look in his eyes, though, would remain with Rachel for the rest of the sleepless night. The look that said it all in a word she had never truly understood.

Incoming.

And Jake was gone.

Jesse remained behind, looking shell-shocked and ill. Rachel felt her heart skip a beat as Big Al's big mike shoved toward her face. She recoiled slightly as Al said, "Can you give us any insight . . ."

. . . and another voice came from the sidelines, saying, "Miss Malloy?" and Jesse half-turned to meet it . . .

. . . and the thick red gouts hit her full in the face, splashing across her chest and even spackling a horrified Al Belsen . . .

. . . and Rachel cried out . . .

. . . as Jesse stood, the eyes of the global jukebox fully upon her, clotted blood dripping from face and hands and breast and hair . . .

. . . and a triumphant Lenore Kleinkind stood, emptied mason jars in each hand, hollering something about the sanctity of human life as two security men grabbed her and wrestled her down . . .

. . . and in front of an estimated sixty million viewers . . .

. . . Jesse screamed.

THE SCREAM

"They that worship God merely from fear,
Would worship the devil too, if he appear."
—Thomas Fuller

"It breaks the cage, fear escapes and takes possession
Just like a crowd, rioting inside.
Make me do this, make me do that, make me do this
Make me do that—

Mother stands for comfort.
Mother will hide the murderer."
—Kate Bush

Alex was still delirious when the chopper arrived at the band's Staten Island estate. For forty-five minutes he had been going back and forth between babbling and whining and moaning and writhing. Somewhere over Jersey, he had emptied his bladder.

The rest of the passengers were silent, Rod particularly so. Walker could understand that. He was scared out of his mind. Every bit of triumphant glee they'd earned through the trashing of Rock Aid had been sucked right out by Alex's collapse. Now they were trapped in a howling machine with a dying man, their future uncertain and their own mortality shoved right in their faces.

It would have been nice to sedate little Alex. It would have been nice to shut him up. Under the circumstances, unfortunately, it was out of the question. Any more drugs in that boy and they might as well bag him. He was that close to the other side.

It took Walker back. Oh, yes, it did. Took him back to the war that had made him what he was. There had been lots of chopper rides like this in those halcyon days. And screams galore.

But it took him back.

Yes, indeedee-doo.

To one place in particular.

November, 1967. In the Central Highlands near Dak To. Some seven months before the real madness began.

In the days before Momma.

One of the many bloody firefights surrounding Hill 875 had taken down eight of his men, and he was feeling pretty fucked up about it. Corpsmen were running all over the place, trying to patch up the casualties. There was hope for a few. But only a few.

There was one kid, a green little piece of shit who he'd known would never amount to anything; and as it turned out, he was right. Something had come from out of the darkness to take a football-sized chunk out of his innards.

And the kid was screaming.

It occurred to Walker that the kid needed morphine. It wouldn't save him—the odds were good that nothing would— but it would spare him some pain, and sometimes that was the best you could do. The kid had no tag—one of those little manila fuckers that reminded Walker of those DO NOT REMOVE UNDER PENALTY OF LAW *tags they hung off the sides of mattresses—so it was clear in his mind that it hadn't been done yet. You always got tagged. It was the name of the game.*

Walker had cornered his corpsman and secured the necessary ampules and works. Then he had returned to the site where the kid still lay, screaming out his heart. You're gonna be okay, Walker remembered saying.

Then he stuck the needle in.

It couldn't have been more than two or three seconds later that the kid jerked to agonized attention: eyes bugging out, mouth yawning wide, body rigid and twitching. It was like someone had stuck a high-tension power cable up his ass. And he was stiff like an ironing board.

Like a tombstone.

And Walker realized that the kid had already been goosed, he already had as much as his system could bear, but some asshole had fucking neglected to tag him . . .

. . . and all Walker could do was watch him die . . .

It was like that again, right down to the screaming; only the kid in question was clearly marked this time. Not with a tag; he didn't need one. It was all written down in the dissipation of his features, the slow but steadily quickening erosion of his body, mind, and soul.

Momma, he silently lamented. *All these years, all this trouble . . . why did it all have to come down to one goddamn blind dying genius-junkie?*

Then the chopper landed, and the door flew open, and

Locke and Keynes were there. There were no smiles or exchanges of greeting, though they hadn't seen each other in nearly nine months. Walker had radioed ahead. They knew what was going on.

In less than a minute the nurse and the gurney bearing Alex Royale were being shuttled back to the mansion. Walker and the rest filed out solemnly, hoofed it the rest of the way. Out across Richmond Terrace, the oily waters that spared them from the Jersey chemical vats gleamed like black glass.

The Scream was, at long last, home.

And, for better or worse, the waiting was almost over.

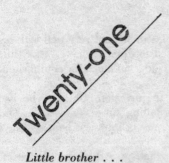

Twenty-one

Little brother . . .

Alex heard the voice, but faintly. A whisper through the screams. There was little in the room that he was aware of: the rustle and creak of the bed as they laid him down, the clink and tinkle of the IV, the prick of the needle, the soft murmur of voices and gently bleeping monitors. Even the warbling sounds he made were background noise to him now.

What senses he had left were directed inward, pulled into the dark place that his soul had become.

And the even deeper darkness on the other side.

Little brother, listen to me . . .

It was Rod. Close now. Waves of warm breath brushing his ear.

You have to be strong, Bucky. You have to. We're right at the palace gates now, and there's nothing to stop us but ourselves.

He wanted to cry out, to cry out warning. But he had no will, no control over his body, the cold and the dark were sucking him down . . .

*If you give up now, it will all have been for nothing.
Do you understand me?*

Down to the place where the hell-thing waited . . .

Can you hear me, little brother?

I need you.

Waited with its cold dark constant smile . . .

Shit.

And then the voice and the breath pulled away, and the sound of his brother's suddenly furious shouts blended in with the beeps and the clinks and the rest of the fog on the outside.

Leaving the inside free.

For the screams to resume.

Rod was royally fucking pissed. It went very well with his terror. The two emotions danced together divinely, a swirling performance at the core of his being. So much for equilibrium. So much for being able to think.

Oh, yes, he was here at the mansion. Oh, yes, he had money and power and freedom falling out of his asshole. Oh, yes, he was the bloody Crown Prince of Darkness he had always envisioned himself to be.

But things were going on that he had no knowledge of. That he had no control of. Behind his back.

And Alex was dying. *Really* dying, this time.

So where did that leave him?

I don't know, he told himself. *But it feels like nowhere*. He credited himself with having that much perception. *If Alex goes, my bargaining power is out the window. They'll be on me in a second. They will fucking eat me alive.*

And I can't let that happen.

I won't *let that happen.*

Rod thundered down the upstairs corridor, away from the room where his brother's life was being held in tender abeyance. It was long and dark, and its pale white walls were sumptuously attired with great bleak antique portraits in massive oak antique frames. Ordinarily he would have loved to linger with the old dead farts; it had been so long, and his soul had been hungering for a deep quaff of the mansion's deliciously sinister atmosphere.

But he was scared, and he was pissed, and homecoming was affording him no joy at all.

There was only one place to take the madness he felt.

There was only one thing to do.

The stairs led down. He followed them to the main floor, the foyer, then doubled rapidly back to his left, steering clear of the huge rehearsal room that dominated the heart of the mansion. Past the black steel door lay the second stairwell, winding down into its bowels.

He had given orders, upon his arrival, for the bordello to be stocked. It was pleasing to discover that, in at least one respect, things had not completely fallen apart. There was two fine specimens awaiting him: drugged, trussed up, and ready for action.

"Ah," he said, stepping inside and closing the door behind him.

The one on his right was a female. Young, maybe sixteen. Very pretty, in an underdeveloped Olivia Newton-John kind of way. They had left on her underwear, as per his request. It was very nice underwear: scanty and lacy and black. Revealing. Good choice. Apparently little Olivia was kinkier than her surface might denote.

Nice body, too. They had damaged it very little in the course of her abduction. Her breasts had just a bit of sag, like a sow in need of milking. Her ass was flat, not as curved as he liked. Then again, so was her tummy, and he liked that quite a bit.

All in all, he found her most satisfactory.

The one to his left was a man. Evidently the abduction had gone a little less easily with this fellow. His eyes were swollen; and though he'd been well cleaned, the tiniest trickles of blood still oozed from the freshly broken nose.

No matter. No one would ever know. And Rod didn't put nearly so high a premium on male beauty as he did on its female equivalent. He had the body type that Rod favored most: tall, pumped up, reeking redneck hostility. Even naked, it was clear that the guy favored Mets caps with their brims turned toward the back.

Rod decided to call him Knute Rockne.

Knute was most satisfactory, too.

"Ah, yes," Rod reiterated, stepping closer, allowing himself a smile. He felt better already. He truly did. He was a sucker for therapeutic recreation. "I'm very happy to see you tonight. I don't know who you are, of course; I don't know anything about you. But that really doesn't matter, does it?"

Neither one of them could speak, as such. The analgesic had seen to that. Nonetheless, he always insisted that their tongues be removed; his wish, as always, had been obeyed. When the drug wore off, he would not want words. He would want raw emotion, primeval and pure.

"You are here for my pleasure." He paused for a moment. Their eyes broadcast fogbound but nonetheless poignant terror. Olivia's eyes, in particular, were inspiring. He smiled and began to unbutton his shirt.

"More specifically: you were *born* for my pleasure. I hope you appreciate how splendid that is. It's not *everyone* who gets chosen to be my honey-love, after all. You should think of yourselves as something rather special."

Rod's shirt was custom tailored and cost an even four hundred dollars. One of its design imperatives had been that it unbutton at the vertical slide of a hand. For four hundred smackers, that was easily arranged. The first stage of his striptease went off impeccably.

"You may have had dreams of your own. In fact, I'm quite sure of it. Who doesn't? I had a dog once. It often dreamed. I figured, 'If Hildegard can do it, anyone can.' Was I wrong?"

Knute moaned. Olivia chirruped. Between them, not a whit of articulation. Rod sometimes wondered why he even bothered to ask.

He slipped off the shirt, tossed it carelessly to the floor behind him. His naked torso gleamed. He liked to tan. He tanned superbly.

He began to unbutton his pants.

"The point is: your dreams were wrong. They couldn't help but be. You didn't know what destiny had in store. You couldn't have. I mean"—and he chuckled—"what in the world would have made you think that you'd get to meet someone like *me*?"

Rod checked to see if Knute's pecker was enlarging. It was, just a little. That was always nice. Big macho homophobes, in his experience, stood an eighty percent chance of getting a hardon in moments like this. The reluctant subconscious poking out, so to speak. He gave it a tweak. Knute's subconscious, at the moment, was a plump kielbasa of dread.

Rod turned his attention toward little Olivia, caressing her shoulder, tracing one long-nailed finger along the sculpted ridge of her collarbone until he encountered the black lace strap of her brassiere. This he slid lovingly over her left shoulder, unfettering her breast and allowing it to sag just a touch to its full glory. He took it in hand, hefting the flesh like a ripe melon at market, careful to avoid the nipple, which was large and pink and fully capable of hardening of its own accord, given the proper mood.

Rod was a master of proper mood. He squeezed the breast and stared into Olivia's spinning eyes. She whimpered.

The nipple went stiff.

He smiled again, broadly, and strolled over to his throne. This was no time for dallying, and his boots required removal. He sat down and slipped them off, one at a time. His socks followed suit. Nobody spoke.

Surprise, surprise.

"*God*, I feel good!" It was true. His body tingled all over, and he was beginning to perspire. *Like the old saying goes*, he said to himself. *If spit don't work, it ain't troo love.*

With his pants undone, his own beautiful bone was showing through his red bikini briefs: eight inches of personal pride. He hoped that Knute was responding. Knute was. Olivia, too. What a splendid pair!

Rod slipped his pants off and stood again. He stretched, flexed, sighed expansively.

And for the first time since his return, drank in the details of his beloved bordello.

It was a good-sized subterranean room, thirty-five by twenty (though it seemed far bigger), with no windows and a very high ceiling. For the convenience of the rest of the household, it was utterly soundproofed. The lighting was excellent, largely on behalf of the three strategically placed vidicams. Two excellent directional mikes dangled from the ceiling. Bose monitors in each corner tickled the air with lush surround-a-sound.

This was not to mention the endless varieties of exotic apparatus that dominated the room. The elaborate chain-and-pully devices that held his guests in place, to begin with. And oh so many more.

And then, of course, there were the mirrors.

They lined the walls, the floor, the ceiling. They arced and angled in geometric perfection, made the bordello a kaleidoscope of reflected light and image. You could see yourself, at virtually every angle, from virtually any spot in the room. This was of the utmost importance.

Watching, after all, was half the fun.

"You know"—he turned back to his audience—"you may find this hard to believe, but I grew up in a place like this. My father was an enthusiastic libertine, a great admirer of the grand Marquis: de Sade, that is. You are familiar with his work?"

Mssr. Rockne and Mlle. Newton-John stared blankly at him, eyes swimming in pain and confusion and terror. Rod noted, with some distaste, that they had both begun to drool a bit. A side effect of the drug: one that he was wholly familiar with, but that he still found somewhat unappetizing.

"No matter." He shrugged. "My father was a surgeon. Of course, his understanding of the human body was superb. What makes it work. What makes it fail. What kind of injuries can be sustained, and for how long.

"Most of all, he was an expert on pain.

"And pleasure."

Rod was definitely getting excited now. He could feel his pulse in the tips of his fingers, and his briefs were under enormous strain. *Hold back,* he told himself emphatically. *All good things come to those who wait. . . .*

There was a table full of implements before him. He savored each in turn. The scalpel. The bone saw. The twelve-inch dildo with the blunted metal studs. The fourteen-inch dildo with the sharpened metal studs. The electric nipple-clamps. And so on. And so on.

He had missed his toys immeasurably. It had been a long nine months, with precious little true libertinage to boast of. It was too easy to get caught on the road; and most of the security had been diverted toward Tara, that bitch. Her, and her little fucking army . . .

But that's over now, he snapped at himself. *I'm home now. And all that is going to change.*

He tried to regain the moment, to shake off the effects of the insidious digression. Too late. One thought of Tara and the poison began to spread: slow-moving, hot, and dark as molten tar. His body still tingled, but the quality had changed.

The rage was back.

The killing rage.

It was time to make his first selections, get on with the show. Tonight it wasn't too difficult. Ordinarily in such cases he opted for chivalry; but there was something about this particular man that made Rod chomp at the bit. There would always be more ladies-first scenarios to enjoy.

And besides, he would be opening the door for her.

Later.

This left the selection of the opening device. Again, the decision was unorthodox but immediate. "Inspector Royale," he said aloud in a convincingly stodgy British accent. "Can you solve the mystery?" Then he smiled and in a different voice said, "Certainly. With pleasure.

"Mssr. Rockne. In the bordello.

"With the instruments of his choice."

The table of goodies before him was one of three, and all of them had wheels. He rolled the first one forward, brought it to rest in front of the stud. "Take your time. Think about each of these items in turn. I'm sure you'll come up with several creative uses for each of them. I'll discuss my own favorite techniques in a moment. Then we'll, you'll pardon the expression, come to an agreement. No problem?"

Knute's red and swollen eyes were as wide as they could get. He let out a piteous caveman sound.

"Delightful. Now you stay right there."

As he turned to fetch the second table, he thought about his father. He often did, especially in moments such as this. What a superior man his father had been! How strong and courageous, how uncowed by the bogus morality of the weak and trembling. Where most men recoiled from the force of their own desires, Father had waded straight in, daring sensation to overwhelm him, daring God to strike him down.

Which of course, he told himself, *was never going to happen*.

Because there was no God; and if there was, Man had misunderstood Him completely. The simple fact was that God *punished* the meek. *Nature* punished the meek, every step of the way. One look at any point along the food chain was proof, and only a hypocritical lying coward would deny it. Only a weak hypocritical lying coward stood to *gain* from proclaiming the myth of morality.

Because morality purported to make men equal; and everybody knew that *that* was bullshit. No fucking *way* were men born equal.

There were the great ones.

And then there was everybody else.

The second table was full of surprises for Knute. Rod gripped it with suddenly trembling fingers and steered it around, turning back the way he had come. Light glistened on the implements. A beautiful sight.

Such perfection in the way things were.

Like Knute and Olivia. How perfectly they hung, trussed to their devices, in absolute accordance with physical law. What perfect specimens of inferiority they were, proving the rule by providing no exception. One had to assume that the Creator, if there was one, knew what the fuck He was doing.

If there indeed was a God, he reasoned, He clearly intended for the fierce and the cruel and the powerful to prevail.

Alex never understood that, damn his pussy soul. Alex had not been able to sustain the privilege of his position. Because he was weak, he empathized too much with the weakness of others. It dragged him down.

And it was pathetic, because Alex was so *obviously* superior to virtually everyone that he met. Playing Mozart at five. Playing Tchaikovsky at eight. A genius computer programmer by the time he was ten. The boy was an absolute genius at everything he touched. There was no instrument he could not master, no system he could not analyze and absorb, no style that he could not grasp and transform, no horizon beyond his reach.

Little brother . . .

Rod found himself in front of his captives again. He was startled and annoyed by the intrusion of flat reality. He positioned the table beside its counterpart, turned away without a glance. He was thinking. He did not want to be bothered with them just yet.

He was thinking.

Little brother . . .

Little brother was a lousy libertine. In fact, he was no real libertine at all. He had no taste for dominance. He had no real capacity for aggression. He got no pleasure from rapine and torture and death. The only way to even get him *down* to the bordello was by force, in a submissive role, and he usually cried all the way through *that*.

Rod and Dr. Royale were confounded. This was not like family. Even Mom—who Rod and Alex had only met on the inside, and who had died giving birth to the twins—had been an intrepid devourer of pleasure in her day. The studded dildos were her legacy.

But there was no precedent for Alex.

One thing was for certain: if he would not participate, he could not be trusted in the outside world. Stupid or not, they lived in a nation of laws; and the dedicated libertine had much to fear from society at large. There could be no Cub Scouts, no day care, no school. Just a tutor, a governess, and a maid, all three of whom were utterly loyal to the doctor.

Alex had his private education, and a damn good one at that. He had his music and unlimited freedom in which to pursue it. He had fine clothing, good food, exquisite shelter.

But he had no friends but Rod, and no concept of the world outside those four sheltering walls.

Poor little Alex . . .

Little brother . . .

The third and last table bore some of Rod's favorite items. The staple gun, for example. It wasn't the kind of device you'd expect to see in a place like this, but he always had a lot of fun with it. You figure: if it can anchor speaker wire into three-quarter-inch plywood, it can do a pretty number on naked skin. A half an inch into tensed abdominals, for certain. Straight through the scrotum, no problem at all. Not a lethal weapon, barring a clear shot through the eye or the temple.

But a great pain-bringer, all the same.

Mssr. Rockne is hanging there, waiting for this, he told himself. *It's not polite to keep him waiting. Leave your dumb old fucking thoughts alone.*

Unfortunately, it wasn't quite that simple.

Rod began to roll the table forward in the hope that each revolution of the wheels would bring him deeper back into the mood. It didn't work. All this thinking, all this backtracking through memory, just rekindled the anger and fear. He felt suddenly ridiculous in his goddamn bikini briefs, trying to fuck his way sane while the world was falling down around his ears.

And the thought of feeling ridiculous in front of these pissants made him almost *unbearably* furious. For a second the roles felt hideously reversed: *he* was the victim, trussed up without a tongue, and *they* were the ones who were free to gloat and cluck at his inadequacies.

The thought was too ugly to bear.

It had to be rectified.

At once.

Rod slammed the table into the other two and then turned to his male receptacle. The staple gun came up in his hand. He jammed the pay end in Knute's hard belly flesh and squeezed the trigger twice. Knute jerked and wailed. Rod brought the machine up and broke the fucker's cheekbone with it.

"Shut UP!" he howled, then pulled back toward composure. There was some panting involved. He tried to keep it under check. "You are on drugs now, asshole," he said more quietly. "Just wait till they wear off. *Then* you can start your fucking screaming."

From that point on, Rod was utterly centered. His memories, his rage, and the moment at hand were one. Purely one. No separation at all.

"You know what it is to be nicked away, a piece at a time?" Rod demanded.

Knute was not capable of a coherent answer. His wide eyes and cold sweat were all the testimony needed. Rod accepted and dismissed it all at once.

"Well, I'll tell you. It's the story of my life. It's what's going on in my life right now. You wanna know why I'm gonna hump you till you bleed and die?

"I'll tell you.

"I'll tell you right now.

"BECAUSE THE SCREAM IS MY FUCKING BAND!" he roared. "IT'S *MY* FUCKING BAND! FROM DAY ONE, IT WAS MINE! I HAD MY BROTHER UNDER CONTROL, I HAD THE RHYTHM SECTION UNDER CONTROL, I HAD THE WHOLE GODDAMN DREAM POINTED RIGHT WHERE I WANTED IT!

"AND NOW THIS FUCKING *CUNT* IS TRYING TO TAKE IT AWAY, AND MY GODDAMN BROTHER IS DYING, AND DO YOU KNOW WHAT THIS MEANS? DO YOU KNOW WHAT THIS FUCKING *MEANS*?"

Rod took five more shots in rapid succession. They made a blood-trickling ladder up the center of his victim's torso, brought the exquisite bucking and yowls.

It didn't matter that Knute didn't understand. There was nothing left to say anyway. What needed to be worked off had nothing to do with words.

The smell of blood was in the air.

Rod stepped back, composing himself. It wasn't easy, but it could be done. He needed respite, distraction. Three tables worth of regalia decorated the tables before him. Lots of serious toys, every one ripe for the using. His erection returned like the dawn.

"So what do *you* wanna do?" Rod asked.

And smiled.

Twenty-two

Of the overlapping worlds upon worlds themselves, only one could rightly be considered a place. It alone occupied space and time and obeyed the laws of physics and form. It had life. Its primary currency was flesh. It was hungered for and sought after, scorned and mourned and fought over. As the playing field. The battleground. The ultimate stage: both for those who occupied its frail boundaries . . .

. . . and for those who wished to.

For many denizens of the other planes yearned eternally for enfranchisement through the coin of the realm. They hovered, ever on the other side, watching and waiting for a passageway to open up. The ways in were few, *and fleeting. And there was a barrier in the way, one that kept the Kingdoms at bay.*

It was not a wall. There was no wall between the worlds, as such. No great stone edifice. No fortress, with gates of pearl and streets of purest gold. Not even so much as a solid black line of demarcation between the heavens above, the hells below, and the Earth so squarely poised between.

But there was something. Intangible, yet real as the spark that could turn soft folds of gray meat into living, thinking mind, or discern order in a whirlwind of chaos.

Some thought the barrier was karmic in nature, an ethereal membrane thin as the line between yin and yang, with a pliancy that allowed it to counterbalance the assault of countless millions of tragedies. Some thought the very life-force of the biosphere sustained it, soul-energy holding it together as it moved across the surface of the planet like patterns on the skin of a soap bubble. Others disagreed, for reasons of theology or conviction or purely mortal dread. And most never thought of it at all.

But whatever it was, one property of its nature was clear to any with eyes to see. It fed upon whatsoever we gave it, for better or worse. The keys to the Kingdoms, as always, lay within us.

Just itching for us to let them out . . .

At two A.M. Channel Four repeated its eleven o'clock newscast, right on time. Sue Simmons and Chuck Scarborough presented the on-the-scene madness with just the right touch of anchorperson angst, keeping track of the rising death toll like emcees on a March of Dimes telethon. Sixty-seven dead, two hundred and sixteen injured seriously enough to require hospitalization. Scores more hurt in the stampede and the parking lot riot that ultimately ensued. Police, rockers, right-wingers—everybody blaming everybody else for the panic that gripped the southern edge of the City of Brotherly Love.

By eleven there had been time to assemble a reasonably coherent video recap of the play-by-play, culminating in The Scream's destructo set. It was a tumultuous montage of images: the white phosphorous grenades, blooming in the distance. Alex, taking his big dive. The band, freaking out and walking off, leaving instruments on and howling. The chopper, lifting off. The bodies, spilling out the gates and over the fences, even tumbling off the top of the amphitheater in a frantic exodus that conjured shades of the fall of Saigon.

And on every network Walker checked, the one image that had been instantly transformed into the day's definitive icon of pop disaster: the woman. Backstage. Screaming.

Through a faceful of blood.

Walker looked up from his desk. The vast expanse of his office was dark, illumination coming solely from the blue flicker of the tube. It was an island of light in a sea of shadow. Walker watched, expressionless, as the shadow swelled. And chuckled.

And spoke.

"Too bad Andy Warhol's dead," Momma said. *"He would've had a ball with that."*

Walker felt his hackles rise instinctively. *She's getting bigger,* he thought, *or maybe just more substantial. . . .*

"Both actually," Momma said. Walker flinched the tiniest bit as her presence touched his thoughts and receded again. *"Oh, dear,"* she whispered, *"I do hope that I can retain my girlish figure."*

The laughter that followed filled his head with a sound like bags of dry leaves and bones dragging across a concrete floor. Walker endured it in silence for about another thirty seconds. The scar tissue on his back and his face and on the knuckle-joint of his missing finger throbbed; the vacant hole where his left eye had been itched horribly. "It's been a long day, Momma—" he began.

"And a fruitful one, too."

"—and if you don't mind, I'm a little beat."

"I'm sure," it replied, *"but alas, there's yet more to come. Miles to go before you sleep, one might say."*

Another cryptic chuckle. Walker groaned and lit another Lucky. There was no escape, he knew. There was no way around it. Only through it.

"All right. What's up?"

"First of all, some good news. Do you see the box on your desk?"

Walker looked down. A small UPS shipping carton sat atop the In basket. "Yes. What of it?"

"It contains something for our boy genius. You will, of course, see that he gets it."

Walker picked up the box and opened it up. Inside, a brand-new E-prom chip nestled in the packing material, copper pins sticking up like the legs of a dead millipede. "Very pretty. I'm sure he'll be thrilled."

"You have no idea."

"Who sent it?"

"Friends. In high places."

"Hmmph," Walker grunted. He was too tired to care. "Anything else?"

"Yes. It seems that our South African mining concern just happened onto a rather large vein of gold in that supposedly mined-out hole in Zimbabwe, a"—it chuckled again—*"a mother lode, you might say."*

Oh, Jesus, he winced, carefully modulating his thoughts. "My, we are in an insufferably good mood tonight, aren't we?"

"We should be. We've done well."

"I suppose."

"All is exactly as it should be."

"Yes, I guess it is."

"Then accept your good fortune, as a token of my beneficence."

"You don't owe me anything."

"Yes, I know; which is quite again more than I can say for you. But take it anyway."

Walker sighed; it was not as if he had much of a choice. The money would go to their agent in Johannesburg, then to their Swiss accounts, then on and on, until it ultimately filtered through the world EFT network and into their Citibank accounts. Just like everything else. Momma had seen to it.

Oh, he did the actual phone-calling, letter-writing and check-signing, giving off every indication of being the genius managerial firebrand with the world's greatest inside information. And he had, over the long haul, picked up a genuinely comprehensive understanding of the machine into which he'd been thrust.

But Momma called the shots. Always. He was the eyes and the ears, the hands and the mouthpiece. But in the end, Momma was the source.

Same as she'd ever been.

Since the beginning . . .

*   *   *

The circumstances of their meeting had less to do with predestinative significance than with plain ol' bad timing. He was the right man, in the wrong place, at the worst of all possible times.

It was another in a seemingly endless chain of secret-missions-that-never-happened; no colorful code name, like Project Muscle Beach or Brass Monkey. Not even a dust-dry designation like Op 34, or its oh-so logical follow-up, Op 34A. Nossir. This one didn't even exist at all. Walker was part of a Special Forces team under Major James "Bo" Strakker—three Americans, an Aussie, and four Nung team members—who were heading far up through the Central Highlands, well into Cambodia. Up to Phnom Dac, a ville that MACV Recon indicated was a pit stop for NVA regiments moving through on their way down the Ho Chi Minh Trail. No big surprises there; Walker had often witnessed the aftermath of the VC incentive program. The possibility of having your belly slit open and your entrails eaten by wild pigs as you died could make anyone cooperative.

It wasn't that the villagers were innocents; they were human beings, after all, with the same penchant for everyday deceit and fuckery that you might find among human societies anywhere else on the planet.

But they were caught, as it were, in the middle of a grudge match between opponents whom it was best not to piss off. They could not serve two masters. They could not escape.

They were doomed.

Going in was comparatively easy. A hot, muggy walk up hills and down hills, through a thick triple canopy of jungle foliage that filtered the sunlight in a thousand subtle shades of green and yellow and gold. They moved, as always, in a disciplined silence, all moving parts on their weapons and gear taped down, all insignia stripped, all identification with the military mechanism that had brought them there excised. They'd smoked Thai cigarettes and eaten rice and *nuoc mam* until their very sweat smelled of the land through which they moved. Their faces and necks were dappled with green and brown streaks of cammo paint; when they moved it was as if no more than a breeze had riffled through the saw grass and bamboo and banyan trees, and when they stood still they seemed to melt into the mother earth altogether.

They hiked for two days. It was hard to tell where Nam

left off and Cambodia began. Not that it really mattered. They humped about sixteen clicks from where the gunships originally deposited them, reconnoitering supply routes for H&I strikes, placing little surprises along the "safe" trails until they weren't quite so safe anymore. . . .

It could have happened any number of times. Like an embolism ready to blow hot blood into all the wrong places, the pressure mounted. At a hundred different places, a hundred times a day, atrocities raged across the land. At a hundred different places the veil wore thin. It was only a matter of time until one gave out.

And at each one, just on the other side, the demons waited.

They knew that it wouldn't stay open long. It never did. The Mother struggled to protect herself, healing the perforations even as they occurred. Closing the holes, shutting them out. Their opportunity, such as it was, lasted only seconds.

But, sometimes, seconds were long enough. . . .

On the afternoon of the second day they reached the hamlet of Phnom Dac. Once there, they rounded everyone up: maybe sixty-seventy people. Men, women, children. Strakker's team was slick, all right. Total pros. He had the Nung team circle around and come in on the north side first; the spotters thought they were NVA. By the time they realized what was up it was too late. Slick.

They found rice, and medicine, and ammo, and weapons. Standing orders were prepare to blow in place. This they did, conscripting the aid of several villagers in piling the ordnance in heaped and bristling pyramids, then wiring it all for command detonation when they'd gotten safely out of range.

Then they came to the problem of the prisoners. Standard mission procedure was to evac civilians to a POW camp, interrogate them till they found out who was doing what, and relocate the rest to a fortified hamlet somewhere in the south. That was what they usually did.

Not here. Not this far over the border, no fucking way. The fate of Phnom Dac seemed cloudy, until Major Strakker stepped in. He made it all crystal-clear. He took one of the ville elders from the huddled mass, held him by the chin and scalp, and very calmly asked him when the next NVA convoy was due in. He got no satisfactory answer, only a stream of appeasing denials. More questions, more denials. Strakker nodded and listened and nodded some more.

Then he snapped the old man's neck, like a dry twig. And he hauled up another.

And another.

And another . . .

The veil stretched. The veil stretched. With each snap of bone and cartilage the opening forced a little wider. Until it was possible to get a little help from the other side.

Until it tore completely . . .

Six dead dinks later, the team got the picture. They questioned a few more. And they lined up the rest. Sixty, seventy people. Men, women.

Children . . .

. . . as the Passage opened, the pipeline between worlds. It was tiny. It took far worse to effect any sort of major opening for more than a microsecond, and this was nothing compared to the gouges left by Dak To or Hill 875, Dien Bien Phu or the Plain of Jars. The horrors here, such as they were, were barely enough to squeeze through. Still, opportunity knocked.

And the demons answered.

Only a few got out, scrambling and clawing through the void, beating each other back in a mad dash for substance. The first through the gap became flame, became smoke, became madness and hate and rage. They tainted the adrenaline-charged moment like a mega-dose of impure speed: amping the panic, poisoning the fury . . .

They shot them. It took five minutes, tops. It was nothing personal.

Walker did his bit like everybody else. The professional in him understood the necessity of it, understood that they were operating in an area where they were officially "deniable," against an enemy that commonly employed women and children as fighters, smoke screens, and sacrifices. They all knew the rap. Every one of them left breathing threatened their odds of getting out of there alive.

But his human side felt it: the schizoid fracture deep within his soul. On the one hand, the urge to waste these fuckers here and now. Every last little slit-eyed zipperheaded one of them.

And totally at odds with that, the glaring sense of *wrongness*. You don't kill civilians. You don't kill *children*. Sixteen years of Catholic schooling had pounded that much into him, and he'd come halfway around the planet to fight the good fight for God and country. He was beginning to realize that he'd become enmeshed in a machine not of his design, one whose purpose evaded him and whose outcome was to transform him into exactly what he'd come here to halt. He stood there with an AR15 smoking in his hands and watched the rounds shimmy and pock into backs, legs, heads. Most of them just laid there and took it.

But one woman—more a girl, actually, but with a babe of her own in her arms—made a run for it. She was near the edge of the woods on Walker's side. She broke through the underbrush and hauled ass down the hill.

Walker shot her, too.

She screamed, a high-pitched shriek, and the baby wailed. But she kept on running. He fired a few more rounds in her direction, slicing through the leaves along her projected trajectory when he couldn't see her anymore. She stumbled, but kept running. The baby kept crying.

And Walker kept firing . . .

Already the gap was closing, healing shut. Of the demons that pried free that moment, only one resisted the impulse to flee, to settle for what could be bought in the immediacy of the moment. It alone remained, one ethereal appendage hooked through the slit between worlds, like some hellish Dutchman with its finger in the dyke. Working the wound. Keeping it open. Gathering strength . . .

The team walked into a clearing less than two clicks out. They'd set fire to the ville and then beaten a guarded retreat back into the jungle, taking a different trail and detonating the munitions when they were safely clear. They couldn't see the fireball through the trees, but they could hear the explosions and feel the ragged staccato tremors as Phnom Dac blew sky-high. Rocks and debris rained down behind them, snapping through the vegetation on its way back to earth. They continued on, keeping a watchful eye for trouble ahead and behind.

But trouble, when it came, came from above.

They were in a valley, little more than a niche between rocky slopes, and had entered a grove of sorts: a hole in the jungle big enough for extraction. They broke squelch and radioed in their position, and then sunk back into the jungle to wait. Walker guarded their rear, scanning the woods for movement. He was tired and uncharacteristically tense. Everyone else seemed to take it in stride, quietly smoking and waiting, and he thought that he should, too.

But nagging, haunting images of the way things went down in the hamlet continued to plague him. As he sat and stared into the undergrowth he kept seeing the bodies twitching on impact, the woman running down the hill, the woman lining up in his sights, the woman screaming . . .

In less than an hour they heard the whine of an approaching chopper. The team lit green smoke. An unmarked, camouflaged UH-1 circled overhead like a big metal dragonfly, then eased itself downward. There were mere minutes left to go when the prop wash bent back the tall grass and revealed the neat rows upon rows of sharpened bamboo stakes.

And only seconds when Walker looked up and noticed a peculiar movement in the trees. Way, way up, in the shadows of green and gold and brown.

Legs. Feet.

He yelled and dove behind an outcropping of rocks. Nobody heard him over the drone of the helicopter's rotor. Nobody turned.

Until the shadows themselves opened fire . . .

. . . *and Walker turned around just in time to see Major James "Bo" Strakker's head vaporize in a cloud of bone and brain less than three yards away; he went down firing, rounds spraying out in a spiraling pivot. Stray nine-millimeter slugs took out two of the Nung team members before they could even blink. The door gunner on the chopper opened up on the treeline in the last seconds before the pi-*

*lot's windshield shattered and the ship spun down to ex-
plode in the field. Walker tried to cover the others, but there
were too many of them; the bullets seemed to be coming
from everywhere. Grenades dropped from the trees like ap-
ples at harvest time, dull metal thuds that threw shrapnel
like molten confetti. Walker screamed as a heaping handful
of it ploughed into the left side of his face and through
the fabric of his Stabo-rig and into the soft skin and hard
muscle of his back, cutting and burning like a sonofabitch
from forehead to beltline. He fired wildly into the trees. The
Huey exploded again as the ordnance caught fire, sending a huge black cloud of smoke and flame into the air . . .*

He blacked out for maybe two minutes. When he came to,
he was blind in one eye and the overall pain was impressive.
He reached up and patted the left side of his face; his hand
came away blood-slicked and full of tiny bits of twisted metal.
The surface of his face was a welted, pulpy mass from cheekbone to forehead; his eye, as near as he could tell, was long
gone. He gradually became aware that he was deaf in his left
ear, too; not even a ringing. Just dead, dead space. Not good.
He fought to control his breathing, to not lose it in the trauma
of crippling disfigurement. Now was not the time. He had to
survive, at all costs. He had to live.

Right then, living meant taking care of business. It took
all his strength just to turn around. When he did, he saw that
two North Vietnamese had lowered themselves from their tree-
top sanctuaries about thirty yards off to his left. They had
knives drawn and were busy inspecting the bodies of his team.
The Australian and a couple of the Nung team were still alive.
They fixed that, quickly and painfully. And they gave the all
clear.

More ropes dropped out of the trees. They formed a
ragged perimeter around the clearing, a perimeter he was on
the barest outer edge of. They didn't yet see him behind his
little stone barrier. He used the fleeting invisibility to his
advantage, pulling open his field dressing pouch, loading an
ampule of morphine, and hitting himself up. Not much, just
enough to take the edge off the pain so he could concentrate.
Yeah, sure.

The morphine hit his already-shocked system like a velvet
sledgehammer, flooding his body and brain with a leeching

euphoria. He took aim and waited. The ropes wiggled as the others descended. He opened up on them when they were about twelve feet off the ground, taking out the two already there and another three on their way. They fell like sacks of wet rags. The rest of them scrambled back up and started capping back at him, pinging little dings out of the other side of his shelter. Walker peeked out. Another one was trying to sneak down. Walker popped him. The sniping redoubled. Stalemate.

Walker started laughing. It was a lovely little situation, all right; he couldn't get out of there, and they couldn't get out of the fucking trees. It was his own little Mexican standoff, deep in the heart of Cambodia.

They remained like that for the next hour and a half. In that time, Walker popped the rest of his morphine and four more snipers. He was dizzy, fucked up, and far from home. Self-cauterization had evidently caused his shrapnel wounds to stop bleeding, which was good. But he had nonetheless lost a lot of blood already, and that was not good at all. It was soon dark, his grip on reality was getting increasingly wonky, and it was only a matter of time before one or more of his tree monkeys successfully escaped from their hidey-holes. Or reinforcements came. Or he ran out of ammo.

Or luck.

The wind shifted, blowing the smoke from the chopper's wreckage his way. The elephant grass had caught fire, too, adding a hempy tinge to the greasy mix of aviation fuel, cordite, melting plastic, and charring flesh. Walker choked, gagging in ragged fits. And as he squinted into the billowing smoke that roiled skyward, he saw it.

A face. No, not even that. Not that whole, not that complete.

Just a smile. Huge, huge; maybe ten feet long. A shadow across the foliage overhead, beaming down on him from above . . .

Hempstead and Jim sat in the woods on the mountain, feeding a small bonfire, the delicately flickering flames making their faces seem otherworldly and ancient, burnished with an amber glow. The melee in Philly was several hours and a hundred miles behind them. It had taken altogether less than sixty minutes to fly back, but the decompression was slow in coming. Technology had moved faster than their emotions. They were in shock. Something majorly fucked was taking place right under their noses, their past beginning to feel as though it were cycling back in on them like the world's worst case of terminal feedback.

They had been sitting in a connected silence for some time, long after the madness had abated for the night. The protesters were gone. The grounds grew still. A three-quarters-empty pint of Jim Beam sat propped in a bootheel-niched swell of pine needle carpet. The pop of kindling and night sounds mingled with the faintly chill breeze rustling through the pine and elm and maple up and down the side of the mountain. It sounded like spirits, whispering in the shadows. Not evil, not good. Just *there*; an intrinsic part of the fabric of night. Watching. Waiting. Listening.

It was a perfect time for the telling of ghost stories.

Which, in a way, was exactly what they were thinking.

Hempstead snapped another twig or three and threw them in, biding time, chewing over the memory like an old dog on an old bone. When he closed his eyes he saw it hovering, glistening in the moonlight, before him.

A forgotten piece from a twenty-year-old puzzle, sliding suddenly into place . . .

Walker squinted up at the beaming shadow splayed across the canopy. Lying in the dirt and leaves, staring one-eyed up at it and with zero depth perception, it was comforting to consider it all the spectacular hallucinations of a dying man. The sun was starting to set, firing long waning rays through the smoke and the trees. The smile grew crooked, almost sardonic. It glitched back and forth in his mind's eye. Now it was a smile. Now, just a branch, just a long shadow in dying light. Now, a smile. A shadow. A branch.

He would have been more than happy to pawn it off as either of the latter. It was possible, even probable.

Until the lips parted.

And spoke to him . . .

"Walker." The voice in his head whispered his name flatly yet intimately, as though speaking itself were new, yet he was an old friend. It didn't even register as sound so much as the tactile sensation of otherness in his mind. The voice was an

alien presence that formed words that burned like white phosphorus in the deep folds within his skull. He was reasonably sure that if he could feel anything at all, he'd be terrified. At the moment, that was the best luck could offer him.

"Wahl-kerr . . ." creakingly langorous this time. He saw the smile distend, like the stretching of old rubber bands. He stared at it, watching the long shafts of light that spilled out when the shadow-lips parted. It moved like the crudely animated images in a flip book: there, not there, there, not there. Flick flick flick flick. It was mesmerizing.

"You're dying." It smiled reassuringly. He heard a snap to his right, turned and pumped two bullets into another sniper who was trying to flank him. A baker's dozen answered back, chipping huge divots out of his sanctuary. They were gradually whittling it down, yessir. Arts and crafts with automatic weapons, yup yup yup . . .

He could hear them calling to each other, could feel the dull moist thud of metal in his back every time he moved. More were certainly on the way by now. Twilight was fast approaching; the forest was filled with the myriad sounds of the food chain in motion. Chirping, creeping, crawling. Beckoning him to join them. The morphine-induced mercy was hinting of its inevitable fade. To agony.

To death.

"I can help you." It purred, a low-pitched rumbling that filled the space between his eye and brain.

Walker grinned, tasting blood. "Fuck you," he said.

"We can help each other."

"I don't need your help." He laughed weakly, coughing up a bubbly red froth.

"Check your ammo."

He felt for his ammo pouch. Empty. Shit. The last clip was already in, already half gone. Time flies. He had a survival knife and a couple of frags and that was that. Maybe two to throw and one to hold. Funny, he hadn't figured on such an ignominious end. Oh, well.

Walker looked up. It had changed shape, it wasn't quite a smile anymore. It looked tense, fretful. The shadows were lengthening; it was getting harder to discern in the gloom. The night sounds seemed louder. "I don't need you," he repeated, but it somehow lacked the defiant conviction of a moment earlier.

"Oh, yes, you do," it whispered. *"Just as I need you."*

A pause. A tremor of pain. Finally, "What do you want from me?"

The smile broadened. *"Everything."*

. . . and it touched him, ethereal fingers sliding in to linger in his mind and eye and heart. Revulsion passed through him in spasms, his body shaking, his throat dry and raw. He saw the rupture from whence it came, heard a tremendous buzzing in his ears, saw the enormity of its intent in a vast, lurid gestalt of grotesque ambition . . .

Walker reeled from the seizure, looked up again. The smile was assured, more defined. "What the fuck's going on here?" he mumbled.

. . . and the grip tightened, became a fist around his heart. He felt his spirit wrenched from its mooring, yanked upward into the trees. He could see his body back on the ground, wedged in its crumbling niche of stone. It didn't look long for this world. He felt no pain, though, felt utterly detached from the goings-on below. His consciousness hovered, disembodied, before the giant grinning lips.

"Your dying is what's going on," the demon said, *"and there's not much time. Do you want to die?"*

"Not particularly." His defiance rallied.

"Then serve me."

"Yeah, right." And slipped.

"I'm serious."

"You're a hallucination." And faltered.

"Not if you believe in me."

Walker blacked out again. He came to, weak and in pain and on the ground. The food chain was feeding. The blood was congealing in the heat, sticking to his face and side and back. The snipers were still sniping. Even if they didn't get him, the flies and the worms very shortly would. Thoughts of new life in his ruined socket flooded his mind; the images were increasingly hard to fight off. God seemed very far away, indeed, and he sure as shit didn't believe in spooks. What he did believe in, though, was survival. At any cost.

"OK, fucker," he said to the shadows in the trees. "You got yourself a deal."

"Then prove it."

"How?"

"*Simple: surrender to me.*"

Easy enough; it was an effort to even keep talking. Walker grunted and went limp, slumping into the earth.

And the demon did the rest.

It was like letting someone else slam down on the gas pedal and steer when you were strapped in the driver's seat: his right arm jerked suddenly, fingers clutching toward the left shoulder strap of his Stabo-rig. Grasping the handle of the blade and pulling it free. Six inches of razor-edged steel slid down and out into the hand, which moved of its own accord now, waving the blade in front of his face like a snake ready to strike. He stared helpless as the left hand came up and splayed, fingers stretching till the thin skin webbing between them seemed likely to split. The two limbs wavered there momentarily, a ritual puppet-dance before his solitary bugging eye.

And then they jerked even further, hauling him into an agonizingly upright position. More shots fired from the trees, pinging all around him. His left hand slapped down and clutched at the rock. The right hand hovered over it, quivering. Walker heard the scream welling up deep inside him, rumbling out from the pit of his soul like a runaway freight train. Out of the corner of his eye he saw a belch of smoke that marked the bullet with his name on it . . .

. . . and the knife came down . . .

. . . and time stopped dead in its tracks. There was a sharp thwop! as the blade severed the first joint of the third finger of the left hand.

The scream died.

The shooting stopped.

The bullet with his name on it fell out of the air an inch from his face as if slapped by an invisible fist. The jungle went utterly still.

And Walker trembled, watching the blood.

It flowed, in thick runnels, down the trunks of the trees. It dropped from unseen sources. Branches snapped as things fell thudding to the ground. First, the rifles, the grenades. Then the hands that held them. Then the arms. Then more, and more: jumbled pieces, unidentifiably mangled. Walker watched, incapacitated, as the grisly rain fell. And fell. And fell.

Warm gouts spurted out of the hole where his finger had been. Control of his body was returned to him; he fell over immediately, crawled right back up. The finger lay right where he'd left it. The demon chuckled as he stared aghast, chuckled again as he picked it up.

And then it said with great relish and solemn dignity, *"Take this."*

It chuckled some more.

"And eat it . . ."

Walker crushed the butt of the Lucky into the ashtray. Momma was humming, over and over, the refrain from Carly Simon's "Anticipation."

"You're so perverse," he muttered.

Momma cackled. *"I understand they even made that one a catsup commercial. How apropos."*

Walker shuddered. The memories were an endless repetition of freak show images: the severed finger, pressed to his lips. The bloody flesh, falling chunk-style. The food chain, resuming its twilight call.

And in the distance, the cry of a child.

He found her. The demon directed him, and he found her. A half click away, nestled in her dead mother's arms. Screaming.

It was the babe from the ville. Walker's aim had apparently been close enough for rock 'n' roll: he'd wounded the girl, she'd fled this far back into the jungle, she'd hidden, and she'd died.

Leaving behind her legacy, such as it was, on the jungle floor. Hurt, by his hand. Crying, in his arms.

He carried her back to the clearing, shambling like a zombie, sobbing shamelessly, stray bits of metal falling out of his back and neck. It was full twilight by the time he found the team's radio. It was in perfect working order, which was more than he could say for the radioman. He broke squelch and sent a distress call. No one answered. He was about to do it again when the voice came like smoking neon letters in his head.

"Relax. It's taken care of. Help is on the way."

"Oh, really?" He was trying desperately to affect an air of blithe indifference. It was useless. He'd opened the door for a moment.

And now he had company.

In his arms the baby made a rasping, wheezy, sick-child noise. Walker looked at its face, distinctive even in the gloom.

Almond eyes in a European face; a little half-breed, the bastard by-product of strangers in a strange land. Tiny little legs wriggled tiny little toes, tiny little arms clawed weakly. With all nine tiny little fingers.

In his head, that dust-dry laugh.

"WHO ARE YOU?!" he screamed, falling to his knees.

"My name is legion.

"But you can call me Momma."

Walker howled, laughter mixing with the tears until he couldn't be sure where the one left off and the other began. Not that it much mattered. Eventually he looked at the waif in his arms again. She was feverish, trembling. *"And who the hell are you?"* he croaked.

The sky smile opened wide. And the voice told him, immensely pleased . . .

The fire was burning brightly when Cody came upon them. He had a bag of prime smoke that he'd saved for a special occasion, and though this wasn't what he'd hoped for, he figured it qualified.

Cody sat down, lit up, and passed a joint over to Slim Jim, who grunted thanks and sucked in a man-sized lungful of sweet, musky smoke. He held it in and stared at Cody as if seeing him for the first time.

"Tell me sumthin'," he said upon exhaling, voice slurring only slightly. "What d'jou do during the war?"

"Which one?" Cody asked.

"Fuck you. You know which. Where d'jou go? College? Canada?"

"College, some. Jail, mostly."

Slim Jim snorted. "Jail, huh? What, d'ja get popped dealin' or sumthin'?"

"Got caught standing up for my lofty principles."

"Hmmph." Jim belched and took a parting hit off the joint, washed it back with the pint. "Me an' him did our bit, fightin' for the damned country."

"Yeah, that's the funny thing." Cody exhaled a fat cloud of smoke. "That's what I always figured I was doing, too."

"Hrrmmmph." Jim was reasonably blasted at this point; it lent a well-lubricated verbosity to his feelings. "So what'd we get for it, all our duty and honor and patriotic fucking freedom-fighting?" he said, more to himself than anyone else. "*Screwed*, is what." He looked back to Cody with a mixture of braggadocio and remorse, as if explaining the fundamentals of fine wine to a connoisseur of the screw-top set.

"We were supposed to be the good guys. We were real good at what we did, I'll say that much. We were trained to go in there and clean up. We *believed* that we were going to go in there and clean up. And we had the goods to do it, too." His eyes flashed with the fires of rekindled memory.

"But by and by, we found out that that's not what we were really there for. Uh-unh. I don't think anybody even fuckin' knows the *real* reason—one that Nixon or Ho Chi Minh or Dow or the Rand Corporation or God Himself would ever even cop to. Do *you* know?!"

Cody shook his head. Slim Jim leaned closer like a great bearded Buddha, smelling of dope and sour mash and Marlboros. "Neither do I," he said.

"But I'll tell you what I think. I think that we were there to raise Hell. Literally. Raise. Hell. Inch by inch. Every day was like a fuckin' Judgment Day back then. Can you imagine that? I mean, *really* imagine it??"

Cody shook his head some more. Slim Jim *harrumphed* triumphantly. "Course not," he muttered, " 'cause you weren't there. But it's the truth. You get past all the moralistic poly-sci *crap* and that's all war is." He sucked back the rest of the pint and laid the bottle in the flames. "It's a chance to make hell on earth. We take everything dark and wormy inside us and turn it loose like wild dogs on a long chain. And we always figure that the chain will hold, that it'll keep the hounds at bay . . ." He trailed off then, as if lost on the track of his own thoughts.

"You can send a man through hell, you know, and he'll go singin' all the way," he continued almost brightly, switching tracks. "*If* you give him good enough reasons. Somethin' worth killing for, say, or dying for. Charlie had 'em, sure enough."

"And we didn't." Cody said. The fire popped.

"Bullshit!" Slim Jim spat. "College boy. *Hmmph*. We had *plenty*.

"But in the long run," he amended, "Charlie's were better. And it don't have nothin' to do with capitalism or communism or any of that horseshit. It runs a lot deeper than that. It's personal."

Hempstead didn't say anything, but he was nodding his head. Jim was on a roll now, the mix of alcohol, tetrahydrocannabinol, and leftover adrenaline acting like a verbal diuretic. "Hell, I guess everybody's experience of it is different, but after a while I just gave up on trying to figure it out and settled for just trying to keep my ass and my crew in one piece. I wasn't fighting to *build* anything anymore. But Charlie was. Charlie still believed.

"Shit, in the end Charlie beat me by out*believing* me."

"So why'd you stay?" Cody asked.

"Try and leave." He laughed. It was the laugh of the righteous lunatic: sharp and hoarse and fast. "You get caught up in a machine like that and you find out real quick that it's got a mind all its own, and you're just along for the ride. And if you've got to do all kinds of terrible things, and there don't seem to be any *reason* for doing 'em, other than to survive and avenge and survive and avenge and survive . . ."

Cody shivered as a breeze stirred through the trees. He tried to teleport the tactile sensations of night and fire and spirit-wind to the other side of the planet, tried to envision the kind of danger that would make you forgo even a small blaze such as this for fear of attracting a midnight mortar round. The whole thing was slopping over the boundaries of drunken, spooky campfire chat. It was starting to get under his skin.

". . . well, you just do it. And you learn not to let it fuck you up too bad; you learn not to *feel* it. But then the very act of *not* feeling it is what does the worst damage of all. It torques out your *soul*, man, and it just makes the whole situation more conducive, somehow . . ."

"More conducive to *what*?"

"I dunno, exactly." Jim sighed as if his entire reality map had caved in on him. "But I swear to God one time we came to within spittin' distance of it. Something dark, moving through the world. Something evil. Like a scout, a fucking Lurp from Hell. You know what I'm talking 'bout?"

Cody realized that the remark wasn't aimed at him; he turned toward Hempstead, expecting a blast of reason to counter Slim Jim's dark mythos.

But Hempstead only stared into the fire; and when he finally spoke a good thirty seconds later, it was as from a distance of years and miles and shadows past. "Yeah, bro'. I know." Then he looked at Cody, and the floodgates cracked just a hair, and the words came out. He spoke them like a man single-handedly wielding a runaway firehose: tight, barely contained clips. It was as if there were no way he was going to let the feelings wash over his reason, and yet there was no way around it. Finally, he shrugged.

"Jimbo and I flew together in the Nam, you know, and we mostly operated out of III Corps, in the Highlands 'long the Cambodian border. One time—we was just heading home off a recon—we get this weird priority distress call, far enough over the line to make you wonder who the fuck was out there, you know?

"Anyway, long story short, we reach the snatch point right near sunset, which is a very nervous-making time to be in the air going anyplace but *home*, and we spot the smoke coming up. All yellow and black, which is not good—the yellow means trouble for sure, and the black meant somebody else found out the hard way. Sure 'nuff, when we get overhead we can't even fuckin' land, 'cause there's one bird already downed in the clearing.

"And bodies. Lots of bodies."

Hempstead spoke in low, low tones, staring into the flames like a gypsy reading tea leaves. "There was only one survivor, and he was fucked up, holding on to something that looked a lot like a baby. We figured we'd hook him and hoist him in on the way, so we lowered a cable and D-ringed him the hell up 'n' out of there.

"We get him up, no sweat. Weird thing is, he had to hand off the child to me before he could get in. I took it." Hempstead nodded. "I held that thing in my arms, man, and I tell you true, when I touched it, it was dead. Stone-*dead*.

"But when this mystery man gets in and sees it, he freaks out. He's been wounded, right, his face is all fucked up and his back's all fucked up and his one hand is bandaged, and he won't let me check him out. He just grabs the kid and starts babblin' shit—not incoherent, more like he's talkin' to someone, havin' a two-way conversation all by hisself. He's leaning against the bulkhead, holding this dead child, and he's off in his own little world, going, 'What do you want from me? What do you fucking *want*??'

"Then he gets this look on his face . . . I can't even

describe it. Deranged, maybe, but *willful*. Dinky-dao. Head cocked, like a dog does when you talk to it.

"And next thing I know, he's ripping the bandage off his hand, and his ring finger's gone, and he's holding the stump up to the kid's lips. Only it's not bleeding anymore, and he gets really agitated, and he whacks his fucking hand on the bulkhead, sayin' 'C'mon! C'mon!!' and goin' *whap! whap!* until it starts bleeding again."

Hempstead broke another stick and shoved it into the fire. "And then he touched the blood to the baby's lips. And it lay there for a minute, and he mumbled some shit. And then it coughed, and it started to cry.

"An' he suckled it."

The three sat in silence, listening to the fire and the woods and the wind. Cody didn't know what to say, was afraid to say anything for fear it would sound stupid. He finally gurgled something to the effect of, "Maybe it wasn't really dead . . ."

Hempstead shook it off. "No way. I shit you not—I've seen dead, and I've *made* dead. I know the symptoms."

Slim Jim nodded. Cody shivered. A gust blew across the fire, sending sparks up into the night sky. "He looked at me then, with that one fuckin' eye, and for a second we had an eyeball war at six thousand feet. Then he went back to his mumbling. And I'll tell you somethin' else," Hempstead offered. Cody wasn't sure he wanted to hear.

"We got back to base, and that motherfucker disappeared, kid and all. That was twenty years ago, give or take a day. And I never seen him again.

"Until tonight. He was on that stage, at the concert."

Jim looked at him, eyes akimbo. "You didn't fuckin' tell me that!" he blurted. "Who? Where? What the hell was he doing there?!"

"He's The Scream's manager."

"He's *what*?!!"

"You heard me. I'll never forget that face. And that makes a whole lot of things make more sense, and a few things a whole lot less.

" 'Cause all the way back, he squatted there, rockin' and mumblin' the same damned word over and over again. It didn't make no sense at the time.

"But, I swear to God, that word was '*tara*'. . .

An empty Lucky Strike pack was burning in the ashtray, caught from a stray ember off his last butt. Momma was silent. Walker watched it curl and flame, unchecked. He didn't care. In fact, he cared less and less about much of anything, the closer they got. It would be so easy to toss in a disposable lighter, wait for it to blow and catch the desk like a miniature napalm strike. The desk would go. The drapes would go. Then the rug, and the chairs, and the thick wooden ceiling beams and the oiled oak paneling, and maybe he could pull the whole miserable house down on top of this bullshit operation, maybe . . .

The puny blaze guttered as a waft of breeze from the opening door blew in. Momma snickered. Walker didn't look up. He already knew who it was, and he could damned well guess what he wanted.

And Walker found some small comfort in the fact that he'd soon be able to give it to him.

Twenty-three

Walker was in there, behind his fatass desk. Conversing with himself, as usual. Rod rap-a-tapped snidely on the opening door as he strode inside, then slammed it behind him.

"I wanna have a talk with you, mister. Right now."

"Okay." Walker swiveled his chair around to face the doorway. His own expression was weary but otherwise inscrutable. "So talk."

"*So talk*," Rod sneered in contemptuous mimicry. "Man,

you are smooth as baby shit, aren'tcha? Too cool for words. How am I supposed to trust a man who talks like that?"

"Let's rearrange the question a little, boy." Walker gave the last word subtle emphasis. "How much choice do you think you have? How many alternatives? Answer me that."

Rod stopped at the front of the desk and thought a moment. He felt much better after his sojourn in the bordello, as always . . . confident, masterful, strong . . . but there was something about Walker that always brought him up short. He hated to think that Walker was simply more powerful. That was too much like concession.

"I just need to know where it's going," Rod began. "I need to know what you have in mind here over the long haul. I mean, all the long-foretold changes are happening hand over fist now: the tour is over; Momma's comin' in on Monday night; this whole phase of The Scream is almost over. Correct me if I'm wrong, but this is right so far. Right?"

"Right. On every count."

"Now you always said that we should take it as it comes, you wouldn't know the future until it got here. And I always believed you," Rod lied. "But now we're standing at the goddamn threshold, and I still don't know where it is.

"If *you* know, I wish you would explain it to *me*.

"I'm getting impatient.

"And the stakes are getting high."

Walker lit a cigarette and dragged on it slowly. From anyone else, Rod included, it would have seemed like an attempt to buy time. But Walker was too fucking cool. He was *stretching* it, to magnify the discomfort of the moment.

"So what do you want to know, exactly?" Walker said.

"Where I stand. Exactly."

Walker dragged again, let a thick plume waft. He seemed to think about it, but Rod wasn't fooled; he knew precisely where everything stood.

"You've already been promised a kingdom," Walker said at last. "The promise still stands. You've seen enough of Momma's power to know that she's good for her word.

"At the same time, everything that's happening here couldn't be done without you, boy. You know that. *She* knows that. And she's not very likely to forget it."

"But once she's here," Rod countered, "what's to stop

her from fucking us *both* over? Have you thought about that?"

Walker smiled grimly. "What's the point? She's still going to need us. It's a big world, and she can't be everywhere at once." He took another drag, blew it out. "You've got to understand. This is the physical world, and all the physical rules apply. Once she gets here, she's just a bigger and better version of us. You know what that means?"

"She can be hurt."

"She can be *killed*." Again: the smoke as emphasis. "You think she came all this way just to die in a second? Think again. She needs warm bodies. She needs us to prime the audience, she needs us to pave the way and guard it. We get them to believe in her until *she* can do that for herself. And then she's here, and it's a whole new ball game.

"Now, you have been loyal to her so far, and it's been to your advantage. It will *remain* to your advantage if you don't piss around and ask too many stupid questions."

A smart-ass response leaped to Rod's lips. He bit it off and swallowed it. There was truth in Walker's words, God damn it. There always was. How much truth and how much bullshit, Rod was in no position to say.

Then again, he was in no position to say a lot of things. As Walker pointed out, *How much choice do you think you have?* He was in over the barrel on this thing, and not just contractually. Walker owned the band, on paper.

But Momma owned them all.

"What about my brother?"

Walker's deadpan gained a sudden, serious edge. "We'll get him through this. We have to. Momma can't make it without him."

"Yeah, that's fine. But what happens to him after she's out?"

"I don't know. I can't promise you anything, because there are no guarantees. *My* feeling is that, after Monday night, the worst will be over . . . but shit, I really don't know."

"Well, that's great, isn't it? That really puts the whole thing in perspective—"

"Let's get something *straight*, boy!" Walker roared, abruptly standing. Rod took an involuntary step back; up close and angry, Walker had that effect on people. "You know as well as I do that you don't give a damn about your brother. *You* sold him down the river on this deal, not me. If you didn't know for a fact that you'd be nowhere without him, we wouldn't even be *having* this conversation."

"Fuck you."

"Fuck yourself, punk. In fact, don't bother. I think you already have."

Rod felt the hot spark of that one, violently igniting off the cold flint of his heart. His whole being began to coarse with sickening heat, seeping out from the core and down into his extremities. "Wha . . ." he tremulously began, then whipped up the courage to continue. "What the hell do you mean by that?"

"I'll tell you what I mean." In that instant Walker vaulted over the length of the desk and came to rest within an inch of where Rod stood. Rod tried to hustle backward, but he needn't have bothered. Walker grabbed him by the throat and *forced* him back, slamming him into the door and holding him there.

"I mean that you've overstepped your boundaries, little man. You have pushed me just about as far as I care to let you. We put up with your little power trips. We stock your little torture chamber. We cover your ass every step of the way.

"But you're in the *big* leagues now, dipshit, and there's more at stake here than whether you're happy or not." Walker slammed Rod's head into the door for emphasis. "You step on Momma's toes . . . or God help you, you step on mine . . . and there's not a thing in the universe can help you. You understand me?"

Rod, in panic, tried to nod. With Walker's hands around his throat it didn't work too well. And no words were forthcoming.

"We *made* you big time, you little ass-licker. And we'll keep you that way so long as there's any point to it. You just play your cards right, and you will have all the power you can handle. *Just do your job,* and you'll be fine.

"But I'm telling you right now, and I'm not gonna tell you again: you fuck up, you cause trouble, you play *one wrong note* between now and the time that Momma arrives, and I will personally snap your miserable neck.

"Have I made a lingering and crystal-clear impression on you, boy?"

Again, Rod attempted a nod. This time, Walker let it come through.

"Well, good." Walker patted Rod lightly on the cheek.

"And since we've come to such a sweet understanding, there's something I'd like to tell you that might lighten your spirits somewhat. Would you like to hear some good news?"

Walker let go and Rod nodded again, completely unimpeded.

"The odds are highly in your favor that Tara won't survive Monday night. If all goes well, and you behave yourself, you can have your band back. Pick your own lead singer. I'll just manage the business, and you'll be bigger than ever. Does that sound good?"

Rod had to agree that it did.

In fact, it was almost enough to bring back his sunshiney smile.

od was full of shit. That was Tara's considered opinion, though she kept it to herself. The few times that it did leak out were in the aftermath of outbursts like the one still raging downstairs. It was then that her eyes betrayed her, narrowing to almond-shaped slits of contempt; and even so, the emotion flashed and faded so quickly that no one in the entourage even picked up on it.

No one but Walker, that is. Walker picked up on everything. He knew, as she did, that Rod Royale's dime store De Sade imitation would buy him little more than a stick to twirl on in the end. He knew, as she did, that Rod Royale was full of shit. She could see it, in the windows to his soul.

Just as he could see, in hers, that she was full of something else.

Soon, now. Very soon.

Downstairs, pandemonium reigned. Rod was babbling, Walker responding in curt, low tones. Alex was upstairs, still out to lunch. Tara wasn't terribly concerned; at the moment she had far more pressing things to think about. She would deal with Alex herself, if it came to that.

She made her way up the winding stairs silently and stepped through the door to her suite, loosening the leather waistlet and letting the heavy dagger drop to the floor. The release of pressure from around her waist was a relief; she was lately beginning to feel very sensitive, the skin of her breasts and belly and lower back tingling in a way that was partly pleasure, mostly pain. It was a sign, unmistakably. Every fiber of her being affirmed it.

Soon.

She was fully in the room now, the scent of incense wafting up to her nostrils. A thickly pleasant smell, rich and pungent. It hung heavy in the air, soothing her.

And masking, very nicely, the taint of Passage.

The chamber was dark, lit only by the dimmest red glow of recessed lighting. It could be raised to a more workable level later, but for now it was best left low. After all, ambience was the critical ingredient, yes?

Yes, indeed. She parted the drapes that surrounded her bed and stood framed by the folds of fabric, staring into the pitch-black slit. Staring and listening.

A low moan, more a gurgling, came from within. Tara smiled, teeth white in the shadow of her face.

"Shhhh," she whispered. "Be still."

She shook her hair back, stretching the tight ligaments in her neck, and then crawled delicately and decisively onto the bed. Feeling the taut strands of hemp that bound the limbs securely to the bedposts. Feeling the limbs themselves, quivering against her touch like beads of mercury on a plate. Tracing them back to their juncture: torso, chill and heaving. Tight, weakly straining neck. Face, features, twisted in fractured comprehension of what lay ahead.

"Ooh, yes," she cooed, "gonna be my baby tonight." Tara stroked his sweat-streaked hair lovingly, fascinated by the degree of will left to this one. He'd survived the transport. It was another sign: outward affirmation of what her inner self hoped to be true. At last, she had what she needed to fulfill her end of the promise.

Another moan: this one louder, more intense. He was a

bit more unstable than she'd been led to believe; it appeared as though he still wasn't taking to the changes very well. She touched the squirming face, felt the tears tracking down each cheek. Poor baby. It all seemed so awful now, she knew. But that would pass in time, this Passage. He was Chosen. She told him that. He cried like a babe in the wilderness, not even words, just a wash of rage and anguish and despair. She understood. She cooed and stroked his hair.

And then she straddled him.

He protested weakly and to no avail. It was four A.M., after all.

Feeding time.

Twenty-five

At four twenty-three A.M. the videotape played through. The VCR, a top-of-the-line model with all the latest features, automatically zeroed off the tape and shut itself down. It left the TV—a lower-grade companion far less inclined toward such articulate self-maintenance—quietly hissing to its audience of one. There were no secret messages in that low white noise; no cryptic encodations, no masked voices. None were necessary.

He brought along his own. He carried them always.

Buried. Deep inside.

Inside, there was blackness welling up like a pool in a clogged culvert. There was the gradual slump as exhaustion and gravity pulled him deeper into the folds of the chair. Every circuit breaker in Jake's body was shutting down, a billion frazzled nerve endings sputtering and winking into darkness.

And then, in a ragged alpha state just prior to descent into REM stage, there was the balancing act: teeter-tottering on the outermost edge of consciousness that marked his entrance to the third dream. The fight to resist it was brief and futile. In his mind he turned: screaming, scrabbling through the billowing shroud of oblivion, back towards the land of the living. In his mind, he fought: until his strength, what little remained, gave out entirely.

And he fell, screaming.

And he fell . . .

Clutching, arms flailing, he pitched downwards into the land of the lost. He landed shoulders-first with a bone-shattering crunch. The bones weren't his; rather, they belonged to the thing upon which he fell.

It was a corpse, and an old one at that, all the juice long gone, the shell dried out and hollow as husks of Indian corn. Jake fell right in its lap. It crumpled on impact, shattering into a thousand brittle fragments; the head tipped forward, wrenched off its spinal perch, and hung suspended by a few strands of ancient neck-leather inches above his face. Its lower jaw distended in a cavernous rictus, the fleshy interior long since dried up or eaten away. Its eyes were likewise missing. But its spectacles remained; big thick lenses, cracked and bent and blasted. X-ray specs.

A spark went off behind them in the twin blackened pits. And the skull tilted toward him further as if in dimmest recognition. As it bent forward, the name tag on its musty fatigues shone black in neon uppercase stencil:

DUNCAN.

"NOOOOOO!" Jake twisted away, scuttling backwards and further into the tomb. The others were there, too: Natch and Sanchez and Claiborne and Willie from Philly and Top Six and on, all lined up against the narrow clay walls like ducks in a shooting gallery. They stirred as he crawled past, the same animate spark burning in the ruined sockets, withered arms rustling as they reached for his head, his back, his legs. Decades-old fingers snapped like kindling as they clawed at him, hissing through gaping mouths . . .

Jake's face screwed up like a raisin under a blowtorch as the weight of the dreamscape settled upon them. *"This never happened!"* his mind howled. *"I never found you! I NEVER FUCKING FOUND YOU!!"*

He fully expected to wake up now. It was the break point: the moment of traumatic frisson that always sent him hurtling back. Semideranged, rocketing out of bed or Barcalounger, he'd wreak havoc on the waking world until the last shreds of guilt and terror evaporated. The nightmare was a recurrent pattern, a three-stage, scar-tissue-tape loop that had become his unconscious harbinger of doom. His conscious self had come to expect as much.

This time was all that, and more. This time, he couldn't get out. This time, the dream wouldn't let go . . .

. . . *and there were more: dozens more, hundreds more in the depths. Not just his squad, but Vasquez and the brown-bar, the child and others. People he had never seen: Asian and American, VC and GI, whole and in parts. All dead. All reanimated. Lining the winding walls, staring blindly through ghost-ember eyeholes, raising dead-branch hands to point and pull and grab. A limbless torso thrust up before him, rusted dog tags still hanging from its mangled neck. He plowed right through it, feeling it come apart like punky, worm-eaten wood . . .*

. . . and Jake writhed in the chair, moaning audibly, unable to break free . . .

. . . *as he slid down and down, the floor of the tunnel gone slick with viscous clotted sludge, the air choked with a hot, charnel stench. He screwed shut his eyes, he screamed and retched and screamed some more, breathing in death and spoilage and despair. And he slid, onward and downward into the esophageal blackness, the walls themselves closing in to grip and push and propel him forth, until he spilled out into a vast, cavernous space.*

It was an arena of some sort: immense, circular, horribly alien, dreadfully familiar. The walls rose up in countless tiers like Gigeresque reptilian ribs; the floor was packed to capacity with the swarming, milling damned. Five stone pillars rose up across the expanse like fingers on an enormous hand, like the points of a star.

And at the far end, squarely between the bottommost pillars, was the stage. Long, black luminescent drapes obscured it from view. The damned clustered toward it in rapt anticipation, hovering on every movement or rustle, mouths hanging open like dogs in high summer. Jake was mesmerized by the throngs, the sea of lost humanity sweeping him closer and closer to the object of his transfixion.

The long black slit in the folds of drape parted, swelled, rippled back from the stage in waves to reveal the man crucified upon it: naked, sweating limbs contorting in agony, broken wires trailing from the electrodes pasted to his shaven skull. Jake noted with horror that he sported a furious hardon. The crowd absorbed every minutae of his grotesque convolutions, feeding on the pain and anguish . . .

. . . and Jake was transported up onto the stage, alternately staring out at the Cheshire cat grin that now floated lazily above the crowd and down at the wretched form squirming away from his touch. He leaned closer, reaching down to help him . . .

. . . and the man's head cocked up, like a crippled animal sensing danger. He was little more than a vandalized semblance of humanity: his eyes gouged out, his features twisted with pain and disfigurement, his body wasted.

But he was recognizable. Dimly, marginally apparent.

And as Jake felt the shock of cognizance, he also felt the sound welling up inside him: more primal scream than any attempt at communication. He felt it like the high-pitched whine of a turbine overloading, hot as the juncture of critical mass before the mushroom cloud, as the thing that was once Pete opened its mouth in a ghastly rasping counterpoint . . .

"NOOOOOOOO!!!"

. . . as the explosions blew the arena to smoking jelly . . .

. . . and the hellish grin opened wide.

And descended upon them all.

Twenty-six

"**G**od damn it," Rachel spat. She had awakened like a shot to the moaning from below. "*God damn it.*" Somewhere between a hiss and a whimper.

Rachel rolled over. Her eyes trailed across the empty side of the bed and rose up to meet the moon: a pale crescent, disappearing over the Caledonia hills. The clock on the dresser said 4:37.

She cursed the empty side of the bed, her own terror. Jake moaned again, more desperate this time. It was getting worse. She could picture him, sprawled in the reclining chair, the blue light highlighting his features as he writhed at the pictures that crawled through his mind.

When the dreams came back, they were always bad, always in threes. Like the sirens of Greek mythology, luring him onto the rocks.

Rachel Adams slid out from between the sheets, padded softly and quickly toward the door. Her bowels felt icy. She brought her fingertips to her forehead and wiped away a thin coat of sweat that hadn't been there mere moments before.

I don't want to be afraid of you, Jake, her mind said. It was honest enough, but it didn't change squat. The third dream was always the dangerous one, the one where whatever tormented him turned outward with a vengeance. Sometimes, it could be abated; sometimes, only endured. It had put chairs through windows and fists through walls. Once, it put him in Bellevue for observation.

Once, it put her in the emergency room of St. Vincent's.

The scars, more than three years old, were still there; the back of her skull pulsed with phantom pain, remembering damage long healed-over and gone. When he moaned again, it was like fingernails dragging along her spine.

And that, of course, was when the baby stirred.

"*Oh, shit,*" she whispered. If the rest of the household wasn't awake yet, it was only a matter of seconds. Natalie had a set of lungs that could unlace your shoes at thirty yards and a hair-trigger alarm system to match.

Jake moaned again, and that made it final.

The well-oiled hinges on the door creaked anyway as she stepped beyond them and into the hall. In Ted's room, sheets were rustling. After all he'd been through, the last thing he needed was a psychotic episode. She would do what she could to spare him that.

At the head of the stairs was a stained glass window she'd designed, constructed, and installed. It was an unsubtle variation on the ol' yin/yang: demon-face as the black dot on the white half, angel-face as the white dot on the black. The moonlight brought the point across, reflected it on the hard-wood floor at the end of the hall. She moved toward and through the icon-light.

Then headed down the stairs.

The next time he moaned, she could see him. Her imagination had been only slightly off. He was, sure as hell, in the battered black recliner. The TV was on, the VCR was off, the dull hiss filled the room with informational emptiness. He was nearly naked in the chair. His face was contorted in plain agony.

There would be no more moaning; that phase had passed. It would be on to full-fledged screaming or violence.

Unless she stopped him in time.

Rachel's gaze flickered down at the scars again. Automatic. *Do you need to be reminded?* her mind asked herself. He had bruised and broken and ripped her up unconsciously, using only his blind, bare hands. There had not been a weapon within arm's reach. She hoped that there wasn't one now.

Rachel finished with the stairs, made her way toward the kitchen. Upstairs a door creaked open. He didn't stir at the sound of it. Good. The thought of getting caught within three feet of him was terrifying.

She slipped rapidly past him and into the kitchen. Like their bedroom, it was brightly moonlit. The towel and pitcher were next to the sink, where she'd left them last night. She turned the cold water on full, let it thunder against the aluminum basin for a moment, then proceeded to fill the pitcher. The noise would help him ease out of the nightmare; the water would finish the job.

She hoped.

He was halfway into a scream when Rachel reentered the living room, halted a full six feet back, and let fly. A quart of ice-cold soaring water sent an electroshock spasm through his body as it hit. He jumped, eyes snapping open, seeing nothing. His hand reached out automatically, with chilling precision, for the hilt of a nonexistent knife.

He sucked in a huge wheezing breath, eyes flicking over at his empty hand, then back. This time, there was no question that his half-crazed gaze was aimed at her. She backed away, trying to take the murderous terror and panic and rage of his expression in stride. It didn't work. It never did. When Jacob awoke from his dreams, it could be the scariest thing that Rachel had ever seen.

Then his eyes cleared, and his expression softened, and he crumpled into himself. The leap from nightmare to Naugahyde had been broached, again. She stood firmly before him, skewered by his sight.

As the nightmare memory slipped tenuously behind.

"Shit," he said throatily, wiping water from his eyes. His body glistened in the blue light.

"I know." Her throat was clogged, too.

"I'm sorry."

"It's okay."

"No, it's not." He looked up at her, his gaze appearing merely disturbed. It was a big step back from crazy. It would have to do.

Rachel stepped forward and tossed him a towel, playing it safe.

"Thanks." He snagged and shook the towel fold-free with a fluid motion. He had remarkably articulate musculature, and it displayed itself in the gesture. She watched the way his body gleamed in the boob tube glare: cut and packed and deadly. She watched him dry off. There was silence between them. Her fingers drummed softly on the empty pitcher in her hands.

He was shaking, too. Even more than usual.

"No. It's not," he repeated, almost to himself. "It was different this time."

"It was worse."

Rachel shuddered, confused. Great. *What could possibly be worse?*

Jake cradled his head in his hands. "I saw Pete." He rubbed his scalp as if to massage away the memory. "He was . . . I think he's . . . no . . . shit, it's too weird." His head shook vigorously. "I don't even know what I'm talking about."

"He was what?" She drew nearer, her fear receding in the face of her concern. For Pete. For Jake. For the mean level of sanity. "What about Pete? What did you dream?"

"That he's dead." He said the words without looking up.

Ask a stupid question, Rachel thought. She touched him lightly, stroking his sweat- and water-slicked hair. "Honey, it was only a dream—"

"BUT IT WASN'T *JUST* A DREAM!" he spat.

Upstairs, Natalie let out a shriek. Ted's door flew open; his footsteps thudded in the hall. "Mom?" he yelled.

"It's okay, honey," she lied. "Everything's fine."

"That's great," Jake groaned. "I had to wake up the whole fucking house, too. I'm sorry." He was serious. The dreams made him ashamed.

"I'll go get the midget." Rachel started toward the stairs.

Jake looked at her anxiously. "Will you come back down?"

"Do you want us to?"

"Yeah." He feigned a smile. "I wanna see my women."

"Both of us?"

"Both of you."

"And Ted?"

"Oh, yeah. Maybe most of all."

She came to him then, pulled the towel from his hands, and brought her open lips to his. If they ever had any doubts as to the status of their love, all they had to do was kiss. Like the old saying goes: You don't need a weatherman to tell you which way the wind blows.

The wind was blowing some extremely bad ways. The bad news from the concert was doubtless still coming in, and it was apt to get a whole lot worse before it got any better.

But the kiss was good. And that, too, would have to do.

"Pinky and I will be right back," she said, pulling gently away. He touched her face: an act of reverence, softly delivered. She smiled again, stepped out of his reach, and turned toward the stairs.

In turning, her gaze swept across the snow-blind screen. It would not be so blank when she returned, she knew. He'd be rolling back the day's noteworthy broadcasts, drinking in the atrocity, relentlessly stroking the tension that drove him. Rachel moved down the hall, smiling tiredly at Ted, who scrutinized her every move. Passed the bedroom and on toward her howling daughter's lair.

Again she cursed the empty side of the bed.

And the war that she slept with instead.

Twenty-seven

SUNDAY, SEPTEMBER 6
JONESTOWN, PA

Pastor Furniss's morning began in outrage, and got steadily more outrageous from there. Never before had he had so much righteous anger at his disposal, so much justification at his beck and call.

Surely the day of reckoning was at hand.

The numbers had upped since the late Saturday night reports; secular TV filled him in on that much, hours before his own program began. He paced around the kitchen in his pajamas, sucking down cup after cup of Brim while the statistics rolled in and his wife Mildred tiptoed quietly around him.

Five more dead, thirty more listed as missing in the Rock Aid aftermath. Increasingly bizarre rumors as to what had actually happened there.

Not the least of which came from within his own camp.

If only he could speak it.

No matter, he told himself. *There's more than enough. More than enough.* He sat at the kitchen counter, impatiently awaiting his eggs over easy and pure pork sausages, his toasted Roman Meal Lite bread and molten Parkay, while the show began to take form in his mind.

Breakfast was served. He shoved it down, offered perfunctory thanks, moved to the bathroom, got ready to shower. His b.m.'s were runny and vile; it burned coming out and took forever to do so. The body, rebelling as usual.

No surprises there. It was the nature of the flesh to betray. With lust. With pestilence. With the simple passing of time. He looked at the roll of his massive belly, the tiniest protruberant hint of his flaccid genitalia, the reeking porcelain beneath, and a wave of revulsion ran through him.

"*Oh, Jesus God,*" he whispered, a prayer for strength.

Then he had squeezed out the last, and he wiped disdainfully, stood, turned away, flushed without looking. There was some aerosol air freshener on the shelf before him. He spritzed it around the room to mask the smell.

He saw himself naked in the medicine chest mirror. It was not a pretty sight. He didn't like thinking about his body, its slow decline into lumpish disrepair. Clothed in the finest that the Lord's bounty could provide was another thing, yes—he looked dashing in a suit—but stripped down like this, it was more than humbling. It was humiliating.

"Vanity," he muttered, and turned back toward the shower. It was not fitting to dwell on his nakedness, nor to bemoan the state or the fate of the flesh. For the flesh was temporary, as was the world; when both were gone, he would linger still in the kingdom of Heaven.

It was just that, every once in a while, he wished that He would hurry up with it.

Because the world was crawling with sin. Oh, yes, it was. Satan was alive in every speck of matter, just waiting to drag you down, and there was no safe place to hide.

Except in fervent prayer.

Pastor Daniel Furniss pulled back the shower curtain, put the hot on three-quarters full, and the cold on just a tad. It would take a minute for the water pressure to build back up. He would use those moments to focus his thoughts, bring himself back into line.

"Oh, Heavenly Father," he began, loud enough to be heard over the water. "Grant me the courage and wisdom and power of faith in you, O Lord. Give me your blessings and your support.

"For today I face the Enemy, and he is mighty indeed. He has brought great suffering and death to our young and then dared to turn it against us. Against *you*, O Lord; for when he casts aspersions onto your Faithful, he makes blasphemous mockery of your sovereignty on Earth, the testimony of the Spirit.

"I beg you, oh Lord, to give me strength today. Cleanse me of sin and sinful thoughts. Purify me, so that I may enter into battle with the radiance of your light around me, protecting me, glorifying me as I glorify the word of your only begotten son."

The toilet's burbling hiss concluded, and the shower shot up to full strength. It was as if God had spoken. He stuck his hand under the water and found that it was good.

"Amen." He stepped under that cleansing rain.

But there were impurities within that neither prayer nor shower could rinse away. This became clear as soon as he closed the curtain, closed his eyes, allowed himself a moment to luxuriate.

Thought began.

And feeling.

There were problems, coming into this morning's show— problems of the world, the flesh, and the devil—not the least of which was the anti-Christian backlash stampeding through the secular media. As if Christians had anything to do with it . . . as if any decent Christian were *capable* of doing such a thing.

No, they were fishing, and without bait at that. All they had going was the Kleinkind woman, who had quite obviously worked alone, and who quite clearly had no idea what was going on around her. So, essentially, they had nothing that would stick.

Pastor Furniss, on the other hand, knew exactly who to blame.

Unfortunately, he had nothing tangible, either.

Because, from a practical worldly standpoint, the whole thing made no sense. Why would the rock industry want to sabotage its own mechanism, make its big statement of principles a bloody disaster? The answer was simple: *No reason at all.*

But if you looked at the big picture . . . ahh. There was rhyme and reason there.

More than enough to let him know that what he knew was truth.

In the big war . . . the *eternal* war where souls lay in the balance . . . the Fallen One had very few advantages. Primary among them was deceit. The serpent had no shame and no loyalties; but it took great joy in panic and chaos, and the greatest joy of all in mocking God. Surely the already dubious credibility of the Devil's music was worth a giant stab at the heart of Jesus.

And if it worked, God only knew what demons could be born.

So yes, he had no doubt: Satan was behind it, just as he was behind the whole of rock 'n' roll. It didn't matter whether the bands or the fans believed; it didn't matter *what* they believed, in fact. Satan had them all by the short hairs. Satan worked *through* them, through their worldly abandon. Just as Satan used our own bodies against us and then gloried at our inevitable destruction.

While the chaos spread.

And the end came ever nearer.

Of course, the question still remained: What earthly vessels did the Vile One use? Demonic culpability notwithstanding, the knives and grenades had been wielded by human hands. Whose hands, precisely, were they? And how much did they know about the Evil One they served?

Which brought him to his own most disturbing problem.

The girl named Mary Hatch. . . .

Furniss became aware of the water thundering down, the pleasure it provided, the purpose it implied. He submerged his head in the spray for a moment, pulled away, wiped his eyes, reached for the Tegrin Medicated Shampoo, poured some onto his palm, massaged it vigorously into his scalp. Tegrin didn't lather well, but within a minute the top of his head was burning and tingling. He could feel those would-be dandruff cells screaming all the way to oblivion.

He rinsed his hands, wiped his eyes again, and reached for the soap. Ivory, same as when he was a kid. Eschewing the washcloth for the first run through, he began to soap himself down. Luxuriously.

And thought about Mary Hatch again . . .

Mary Hatch lay curled in the Quiet Room, face to the ceiling, staring into the light of the solitary sixty-watt bulb with her eyes open wide. Her breath was close and hot and stifling, and the thick-padded walls so close around her did nothing to alleviate it.

Paul had put her in here for getting him in trouble with the pastor. Just her and her Bible and a chamber pot, in a sound-proof, windowless padded cell the size of a small walk-in closet.

The Quiet Room.

She'd been in there all night, but it didn't matter. It was

stifling in there, but that didn't matter either. She couldn't feel it. She barely felt the hot sweat of her own body.

Because she felt so cold inside.

Somewhere, she thought, *on the other side of all this cold, a message is waiting for me. If only I could see it, I'd know how to tell people. I'd know what to say.*

But I can't, and I don't.

And—forgive me, Jesus—but I'm so goddamned scared. . . .

One thing was for certain: Aunt Elaine was right. These people did not understand. Pastor, at least, seemed firm in his beliefs, so far as they went; but that wasn't nearly enough. And then Paul Weissman, with the hate like a cancer within him. Jesus would have had to be a contortionist to fit on the cross that *he* worshipped.

But they were only the smallest part of the cold within.

The crux of it, she knew, lay with The Scream.

The Scream. Just the thought of the name made her shudder, brought the images back in full-flooding Technicolor: no longer just the Diamond Bar massacre, but Rock Aid as well, the two merged inextricably by the three factors they held in common.

The music.

The murder.

And the presence of Cyndi Wyler . . .

The girl's story was lunacy, even for a man of the Spirit. It was one thing to claim that her missing friend had shown up at Rock Aid, quite another to claim she was a walking, talking corpse. *Damn* that idiot Weissman! Furniss didn't know much about mind-destroying drugs, other than the obvious connotations; but he had heard about flashbacks, and there was little doubt in his mind that Mary had gotten away from him at the concert and experienced exactly that. Probably smoked some pot or crack or God knows what! He wondered how prudent it was to allow a girl like that to remain at the Village.

The water splished down. Still, there was something compelling about her. He thought about it as he rinsed away the soap and shampoo. Her commitment to the spirit, *whatever* its original inspiration, was truly impressive. Ever since she'd arrived at the Village, she'd done little other than study the Scriptures, day in and day out. That drive, that level of scholarly intent, was almost unheard of at LCV.

That, combined with the terrible aura of sadness around her, made her an object of powerful fascination. (This he mused as he lathered up once again, this time with simple Prell.) She had experienced true Christian suffering, and its mark was upon her. It made her seem so vulnerable, so pure. . . .

It was the smoothness of the lather, the gentle warm rushing of the water, that put the thought in his head. It was the simple fact of his nakedness, his isolation.

It was the Devil Himself.

Suddenly, in his mind's eye, she had come to his arms, and the sun was shining, bright and warm, and she was naked against him, he could feel her tight young flesh against his own . . .

"No," he muttered, wiping and opening his eyes. The familiar pale aquamarine tiles of the shower stall greeted him, pulled him back toward safety.

But it was too late. Too late. The seed had awakened, and every steaming molecule of air in the room was charged with that knowledge. This wasn't like the other times, no . . . not like the sinful weakness he'd felt toward the Anderson boy (Lord, forgive me!) or any of the other times he'd yielded to the lusting of the foul animal within him. He could feel the slow stirring in his male organ, like a long-slumbering beast aroused from hibernation by the scent of fresh-killed meat.

"No," he repeated, and then his eyes went shut again . . .

. . . and her long blond hair was in his hands, flush against her smooth back as he stroked its length, down to her glorious hips, the great round globes of her . . .

"NO!" Furniss shouted, slamming his fist against the tiles. A pointless gesture. The pictures were still there, even with his eyes open: a ghost image transposed over the shower's reality, the sight of suds cascading down his belly and to either side of his burgeoning erection . . .

. . . and she made a little noise, so sweet, as his tongue caressed her ear, while her own hands came up and around to take and stroke him gently . . .

He was stroking himself. He stopped, stared at the offending hand. Sweat began to form under his skin despite the water, as if, in fact, it had suddenly hiked up thirty degrees. "Dear God," he began, "please help me. This is wrong. . . ."

. . . and she was sliding down the length of him now to take him in her mouth . . .

". . . Jesus, please . . ."

. . . her fine ripe succulent fifteen-year-old mouth . . .

". . . have mercy . . ."

. . . and he could feel the motion, was slave to the motion, the deep and shallow and deep and shallow and deep . . .

. . . and he was committed now, God help him, there was no turning back, he was fully erect now and aching for release as she worked him and worked him, shallow and deep . . .

. . . and he leaned against the wall with his free hand, no longer praying, eyes squinted against the tumbling water and his own deep-seated shame . . .

. . . as he entered between those beautiful hips from the rear, entered her deeply, wrenching great sweet sobs of joy from her as he ground inexorably toward his own massive conclusion . . .

. . . and then he watched, grim-faced and panting, as the last few strokes of his hand produced the driblets of squandered seed that were his just reward. Even as the passion gripped him, caught the breath in his lungs and then bucked it out in spasms, he was disgusted.

He saw himself, his fantasy gone: a pudgy middle-aged man of God, clutching his reddened pud while his heart hammered in his throat. He watched his semen spiral around to catch in the hair-clogged drain, and a physical wave of revulsion ballooned in his gut.

A man of *God!*

For surely this was the Devil's work. The Devil, working through the weakness of the flesh and the soul's own sinful nature, dragging him down to the level of the animals and *worse!*

Because he knew better.

Because he was a man of God, annointed in the blood of the Lamb . . .

"Give me strength," he croaked, then cleared his throat and tried again. "Give me strength, O Lord, and forgive me my weakness. For I have fallen short of the Glory of God.

"But I am your servant, chosen by You to lead Your flock in the ways of Your love.

"Help me, O Lord, so that I might save them from themselves."

Then he turned off the shower, toweled dry, and—almost as an afterthought—eliminated all evidence of his crime.

Twenty-eight

The target range was directly across the trail from Cody's shack, roughly equidistant between the lodge and the house. The trenchlike slice had been carved ten-feet deep into the clay soil of the mountainside around nineteen fifty-two, back when little Cody was glued to a black-and-white Zenith somewhere in Arizona, watching Davy Crockett, King of the Wild Frontier. It had long fallen into disrepair: the timbers that lined its thirty-meter length rotting away with each successive season's cycle of decay, brush and branches falling to clog the clearing.

Cody had fixed all that, damned near single-handedly. He cleaned out the flora, replaced the rotten beams and put in a variety of fresh targets. It was set up to accommodate all manner of projectile-throwing implements: rifles, side arms, or bows. Pennsylvania's weapons laws were significantly more accommodating than the Big Apple's, and quite a few members of the crew had availed themselves of that fact and either acquired weapons or legitimized ones already in their possession. Most of them, anyway.

Personally, Cody preferred more subtle, if no less lethal, devices. "This here," he lectured, "is yer basic Magnum Force Trident." He brandished the bizarre weapon: a black, high-tech-looking crossbow pistol, replete with cross-haired scope. "It's twenty-four-ounce, heavy-gauge aluminum, with a laminated fiberglass bow strung with forty-five pounds of tension, and it's accurate up to sixty feet." He aimed it at a sandbagged target halfway back and squeezed the trigger. An eight-inch bolt whizzed out and away, sinking into the bull's-eye with an abrupt *thwok*!

Slim Jim whistled appreciatively. Hempstead just shook his head and laughed. "Not bad, but somehow it would be a whole lot mo' fearsome if you didn't boost yo' sales pitch straight outta the *Sharper Image* catalog."

"Yeah, well"—Cody grinned—"you take it where you find it, dude."

"You got this from the *Sharper Image*?!" Slim Jim asked incredulously, taking the weapon into his hand and hefting it. "Who the fuck are they *selling* 'em to?"

"Same yups that buy the fake samurai swords, ah guess." Hempstead nudged; Cody winced. "Seriously," Hempstead continued, letting the ribbing drop, "I prefer something with more of a *kick*."

He held up his hunting rifle like a kid at Christmastime and looked very serious. "Kleingeunther K-fifteen two seventy Winchester, Frontier one forty-grain boat-tail spire-point interlock ammo, Redfield Illuminator 3X-9X scope." He finished the dissertation, shouldered the gun, sighted in the target, and said, "Go 'head, homeboy. Fire another bolt."

Cody looked at Slim Jim, shrugged, and loaded up another one. He took aim, said, "Puttin' it in at three o'clock," and squeezed the trigger. The bolt flew out; Hempstead squeezed off a shot a split second later.

And blew the bolt out of the air not five inches from the target.

"Whoa," the voice behind them said, "nice shootin' thar, Tex."

They all turned. Jake smiled wanly as he stepped off the trail. "Nice day, huh. You boys rehearsing for World War III or something?"

They all grinned and kicked at the dirt. Cody lit a joint and passed it on to Slim Jim. "Could be," Hempstead replied, "given our current situation, it's not the worst idea in the world. You joining us?"

He nodded toward the Cordura bag slung across Jake's right shoulder. Jake shrugged and laid it down on the rough-hewn balance beam, unzipped it, and withdrew a lever action Marlin .30-06, also scope-mounted.

"Just thought I'd do a little target practice, is all."

"Uh-huh. Looks like you're not the only one."

"Looks like things are getting a little tense around here."

"Uh-huh."

"Do you want to talk about it?"

Jake was staring at Hempstead quizzically when he heard the metallic *claack* of a machine-gun bolt pulling back. Every hair on the back of his neck went static-upright. He turned around to face Slim Jim, who cradled an Uzi in his arms.

"I do believe," Jim said, "that we need to do a wee bit more than talk."

Walker felt the shadow fall across his face like an ink-black pillow, threatening to smother the life out of him.

"Walker," Momma hissed in a voice like rope twisting in a high wind.

"WALKER!!"

He sat up, rumpled and sweating. Beads of perspiration trickled into the indentation in the leather upholstery of the couch, where his shirt could better absorb them. His neck hurt. It had not been a nice dream: short and violent and born of sleep not deep enough to ease the fatigue. His scars throbbed. He looked across the office.

The drapes sealed out ninety-nine percent of the afternoon sun, but several valiant beams had weaseled through a slit in the drapes to shine across the ancient carpet; dust motes floated langourously in the swaths of golden light.

"Get up."

The dust swirled turbulently. The sunbeams halted in midair, sliced off and swallowed by the blackness that loomed toward him. "What is it? What's going on?"

"Trouble."

"Great," he spat, sitting fully upright. "What, specifically?"

Momma told him what she knew. It was limited. He was still her eyes and ears, and her "other sources" operated on much more obscure levels of perception. But they were usually right, and it could indeed be dangerous.

Walker ran a hand through his hair; he was exhausted. "Can it wait?"

"I think not."

"So what should we do?"

"Take care of it. Make a call. Head 'em off at the pass. "Just fix *it."*

"All right." He sighed, standing and walking to the desk.

The number was already loaded into the phone's memory. The arrangements were made in less than three minutes.

Walker sat back in the big leather chair. The shadow was a jack-o'-lantern slit in the middle of the floor. "I had a dream. It was about—"

"*I* know *what it was about*," Momma said. "*Remember the old saying, Walker: Be careful what you dream . . .*"

Yeah, he thought.

It just might come true.

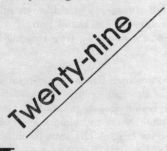

I
t was the Symphony of Life: her own soul-music, sweetly redefining the air itself with sound. Jesse let it flow over her, catch her in its rhythms, propel her as she rose and fell and ground and writhed and rose to fall again upon the sweet hard love inside her.

And Pete was beneath her, smiling up at her, then closing his eyes and making little Pete-noises. They mingled with her own, the sound from the speakers, feeding life back into the symphony.

Just as the electrodes attached to them fed living pulses back to the master translator.

Back to DIOS.

She rode him, with heat and deliberate abandon, anticipating the flood within her that would signal his release, anticipating her own wild ride's conclusion. It was building now, and she picked up her pace, giving herself over more fully to the pull of the waves.

For that was the essence of the cosmic dance, the fabric underlying all creation. That moment of release and abandon.

When all of the barriers break down.

And the mysteries reveal.

On the subatomic level there are no barriers. On the

subatomic level even the binary code is subsumed. No more on or off, yes or no, life or death. Just an endless continuum of being, neither isolated as a particle nor undifferentiated as a wave. Quantum theory calls them wavicles; and they join all things together into one infinitely multifaceted Whole.

Within that Whole, all things are contained. Every choice. Every option. If it exists anywhere in the universe, it is there. If one can imagine it, it is there.

The only difference is in the rate of the vibration.

And that rate of vibration determines everything. Determines shape. Determines sound. Determines density and the characteristics thereof. Determines, even in dreamland, what is bed and what is bedded, what is solid and what is gas, distinguishes between vagina and penis and the chemical structure of the lubricants between.

If one could listen in, at the subatomic level, one could hear the infinite timbres come together in exquisite song.

The music of the spheres, as Pythagoras dubbed it.

The Symphony of Life . . .

It was that symphony that she moved to, as the moment came near. It choreographed the rise and fall and grind and writhe, drove her closer and closer to that moment of ultimate merger when she was Pete and Pete was she.

And then she saw the cervical cap—not in her at all, but off to the side, torn and bubbling and sinking into the pillow beside Pete's head—and panic jolted through her like a shot of methamphetamine. She tried to pull off of him. He held her firmly at the hips. It's already too late, he said.

He smiled.

And it was true, not because he'd come, but because she was already pregnant. How could she have forgotten? She was so fucking big . . .

. . . and as she watched, her belly swelled and burgeoned, as if his cock were a faucet turned on full and she were a water balloon, her flesh distending like rubber . . .

. . . and the music changed, subtly at first, then faster and faster as harmony mutated into dissonance and major shifted to minor, beauty turned to slavering beast . . .

. . . and there was no pain, there was only the horror, filling her belly and frying her mind as the first red spritzing cracks appeared and she felt the growing thing begin to claw her, claw her from within . . .

. . . and in the last moment before she burst, she saw that Pete was crying, big viscous tears, like egg whites surging out of a fractured shell . . .

. . . and then she was screaming into her pillow, with the warm light of morning burning into her open eyes.

The time was 11:34.

Time to face the music.

Everybody steered clear of her when she emerged from her room: Pete's Gram, Bob and Bob, all the guys from the crew. It was as if they could feel her pain coming, an invisible buffer zone that preceded her by a good twenty yards. She could feel their embarrassment for her. It simply drove the wedge in deeper. Like a ghost, she moved through the corridors, down the stairs, past the rehearsal room, and out the front door.

The first thing Jesse noticed, as she hit the great outdoors, was the sound of gunfire. It hadn't really registered from inside for some reason. Maybe because she didn't expect it. Maybe because her head was already full of cotton and cacophony.

The second thing she noticed was the absence of submoronic singing. It was the first time in seemingly forever that the day hadn't greeted her with a round of *holy, ho-lee*. She glanced, unsmiling, in the direction of the gate. No assholes. Amazing.

Jesse started down the hill, away from the gate, in the direction of the shooting range. The odds were good that they wouldn't even notice her, whoever they were; their backs would be facing the trail. The odds were good that they were shooting at the targets, not each other or some unnamed thing. If she was wrong, so what. A bullet in the head might be an improvement. . . .

No, no, no, she told herself. *This is not healthy. This is not sane.* She got a flash of the Jesse to whom she was accustomed: a strong woman, not at all self-destructive, willing to stare down any obstacle until it shied away.

She could not seem to find that Jesse within her.

The dream came back, and with it the despair. Her hands came to her stomach, confirming the relative flatness. No, she was not bursting her seams. At least not abdominally. Whatever was taking form in there, it was still very small: more like a tadpole than a human being. . . .

"*Shut up!*" she yelled, and stopped in her tracks. The sound of her own voice startled her. She had not meant to say it out loud. The fact that she had done so meant that, yes, she was really fucking losing it now. Which meant that there were no holds left to bar, and control was history out the window gone . . .

The face of Lenore Kleinkind appeared: kindly, conde-scending, genuinely compassionate as a yellow-faced HAVE A NICE DAY sticker. It has a right to live! she insisted, *waving an open quart jar of pig's blood before her for emphasis. . . .*

Pete, then: loaded out of his mind, red eyes wrestling themselves into focus. You're talking about a human *life* here! *he bellowed. In one hand he held an empty vial of coke, in the other a loaded and dripping condom. . . .*

"Leave me alone, God damn you," Jesse muttered, forcing her legs to move again, forcing herself onward. The trail wound downward; she followed it, barely looking. The external was largely a matter of course.

It was the internal that owned her attention now.

There was no other way to view the grande dame of the Susquehanna Women's Services Center, that miserable treach-erous twat; but her assessment of Pete wasn't fair, and there was no way around that, either. Lumping them together only twisted things worse than they already were.

Pete—whatever else could be said about him—was at heart a beautiful man.

And he had loved her. In his own way, he had. He wasn't all that good at it—it wasn't the kind of thing you auditioned for, after all—but insofar as his immature, dashing, unspeak-ably handsome, funny, charming, and prodigiously gifted little weenie ass had been capable, he had dedicated himself to her in a way that he clearly had never dedicated himself to a woman before. He had admired her talent. He had admired her work. He had admired her worldview. He had admired her body. He had gone to her often, in open admiration of all of the above, and rarely come away with less than a satisfied and utterly Pete-like grin.

He had even *said*, on more than one occasion, that he loved her. . . .

God damn it! she howled at herself. *Why am I thinking about him in the past tense?*

The answer to that one was simple.

Pete was fucking dead.

And, of course, there were only a couple of dozen problems with that hypothesis. Most of them had to do with the issue of subjectivity. *He's not here; therefore he must be dead*. It sounded like one of Eugène Ionesco's syllogisms: *All cats die, Socrates is dead, therefore Socrates must have been a cat*. It made for nice absurdism, but it had about as much to do with reality as a David Lynch film. Logic made stupid.

Logic made irrelevent.

But it didn't change the fact that Pete had no reason to disappear. He was not the kind of person who ducked and ran. Maybe for one night, one brainless liaison with an equally brainless chippee. That was very likely, in fact.

But he would have been back for Rock Aid.

And he would have been back for her.

So that narrows down the options, she continued. *Either he's dead, he's been kidnapped, or he's in a coma. Maybe even all three*. This was not a cheerful realization to come to. It took a chunk out of her, made her steps falter.

She was even with the shootists now, and she had been correct: they were shooting at the targets, and they hadn't noticed her at all. Knowing that she wasn't being watched enabled her to look at them: Jake, Cody, Hempstead, the copter guy. They seemed to be deep in intense conversation, punctuated by gunfire. Make a point. POOM! Make a point. POOM!

She thought about going to talk with them, find out what's going on; from the look of it, they weren't exchanging recipes for Sunday Delight Supreme. Then Hempstead fired, and it made the fillings in her teeth rattle, changing her mind rather abruptly. Whatever it was, she could discuss it with them later.

Maybe later she'd be able to think.

She continued down the hill, toward Jake and Rachel's house and the woods below. It was probably best that she not speak with anyone right now, after all. It was probably best that she be by her lonesome. The things she had to work out, nobody could help with. The trees, maybe. The birds.

The trail was simply worn-down grass with sporadic pools of rock and soil. It had a nice down-home wilderness feel. Injuns, no doubt, had traipsed along it back around the birth of the nation, back before they traded their rings and beads for anthrax-smothered blankets, that is. . . .

"Nice," she muttered, shrugging it off, letting one foot fall after the other. Another shot rang out; it was almost as if the shock wave of it pushed her forward, away from them, further down the hill.

And that was when the bug began to scuttle across her path.

It was a big black ugly sucker: a beetle of some sort, awkward and clunky and roughly the size of her thumb. She froze in her tracks and stared at it, while something primordial tugged at the muscle strings in her chest. It was the same low-grade revulsion that had always seized her when she turned on the lights in her New York kitchen and watched the roach Rockettes rehearsing in the sink. Insect-loathing: cornerstone of civilization.

The first impulse, of course, was to squash the bastard. Better yet, to get somebody else to do it. She'd always disliked the moment of impact: the feel, the sound, the fact that she was actually killing something, no matter how repulsive it was.

Then, of course, came the guilt. It was alive, after all. It had a right . . .

And that, of course, was the end of the line; and before she knew it she was running, sidestepping the goddamn beetle and making a beeline for the woods, barely watching where she was going because her eyes were filling with tears, brimming over with tears for the baby Jesse and the baby within her who would never get to be, never get to be because she didn't want it, she couldn't *deal* with it now, Pete or no Pete there was no man to support her while she took a year or two off that she didn't even *want* to take off, she didn't even want the man, but now there were all these people trying to make her feel guilty for making her decision, setting her up for fake abortions, throwing blood in her face on national TV, saying it has a *right* to live when *she* felt it had no rights at *all*, since when did kids ever get to vote on *anything* their parents did, and besides that it wasn't even *here* yet . . .

. . . and she ran, and she ran, but she couldn't shake the knowledge that she could abort a fetus but she couldn't step on a goddamn bug, which just made the tears flow all the more because it told her something about herself that she didn't want to know, *several* things about herself, and one of them was that she was surely a selfish bitch, and another was that she *had* to be, because God and Nature and Fate had all conspired to turn her into her mother if she did not remain *absolutely fucking resolute* as to what she would or would not allow to happen to her body, and the simple fact was that she would not have to raise and support and protect that bug, and that nobody was going to help her raise or support or protect her baby either so they had absolutely no right to talk, but it didn't change another, *equally* simple fact, which was that there was a budding human being inside her that she was going to kill before it even knew what hit it, and when you killed a human being they called it murder, because that's *exactly* what it was . . .

. . . and as she came up even with Jake and Rachel's house, Natalie began to crawl out from around the back, and Jesse looked for just the split second that it took for her left foot to hit the half-buried rock, smashing the three biggest toes and sending the rest of her careening down, face-first, into the dirt and stones, hands coming up to catch the brunt of it as she landed, the flesh tearing open and skinning back in dozens of tiny places as she shrieked out her frustration and rolled onto her back, hands coming up so she could dimly survey the damage, *other* hands coming down to hold her, help her up, take her by the shoulders as she fell forward into Rachel's embrace and cried and cried and cried . . .

"Jesus Christ," Rachel muttered. "I didn't know . . . I mean, I had no idea it had gotten that *weird*."

"Well, it has," Jesse countered. "And Jesus—"

"—had precious little to do with it," Rachel said, finishing the sentence. "That's for sure."

The two women sat across from each other at Rachel's kitchen table, a vase of fresh-picked flowers between them and just to one side. The baby was down, and so they were alone: not so far apart that they could not touch, though they abstained from it for the moment. All myths of instant feminine intimacy aside, they did not know each other all that well; and none of this was easy.

It was 1:05 in the afternoon, but they were sharing the day's first pot of fresh-ground Columbian blend while the high sun shone through the windows and danced through the many fine crystals dangling in the light. That same light sparkled in the tears on Jesse's cheeks, filtered through the cigarette smoke that emanated from her free hand.

She had told about the dream, the night of impregnation, her fears both for and about Pete. Now she had just finished the story of the Little Abortion Clinic That Wasn't. It was the first that she'd spoken about any of it to anyone, and it didn't sound any better in the telling than it was in the flesh. The only good thing was that she got to work a lot of her feelings out. Crying was easy in front of Rachel; so was screaming and slamming her fist against the table. There would be no demerits for excessive emotion in this conversation. And that was refreshingly nice.

"Will you take them to court?" Rachel asked.

"I don't know. I . . . I can't think yet. I haven't had a chance." She rolled her eyes, dragged on her smoke, continued, "I mean, on the one hand, I'd love to sue. I'd love to sue her tits off. On the other hand, she'll probably never get to pull another scam like that again. There'll be a big investigation; they'll shut the clinic down. With any luck, she won't have any tits *left* by the time I get around to pressing charges."

Rachel laughed. "This is true, and that's the funny thing. People such as her and Pastor Furniss are small time. They're *wanna*-bes, you know? It's like, there's nothing on the planet she'd rather be than Phyllis Schlafly; just like he'd probably trade his Liberty Christian Village and the souls of everyone he's ever *known* for one second in the shoes of a Jimmy Swaggart."

Now both of them laughed, and that was nice too. It had a very short half-life, however. All too soon, the all-too-uncomfortable silence returned.

"So," Rachel began at last, "where does that leave you?"

Jesse said nothing; but from Rachel's view, the psychic retreat was more than eloquent. This was the *really* difficult part. This was the landscape at the heart of the pain.

"We can stop now, if you want to," Rachel persisted gently. "But I've got a feeling, since we've come this far, that you might want to go all the way."

Jesse stalled for a minute, snubbing out her cigarette, reaching for another, refraining at the last moment. Her eyes, which had seemed on the verge of drying, began to fill again. Her breath hitched as she prepared to speak.

"I guess," she managed at last, "I'll have to find another place to get it done. I mean . . ." And then she lost it again.

Rachel reached out her hand, took Jesse's free one in her own: a gesture of solidarity. Jesse flinched for a moment and stared at the clutch; then her eyes overflowed, and she stared off into the never-never land to the right of her knees. Rachel watched her, gauging the pain, deciding whether she had the requisite empathy. Sometimes, after all, good will wasn't all it was cracked up to be. She needed to know if she was going to make things better or muck things up.

Only one way to find out, she told herself, and then went with the flow.

"Listen to me, kiddo. You have a couple of choices. Not all of them are pretty, but that's beside the point. You'll want to think about them all—"

"No. You listen to *me.*" Jesse yanked her hand away. Anger underlied the sudden power in her voice, the straightness of her spine, the intensity of her gaze. "If there's one thing I don't wanna fuckin' hear, it's anybody tryin' to talk me out of it! Okay? I mean, this is hard enough as it is!"

"I know what you mean—"

"*Do* you now!" Jesse could feel her defenses slamming home now within her, like the huge steel doors thundering shut behind Don Adams in the *Get Smart!* opening credits. "Rachel, no offense or anything, but you decided to *have* your kids. There's a big difference between a baby you want and a baby you had forced on you—"

"Jesse, let me put it to you this way." She gracefully withdrew her hand from where it had been abandoned, used it to push back her long red tresses, used the seconds to subdue her own anger. "When I got pregnant with Ted, it was in the days just preceding *Roe* versus *Wade*, which means that there *weren't* any listings in the yellow pages. It was illegal, you understand? The only legitimate way to get an abortion was with a doctor's excuse, which means that you either had to be at death's door or be a fucking psychotic. You know, either it was a certifiable health risk, or you had to threaten suicide.

"Of course you could always do it through the underground; but somehow, the thought of getting scraped in a back alley by some guy named Paco was more terrifying than the pregnancy itself.

"You follow what I'm saying?"

Jesse nodded. The anger had fizzled, at least for the moment. She listened, tense but most certainly attentive.

"At the time I was involved with this guy named Sam; and let's just say that Sam was an underachiever. He had a great voice, and he played a mean guitar, and he wrote me some beautiful songs . . ." She trailed off, wistful for a moment. ". . . but, bottom line, he was a deadbeat. Liked to sit around stoned all day, playing the guitar and bitching about how *commercial* FM radio was getting. Not what you'd call a good provider."

She smiled. Jesse did not. Her concentration at that moment was enormous.

"I would *very much* have liked an abortion just then. I'm pretty sure that I felt a lot like you do now. I was right about your age, in fact. You're twenty-three?"

Jesse nodded.

"Okay. I was twenty-one-anna-half. Big difference." She smiled and swigged her coffee again. "I have to admit I wasn't nearly as focused as you are, or nearly as talented; but I still had dreams, and they didn't involve carrying an infant around to job interviews, and they didn't involve going home to Mother or collecting welfare, and they *also* didn't involve spending my life with good ol' Sam. Unfortunately, I was up against a brick wall, and my dreams didn't seem to carry a whole lot of weight.

"So I went ahead and had Ted by myself. I really didn't *have* any choice. Fortunately, southern California was Midwife City around that time, so at least I had some support. Sam hit the road by the fifth month, which saved me the trouble of giving him the boot.

"And then I just struggled like crazy for the next eight years: me and Ted, against the world."

"But, my God," Jesse muttered. "What did you *do*?"

"My God!" Rachel laughed. "What *didn't* I do?" She shook her head, less wistful than rueful this time. "Well, lots of little counterculture jobs, for the most part; they were really good about babies, but they didn't pay for shit.

"Remember, these were the days when 'pregnancy leave' in straight America was an impossible dream, as opposed to the highly improbable one it is now. I mean, if you think *this* is a man's world, you shoulda been here *then*. There was no slack. There was no leeway.

"So I worked my way around the fringes. I'm talking food co-ops, stained glass, some political canvassing and stuff. Probably the straightest thing I did was spend a couple months working for George McGovern."

"Anyway, that was the straight stuff. Then, of course, I picked up a lot of Gerber's Strained Beets and Oscar Meyer Weiners on the ol' five-finger discount plan. I did some dancing and hustling for tips. I had a couple old men along the way, sort of low-grade sugar daddies." She paused, as if weighing the next batch of words. "I even turned a couple tricks at one point."

"Ohmigod."

"Hey." Rachel's face was ultrasober as she said it. "When it comes down to survival, you do what you have to do. At that point, I just considered myself lucky I was cute enough to pull it off. I *had* no backup: just the love of my son, the love of my friends, and the love that I felt God had for me."

"Yeah, that's some kind of love, all right," Jesse sneered. "Direct from that big bearded guy in the sky. Man, I've heard enough of *that* to last me the rest of my—"

"You been around long enough, you realize how unreasonable the whole *world* is. It's like there's this vast matrix of illogic that permeates everything; and once you realize that *we* don't make the kind of sense we presume to make, then you start to wonder about the image of God that presupposes that order.

"I went through that real heavy, the whole Christian thing. I had incredible faith, and I had incredible doubt. The beauty of Christ, on the one hand, was undeniable. What thinking, feeling person can deny the power of forgiveness, of unconditional love, of standing bravely and selflessly up against the forces of injustice and intolerance and hate?

"But on the other hand, there was the Church. Too much. All its little cliques and subcults of organized belief. And the more I saw of them, the more I realized that they had *less* forgiveness, *less* unconditional love, *less* tolerance or sense of justice than a lot of the undogmatic unbelievers I met.

"So I retained my love, and I retained my faith, but I gave

up on being a Christian. It seemed evident to me that Christ had, to a large extent, *failed* when he died. He left His Word wide open to mutilation by the very people He'd made mincemeat of when he lived: all the power hungry high priests and multimedia rip-off artists of the world."

Jesse just stared at her now, saying nothing.

"And once the faith you had gets stripped down to that, you start to embrace a larger order. One that draws on a larger number of sources. One that doesn't draw the same kind of lines. Do you know what I'm saying?"

"I'm not sure . . ."

"Yes, you do. Just listen real hard. The fact is, *nothing makes any kind of real sense at all* until you embrace the irrational. And beyond that, the wildest extremes: the things more beautiful or monstrous than you ever dared imagine. Try to make sense of your emotions without that sensibility; try to make sense of your deepest feelings.

"Try to make sense of your *music*, for God's sake! You've already explained your music to me, what your Symphony of Life is supposed to represent. You already understand all this stuff. You're just so damned pragmatic about it, you seem to forget what it means."

"Okay." Jesse's hands were trembling slightly as she clasped them together before her. "So what does it mean?"

"It means that whatever it is that's Out There will love you, whatever you choose to do. It also means that it will mess with you, whatever you choose to do.

"*Mostly*, though, it means that any choice you make is between you and it, and nobody else has a right to say one goddamn word about it."

Yes, definitely trembling now, as Jesse brought her arms down to hug her belly. Very quietly, she spoke.

"So what do *you* think I should do?"

"I don't know what to tell you, Jess. I really don't. On the one hand, you'd have a much easier time bringing up a kid than I had with Ted. You can still write and record and play; you aren't scheduled for another tour until next year; you could afford an au pair girl to cover you while you work. I'd even help out, as much as I could.

"But just because you could handle it, that doesn't mean you should have to. Like I said before, I would have *loved* an abortion way back when. I wouldn't blame you a bit if you had one now. It's just a matter of what you can live with."

Jesse said nothing. Rachel followed suit, waiting.

A weighted oasis of silence followed.

Jesse broke it at last with the skritch of a match. Her face was seriously pale as she spoke.

"I'm scared."

"Okay." Rachel left it there.

"I mean, I'm really scared," Jesse persisted. Her eyes were almost luminous red as she began to cry again.

"So go on. Tell me."

"I'm scared to have the baby. I'm scared *not* to have the baby. I'm scared"—pausing to choke back the sobbing—"that this thing inside me might be all that's left of Pete in the world."

And then the sobbing came, full force. Rachel waited it out, suppressing the urge to go over and hold the girl. This moment of pain and catharsis was Jesse's and Jesse's alone. When it was done, they could go on.

Or they could leave it, for now.

"And you know what keeps coming back to me?" Jesse moaned through her tears. "That stupid woman and the thing she said: *'It has a right to live!'* "

"No, it doesn't," Rachel said. "Not at all.

"It merely has a chance."

Thirty

Sunday afternoon's big *Call to Glory* telethon was just getting revved up when Mary Hatch tipped over. As always, it had been made direly clear to everyone in the preshow power prayer debriefing that this was *the* most critically elemental segment of LCV's weekly Faith Outreach programming lineup.

It was more important, they stressed, than the chatty downhomesiness of *Triumph Tonight!*, more important than *Rock of Ages* (their admittedly marginal Friday-night competition against the glut of late-night Murder Music venues), which featured primly dressed and smartly suited youngsters singing Pastor Furniss's favorites from the ol' time gospel hit parade. Yessir, it was more important than just about anything, because on a good night *Call to Glory* could really rake it in for the Lord, hallelujah, amen.

Especially in the wake of yesterday's stunning defeat for the Enemy.

Yessir, Satan had really done it this time, and Pastor Furniss was fully expecting the joint to be jumping, with all those lights on all those phones *blazing*. Everyone smiled a lot and assured Mary that it was quite the honor to be chosen as one of the smiling Faith Outreach volunteers for such an important event. It meant that they were really on the way to accepting her into the fold; it meant that she could be personally trusted to spread the Good News to those who called in their darkest time of need, praise God, that she could be personally trusted to speak for the Lord, giving comfort and getting at least one major credit card number.

It meant that they were hoping to high heaven that she'd be all right.

Mary's knees were still stiff as she made her way through the cinder block basement facility that comprised the realms of Studio B, the heart of Liberty Christian Village's multimedia complex. There was, in fact, no Studio A, nor any complex to speak of; and in fact, there never had been. But it was coming; oh, yes. Soon, soon. Just as soon as they could amass enough faith to beat the Devil back and get their financial heads above water, they were gonna be a *beacon*: shining into the morass of sex and drugs and murder music to CALL the teenagers of North America back home to GLORY!

AMEN! THANK YOU, JEEZUS!

Mary stood before her preordained space, a red plastic bucket-style chair at the end of a long bank of red plastic bucket-style chairs, each facing its own pair of bright red telephones. It was the same fragile fiberoptic lifeline that she herself had been on the other side of not so very long ago. With any luck at all, dozens of lost and floundering souls would be reaching out tonight, praise God, and would find Him through her.

Mary sat down. The chair was maybe an inch or two shy of comfortable height for the table, and the enormous Faith Outreach button she'd been given clanked against the table rim like a giant metal cookie. It was a bright yellow 3-D disk that shifted as you looked at it, with a big frowny/smiley face and the legend GET SMART! GET SAVED! alternating in boldface along the bottom. They must have figured that the trauma of yesterday would fade a little faster if she were given a little piece of the Lord's work to do. So it was given to her, along with the pledge forms and the training manual that she was supposed to have stayed up with, memorizing. It was hers to keep, an honor conferred on a chosen few. It was almost as big as her left breast.

It was ludicrous in the extreme. And she hated it.

Because Mary Hatch was well beyond having second thoughts about her future in dear old El-Cee-Vee. Mary Hatch had come, through a painful process of self-realization, to the inescapable conclusion that she was more likely to find Jesus hanging out with the hookers on Hollywood Boulevard than haunting the dreary hallowed halls of Liberty Christian Village. To be sure, there were numerous scared and scarred hearts there that sought Him, hers included. But if He was to be found at all, it was through no help of the institution that bandied His name so freely. At the ripe old age of fifteen, Mary Hatch had figured out that Liberty Christianers weren't about Christ at all. They were about *control:* control their thoughts, control their actions, control what they see and read and hear and think, and you control their souls. Save the poor, innocent, brainless children by *controlling* them, making them into God's little robots. Do what you're told. Just say no. No no no bad bad bad sin sin sin . . .

Jesus, she thought. This place was too much. A very big joke with a very unfunny punch line. There came a point when she realized that she'd felt closer to God watching Ed McMahon sell life insurance on TV.

And a lot less scared, too.

Because she didn't have to *buy* Ed's bullshit. She could switch off Ed any ol' time she pleased, blip his laughing face straight into the stratosphere. And perhaps worst of all, Ed

McMahon hadn't been given legal guardianship over Mary Hatch.

Whereas Pastor Furniss had.

It had snuck up on her when she wasn't looking, which was the preferred method of virtually everything else in Mary's young life. Trina, the potato-faced girl who worked in the administration office, had cheerily noted that Mary would be joining them for the fall semester, after all. This came with all the subtlety of a rubber mallet to the forehead: Mary had been wandering around in a semidysfunctional daze for most of the summer, true, but the unconscious assumption was still that she would somehow be back in Diamond Bar High come the first week of September.

Apparently, Pastor Furniss felt otherwise. Apparently, he had successfully communicated his feelings to her folks, who had shelled out the fifty-five hundred dollar tuition-plus-room-and-board that went with the privilege. Apparently, she'd more or less sat back and let it all slide by as if it didn't really matter. She hadn't really kept in touch, beyond the carefully regulated Family Interface Program. She hadn't really had much to say.

Apparently, Pastor Furniss and her parents had.

Save the children. *God*, she realized, *how could I have been so stupid?*

Easy enough: she was in shock. They were ready for her. She was vulnerable.

And they were determined to keep her that way.

For her own good, of course. Outside communication at the Village was kept to a bare-bones minimum, the better to allow the youngster a chance to purge the debilitating influence of our X-rated society, and to let the family-oriented, value-intensive curriculum at LCV take firm root in the soil of impressionable, PG-rated minds. Undoing the damage could often be an arduous task, particularly in young Mary's case with the trauma and what have you, and so contact, both in and outside the facility, was scrupulously controlled. As were phone calls. And television. And radio. And newspapers.

And everything.

By the time it dawned on Mary that dear ol' Liberty Christian had about as much to do with liberty as it did with Christ, things had once again descended into the realm of waking nightmare. *Something* had happened on Saturday, when

The Scream came onstage. She felt it from a distance of several hundred feet.

Worse yet, she *saw* it . . .

. . . rolling off the stage in neon-bright flashes of kinetic energy, stroking the swarming masses filling the arena. For one fleeting, hypnotic moment she saw people not as flesh and blood, but as light: heart-fires burning as brilliant white whorls no bigger than pinpricks in the vast configuration of space before her. The stage pulsed in rhythm with the music, which was filling her, insinuating itself through every opening to her interior: as sight, as sound, as smell as taste as flesh as flesh . . .

Mary stood bolt upright, knocking the red plastic chair clattering over. And she stayed like that: swaying, eyes closed, as the images flashed back over and over, and she felt the Spirit moving through her . . .

. . . as the light went red, then purple, then glowing, squirming black as a crevice split the floor of the arena and the mouth of Hell itself opened wide, and she clamped down hard harder than she knew how and she prayed to Jesus please God no please no make it stop maaaaake it STOPPP!!!!!

She gripped the rim of the table, felt the wave of nausea rise and crest and recede without spilling out, and managed to hold in the sound that threatened to come wailing out of her. She kept it down to a compressed squeak that was laughable in the face of the terror that propelled it.

All eyes were upon her. Suddenly she felt too absurd, standing there lobotomized with a stupid smiling plate stuck to her chest and the big clunky TV cameras staring at her as though she were a Nancy Reagan poster girl: *See What Drugs Did to Me. Just Say No.* It was too much.

She gazed across the crowded confines of Studio B and saw Paul Weissman waddling toward her, petulant as ever, a technician's commset perched on his head. It wasn't connected to anything of importance, the unplugged cord sticking out to one side like a lopsided neoprene antler.

Paul was one pissed-off penitent. He'd violated policy by actually taking a group *into* the concert, instead of staying safely out in the parking lot, and she'd heard he'd gotten a royal drubbing for it. He had, in turn, taken it out on her, in ways that would leave no telltale marks, and then he'd locked her in the Quiet Room for thirteen hours. He'd turned every cheek she had, and she hated him. That hatred burned bright inside her, warming the cold places that she couldn't otherwise reach. It was something to hold on to. It was a start.

"Mary!" he sniffed, voice redolent with ersatz compassion.

She had to get out of there.

"Mary, are you alright?"

She had to get out of here, *now*. She unpinned her button and laid it on the table. The legend shifted; the smiley face frowned.

GET SMART!

She turned, all eyes upon her, and started walking.

"MARY!"

And then she ran.

It was impossible to get out of the chair.

Across from him, on the edge of the bed, the ghost of Chris Konopliski was rolling another joint. Or trying to anyway. His fingers kept going through the papers, the smoke, the open album cover. "Son of a bitch," he would say, shrugging in confusion.

And then the blood would fly out of his mouth.

"*Stop*," Ted hissed, but it did no good. If it wasn't one vision, it was another. It had been that way for the last nineteen hours or so.

And it was impossible to get out of the chair.

Once, in the middle of the night, when Jake had begun to scream. That time he had been terrified, thinking of the Screamer with the grease-slick skull. And once, when everyone was asleep again, he had gone to piss: terrified again, of the silence this time, and of the darkness that seemed to be everywhere.

To just sit in the chair was terrifying.

But to leave it was even worse.

That was why he fought the clouds of sleep when they came to claim him. Awake, he at least had his body to distract him. Asleep, anything could happen. Like a visit from Freddy Krueger, without the shoddy saving grace of a John Saxon or Heather Langenkamp performance, the nightmares would come . . .

    . . . *and he would be back in the crowd, with the knife*

going in and the blood coming out and the face coming off. And he would once again be struck with the helplessness, the no-time-at-all-to-react, the cringing cowardice that had allowed him not only to do nothing, but to run away after . . .

NO!

So he would not sleep, and he would not dream, and he would not leave the chair.

That way, nothing could hurt him.

That way, no one would ever know. . . .

Ted punched up the volume on the Sansui's remote control, letting the music wash over him, as if the decibels could drown out the nattering voice of guilt. He took another hit off his skull-bong, and listened to the dirgelike chant that opened Side Four of the album that Chris's murderers had provided in the hope that he might better understand.

And he stared, intently, at the tickets in his hand. Then at the lyrics embossed on the album's jacket.

The words to "The Critical Mass."

The words themselves were right there on the back cover, laid out in a raised, quasi-archaic, blood-red script, repeating and overlapping as they traced the shape of a pentagram. It overlaid a bastardization of the classic Da Vinci anatomical study of the-man-in-the-circle: legs spread, arms outstretched.

Except the figure on the jacket was that of a gloriously naked Tara, facing backward in mute supplication, head thrown back, wild black hair cascading all the way down to the juncture of her succulent buttocks. Her skin glowed red in the sheen of the fire that ringed her. One hand gripped a microphone, the other a dagger. The glint of razor-thin Band-Its crested the top of her skull.

Ted stared at her—an illusion on glossy paper and cardboard, product of slick art directors from Bedlam—and his drug-heightened synapses saw the figure shimmy and tremble with life, heard the worlds layered within the stereophonic folds of state-of-the-art digital mastering that pounded out of his Advent speakers:

"Magdhim Dios! Satanas Dios!
Asteroth Dios! Ellylldan Dios!"

The bass and drums pounded in droning syncopation.
Ted started to cry.

"Sancti Dios! Omnitus Dios!
Malebog Dios! Baalberth Dios!"

The chant swelled in a wash of reverse-gated, reverberating sound; the beat picked up by the microsecond.

Ted lost himself in thoughts of vengeance, the urge to rend and smash and tear uncoiling inside him.

As the tempo picked up.

And "The Critical Mass" kicked in . . .

Thirty-one

tickticktickticktick . . .

The second hand chugged through its ultramagnified paces, sandwiched in its customary between-teaser niche. It punctuated the break, as yet another segment on CIA/Contra drug-running in and out of El Salvador gave way to the full-tilt energy of The Scream, transforming their audience into a mob.

"It began as 'Rock for Rock's Sake,' and ended in disaster . . ."

Cut to a jerking journalist's frieze of smoke and fire, flailing limbs and howling feedback, then to a gaggle of whey-faced teens torching shattered vinyl as the dulcet tones of Harry Reasoner concluded, ". . . *now many people are saying it's time to 'Knock Rock' altogether*."

tickticktickticktick . . .

"Nice," Jake said under his breath. The room breathed a collective sigh of unease as the voice-over concluded by promising all this plus much more, when they came back with another edition of *60 Minutes*.

Jake felt like shit. He had good reason; *60 Minutes* was about as subtle as the stamping on a claymore mine when they went after something. *FRONT TOWARD ENEMY*. You could tell by the teaser where they were going to point these things.

And this setup had none of the glowing reverence they

had reserved for their report on Bob Geldof and Live Aid; indeed, the ticking of the stopwatch sounded more and more like a time bomb, about to blow up in all of their faces. All day, the damage reports had displaced the trade deficit and Central America in the news, and they had been condemnatory in the main, and the free-for-alls on *Washington This Week* and *Face the Nation* made it look as though the esteemed senator's legislation was gonna ramrod home. He felt like a blast victim, just coming up from the anesthesia and wondered what all was missing. He vaguely wished that he'd stayed in bed this morning. He vaguely wished that he'd stayed in the womb.

Too late now.

Some of the band and most of the crew had departed for downtown Harrisburg to hit the clubs and drown their sorrows in bright lights and beers; Jake, Hempstead, Junior, and Bob Two hung back and now huddled around a freezer chest of Heinekens in the Twilight Zone, savoring the slow-rake-over-hot-coals that was imminent. Gram was not present, which surprised no one.

Neither, not surprisingly, was Jesse. *And Pete*, the voice in his head added. *Mustn't forget ol' Pete.*

He winced and shifted uncomfortably, as a Coke-hawking Max Headroom blipped onscreen, all digitally enhanced winsomeness and wit. It was lost on Jake, who stared fixedly inward as he contemplated the basic truth that said Pete's continuing absence was beyond merely inexcusable. It was crazy. It was scary.

And getting worse, practically by the minute . . .

Because deep down inside, Jake knew that Pete's disappearance signaled big-time weirdness. Just as sure as he knew that that dream last night was some kind of warped message, a subconscious cue card that he couldn't quite see to read. It went light-years beyond the guilt rationale of survivor's syndrome. It was tangible, sensate reality.

"Rock and Roll." Harry was back. *"It's been called Devil Music, Drug Music, Porno Music, Murder Music . . ."* Harry intoned, seated before the iconographic freeze-frame of a strutting Tara Payne vis-à-vis a preening Pastor Furniss. *"Depending on whom you listen to, it will lead you to have sex, use drugs, kill yourself, or simply sell your soul."*

Harry paused bemusedly for effect, then set up the critical question.

"Certainly many bands today go out of their way to reach extremes.

"But how much is 'too much'?"

Derisive snickers rippled through the room. Junior muttered, '"Too much is never enough!" and ceremonially clinked bottles with Bob Two. Hempstead fingered his sax and blew a short, rude *blaaat!* It was defensive posturing at its finest, but Jake couldn't bring himself to join in.

". . . and increasing numbers of people are wondering just that, in the aftermath of an event that was supposed to bring a generation together . . . and wound up tearing it apart."

The frozen image animated then, Tara exhorting the crowd to madness. Jake stood up. He suddenly decided that he couldn't sit through another ten seconds, no less ten minutes, of this. Cody was taping, if he needed any of it. What he needed much more, right then, was fresh air.

He walked over to the back door and stood at the screen. It was twilight on the mountain: a magical time, eerily beautiful. The sun going down in flames, streaking amber and orange and gold through the descending canopy of night. The Susquehanna River snaking like a ribbon of fire to the west.

Standing there, breathing in the night, it was almost possible to believe that this entire thing was going to blow over somehow; that Pete would wander in eventually, wasted and disheveled, and Jake and the band would take turns kicking his ass and razzing him about it for the next six months or so, but otherwise let it slide; that the enormity of the disruption and destruction would eventually disperse, like a monsoon rain that goes for days and days on end, only to yield to the sun.

Fat chance. It's monsoon time, now and forever, amen. Jake cursed the dour sullenness of the thought, but he couldn't shake it. And though it was bad enough that he felt crazy himself, both Hempstead's rap and Slim Jim's proposed solution were entirely over the edge.

Jake stepped outside. Jim was out there, dangling his feet off the end of the porch, puffing on a meerschaum pipe. He walked up and sat down beside the chopper pilot, who exhaled a long, philosophical trail of vanilla-scented smoke and squinted into the sunset for a while before he spoke.

Finally, "Well, bossman, whaddaya say?"

"Don't know, man. It's too complicated. Too weird."

"Ain't nothin' complicated about it. These people are what's weird, and when they find out whoever torched Rock Aid, I'll betcha my bird there's a trail of bread crumbs leadin' right back to The Scream. Them and their spook manager." He spat into the dirt. "Oughta just ice the little fuckers."

Jake shook his head. *Ice the fuckers.* He made it sound so easy. Maybe it was, a long time ago. As for now . . .

"I don't know if I can do that."

"So call a professional."

Jake looked at Jim, slightly annoyed. "You've just got an answer for everything, don't you?"

"Yep. Phone numbers, too."

Jake looked at him. "You're serious."

"Yep."

"That's murder."

A pause. A sigh. "Yep."

Neither man looked at the other; Jake stared at the ground, Slim Jim at the receding sun. A scant twenty-four hours had passed since Rock Aid blew up. In that time Jacob Hamer had come in contact with more carnage than in the preceding twenty years. And here he was thinking, however speculatively, of coming even closer. A lot closer. Too close for comfort or sanity or maybe even survival . . .

It was stupid, he decided. Stupid. He wasn't some wacked-out war vet creaking under the weight of his own emotional scar tissue. He'd busted ass to build a dream and make it real. He had a home and a family he loved, a career he loved, and a community that damned near depended upon his viability for its very existence. He couldn't risk all that on the basis of a few weird dreams and some scraps of decades-old memories. They had no proof. They had no probable cause. He couldn't even safely say that Walker was the same guy; and so what if he was? So fucking what. *Lots* of guys torqued out over there, but they readjusted to The World just fine, thank you very fucking much. Contrary to the popular myth, not everybody ended up as fringe-element junkie psychopaths or road-warrior rejects, shouting out their rage from the dark edge of the world. Some of them went on with their lives. Becoming lawyers or truck drivers or doctors. Or rock stars even.

Such were the thoughts racing through Jake's mind. They were cool, solid, rational: the stuff that clearheaded game plans were made of. Jake believed them with all his heart. And he was about to tell Jim exactly that.

When the shouting from the Twilight Zone began.

It lasted for no more than three seconds.

They were the longest three seconds of her life.

"Oh, my God," Jesse whispered, not wanting to accept the image on the screen, unable to deny it. She stood in Rachel's living room and stared helplessly at the *60 Minutes* concert footage, taken from the Spectrum press box.

It was footage from Friday night's Scream performance.

And Pete was there.

Pete was there. The knowledge pummeled her with fists of lead, slid through her nerves like mercury. She watched his face pop in and out of the picture: not the focus at all, a peripheral detail sandwiched in with the rest, its significance utterly unspoken. Harry Reasoner made no comment about the missing rock star, his surprise appearance there, the fact that he had not been seen by anyone since.

But suddenly, Jesse couldn't hear what Harry Reasoner was saying at all.

Because Pete was there. Smiling. Wasted. Less than three hours after their final meeting in the lobby of the Penn Towers Hotel. Poking out from behind a corpulent Bedlam Records exec, cigarette in hand, laughing inaudibly. Disappearing for a moment. Reappearing to bounce up and down in his seat to the rhythm of the thundering music from beyond in typical Pete-like fashion.

And then he was gone.

In the next room Natalie was noisily resisting dinner. Rachel could be heard over the prattle on the tube, saying, "C'mon, Boobie. You *love* your yummy SpaghettiOs! Eat up, dammit! Go ahhh . . . ahhh . . . MMMM!" It was a combination of sounds that threatened to drive Jesse mad.

"I gotta get out of here," she told herself, the room at large. Her belly came alive with sudden pain. Tension. Dread. Terrifying suspicion. She stood, moved unsteadily toward the kitchen. A wave of dizziness hit her, and she whined, low in

her throat, staggering into the doorframe with a mute thump
and leaning there for support.

"Jesus," Rachel said. "Are you okay?"

Jesse turned to look in the direction of the voice. Both
Rachel and Natalie stared back at her. The overhead light in
the kitchen was piercing. It borrowed some of the pain from her
belly and placed it squarely behind her eyes. She could feel
the blood leaching back from her flesh, feel herself grow faint
and pale.

"No." It was only partially in answer to the question. She
had only partially heard it. There was a void at the core of her,
and it was sucking her toward it, pulling the outside in. "No,"
she repeated, and her eyes pinched shut.

In the sudden darkness she heard the back door open.

And heard Rachel mutter his name . . .

"LADIES!" boomed the voice from the doorway, jerking
Jesse's eyelids open. "IT'S SO GODDAMN GREAT TO *SEE*
YOU!"

Natalie began to scream then, cringing back instinctively
in the tight confines of her high chair. Rachel had the baby up
and in her arms within a second, backing rapidly away. The
bowl of baby SpaghettiOs clattered noisily to the floor. All this
went on in the periphery of Jesse's vision.

Her gaze was fixed upon the dead man in the doorway.

"EEYAAOW! YOU IN *PARTICULAR*, JESS! GOD, ARE
YOU A SIGHT FOR SORE EYES!"

He laughed, and it was all wrong: a high-pitched trilling,
like a gale wind blown through a rot-clogged pipe. There was a
burble at the back of it that sent the taste of bile to her tongue.

"Pete, no," she croaked. She wanted to back up as well,
but her back was already to the wall. There was nothing to do
but look at him while the weakness in her body intensified,
magnified, consumed her.

Pete laughed again, in the flesh. His flesh looked bad:
pasty-white and blotchy, like a loaf of molding, uncooked
dough. His teeth, exposed, were yellow and brittle as Indian
corn. Silver shades concealed his eyes.

"Yes," said another voice from behind him. "Believe me.
All the way here, he's been talkin' about nothing but you."

Two more Screamers came in. The speaker was older, tall
and thin. He looked like Keith Richards and talked like Bruce

Dern. He was the only one who appeared even remotely alive. The other one was just a kid and looked even worse than Pete.

Rachel had retreated to Jesse's side at the far end of the kitchen, her screaming daughter tight in her arms. "What's going on here, Pete?" she said, her voice taut to cracking. She was scared. She was trying very hard not to show it. She took another step back. "I mean, wh-what are you people doing here?"

"*Well, shoot, Rachel!*" Peter howled, stepping forward. "*Just about anything we WANT, I guess!*"

Rachel bolted and ran. The littlest Screamer started after her. For the first time, Jesse noticed the knife in his hand. She shrieked, pressing against the wall as they hurtled past her. For one lunatic second, she thought about running too.

Then she stared into the black gaze.

Of the barrel.

Of the gun.

"You stay right there, little missy." Kyle said, "Mr. Peter would like to share a moment with you."

Upstairs, Rachel began to scream.

And Natalie, suddenly, stopped.

If not for a defective soldering iron, Cody never would have seen them at all.

He was down at the shack; the lodge had gotten too weird. Until the boys settled down, he didn't want to be near them. They were putting out some scary vibes.

Dinky-dow, as Hempstead said. Vietnamese for *crazy shit*.

There was, of course, always work to be done. It made a great excuse. It was also excellent therapy: there were very few things in Cody's life that couldn't be cured by a couple hours of zen and the art of circuit board maintenance.

Which he would have happily gone on with forever.

Had the iron not fritzed out.

It was a budget Radio Shack model; and when it went, it took the lightbulb over his work bench and everything else on that circuit with it.

Including all the other lights in the shack.

Including the VCR feed to the lodge.

"*Shit.*" He sat there like a fool in the sudden darkness. He cursed several more times before he found and fired up his flashlight. Then he put down the board and made his way over to the circuit box to trip it back. His glance through the window by the box was strictly casual.

It was the movement that caught his eye: out in the woods, furtively menacing, like a pack of stalking wolves. The shadows rapidly consumed them as they moved up the hill, but not before Cody sighted three: two skulking Screamers in black leather and longcoats and a big guy carrying what very much looked like an assault rifle.

"Holy hell," Cody whispered, clicking off the Duracell. It was the afternoon's paranoia made flesh; whatever these people were doing, it was not likely to involve the spread of world peace. *"They were right."*

And then he started thinking. Fast.

It was roughly three hundred yards from the shack to the big house, most of it a steep incline; they would have a precious few minutes grace. Cody felt his way through the darkness to where the intercom mike was sitting and keyed it on.

"Jeezuz, I hope you guys are nearby," he said by way of prayer. "Preferably armed."

". . . 'cause we sure as shit got company."

Cody's voice crackled through the intercom in the lodge, rupturing the media silence that had come when the big TV shut down. That silence had lasted for fifteen seconds, leaving a load of confusion in its wake.

That confusion was almost fatal.

"CODY!" Jake yelled. "WHAT THE HELL IS GOING ON?"

There was no answer. Junior and Bob Two stood frozen by the pool table, cues in hand. Hempstead was already moving toward the closet where the rifles were stashed. Jake looked over to the doorway. Slim Jim was nowhere to be seen.

"CODY!" Jake repeated. "WHAT THE HELL DO YOU MEAN?"

"*Shut up.*" Hempstead hissed. He had chambered a round in the Kleingeunther by the time Jake started to turn toward him.

And then the Screamer stepped into the doorway.

He was a big greasy fucker with a face like hamburger

and a crudely rendered mohawk. He had a True Value Woodsman Special hatchet in one hand. "EEYAAOW!" he howled. "BOOLA BOOLA!"

And charged.

Hempstead turned toward him, aimed, and fired twice.

The Screamer went out the door backward, minus the hatchet and about five pounds of the flesh below the solar plexus. The 140-grain boat-tail spire point was a big bullet, better suited to bringing down elk or caribou: the sheer shock of impact blew a crater-sized hole in the Screamer, pitching him violently onto the redwood porch.

"Get your fucking gun," Hempstead said, moving toward the door.

Jake didn't need to be told twice. He raced toward the closet, got his weapon in his hands, ran to where Hempstead was standing, and stared at the Screamer.

Who should have been dead.

But wasn't.

The Screamer lay in a long skid mark of gore, twitching and flailing. His spinal column had been sheared away between the fourth and sixth vertebrae; his lower half dragged uselessly behind him, connected only by tendrils of ruined muscle and skin. The white fluted ends of his shattered spine jutted out into the cool night air.

There was obviously pain: that much had, clearly, not been stripped away. But the lunatic sound that spewed forth from his lips was somewhere between a laugh and a howl, as though this whole thing were somehow insanely funny.

Then Jake heard the windows begin to crash in from behind him.

And nothing was funny.

At all.

She had slipped and fallen near the top of the stairs. She hadn't planned it. She was helpless to stop it. At the rate she was moving, there was no time for thought.

She slipped. She fell. She hit with a thud.

And Natalie went horribly silent.

There was a second then, unbelievably long, when Rachel Adams felt her sanity fly out of her like a torpedo. Then the footsteps began to thunder up behind her, and she knew there was no time for insanity, no time for dicking around. Her baby was fine—her baby had to be fine, there was no way she could live if her baby was not fine—and so she hauled herself, screaming, to her feet.

The tip of the utility knife caught her behind the knee-cap, a glancing blow that slashed its way diagonally down across her calf. She stumbled again, now at the top of the steps, screaming even harder, the blade snicking another shallow groove out of her flesh, making an X as she dragged herself, bleeding and tearing, forward.

The door to Ted's bedroom flew open. The sound of The Scream thundered into the hall. Light formed a wedge on the hardwood floor, then filled with shadow. Ted flew into view.

Rachel tried to scream for help. The word was super-ceded by the rending of her flesh as the Screamer began to enjoy himself now, blade going snik and snik and snik, carving out little divots from the small of her back. She rose up from the waist, screeching, then fell back down again, her ear pressed to the infant chest of the limp form in her arms. She swore she heard a heartbeat there, even over the sound of her own shrill screams.

"YOU CAN'T HAVE HER, MOTHERFUCKER!" she heard herself howl, releasing Natalie to the wood floor and whirling, exposing her belly to the killing blade as she grappled for the arm that held it. . . .

Logan was positioned on the outskirts of the parking apron, belly down with an AK47 in his hands. Things were already out of control: Burger Boy hadn't even made it through the door before they'd popped his dumb dead ass. Now Hamer and the big nigger were standing over him like a couple of sitting fucking ducks.

Logan cursed as he set the selector switch on semiauto and pulled back the bolt on the Kalishnakov; he'd tried to tell Walker that you shouldn't send boys to do a man's job, and *piss* on the loose strings. Now he'd just have to go ahead and prove it.

He already had Hamer's hairy head sighted when a crash came from within the lodge; they both ducked in before he could squeeze off.

"Dammit!" he hissed, and raised up on his knees. Now he'd have to go inside.

He was just standing to do so when the shadow swooped down behind him like an angel of death. One hand grabbed the top of his skull; the other slammed a gun barrel into the hollow behind his right ear. His sight starred over in a billion bright pinpoints of pain, blinding him. The click of a revolver's hammer pulling back was louder than life itself, the voice of doom that followed even more so. "Don't even think about it, asshole.

"Don't even think about it."

Cody was fumbling with the Trident when the first reports echoed down the trail. It was hard in the dark, but easier than dealing with the instantaneous unraveling of the fabric of higher consciousness: shoot now, philosophize later. Great choices.

He was terrified. The aesthetics of archery were of small comfort against the prospect of unknown gun-toting maniacs roaming the grounds. He knew the territory; they could reload faster. It didn't even out.

He got the Trident locked and ready and fell back into the furthermost shadows of the shack, heart pounding wildly. He could hear them yelling up the hill and down, wondered wildly if anyone else would hear it.

He doubted it. The downside of seclusion: no neighbors around to call the police or the cavalry or the Marines or . . .

A shadow passed across the window. Cody's heart froze. Someone was directly outside the cabin. He sunk further back into a recess between two audio racks until only his left hand extended, the crossbow pointed at quivering head-level to the door some thirty feet away. Random vestiges of reason whirled like dervishes in his mind, going *oh my god what am i gonna do i can't really kill anyone can i don't even eat meat please god damn i can't deal with this i*

The door kicked open. A crossing shadow filled it.

And Cody fired.

He didn't even mean to: the action was closer to premature ejaculation than premeditation. Eight inches of steel-tipped fiberglass went singing through the air in a kinetic parabola, tracing a deadly arc from Cody's hand to the shadow's head. The impact of the bolt knocked the thing right back into the doorjamb, where it remained. Spraddled. Struggling.

Pinned.

Cody squirmed out of his hiding place and threw the circuit breaker. Light flooded the length of the shack.

And his target became horribly clear.

The bolt had entered through the left eye socket and punched clean through the back of its head, embedding itself in the splintered wood of the jamb. The thing was effectively nailed.

But the thing was still alive.

And the bolt through its head had only slowed it down. The wound just seemed to piss it off. It snapped and spit and grabbed at the back of its head, twisting and straining against the shaft until it made a sound like a crowbar ripping through rotted cantaloupe. Its other socket, equally eyeless, squinted at him with total, killing rage.

Cody was scared; scared that it would any second wrench free of its skull-mooring and come screaming toward him; afraid to try to scramble past. Inadvertently, Cody froze. The thing in the doorway pulled and growled.

And the bolt held.

For the moment . . .

There were two of them in the room, surrounded by the broken glass from their entry. Both of them were Screamers. Both of them were armed: bowie knife on the left, length of chain on the right. Jake sized them up in the second it took to lever a cartridge into the chamber. Hempstead, to his left, was already aiming. There was no question as to who should shoot whom.

Then the third Screamer came through the doorway behind them and fucked up everything.

Hempstead was the first to whirl, just in time for hand-to-hand. Jake turned just in time to watch it happen, remembered where he was, turned back again. The Screamers had not stood still. The one on the left was moving toward him. The one on the right was six feet from Junior and closing.

Bob Two and Junior had been frozen throughout. Jake understood it, even as he brought the scope to his eye and lined the cross hairs. It was the difference between people who'd been there and people who hadn't. That simple. Until it happened, you didn't know.

And once it happened, you never forgot.

Pulling the trigger was easy. Automatic. Jake could see the hole before it happened, and that didn't even matter. He squeezed. The hole appeared. Wet brain and bone sprayed out the back to sparkle in the light.

Behind him Hempstead fired, just once. It gave Jake a nice warm feeling inside. *Another one down. All is right with the world.* He ejected the spent casing, fed in another shell.

Just as Bob Two's paralysis broke, and he caught the whirling length of chain with the fat end of his pool cue. Junior seemed suddenly to understand as well. His own cue came up to hit the Screamer in the teeth.

They were bunched too tight for Jake to fire. He watched them struggle for a moment. His own Screamer was not even twitching: understandable, given its absence of head. For the moment, things seemed to be under control.

And then he remembered Rachel . . .

Another sound from the main room: the crunching thud of expensive things falling over. Somebody was ransacking the studio. Somebody was about to die.

Hempstead took a deep breath and readied himself; he couldn't tell how many were in there, but it was at least two. Maybe armed. Probably armed. His mental scorekeeper tallied that there were three rounds left in the Kleingeunther. Not good. Unavoidable.

They were really ripping into shit, more like a destroy than a search, but with plenty of both. Hempstead considered falling back to reload, decided against it. *Dinky-dao*, he thought. Oh, well.

He stepped into the doorway. There were two, all right: a ferret-faced Screamer who looked fifteen, tops, and an older, mercenary hardcase-type. The latter was by Jesse's keyboards, digging around and cursing. The ferret was tipping over speaker cabinets and laughing. The man took one look at Hempstead and the Kleingeunther and bolted for the door, clutching a small box like a tight end at the thirty-yard line.

Hempstead fired and missed, the bullet smashing into the wall inches behind the fleeing man. He chambered another round and aimed. The hardcase hit the screen.

And the ferret went wild.

In the split second of inattention he had grabbed a stray

mike stand, which he hefted and swung. The tubular steel rod connected with Hempstead's forehead with brutal force, smacking him in the temple and sending him careening into the wall. The Kleingeunther fell clattering to the floor, its breech still opened, its round unchambered. The world went sideways and down; Hempstead joined it, crashing to the floor. A hot gout of blood spurted from the gash that had opened up on the side of his head.

The ferret straddled Hempstead, grinning maniacally, the mike stand still in hand. He raised it like a posthole digger, its heavy metal base directly over the fallen man's skull.

"SEE YOU IN HELL, ASSHOLE!" the ferret screeched.

He raised the stand higher, screaming "EEAYOWW!" . . .

. . . as twin explosions blew from the top of the stairs, sending double-barreled buckshot firing into the ferret's straining back. Lead-flecked goo punched through the rancid fabric of his shirt to spatter Jackson Pollock designs on the wall. What remained pitched forward in a hundred-pound heap, landing squarely atop Hempstead.

"GAHHHH!" he screeched, squirming out from under it. The stench was incredible, like having a sack of sun-ripened road-kill dropped on your head. Its death was a foregone conclusion. He pushed it off and looked for the source of his reprieve.

He found her at the top of the stairs, an ancient double-barreled shotgun propped on the banister for support. Gram looked down at him, eyes wide with fear and a flinty moral resolve.

"Burglars," she said.

. . . and Jake was running, running down the hill, his mind a blank that screamed her name as he thundered down the path, praying to God that he wasn't too late . . .

. . . and when one of the Screamers charted an intercept course, he blew out its breastbone without missing a beat, one foot after another, nothing getting in his way, God help the whole world if one single solitary goddamned thing got in his way . . .

. . . as, from the house below, he heard the last of the screams . . .

* * *

. . . and it all went down in a matter of seconds: the short race down the hall to the top of the stairs, past the tiny still form of his sister, his black boot coming back, then up, driving into the Adam's apple of the Screamer, who whooped and flew back as his neck pulped and snapped, the knife flying backwards, the Screamer as well, careening down the staircase and into the rail. Ted followed, taking the steps two at a time, scooping up the knife as the Screamer lay there twitching like a beetle on its back, belly up and open as the knife came down and tore it open, came up, came down, came up again.

And he could see Chris Konopliski when he closed his eyes, could see his best friend spitting blood, and he didn't want to see that so he opened his eyes and saw that the Screamer was *not* spitting blood, wasn't bleeding at all, and the sight made him so crazy that he brought the blade down to the ruined throat and began to saw his way through it, down to the bone, ignoring the flailing spastic limbs, sawing down *through* the bone and into the hard wood beneath as the limbs went still and the head tore loose to go *thumpity thump* down the remainder of the stairs.

But there still was no blood, so he dropped the knife, brought his hands to his face and began to cry, crying for the impotence that had kept him still before, crying for the vengeance that wasn't enough, crying until he had no more tears left and then tapering off, the world filtering in, the sound of other voices in the great dying night, the voices of his mother and his sister, crying too. . . .

Thirty-two

They dragged all the bodies down to he shooting range and piled them in a heap. It was a maddening task. The Screamers all seemed to break down into two basic categories: long dead, and not nearly dead enough.

The former had rapidly given up the ghost, and even more rapidly disintegrated with the onslaught of overdue decay. The ferret-faced one, in particular, had to be carried down in hunks. One bootlace had gotten snagged on the way down the trail, and before they even realized it, his leg had pulled apart like an overcooked pot roast, the meat stringing away with the wet snap of frayed rubber bands as hip and pelvis parted company and the entire limb slid out of its pants leg.

It lay there leaking onto the path while Junior and Bob Two dry-heaved into the bushes, until Jim came along. He had Logan in tow; the AK slung over one shoulder, Logan's arms tied painfully back with speaker cable, the gun still wedged in the hollow behind his ear.

"Pick 'im up, boys," Jim said. "Move it."

He shoved Logan down the trail. Junior looked at Bob Two, both of whom wished that they had gone out for beers with the rest of the band, after all. It was hard to say which was scarier: the unremitting nightmare of what had just happened, or the paramilitaristic aftershock that it had clicked on in Hempstead, Jake, and Jim. It was like Bob and Junior had suddenly been demoted to the lowest possible rank known to the military mind: civilian.

They scooped up their load, trying to ignore the stench and the sound and texture. It was, perhaps, the worst experience of their lives.

To date, anyway.

Because as bad as the dead Screamers were, they absolutely paled in comparison to the one in the latter category. The one who wouldn't give it up. The one who *wouldn't* die.

That was the one who was as yet still pinned to the inside of Cody's shed. With Logan, that made for a grand total of two prisoners of this little war.

Which is exactly what they were in, Junior realized: a war. The thought was perhaps more unsettling than the grisly chore at hand. It lent an air of permanence to the madness, as though this were less an aberration than a preview of coming attractions: the next lurid installment of the future as told by George Romero. *Evening of the Dead.* Special effects by Tom Savini. Soundtrack by The Scream. Coming soon to your living room, whether you like it or not.

They finished dragging their load over to the far side of the shooting range. The arc lamps mounted on surrounding trees were lit, filling the clearing with a harsh, glaring light. Hempstead was standing over the bodies, stripped to the waist, a swath of white gauze around his forehead and the rifle on his hip. He was holding a pair of shovels.

"Here." He handed them each one. "Best you both start digging."

"What do you mean?" Bob Two asked, more than a little aghast. "What the hell's going on here?"

"I don't know," Hempstead replied, "but we're about to find out. In the meantime, start digging."

"We can't just *bury* them here! We should be calling the police or something!"

"Oh, yeah, well, hey, why don't you go do that! And when they *get* here, you can point out the one whose head *you* personally beat in with a pool cue!"

Hempstead prodded with his boot at the one with the crushed jaw and flattened skull. Its own putrefaction was no less exponential: its skin was already sloughing off in soapy, adipocerous clumps; a noxious whiff of methane and hydrogen sulfide pooted out of its bloated torso. Bob Two felt sick all over again. "But that was self-defense," he muttered.

"Yeah, I know," Hempstead said. "And so is this." He thrust a shovel at each of them.

"Now start digging. And make it deep."

Bob Two was tempted to say something else, but it faltered before he could even voice it. He really wished he'd taken that gig with The Del-Rays.

Junior was already at it, shovel sinking and rising, sinking and rising. He didn't look up, he didn't say a word. Bob turned his back to the bodies, tears welling in his eyes.

And he started digging.

Jake could not allow himself to feel. To feel would be to cave in. To feel would be to die. He could not afford the luxury. Not yet.

So he let the cold take over.

And concentrated on the facts.

The fact was that Natalie would be okay. Jake checked her for signs of serious damage: unfocused eyes, disorientation, drowsiness, bleeding. She checked out positive, in the best sense of the word. A nice bruise forthcoming, and some serious nightmares. But no trip to the hospital.

Which led, of course, to Rachel.

She had been sliced, oh, yes, no question, but she would be okay, too. No major cables severed, no major muscle groupings: just a series of painful and ugly flesh wounds. Thank God for the denim of her pants and vest.

She wouldn't even need stitches, from the look of it. Just a lot of love and Jake's patented field dressings. The latter he whipped up in an instant.

The love would have to wait.

Sticking to the facts:

Three. Chris was dead. Ted had not told anyone, but now it came out. Chris was killed by a Screamer—by one of those things—at Rock Aid.

This explained quite a bit.

Four. Ted had a copy of The Scream's two-record set. It was an interesting piece of work, the way Ted described it. Ted was terrified.

Jake borrowed the album.

Five. Ted had killed the Screamer. Jake was very proud of him.

Or would be soon.

Six. Pete had come to the house tonight. Pete was one of those things.

Jake would not allow it. Not allow himself to feel.

Seven. Jesse was gone.

Eight. Rachel needed to be held, very badly. So did Natalie. So did Ted. Jake could manage that all right. He could even utter the right assurances.

But the cold had taken over.

While the facts spoke for themselves.

At the shed, mayhem still reigned.

The Screamer's head was still nailed to the door jamb. The feathers at the end of the shaft were tickling the back of its left eye socket. Coochie-coo. The other socket was just as empty, but it seemed to be watching them closely all the same.

Cody was still stuck inside, the crossbow in his hand. He was keeping his distance. An understandable thing. The Screamer was pissed off in general—growling like a pit bull, tugging fruitlessly at its mooring—but it seemed to have a special affection for Cody.

Logan was trussed like a Thanksgiving turkey, eighteen-gauge wire stretching across his chest and down under his crotch and back up to his wrists, which were pulled back so tight that the elbows almost touched. His chest jutted under the strain, which threatened to dislocate both shoulders if he so much as breathed wrong, and the wire between his legs had neatly bisected his scrotum into two one-way tickets to the Vienna Boys Choir.

Slim Jim held him as Hempstead came running up the trail. It was true, all right. Jesse was gone, and whatever else Pete was, he was on the other side now. He relayed the information, then asked, "So who's this asshole?"

"Says his name's Logan." Jim flipped him a billfold. "ID checks, but it could be faked."

"Close enough." He shouldered his rifle, walked over to Logan, leaned in, and said, "Okay, fucker, I ain't gonna ask you twice. I want some goddamned answers. I *know* who sent you. What I want to know is, why? What were your orders? Where is Jesse?"

"Piss off, nigger!"

Hempstead nodded, then grabbed Logan roughly by his bonds and hoisted him horizontally up to waist level. Logan shrieked, a high-pitched wheeze of agony, as his legs left the ground.

"Wrong answer." Hempstead then dropped him like a hundred-and-sixty-pound sack of potatoes. The snap of elbow joints was clearly audible. The mashing of his testicles was a much quieter, though infinitely more painful process. Logan laid there sucking wind for a couple of minutes, unable to speak or think or move. The pain settled over him like a blanket of fire, every cell in his brain screaming for the release of death.

And hoping, when it came, that it would go unnoticed.

Hempstead leaned over him. "Okay, let's try it again. The Scream's manager sent you. Yes?"

"Uhhhhh . . ." Logan moaned. The pain was a smothering black veil of stars.

"Answer!" Hempstead prodded one shattered arm. "Yes?"

"Y-y-yuh."

"Why?"

"Geh . . . geh . . ." The pain shifted, black waves spinning. "Get . . ."

"Get." Hempstead reiterated. "Get what?"

"Bih . . . bih . . ." The pain took shape in his mind. "B-Bitch."

Hempstead and Jim exchanged glances. *Jesse.* "Okay. Get bitch. Why?"

Logan whimpered; the pain folded in on itself.

Hempstead prodded. "Why 'get bitch'?"

"Mah . . ." Logan's face screwed up horribly. The pain intensified a million times, the fold deepening into a huge, sucking void. "Mahhhh . . ."

"Mahhhh-mah . . ."

Hempstead felt a strange chill uncoil in his bowels. Logan was crying now, great wet tears squeezing out of the corners of his eyes. In his body, in his brain, the pain spread. The pain smiled.

The pain opened wide.

"MAHHHHHHHHHHHH-MAH!" He screamed, voice climbing from grown-man deep to little-boy screech in one long keening squeal.

"MAHHHHHHHHHHHHHHH-MAHHHHHHHHHHHH!!!"

Hempstead fell back involuntarily as Logan started flopping in the dirt like a cat in a burlap sack. He bounced literally off the ground, landing again and again on his pulverized joints as though whatever he was experiencing inside utterly dwarfed the exterior wreckage in intensity.

A sympathetic vibration seemed to pass through the Screamer as well: he stopped in mid-growl like a dog at the sound of its master's voice, as Logan did the hell-bound hokey-pokey at their feet.

Then he started screaming, too: clipped, hyper cries. Cody's Screamer lurched forward violently, pulling the shaft through the back of his skull, and collapsed on the floor, going "EAYOWW! EAYOWW!"

Cody, Hempstead, and Jim fell back and pointed their weapons, but nobody fired. They were spellbound by the phenomena playing out before them. The two captives seemed gripped in the presence of a unifying field that was overloading them all; turning their attentions wholly inward.

Logan, personally, knew of nothing beyond his own frail boundaries. The release his brain cells had cried for was coming, yes. But it had not gone unnoticed. He had disobeyed orders, and he had fucked up.

Worst of all, he had broken the vow of silence, and the little he had revealed was more than enough to introduce him to a whole new world of hurt.

The smiling void revealed that to him as it opened wide. It would reveal much, much more, in the dread fullness of time. Logan screamed, one last long "MAHHHHHHHHHHHH . . ."

And it swallowed his soul.

A buzzing in the hive-mind: calling out to the faithful, making the many One. A time to retreat.
A job done.
And to Hell with the lost.

Logan was one dead fuck. Only the husk remained, an expression of bottomless anguish etched into every line of his features.

"Jesus," Jim whispered. "What just happened?"

Hempstead leaned over Logan's corpse and shook his head at the sixty-four-thousand-dollar question.

In the doorway, on the floor, the Screamer laughed.

It was a coarse, husky gurgle, halfway between a chuckle and a sob. It flashed Hempstead back to a time years past, when he and Jake had tripped and gone to see *The Exorcist*: the way Mercedes McCambridge's demon-voice had issued from Linda Blair's child-face. It had caused every hair on the nape of his neck to do the fandango back then, and that was only the relative fantasy of the silver screen.

This was indescribably worse. Even the rules of fantasy didn't apply anymore; fantasy had flown right out the fucking window. Like it or not, this was *reality*, and Hempstead had seen enough of the dark fringes of reality to guess that conventional, rational logic no longer applied.

All of which meant, tactically speaking, some kind of new logic. That meant new rules. And embracing those rules would allow him to think strategically. Embracing the irrational would allow him not to lose his mind.

Which he was not about to do.

So he studied the situation, which at the moment included the thing on the floor. It had grown weaker in the aftermath of whatever killed Logan; the veneer of terror had stripped right off of it, leaving what looked very much like a sixteen-year-old undead waif. It no longer appeared fearsome so much as abandoned, as though it were suddenly marooned here, cut off from its source of power.

He thought about that, as he watched the thing laugh and cry and writhe on the floor. He wondered if it could speak.

One way to find out.

He reached over and gingerly rolled the quivering thing over onto its back. Cody and Slim Jim drew closer. It curled like a thalidomide baby into his grasp, still rasping its laughing, halting cry. If it noticed their attention, it gave no outward indication.

He studied its face: sunken, drawn features, breath hitching through tightly stretched jaw ligaments. Its jaw locked up periodically, clicking as it tried in vain to close. Its expression was one of intense confusion, intense sadness, intense pain. It stared upward, eyelids opening wide.

Pockets of thin, vaguely luminescent red worms squirmed wildly in the holes.

Hempstead studied it. *New rules*. He had seen them before; they were a natural segment of the food chain. They usually waited until their host wasn't breathing.

New rules.

"Do you have a name?" His voice was soft but insistent, less the inquisitor than the hypnotist. "Do you have a name?"

The thing nodded weakly. "D-d-dickey . . . ," it managed, barely a whisper.

"Dickey . . ."

It started to cry then, gulping air to feed its lamentation. The thalidomide curl turned fetal in position; the wormy tears fell.

"Where'd they take Jesse, Dickey?"

A flash of schizophrenic grin cut across the sorrow; Dickie giggled grotesquely in his grasp. "T-took her for the s-sh-show."

Hempstead frowned; the kid's mind was cooked. He looked up at the bolt wedged in the doorjamb and saw where some of Dickie's brain cells had been left; he wondered where he'd left the others. Dickey started humming some atonal melody, blinking back the worms.

"Why, Dickie?"

Dickie laughed, coughing thickly. His jaw locked up again. Hempstead shook him.

"Why??"

It was no use; he was almost used up. The coughing laughter became violent, racking sobs; Hempstead was about to just give it up when the Screamer stopped in one last gasp of fractured clarity and spoke. Two words, cryptically out of context.

Two words: both anthem and answer.

"Raise . . . hell."

When Jake came back up the hill, the bodies were gone. Very little was said. Little needed to be.

Jake went back up to the lodge.

Jim had a couple of calls to make.

Thirty-three

I t was close now. Very close. The only thing between
him and the heat from its jaws was the cooling spark
of life that held him to his body.

But it was time to die.

Alex Royale lay on the bed, in the space between his
blindness and the darkness deeper still. If there were others in
the room, he could not hear them. If they were touching him,
he could not know. The outside . . . even only so far as his
skin . . . was fog and miles of distance.

But inside was radiant clarity: sound and light and taste
and heat and smell. All of them wicked.

All of them Hell.

And the thing was smiling, smiling with its teeth so long
in its jaws so wide. It talked to him, confided in him, showered
him with praise and molten breath, thanked him profusely for
what he'd done and told him how much it loved him.

It will all be over soon, it said, *and then we can be
together.*

But first I have to tell you about what I'm bringing you.

And the wonderful completion it implies.

There were no more screams left inside Alex. His cancer
was of the spirit, and it had eaten away his bones. No more
legs to stand on. No more spine to hold straight in the face of
adversity. What muscle remained was slack and limp.

Bearing no more fight.

At all.

I've brought you something you just won't believe, the voice
continued. A black tongue licked cankered lips. *I've brought
you . . . no, don't thank me yet . . . an actual sample of the*

*moment of conception. Can you believe it? Myself, I was too
stunned for words.*

*But you know what I always say: Pray hard enough, and
the Good Lord will provide.*

The thing laughed, its teeth so close that he could feel the
razored whistle of their movement.

That's only the beginning, though, it continued. *I also
brought the one who made it. She's wonderful, brilliant, a real
musician. Almost as brilliant as you are.* It laughed again. *And
beautiful, too.*

I really think that you'll like each other a lot.

Alex had thought that he was beyond pain. The moment
proved him wrong, once again and forever.

In his mind's glowing eye, he could see her clearly.
Momma wasn't lying. She was truly beautiful. The fact of his
life's long loneliness jammed itself through his core like a hot
lightning rod.

And it was too late, too late . . .

*Best of all, though, is the fact that she's pregnant. That's
right. She's still bearing the little shaver that's sampled on her
disk. Just think about that for a second, Bucky: you can get it
coming in and going out, all at once.*

He tried to work up a scream. It would not come.

*Of course, I will need you to modify things. The signal she
brought is too clean. It's too . . . nice.*

*But, of course, I will need you to be strong for this. And
you are so close to me. Your strength is nearly gone.*

That's why I've brought you something else.

That I want you, now, to see.

The vision changed, in his inner eye. He could see
himself. He could see the room. He could see the IV, his
needled arm. He could see the flagging waveforms on the
monitors beside him.

He could see the door as it slowly opened.

And Tara stepped inside.

It was the first time that he'd ever seen her. The blindness
had come to him years before. Retinitis pigmentosa: a degener-
ative disease, eating away at his vision's periphery. Narrowing
it down, a centimeter at a time, like the walls closing in on the
heroes in an old Universal Pictures horror film. Several feet.
One foot. One inch. One microscopic sliver of light.

And then gone.

Leaving him open to the other side of darkness.

And in that darkness she came to him. He knew it was her. He knew her by smell. He could see, now, exactly why she frightened him so . . . why the human fodder of fandom was so willingly drawn to her oven for the slaughter.

She was beautiful.

Too beautiful to be real.

And she was coming toward him now, expressionless as she slipped the tie on her robe and let it fall open to unveil the exquisite nakedness beneath. Her breasts were perfect, not too large or too small. Her hips held sway over his inner vision. The triangular fur that crowned her depths was dark and yet revealing.

Her eyes were only for him.

This is the moment of ultimate giving, she said to him, in a voice as soft as silk. *This is the time where I give to you, as you have given to me.*

She touched him then. So soft. So sweet. For a moment he could almost forget the teeth behind the apparition.

I love you, she whispered. *I always have. I never meant to hurt you.*

But we were born for this moment, you and I.

And so we must come together.

Erection was beyond him now, no matter how hot her charms. He simply didn't have the wherewithal; his body was too far gone. Evidently that didn't matter. She straddled him anyway, her wet crease taut against his impotence. She ground there, meticulous, her hands on his chest, and lowered her left breast to his lips.

Miraculously, his lips began to suckle her.

Miraculously, he began to grow hard.

Oh, yes, she sighed. *Oh, yes, my love.* She kissed him on the forehead, and he grew harder still. The spark within him began to flame. His arms came up. His fingers came to light upon her perfect ass and held there, caressing, as she brought her mouth to his.

We were born for this moment, she whispered once more.

Then her lips parted to take him in.

And her own eyes gave way to her fingertips.

And, together, they were reborn.

Side Four

RAISING HELL

"No skill in swordsmanship, however just,
Can be secure against a madman's thrust."
—William Cowper

"Lord, here comes the flood,
We'll say good-bye to flesh and blood."
—Peter Gabriel

MONDAY, SEPTEMBER 7
LABOR DAY
PHILADELPHIA, PA

7:06 P.M.

Click

. . . and as opposition mounted in an eleventh-hour effort to halt the scheduled Scream concert in the wake of the Rock Aid riot, the ACLU and Bedlam records attorney Denny Isham again refuted any connection between the band and Saturday's violence, in which sixty-seven people were killed and scores more wounded. No one has yet claimed credit for the attack. The governor has refused to order a halt, stating that it would be unfair at this time to penalize the victims of the attack, although he has suggested that Philadelphia's mayor boost police presence at the Spectrum. The mayor responded in a press conference earlier today that the governor's recent budget cutbacks have left a serious manpower allocation problem, and additional police presence will be difficult. This has been a WYCS news blip. . . .

Click

7:07 P.M.

Buzz Duffy was a blue-haired boy with eyes to match. It was a radiant cobalt hue that offset his sunken cheekbones and stubbled temples. Both eyes and hair were flecked with the barest hints of green and red as well. It was either a cosmetological mutation or a political statement, depending on how you looked at it.

Buzz knew how he viewed it. He also knew how his parents saw it; and their pastor, and his stupid goddamned probation officer. In fact, most of the authority figures in his life considered it rebellious or sinful or socially maladjusted.

What the hell. Buzz Duffy wasn't there anymore, and they weren't here.

Lucky for him.

Because here, on this day, Buzz ruled. He was in his element, which was a crowd currently estimated at about fourteen thousand and counting.

Technically, he'd run away from home again, seeing that his folks wouldn't allow him to come legitimately. Technically, he was in a shitload of trouble. So what the hell. It was worth it.

He'd been here all day, watching the scene grow from circus sideshow proportions to near-mythic status. The parking lot was jammed up by noon and had even started spilling onto Pattison Avenue. There were news crews and Holy Rollers and cops and protesters and vendors and scalpers and dealers and cops.

But mostly, there were kids. The kids outnumbered absolutely everybody, and the kids were really rocking. White-hot metal thundered out of scores of car stereos and boom boxes as thousands clustered around their cases and kegs and pipes and bongs, getting stoked for the evening's big event. They threw Frisbees across the parking lot. They threw bottles at the Dumpsters. They blocked traffic. They scared the piss out of passersby. He'd heard ambulances go by three times, heard stories of overdoses and a couple of fights. But no arrests. Not yet.

It was like the hordes of Genghis Khan had overrun the Spectrum Sports Arena, and anybody who didn't like it could suck eggs and walk on the shells. And it was like they knew it, too.

Hell, not five minutes ago he saw six guys mosey up to "the weeping wall," the flat expanse of poured concrete on Spectrum's southern side—brewskies in one hand, wangers in the other—and whizz their way to stardom while some geeks from Channel Four caught it all on tape and a cop on horseback just sat there, watching 'em. They peed out a big wet message for the nightly news:

H-I M-O-M-!

Then they just walked away, laughin'.

Yeah, he could feel it, all right. *Try and stop us.*

Cop didn't do shit.

It was great.

There was an edge in the air, potent and electric. It was the sense of Something Coming. Buzz couldn't rightly say what; but whatever it was, it was gonna be a blast. And Buzz could hardly wait.

This was his lucky night.

He did, after all, have something that his so-called best friend—that stupid little chickenshit Tommy Schaeffer—didn't. Namely, Tommy's ticket. He'd picked up both tickets at the Ticketron yesterday; Tommy was supposed to drive down in his old man's Malibu. It was gonna be a blast.

Until Tommy's old man caught wind of it, that is, and restricted him until sometime just before the dawn of the next Ice Age. Of course, Buzz's folks did, too, but that didn't stop him.

He just ran away again. No bigee.

Whereas Tommy Schaeffer wimped out, leaving his best buddy Buzz to fucking *hitchhike* all the way down from Wilkes-Barre alone. Took all damned night. He figured that forfeiture of the ticket was the least Tommy could do, under the circumstances. It was doubtless for the best.

It was also doubtless what got him his mystery date.

He'd first seen her hovering near scalper's row, looking all willowy an' lost an' stuff. Buzz prided himself on his ability to read a person's body English, and he had amused himself all day by guessing at each person's secret iden-

tity as he cruised the lot, thinking: Head. Head. Dealer. Head. Slut. Scalper. Narc. Head. Scalper . . .

And then he saw the girl. She didn't fit into any of the aforementioned categories. In fact, the only category she did seem to exemplify was one that seemed glaringly out of place amongst the hucksters, druggies, con artists, and cops.

Damsel.

Like, In Distress.

Now there was something you didn't see every day. So what the hell. He talked to her.

She said she really needed to get in to the show, but she didn't have a ticket, and she didn't even have any money, and she didn't seem to have much of anything going for her beyond a kinda decent body and a kinda cute face and a look in her eyes that made him feel like maybe this was his lucky day, after all.

So what the hell. Buzz Duffy to the rescue.

The doors were opening. The crowd pressed toward the series of big blue sawhorses the police had set up to sort of funnel the hordes down through the search points. Security was ultratight since all that shit went down on Saturday. Buzz had only seen it on MTV, but it was enough.

Hell, it was half the reason why Tommy and him had wanted to come in the first place, and most of why their folks wouldn't let 'em. They were afraid their little babies would get hurt or something. It was, in Buzz's estimation, a waste of some perfectly good fear.

They queued up to go in. His mystery date stood beside him. Buzz thought about it for a second, decided what-the-hell, and slipped his arm around her waist. She let him. It was a nice waist. His hand, for want of a better place to rest, found her hip. She let it stay.

This was Buzz Duffy's lucky day, after all.

They were almost inside.

"Hey, I fergot to ask ya," he said. "What's yer name?"

She didn't look up, just said, "Mary." Her voice was real soft. He liked that.

They were next in. Buzz handed over the two tickets with a flourish and said, "Well, Mary, don'tchoo worry 'bout a thing." He smiled. "This's gonna be a blast."

7:11 P.M.

Walker didn't have time to answer questions. The operation was too complex; there were too many places where things could go wrong.

The crew had trained for this well in advance. Everyone knew exactly what to do, how to do it, where and when. Since ten this morning they'd been at it; only a handful of minutes till showtime remained. He had time to check and double-check, to nudge and ride and stay on top.

But no time for incompetence.

And none whatsoever for questions.

So when Debbie Goldstein from the Spectrum front office appeared in the backstage corridor, looking so cute and perky but for her occasional nervous ticking, he suppressed the urge to slit her pretty throat. Not a good idea at this stage of the game.

Besides, he understood her dilemma. She was being very professional: he had to give her that. She had to treat him with the same respect she granted the folks from Disney on Ice, for example, and she did so.

Or tried to, anyway. She had never been anything less than courteous and helpful. But it was clear that she was frightened in some vaguely irrational but indisputable way that he knew she'd be hard-pressed to voice. Oh, well. Most likely, she would not survive the hour.

Play nice, he told himself. *What have you got to lose?*

Walker slipped immediately into his Mr. Friendly-Enough-but-Too-Busy-to-Talk mode, pretending not to see her, studying his charts, letting her take the first tentative step.

"Umm . . . Mr. Walker." She came up beside him.

"Yes?" he said, gaze still on the chart.

"I . . . we've got a situation out in the parking lot . . ."

"I can imagine." Noting the spaces checked off under the pyrotechnics heading. "And?"

Ms. Goldstein tried to compose herself, her prefab smile askew. "Well, we're a little concerned. Especially in light of this past weekend, well, we wouldn't want there to be another riot or anything."

"Don't worry." He turned toward her now. He liked the way she shook under his gaze, wondered what exactly had her so worked up. Was it the kids outside or the crew within or the set they had erected? Or was she sensitive enough to smell the death already in the air?

No time for questions, he reminded himself and continued.

"I promise you, once the place fills up and the show starts, we'll have everything completely under control."

It was his sincerity that brought her around. That, and the look that he flashed to her before he turned away. The light in his eye was direct and succinct.

She was touching her throat as she left.

7:17 P.M.

Hook waved good-bye to the fire inspector and paused in the middle of the auditorium, the better to let the full effect sweep over him. It was the last few seconds before the teeming swarms came through the ramps like ants on a Sunday picnic. His work was nearly completed.

And it was glorious.

He was ringed by five towering columns, all laid out like the points of an enormous pentagram, each one a fucking masterpiece of artful deception. From this distance they maintained every illusion of being built of rough-hewn stone. And close up, they appeared to be harmless chicken wire and papier-mâché. He should know: he had personally overseen the masking and painting, especially of the most critical front pieces.

He had also overseen the hard-wiring and camouflage of the det-cord, which was tucked into the bundles of cable that snaked across the floor, linking the columns to the floating island at the very back of the floor opposite the stage, where his sound and light boards lay.

And he had personally taken the fire inspector on a tour of the sight, showing him what careful pains they had gone to, the better to build this set with state-of-the-art precision. He'd shown him the wiring diagrams, which were meticulously detailed. He'd shown him his electrician and demolitions credentials, which were Class A and up-to-date. He'd shown him how each column's flashpots and lasers and smoke machines could be precisely controlled from his station. He had shown him everything.

Well, almost everything.

He had neglected to show him some of the really interesting bits. Like the enormous length of hose that would soon house his secret recipe, the special sauce. Or the pheromone sensors. Or the one hundred and sixty-five six-pound surprises artfully deployed across the canvas of his masterpiece.

Yep, Hook plumb forgot to bring those up.

Oh, well.

He was sure the fire inspector would hear about it later.

7:24 P.M.

"Excuse me," Pastor Furniss began, "but I have a bit of a problem."

The security guard silently stared at him from behind the glass of the information booth. He was a colored man in his late fifties, gaunt and mean as a half-starved rattlesnake. It took a minute for Furniss to realize that the man wasn't going to respond.

"What I mean to say is . . ." He was nervous, off-balance, unused to being intimidated. ". . . that I believe a runaway girl may be on your premises."

The security guard said nothing.

"And what I was wondering is, might I be allowed to go inside and look for her? That would be such a blessing—"

"Do you have a ticket," the man interrupted, no upward trill at the end to imply it was a question.

"Well, no, I don't," Furniss stuttered. "And, you see, that's my predicament. I need to get inside there, and see if I can find her before—"

"So buy a ticket."

The pastor was appalled and sweaty. Both lay cold against him, burning. He tried to imagine such callousness in his own body. He couldn't, praise God. Were there not such a need for secrecy . . .

"Surely you must understand the importance of this," he began again, putting some power behind it. "A young girl has run away from home. We suspect that she might be on your premises. It is *absolutely imperative* that I be allowed entrance before she has a chance to mingle and . . ."

The security guard pulled out a cigarette and lit it.

Quiet rage set in: a righteous fury, aimed at the self-serving and the blind. It was obvious that this man didn't care about people, the morality that bound decent civilization. He was concerned with his paycheck, the things of the flesh. No doubt, he had *orders* to bar God's will.

This was Satan's place, no question about it. But it would be brought down.

He believed that with all his heart.

Praise Jesus.

"Good day, sir." He turned away from the window. There was no point in speaking further. He moved past the row of empty windows with the SOLD OUT banners slung across them, achieved the door, stepped through.

The heathen hordes awaited.

Paul Weissman was there, too.

"So far, no good," said the chubby young man. His face was grim. Furniss knew how he felt. "Nobody has seen her. I'm having my doubts."

"She's here. Trust in the Father. We'll find her."

But even Furniss was getting discouraged now, his own faith flagging. Their avenues of approach were closing off one after another.

The pastor had hoped to avoid this situation. He'd hoped to apprehend her before she got in. Six pairs of stalwart Liberty Christian youth had been brought for that reason, scattered near the gates, distributing pamphlets, keeping their eyes peeled for that long blond head of hair.

It did not appear to be working. More than half of the crowd was already inside. His guess was that Mary was among them.

Not calling her parents immediately had been a mistake. He knew that now. But, after all, his expectation had been that they would find her.

They almost always did.

And when things did go wrong—as with the Anderson boy, the parents calling first and demanding to know just "what in Hell" was going on—he'd been able to explain the situation well enough to stave off the lawsuits. Barely.

But this was more than bad. This was a dangerous place. If all rock concerts were like this, then Lord have mercy on our souls. All of the pastor's worst suspicions were confirmed by these kids. He'd never seen such potential for violence and outrage, such rampant moral decay.

And if anything happens to her, he mused, then cut it short, disallowing the thought. There were more important things to concentrate on. Like how to get inside.

"Hey, mister," said a voice from behind him. He turned. "You needa buy some tickets?"

The speaker was maybe fourteen years old. He was sitting above them on the concrete wall outside the door, one leg dangling lackadaisically. He had hair like a rooster. He was drinking a beer.

Dauntlessly, Paul Weissman leaped into the fray. "Let me handle this," he whispered to Furniss, then, "Yeah, *sure*, dude. We'll take two. How much are they?" He advanced, digging a hand into his pocket.

"Hundred bucks."

Paul stopped dead in his tracks. "A hundred bucks for two tickets?!" he gasped.

"No, dickhead," the kid drawled. "A hundred bucks *apiece*."

"That's obscene!"

"Free enterprise, dude. The American way." The kid took a long pull off his beer. "You wan 'em or what?"

"Let's go," Furniss said. "The Lord will provide."

"I wouldn't hold my fuckin' breath," the kid said, then turned his attentions elsewhere. Furniss's heart went out to him, replete with visions of the dear boy in proper clothes, with a proper haircut, after a couple of days in the Quiet Room with the Good Book and plenty of time to reflect on his sins.

But at least he'd narrowed his possibilities. Soon, the

Lord would show him the path of least resistance, and there he would go. He had no doubt that God was guiding him. The only real question was where.

"Are there any other entrances we haven't tried?" he asked Paul Weissman.

And lo, Paul provided the answer.

7:32 P.M.

"God, these are beautiful." Alex listened as the patterns shimmied in his ears and on the screen. "Just beautiful."

He sat at the computer console, a commset hooked delicately around one ear, hands deftly fingering the keys on the MIDI controller. The DIOS sat on its stand, LEDs strobing as the data fed in and the data fed out. The signal was strong.

And so, for the first time in ages, was Alex.

He felt superb, truly superb. It was as though an enormous cloud had been lifted from his eyes. And while that might not be so in the most clinically literal sense, it was true that he was seeing things he had never seen before.

There, in the darkness in his mind. Getting clearer with every note that he played.

"Okay," he whispered into the commset's mike, "let's run through our feed sequences again, shall we?"

"Roger," came the voice from below the stage. *"Feed sequence A coming on line."*

"Okay." Alex smiled. His fingers moved over the keys like speed-reading braille. "Switch on my command."

"Roger. On your command."

Alex nodded. *On my command.* Had a nice ring to it. He could get used to that. Father would be pleased. Momma certainly was.

"Give me pulse . . ."

"Check."

"Respiration . . ."

"Check."

"Galvanic response . . . EMG . . . MEG . . ."

"Check . . . check . . . check . . ."

These were the best yet: sample-wise, they were looping superclean and clear, with not a trace of harmonic distortion, and most of all—*fast*. With his mind clear at last he had been able to finish the control program and load the sequencers and the coprocessors, which even now were number-crunching megabyte whole body gestalt complexes to beat the band. Walker's new E-prom was just the ticket, bless his black heart. If Alex had any doubts about the efficacy of a live feed, they were dispelled forever. The studio was fine, but he had a feeling that nothing would beat a live performance of the Symphony of Death.

"Okay, now for Momma Bear. Is she ready?"

"Coming right up."

Momma Bear's vital signs, too, were right on line. Alex couldn't be more pleased.

"Okay," he said, "this is critical. Slip her the probe and give us little Baby Bear."

There was a pause. *"She's fighting us."*

"Then sedate her again. But *lightly*. We don't want to suppress her reaction time too much."

"No problem."

Alex turned his attention inward as he waited for them to bring her under control. It was closer still, responding to even the scantiest snatches of manifested sound as he did this last check. He stretched and tilted his head back.

In his mind's eye he saw the huge centerpiece of the stage, towering over him. The cloud was dissipating, now little more than a smoky film, obscuring the details like an underexposed Bob Guccione centerspread. Still, he could make it out. It was big. God, yes. It was smiling.

And getting clearer by the second.

And as for beauty, he thought, *well, that's in the eye of the beholder, isn't it?*

"She's under."

"Wonderful. Now remember, this is going to be a very delicate, very tricky operation. In order to generate the proper feedback level we need to get a good representative signal from all the members of our happy family, and I'm getting a little glitching up here. We need better contact."

"Sorry, but it's hot down here. She's sweating like a pig, and he's getting kinda gamy. The adhesive just gives out after a while."

"Oh dear," Alex murmured. "Well, get a fan down there. And see if anyone has some Crazy Glue."

Another pause.

Then, "Roger."

Alex giggled a little. He'd almost forgotten just how much he enjoyed the hustle and bustle of the stage. Already he felt invigorated, refreshed. Like a new man.

He felt the presence an instant before she made contact. He leaned his head against her belly as she pressed up against him. "Having fun?" Tara asked.

"God, yes."

And the fun was just beginning.

7:40 P.M.

His hair was perfect, his makeup was perfect, his costume was perfect, but Rod could not get happy. His warmup exercises were not going well. More specifically, his hands were trembling so much that he was blowing his riffs. This was bad, especially when the show was this close to starting.

"Damn!" He set down the guitar for a second and paced around his dressing room. He couldn't shake the paranoia. As always, something strange was going on behind his back. He expected as much.

But the change in Alex was a wee bit too extreme to be ignored.

Sure, it was great to see the boy up and around again. At first it had been cause for outright celebration. But to see him bounce out of his deathbed so chipper was its own kind of frightening. It didn't make sense.

First thing, of course, Rod had checked his brother's eyes, thinking *if Tara did this to you, man, she's fucking dead and it's all over*. The big surprise was that they were still intact. After what she'd done to the rhythm section, Rod wouldn't put anything past her.

But no. Little brother was fine. In fact, he was primo. The wheels were in motion. The sounds he was weaving were too good to be real. His playing was sharp. His wits were like a razor. He was laughing all the time.

So why was he so scary?

Rod reached into his pocket for the vial of toot, laid a sixth of a gram out and sucked it up. One thing was for sure: he would want to be aware. Nobody was gonna slip nothin' by him tonight. When the Earth opened up for inheritance, Rod Royale would be there.

But if you play one wrong note . . . , Walker said in his head, and that brought all the paranoia pinwheeling back. The question *What exactly* do *you stand to gain from all this?* occurred, for at least the millionth time; and again, it was Walker's voice that answered.

How much choice do you think you have?

"All the choice in the world, man. Anything I want." Rod laughed as he said it, the sound unconvincing. "I play my cards right, and the kingdom is mine. You promised me that.

"You promised me."

This was all true, so far as it went, but the creeping doubt remained intact. For one startling second, it occurred to him that he was an absolute and thoroughgoing chump; that Walker and Tara and Momma Herself were luring him onward with a carrot on a stick, only this one was fourteen karats, har, har, promise him riches and he'll follow us anywhere, even down to the mouth of Hell . . .

. . . and this was not a good thought, it did nothing for his confidence and control, and if there was one thing he knew it was that he dare not screw up, therefore this line of thought was anathema and he'd better straighten up. There were other quotes from the Walker litany that served him much better, and he brought them to mind.

She needs warm bodies.

She needs us to pave the way and guard it.

That was better, yes. That was much more helpful. Put that together with a farewell to Tara, and he could almost cheer up, see the end of the rainbow.

"Okay." He addressed the room. "Let's do it. Let's kick

some ass." He grabbed his guitar off its stand, strapped it on, wiped his sweaty left palm against his pantsleg before bringing it up to hold the neck. It was time to go out there and meet his destiny.

If only he could make his hands stop shaking . . .

7:45 P.M.

Heimlich hung up the payphone, wandering gradually back toward the jet-black van. He took his time, pausing to light an unfiltered Camel, watching the last thousand kids or so straggle in toward the gates and the cops and vendors cruise the lot like sharks when the fish leave town. It was still way too hot to make a move. Now that he knew they'd be waiting awhile, the important thing was to stave off boredom. That meant staying out of the van as long as possible.

Heimlich's eyes were dark and impenetrable. There was little that they missed. His hair was dark and cropped close to his skull. His skin was the color of bronzed, cracked leather.

He was a big man, and he moved big. Air got out of his way when it saw him coming. So did people, unless they were very drunk or very stupid. Few people were good enough to stay in his way for long.

Heimlich was a professional, a warrior for hire. He was working right now. A very strange job indeed: hired by a rock star to blow the tits off of some *other* rock stars and to rescue some bimbo in front of over fifteen thousand people.

The job was so strange, in fact, that he had almost considered turning it down. Instead, he'd simply doubled his price: two men, two thousand smackers apiece. Plus expenses.

When Hamer had made the first payment in cash—half the money right there on the spot, with no hesitation—Heimlich had called it a deal.

And the real craziness had begun . . .

They had run a recon on The Scream's Staten Island stronghold at eleven-thirty this morning. They had found it abandoned. That had been a bad sign. Whatever the twisted fucks were up to, it was clear that they had no intention of coming home again.

It didn't take long to figure out why.

The inside of the mansion was bad enough. The torture chamber. The recording studio. Heimlich didn't know shit about music, but it was clear from the reactions of Hempstead and Hamer that you didn't need blood gutters and drains in the floor of your average recording studio.

But the best part, without a doubt, was the garage.

It was roughly the size of a small airplane hangar. Parts and tools and garage-style detritus lined the walls. There were no vehicles parked inside.

But there were lots of bodies. Maybe a hundred. Mostly goats; but that still left thirty or more dead people.

All of them, ex-goats and humans alike, dangled naked by their hind legs from the rafters. Their throats had been slit, the blood drained and removed from the premises. There were children in there. Babies.

There were also a couple of women strung up that made Hamer's olive skin blanch. Upside down like that, with dried blood on their faces, they were hard to recognize. He'd had to wipe one of them down before he knew that, no, she was not the bimbo they sought after all.

But that didn't mitigate the extent of the slaughter.

Or the carelessness . . .

"Sloppy," he muttered. It was the only word that fit. Heimlich hated slovenliness, especially in killers, especially in *butchers* who made such extravagant overtures to style. Rich fucking rock stars making big-budget mayhem with a Z Grade mentality, playing a man's game by Little League rules . . . killing them would accord him a depth of pleasure his line of work rarely permitted.

They thought they were good. That was the big thing. Going public like this, not even covering their tracks . . . it was clear that they thought they were pretty goddamn special. Either they had one motherfucking ace in the hole or one motherfucking case of diarrheic self-esteem. In which case they were cake.

And Heimlich could practically taste the frosting.

The van was parked ten feet from the exit of parking section S6, maybe two hundred yards from the lip of the backstage loading ramp. That was far enough away from The Scream's vehicles to avoid detection, close enough to get there quickly when the time came.

The van was ten feet away from him now. Heimlich could feel the tension radiating through the sealed steel doors. He dragged, exhaled, took a deep breath of air. Sloppy target or not, if this was going to work, they would have to wait a little longer. Pennycate, his trusty pard and currently their man on the inside, had made that exquisitely clear.

Jake wouldn't like it, but he'd better get used to it.

When you hired the best, you were best advised to listen.

7:49 P.M.

There were two unsavory-looking types at the bottom of the loading ramp, pacing back and forth like bored guards in a prison camp movie. They both appeared unarmed, an illusion largely due to the combination of bold-print Hawaiian shirts and figure-flattering belt clips. Either one was actually packing enough firepower to make an intruder do the Big Shoe, if need be. And neither of them was above using it.

Their names were Dingo and Slick, and they were disposable. They both scored low on the placement exams of life. They asked very few questions. They did largely as they were told. They were told to keep out all creeps.

And it looked like two were on their way now.

Dingo scritched at the stubble on his long-chinned face. His ponytail swished as he turned toward his shorter, grungier companion. "Hey, Slick." He nudged. "You see what I see?"

Slick smiled and crossed his hands behind his back, palms grazing the button of his weapon. "I dunno. Whadda you see?"

"I see two creeps coming down the ramp."

"Me, too."

The creeps waddled closer. Dingo and Slick watched impassively. When they were about twenty feet off, Dingo squinted and said, "Oh, shit, man. Walker ain't gonna believe this."

"What?" Slick squinted harder; his night vision was for shit. "B'lieve what?"

"Oh, man, this is too much!" Dingo laughed. "The big guy? I seen him last week, on the tee-vee. On Dick Moy-neehan."

"No shit." Slick seemed genuinely impressed. "Is he famous?"

"He's an asshole."

"Oh." Slick was dumb as a pie tin. "So what do we do with him?"

"See what he wants, I guess."

"I guess."

Dingo laughed again. It lent a false sense of good fellowship to the approach of the famous asshole and his roly-poly pal.

The old guy hastened to explain his situation in nervous, earnest tones: sometimes real man-to-man like, sometimes calling on the spirit of brotherly love to open their hearts to his plight. He smiled a lot. He called on them to do the right thing.

Dingo and Slick smiled, too. He really *was* an asshole. And certainly a creep.

But in truth, this was too good to dismiss outright. Dingo knew for sure that Momma would appreciate the humor. "You just hang on there a second, sport. I'll have to ask permission." Then with a nudge in the ribs to Slick, Dingo turned and ran back to find Walker.

It only took a minute. He was right backstage with the band, who were about to go on. Walker looked annoyed for a second, then listened; and after a moment's thought, did a rare and wondrous thing.

He laughed.

"Oh, that's beautiful. They need passes. Here." Walker dug into his pockets, then threw back his head and yelled, "Hoo, Lawd! *Thank* ya, Jeezus!"

When he laughed again, Dingo joined right in.

It was good to have done the right thing.

7:52 P.M.

There was a moment—a split second, really, hardly worth bringing up—in which Rod Royale felt the sudden, desperate urge to bolt, just hang it up and head full tilt for the exit ramp. It was especially strange in that it didn't quite connect with the moments before or after: it just hung there by itself, flashpot-bright and compelling, then blanked out and was gone.

What it left him with was aftershock, confusion. It was, after all, the dumbest flash he'd ever had or probably ever would. This was *it*, this was the *big* one, the moment they'd all been waiting for. The gates of the Kingdom were opening now. He was gonna run away from all that? Was he crazy?

And besides, there were all those guys with guns. . . .

Shut up, he told himself. Walker was talking. *When Walker talks, people listen.* He knew that with his shades on nobody could tell if he was listening or not, but that wasn't quite the point.

Then the second flash of dread went off, and he realized that, yes, maybe that *was* the point, because everybody in the band was wearing their shades and he couldn't see their eyes. Alex always wore his, of course; besides, Rod had already checked. And with the guys in the rhythm section, Gene and Terry, it hadn't mattered since Phoenix, when they'd tried to jump ship and wound up, no-eyed, on Tara's team.

So maybe it was Tara that made him want to run, but he didn't think so. She was acting the same as ever: cool, silent, oozing dark wet serpentine power. She looked at him, as Walker talked, with the same superior smile he'd seen a million times.

Maybe it was the fact that they were all smiling like that. As if they weren't even listening. As if Walker's words were for him alone.

Because they already know . . .

He glanced at the exit again.

And the third flare ignited, but there was no time to think about it, because Walker was in front of him now, holding him by the collar, with his lone eye visible and eloquent as hell, so eloquent in fact that the words from his lips were like foreign language subtitles as they spoke to Rod's ears.

"Don't even think about it, boy." The eye, the voice, in perfect accord. "All you have to do is get through the first movement. That's four simple stages. *Tick tick tick tick.* You pull that off, and everything will be gravy.

"And you will do it. Right?"

Rod nodded his head, and the band smiled winningly. As one. A fourth warning flare tried to spark in his brain, but the humidity was such that it never got off the ground.

Little brother, he thought, as Alex tossed him a sparkling smile that was not his own and control flitted irrevocably away like tweetie-birds from a magician's top hat.

Then he turned to where the stage awaited.

And began the long walk up to his rightful place.

At the opening of the Way.

7:56 P.M.

Kyle looked at his watch and felt a thin trickle of sweat roll down the back of his neck. They were scrambling in the throes of last-minute prep. It had been hyped as the most elaborate show ever taken on the road. That was total bullshit.

He knew exactly where this show was going. And it wasn't on the road.

Kyle rapped nervous little rhythms on the big metal drums stacked on the pallet before him and watched as the crew hustled like Olympic speed-freaks, running on too little sleep and too much adrenaline and the promise of the payoff at the end of the line.

It was risky, he thought, to be pushing them so hard.

But it couldn't be helped.

There were sixty-three men in the crew. Seventeen of them were actively involved in running the lights, the sound, and the standard special effects that The Scream toured with, which included the giant inflatable claws, which included the laser-cannons and the Cobra, which included the smoke guns and strobe lights and all the other bells-and-whistles they fed the kiddies to get them nice and lubed and make them think they were getting their twenty-bucks-a-pop worth of showbiz.

Another fourteen were required to work in tight-knit synchronization on the computer-controlled hydraulics that animated the humongous articulated stage prop they'd set up, plus the crane operators for her arms. Knock off four to guard the front of the stage, another four for the rear, and that left him two dozen warm bodies with which to take care of his end of things.

Of course, he could have as many *cold* bodies as he desired. Momma had made that very clear. But he couldn't trust them.

Not anymore.

They were too fucking weird. Unstable, and getting worse the closer things got to the end. Kyle didn't like playing nursemaid to a roomful of psychotic budget cuts anymore. There was too much at stake. They had to play things too close to the vest. When the shit hit the fan he had to get his men deployed and hold the fucking perimeter, until Momma was strong enough to hold it herself. They had the goods to do it—M-60's, M79 grenade launchers, RPG7s, a regular smorgasbord of death—but manpower was critical.

"I don't want any of those fuckers out on the concourse," he had said.

And Walker had said *no problem*.

His men dragged the great flaccid sections of fire hose into position and connected them; assembled, they formed an enormous loop that filled the center of the arena floor and completely encircled Hook's five columns. Before him sat a hand pump and the fifty-five-gallon containers that housed Hook's special sauce.

He pried the cap off the first drum; the smell that leached out was as offensive as it was identifiable. It contained three very common, very plentiful ingredients, not very secret at all. And none of which were particularly hard to come by.

Just gasoline. Liquid soap.

And lots of fresh blood.

Mix it all together till it's just a little thicker than a good

10-40W motor oil so it will fly high and spread wide and what's that spell?

The special sauce.

And, boy, did it stink. Kyle looked up at the T-shaped lighting scaffold that jutted out and hung over the front of the stage. Three of the light crew were inching carefully toward their positions along the catwalk; agile as spider monkeys, olive-drab ammo boxes firmly in tow. This was gonna be some show, alrightee.

Kyle wiped the sweat off his neck. Checked his watch. Hooked the pump to the feed end of the hose.

And got ready to rock 'n' roll.

7:58 P.M.

Mary Hatch stood in the tiled doorway of the Section G ladies' room, nervously waiting for Buzz to live up to his name and buzz off. She wished he would. She even prayed he would.

But no. He stayed right where he was, waiting at the foot of the east stairs, looking antsy and anxious to get back to the arena. The warmup videos had started, their beat thudding along the corridor tiles. He was attracted by the sound along with everybody else, like iron filings to a magnet.

She wished he would just *go*.

It wasn't anything against him personally. He was actually a nice guy. He had given her a ticket, lent her his jacket—which was a real blessing, since the culottes she was wearing drew stares at twenty paces and the jacket at least looked cool—and had otherwise been as best a gentleman as he knew how.

He'd even bought her a drink and some popcorn and filled the last hour with enough ambient small talk that the nattering voice in her skull faded for whole minutes at a stretch.

But it kept coming back.

She felt guilty and very sad at the thought of just leaving him in this place; he had the same sweet loser quality that she used to find herself drawn toward.

But she couldn't help it. She was being drawn toward something much stronger.

And a whole lot less pleasant.

She peeked out again as two fishnet-clad, teen queens looked haughtily around her. She was surprised at the co-mingling of detachment and terror she felt: for them, for him, for herself. It was as though she were simultaneously elevated to woman-with-a-mission and reduced to a cog, deep in the mechanisms of a far greater process.

Either way, it was time to get the heck out of there.

And the girls' tight little bouncing buns, as it were, formed the perfect diversion. Poor ol' Buzz; his neck craned wanly to watch them wiggle by, and Mary took the chance to dart from her sanctuary and skitter up the western stairwell.

She burst out onto the mezzanine heading in the completely wrong direction for her seating section, but that didn't matter. What mattered was to put as much space as possible between them. She hoped Buzz would forgive her. It really wasn't his lucky day after all. She was going someplace that he could not follow. So she'd gotten him out of that particular frying pan.

And into an altogether different line of fire.

7:59 P.M.

Hook scanned his console. Everything was powered up and purring, hundreds of happy little LEDs twinkling like tiny red stars, like the distant lights of the promised land. He sat down on his swivel stool and surveyed his handiwork. *Just like Christmas morning*, he thought. *Before you rip the presents open.*

He turned to his assistant, beaming. "Chuckie, m' lad. What's the level on the pheromone sensors?"

Chuckie hunched over the screen for a moment. "Three point one nine oh and rising," he called back.

"Hmmmm," Hook grunted. He was genuinely excited.

And, he thought, *it looks like I'm not the only one.*

He drummed his fingers delicately across the sliders on the special subsection of the soundboard, the section only his hand was authorized to touch. The section that controlled the volume of the signals coming back from the stage. Coming back through the system.

Coming back through DIOS.

He'd waited years for this. He understood the beauty of his place in the structure; what Momma hadn't made clear, common aesthetic sense did. Little Alex had his studio samples and his live samples, and he did his Alex-thing with them, making his little black soundtrack, his symphony of death.

But Hook was next in the chain of command.

And Hook made it all real.

It was Hook who decided how much of what came through the mix and when. It was Hook who designed the impact of the sound, like charges in a daisy chain.

True, little Alex had written the symphony. Momma had inspired it. And Walker himself had laid out the strategy.

But it was Hook, in the end, who was able to make it happen. He scoffed at the mystic trappings of the stage and set, all the expensive trashy mumbo jumbo. Hook knew from experience that, given the will to do so, you didn't have to conjure hell on earth. You could build it, with your bare hands. It was frighteningly easy.

Not to mention surprisingly affordable.

His right and only hand drummed across the sliders.

It was the hand of an artist.

8:00:00 P.M. SYMPHONY OF DEATH

Ted was almost in front when the lights went out.

It happened all at once, as if a thick black curtain had been thrown over the Spectrum. The effect was shocking; the voice of surprise rang out from ten thousand invisible throats. *"Omigod,"* he whispered, abetting the din with what little wind he had.

It was the moment he had come for.

And now the moment had come for him.

Ted stood, twenty feet from the front of the stage, sixteen from the hurricane fencing that separated the crowd from the curtain beyond. He stood and did not move a muscle. Paralysis, cold, had taken hold. *Like rigor mortis in advance,* he told himself, but he was not laughing. There were shapes around him, the bodies of strangers he didn't know and couldn't see.

The terror was second to none.

The floor of the arena was still half-empty; lots of kids were still up cruising the mezzanine, standing on line at the concessions or buying T-shirts or taking that one last leak. Right now, one last leak would feel really good. Preferably not in his pants and down into his boots . . .

His knife was hidden in his boot.

He thought about how much better it would feel in his hand.

Because the lights had just gone out.

And there was a moment of silence, as disturbing as the dead air that always preceded the this-is-only-a-test-for-the-next-sixty-seconds emergency broadcast blurbs on the radio. The silence where you wondered, however briefly, if this time wasn't really a test at all.

As dead air goes, it wasn't very long: a split second at best.

But it was long enough.

There had never been a question as to whether he was allowed to go. A part of his brain, with teenage cunning, had sussed that out long before his flapping jaws could betray him. Shut up, he said, and let them tell you: "It's too dangerous, it's under control, you stay home and protect your mother."

Which, of course, they had done.

Well, piss on that. You didn't live through as much as he had—the death of a friend, the slaying of a monster, the kidnapping of Jesse—and then sit on your fucking hands while somebody else did the dirty work. No way in hell.

Not when you were sixteen years old.

And not when they had Jesse.

So you pretended to go along, and you gave up your ticket for the greater good, and you waved bye-bye when the moment came.

Then you waited for your own moment.

And when it came, you took it.

Taking Chris's ticket with you.

That had all sounded great at the time. Now he wasn't so sure. His knife was as close as his foot, and he couldn't stoop to reach it. It was worse than the time that he'd spent in his chair, fearing the shadows. Now the shadows were near.

Now the shadows had teeth.

The split second of silence had ended. Nervous laughter and dull murmurs took its place, punctuated by shouting and commotion in the distance. "Holy fuck! They're startin'!" called one moron from the balcony.

And then the sound began.

The sound was leviathan, filling the room and rattling the rafters. A low bass drone, synthesized in origin, but with a little something extra.

It was not just any sound. To the initiated, it was a trigger, Pavlovian as a ringing bell. Ted knew from the moment it started just exactly what it was. He'd heard that type of sound before.

"Omigod," he whispered again, and it was lost in the roaring wave of motion, and the crowd was pushing against his back, pushing him up and into the fence, against the fence, nearly through the fence as the faithful poured down from the mezzanine.

To attend the Critical Mass.

8:00:31 P.M. EXPOSITION

Hook pushed it a little more.

Just a hair; there was no need to overload them yet. They had plenty of time. It was still ethereal; no drums yet, no rhythmic syncopated headlong drive. It was the intro, and it was still building: chanting in layers, thousands of shifting voices, each one a single, frozen moment. Suspended in pain, suspended in suffering, suspended in ecstasy and agony and dawning awestruck realization.

Then transposed. And synthesized.

And amplified.

The effect was awesome. It was the twentieth-century extension of the same primal power that could drive human beings to pile one stone atop another, to vault the first cathedral ceiling, build the first temple in which to let loose and howl the first praise to the first god.

The voices shifted, shaping into syllables, then words . . .

"Magdhim DIOS! Satanas DIOS!
Asteroth DIOS! Ellylldan DIOS!"

It had the mounting fury of an electrical storm, the force swirling through the arena like storm clouds in a cavernous void, the words crashing like waves against crumbling seawalls . . .

"Sancti DIOS! Omnitus DIOS!
Malebog Baalberth DIOS! DIOS!"

From Hook's privileged vantage point it was glorious; his island was the calm in the eye of the hurricane. His was the hand that held the hammer, and he was about to let it drop.

But not quite yet.

Stage One was just beginning.

8:01:02 P.M.

The arena was filled with the lost. They were drawn to the sound like moths to a flame, willing to burn for that moment of glory. For the first time in his life, Pastor Furniss had an inkling as to what brought the children here.

And, in understanding, knew the meaning of fear.

Because the sound not only surrounded him, it filled him. It wrenched open his defenses, came sluicing in through every sense, every pore, filling the chambers where his demons were chained. They wailed up inside him like abandoned asylum inmates, howling for release.

And he would die before he'd allow that.

The sound became a Presence. It rooted him in place while the darkness swirled around him. It spoke to him personally, confidentially, intimately. More intimately than God in their private talks together. In those conversations he did most of the talking. While God, in His infinite patience, had listened.

The roles had reversed now.

It was the sound that spoke. He listened with his body, but his soul was the one that discerned. It could hear beyond the sound itself, connect with the endless longing-turned-to-anguish that was its substance, feel the Presence at its core.

As the sound assumed a voice that spoke to him.

Spoke to them all.

"IN THE BEGINNING, THERE WAS THE WORD," it began; ambisexually, impossibly deep and lush and resonant. "AND THE WORD WAS LOVE."

"Oh, Lordy," Furniss whispered, as his first chakra blazed up like a safety flare.

"BUT THE WORD ALONE WAS NOT ENOUGH."

The Presence stoked the flame. He fought to dampen it.

"THERE WERE OTHER WORDS, TO FILL THE GAP. THERE WERE WORDS LIKE BLOOD. THERE WERE WORDS LIKE FLESH."

Echoes trailed off the blasphemy like vapor trails. "Our Father," he murmured desperately, "Our Father who art in heaven . . ."

The curtains began to open.

"Hallowed be Thy name. Thy kingdom come, Thy will be done . . ."

"BUT OF ALL THE WORDS EVER CREATED OR SPOKEN, THERE WAS NEVER ONE QUITE LIKE MOMMA."

"On earth as it is in heaven . . ."

Blue light filtered through the slit in the drapes. The choral crescendoed. The voice grew stronger.

"THEY LIKE TO SAY THAT GOD IS THE FATHER."

The slit folded back like black velvet lips.

"Give us this day our daily bread and . . ."

"BUT WHO GIVES BIRTH? WHO GIVES LIFE?"

"And lead us not into temptation but . . ."

"THE FATHER IS ONLY HALF THE TRUTH."

"Lead us not into temptation but . . ."

"IT'S TIME TO KNOW THE OTHER HALF."

"Into temptation, but . . ."

A blue-red glow washed across the stage.

"THE BETTER HALF."

And Pastor Furniss saw his devil made flesh.

It was all he feared it would be.

"But deliver us from Evil!!" he cried, and turned to run. Something grabbed him by the arm.

"DELIVER US FROM EVIL, LORD!" Furniss screeched, wheeling around. Paul Weissman had already run, but the pastor was not alone.

A bony face smiled at him.

"EEYAOW!" it cried. "TOO LATE!"

Another one appeared behind him, grabbing him roughly by the shoulders. Furniss screeched again as they twirled him about like a squeeze toy and thrust him down into a ringside seat. He grabbed the armrests instantly, trying to vault back out and away. He would have done it, too.

But the Screamers put an end to that rather abruptly.

They both had knives with sharp steel blades.

Two swift and brutal motions and his hands were pinned to the wood.

The shock of pain eluded him at first, so sudden was the impact. They held his wrists firmly the whole while, as if to ensure his continued cooperation. He realized the full implication of the action at roughly the moment the pain slammed in. "JEEEEEEESUS *CHRIST*!" he squealed, his baser self going haywire.

"Showtime, dude!" one of the creatures croaked. His breath stank of the pit. Furniss's fingers spasmed in purely biological comprehension.

And he stared, wild-eyed, the blood running between his fingers, as the curtains opened . . .

. . . and he saw the thirty-foot-high voluptuous monstrosity kneeling on the stage: its head bent forward, its knees spread twenty feet wide. It was nearly naked, skin glistening in the hot glow of the floodlights. Its hips were lewd and wide as the Great Whore herself, its belly taut and round, its fat-nippled breasts full as sacks of ripe fruit.

It was the Song of Solomon, the Whore of Babylon, magnified a millionfold. It was Ishtar and Isis and Aphrodite, feral fecund idolatry incarnate.

It was the biggest obscenity he had ever seen.

She abased herself in a posture of depraved surrender against the backdrop of an endless Gothic cathedral; the vaulted ceiling extended out into infinity, and at the apex of each razor sharp arch there was hung an inverted Christ, cruelly nailed to an inverted cross; and from the Christ directly above her head, the blood of sacrifice rained endlessly down . . .

Furniss squirmed, awestruck and terrified. He couldn't see the face, obscured as it was by thick coils of hair that draped all the way to the floor. Neither could he fully view the temples behind her veil, their halves ripe as rotted pomegranate, secreted behind the sprawling mass of gleaming chromed-and-blackened drums.

But something told him that that was all about to change.

. . . because her arms moved then, he saw that now, she wasn't real, not real at all, just a trick just sinful hollywood special effects those were cranes moving toward the ceiling.

Furniss's senses were swimming. The physical shock was wearing off, hot sticky agony burning red in the center of his crucified palms. But the other shock—the wrenching expansion of boundaries forever exploded—that just went on and on.

The crescendo reached its zenith. The stage glowed. The arms of the stage prop raised with it, hands clawing toward the cathedral arches. Furniss's face was bathed in sweat; his hands twitched against the blades, drawing fresh blood. He was afraid to look down. He was afraid to look up.

And as the head came up, hair falling away to reveal the face, he was most afraid to look there . . .

. . . because it wasn't a human face at all, it was part human and part goat and mostly bone, ash-skin on a horned savaged skull but with human jaws and pointed ears and eyes of smoking embers . . .

. . . and the face raised up with mouth falling open and howling.

And the lights came up to reveal the band in position.

And the crescendo screamed down.

And the rhythm section kicked in.
And sixteen thousand souls entered Stage Two.
En masse.

8:03:30 P.M. DEVELOPMENT

Hook spiked it up another notch.

They had never gone this high in any performance, any-where. It was a calculated risk. If they could handle it, they push it further in Stage Three, and Four.

And more.

He beamed. They could do it; he had faith in them. Momma had faith in him. Seeing was believing, and they so wanted to believe, and why the hell not?

They were begging for it.

His hand was a five-fingered flurry, each digit articulating the incremental increase of a different instrument's blend. His assistant scrambled behind him, tending the mounting storm.

"*What's the pheromone status?*" Hook yelled over the din, looking back.

"*Six point three oh and counting!*"

"*Tell me when it reaches the magic number!*"

"*You got it!*"

Hook cranked the levels. A visible shudder passed through the crowd, like the rippling shock wave on a lake when you lob a stone in.

He smiled.

And lobbed another.

8:04:00 P.M.

Buzz couldn't believe his good luck.

He no longer mourned the loss of his mystery date. So what if she had ditched him. In a big way it was for the best; he could get closer rogue-style than he ever could towing any girl he ever met.

Even so, he hadn't expected *this*. Right the fuck up front.

And the band was wailing, live.

Before his very eyes.

"EEEEEA*YOWW*! YEAHH!!" He screamed till he was hoarse. It sucked right up out of his lungs and on into the full gestalt of the arena. He felt great. The stage was fucking great. The band was fucking great. Tara was fucking great, dressed to slay in very fucking little.

And *God*, were they tight.

Buzz had seen The Scream exactly six times: Philly, Jersey, Jersey, Long Island, Pittsburg and tonight. But tonight was by far the best. He wasn't even stoned or anything and it seemed more fun, more intense, than he could ever remember.

Every sound had an edge on it. The drums pounded against his rib cage, regulating his breathing; the cymbals cut through his head like satin buzz-saw blades. The bass was so viciously crisp that his brain bled in joy at every popping speed-run.

And the keyboards.

God.

The record paled in comparison. Reality paled in comparison. Nothing sounded that good; life didn't get that good. It made cranking the volume to eleven on the CD with the headphones strapped on seem like elevator music from a Soap 'n' Sing. Alex was on fucking fire; Alex hunkered in his elevated niche, which was built to look like Victor Frankenstein's castle after the peasants had trashed it, and he *burned*.

And Buzz burned right along with him.

The intro power-shifted into the groove-proper of the song: a steady, crazed four/four chug with a half-time backbeat. And while the sixteen thousand Buzzes in the audience might not have understood the musical particulars of the structure, they recognized the effect at once. Years of inculcation, from Jerry Lee to David Lee, had imbedded it in their goddamn DNA.

It was cruise music. It was the heart of rock and roll.

It was their lifeblood. And it was pumping.

Just in time, too.

Because Tara had started to sing.

8:04:30 P.M.

. . . and this was sweet, oh, momma, sweet power and freedom, the calves lining up to eat from Her hands, unaware of the hammer, focused in on her as She swayed and She cooed and dripped black honey in their ears . . .

"You need to believe, and
You believe what you hear.
Lord, I won't interfere with that."

. . . and Tara felt the Presence in her, delighting in the feel of her body as She flowed through her veins, made that perfect body arch and writhe and dance and drive them all to madness . . .

"You mean what you say, but
You don't know what you're saying,
I won't interfere with that."

. . . and the world was so close now, so close She could taste it as they sang . . .

"Babes of the Modern Age
Got such a killing rage.
Twisted by lies and deceivers."

. . . and they sang . . .

"Babes of the Modern Age
Waitin' to set the stage
Ready to be the believers.

*. . . and Rod stepped up to the mike to join her, as they
sang . . .*

> "All that we ask
> Of the Critical Mass
> Is believers . . .
> All that we ask
> For the Critical Mass
> Is control . . ."

8:05:00 P.M.

And the solo flew off his fingers like lightning, skewering
the hearts of all who stood before him. He could see the
impact, he could *feel* the impact of the notes striking home,
hammering down to the bone.

He hoped that Walker was paying attention.

This was, without a doubt, the performance of his life.

It was beautiful, now that he'd gotten beyond the terror. It
was everything that his little heart could desire. Could there be
any doubt that he was born for this moment: death thrumming
through his strings, twisted and bent to magnificence, presided
over and delivered by the grace of the sovereign Rod Royale?

The band was pumping behind him. Dead or alive, they
sure kicked ass. He fired off a spitfire flurry of thirty-second
notes that left the audience *aaahhh*ing at his technical virtuosity,
then he leaped three feet in the air and came down in a
perfect split, let them *aaahhh* again, pulled some screaming
harmonics off the top of the neck and rose to his feet, twirling,
wailing, letting the awe and acclaim slide over him as he put
the finishing touches on his solo, melodic now, slipping gracefully
into the primal pulse that bespoke that most critical part
of the first movement of the Mass.

The altar call.

Already, another pisshead was scrabbling toward the stage.
Evidently he hadn't spent enough time with the album. Everybody
knew it took at least three minutes of pumping and

chanting for the sacrifice to begin. Some people just couldn't wait for a beautiful woman to sit on their face.

Well, here comes one asshole who will never get the chance, he mused, as Keynes and Locke intercepted like pit bulls and Keynes whisked him away, and Rod couldn't resist grinning into the polished snoot of the camera as he began to chunk along with the heartbeat of the ritual, power chords punctuating the rhythm. He knew that his fans wouldn't mind. They lived for his smile.

It was the least he could do.

For all those little people . . .

8:06:00 P.M.

The guy was maybe thirty-five, but he sure enough had the spirit. Too much, in fact. He was up and over the hurricane fencing before Locke or Keynes could so much as whistle, clambering toward the stage.

This was not the first time. In point of fact, it was the fifth time tonight. It had been a while since they'd been on the road with the band, what with taking care of the home front and all, but they remembered very well what to do.

When the kids went nuts and tried to make the stage, the name of the game was Scoop and Sling.

Of course, tonight they were doing it somewhat differently.

The aging kid was four feet from Tara. Keynes was closer. He closed in fast. He was six foot two with eyes of blue, and they sized up the interloper lickety-split.

Brown hair, longish and thinning and scraggly. A black, inch-thick headband, knotted into place at the back. Dark eyes, drunk and swimming. Weathered and unshaven pretty-boy face. Small-bodied—five foot six at the max—but lithe and powerful, given the shortage of mass and the obvious drunkenness governing it. He had a muscle shirt under his oversize army field jacket, and the muscles were pretty self-evident.

In the hands of Keynes, the boy was cake.

He hoisted Lil' Rambo up onto the stage by the armpits and started hauling immediately to the left. The cameraman danced around him, going for Tara's profile. Locke nodded, resumed his vigil. Lil' Rambo made one last desperate outreach for Tara before his feet disappeared offstage. "LEEB ME 'LONE! I GOTTA FUCKER *NOW*, MAN!"

"I bet you do," Keynes responded, dragging the little man down the backstage steps. "But tell me, what do you think the odds really are on that?"

His captive hollered something unintelligible about vaginal penetration. Keynes nodded his head and maintained his pace, heading back toward the pile behind the stage. Lil' Rambo would look very nice on top.

Until the next one came along.

"Hey! Where the fuck you takin' me, man?" the guy wanted to know. "Hey!"

Keynes shrugged and quickly assessed his surroundings. The corridor leading out to the loading ramp was empty. Kent and Barryman were nowhere to be seen. And of course Spectrum security had already been dealt with. The little pile was to his right. His Beretta was in its holster, waiting.

"It's time to go now." Keynes let go of Lil' Rambo's armpits, reaching for the gun, but the words didn't quite come out because suddenly there were a pair of very hard elbows jamming into his solar plexus from either side, and in the second it took to whoof out air Lil' Rambo had spun and withdrawn a knife in what Keynes would have to say was a very professional move.

One second later, his throat was slit. There was another second lost as he reached up to meet the outgoing blood. Pennycate made good use of the three seconds following, grabbing the big man by the hair and driving the blade through the temple. Death was instantaneous. He let the body slump down on the top of the pile and wiped the blade clean on the dead man's clothes.

"OKAY, MAN! OKAY!" he bellowed, backing off and slipping the knife back into its sheath. "OKAY, SO I'LL JUST LEAVE, MAN! I'M SORRY! JESUS CHRIST!" He turned and staggered briskly down the loading dock corridor, noting the position of the generator room before heading past the enormous stacks of road cases, seeing the two men that he'd expected at the end of the hallway, their backs to him. There was no longer any point in shouting. From this moment on, surprise and silence were the ticket.

He had seen what he needed to see. He knew all that he needed to know. The implications bespoke something far worse than he'd expected, but it wasn't the first time.

Though it was probably the weirdest.

He was twenty feet from the mouth of the exit now. There were two ways to go out: staggering or lethal. He decided on staggering. Every moment from this point on was critical. If he made decent speed and kept his corpses to a minimum, the whole thing would go down clean and in less than five minutes.

Ten feet now, and closing. He thought about what their reactions would be when he pushed between them. As crazy as they were, it was entirely possible that they'd gun him down on the ramp. On the other hand, that would be a remarkably stupid move, given that the outside had no idea what was going on inside. So the odds were technically, if you were dealing with even reasonably sane insane people, in his favor.

Six feet, the hilt of the knife never more than a split second from his hand. There was the tall one with the ponytail and the greasy little lump. Pennycate estimated that the skinny one would be tougher to tangle with but would go down easier if caught from behind, if only because there was less meat in the way, and as he closed in to three feet his hand was wavering in the direction of the hilt of the blade, but at the last moment he chose not to draw it because there was a very good chance that he'd be five feet past them before they knew what to do and ten feet past before one of them started to pursue him, barring an instant death by gunfire that the odds were against, and by that time Heimlich would have signaled the van, which would pull up to the lip of the loading ramp and surprise the shit out of them, at which point the door would be open for them to roll right in.

All this trundled through his mind in the moments before he pushed between the guards, saying, " 'Scuse me, this place sucks, you people give me the shits," and started meandering at a considerable rate up the ramp, counting the seconds, waiting for the holes to open up in his head or his chest or his belly, clenching his teeth right up until the moment that he heard the word "HEY!" and the footsteps slapping their way up behind him, at which point he knew that he was home free, because even though he couldn't see Heimlich he knew that Heimlich was there and the van was coming so fast that it was not to be believed and all he had to do was keep walking, arms swinging free, giving no indication whatsoever that he was counting the footsteps behind him and waiting for just the right moment to strike.

And all of this was fine, right up to the point that the footsteps started closing in severely and the van was nowhere fucking in sight, at which point Pennycate allowed his all-or-nothing philosophy to prevail, measuring the millimeters between his pursuer and himself and his hand and the hilt of the blade as he reached upward with practiced speed and took the hilt and withdrew the blade and turned just in time to set the process of gutting the ponytailed man in motion, driving in and lifting upwards, feeling the soft organs give and the fluid pour forth while he waited for the sound of gunfire to interrupt his reverie, and when it came it was from somewhere above and behind him, which was good, because the greaseball at the bottom of the ramp had his gun out now and would have gleefully fired were it not for the *phut phut phut* that made his face evaporate with barely a sound.

Thank you, man, Pennycate psychically sent to Heimlich as he finished up with the ponytailed man and let the wet husk collapse to the pavement.

Then the van pulled up, and the doors flew open, and the men in black ski masks came running down the slope. One of them came up beside him, handing off the Uzi, the ammo and a ski mask he could keep all for his own.

"Everybody's bacon is crisped in there if we don't move right now."

"So get your mask on, you beautiful little motherfucker," Heimlich said, smiling. "And lead the way."

"This . . . is our . . . last," her voice halted and stammered, *"con . . . versation . . . till . . . we meet . . . face . . . to face."*

"Yes, I know," Walker replied. Strange. She sounded perfectly lucid for whole minutes, then contact would suddenly frazz out. It was happening in cycles, the last two of which he'd actually timed. It was happening.

"Every three minutes now," he said.

"DID YOU SAY SOMETHING?"

He turned toward Debbie Goldstein, who was standing beside him in the narrow confines of the press box. He shook his head and said, "No, dear. Nothing."

"WHAT?"

"I SAID, *NOTHING!*"

"OH."

At one hundred and twenty-five decibels conversation was reduced to its most fundamental building blocks. She nodded, and Walker watched as her head kept right on nodding with the beat.

She was enjoying herself: apparently she'd loosened up a little as the evening wore on. He was surprised; he would have thought her too delicate to appreciate the grotesquerie that played simultaneously across the full view of the hall and in excruciating close-up on the giant ArenaVision screens. The cameramen were doting alternately on Tara's crotch and Momma's face, with only the occasional reference to Rod or Alex or the rhythm section tossed in as a sweeping blur of sound and color and motion.

And everyone was eating it up, dear sweet Debbie included. He found himself seriously contemplating letting her live, which might not be the kindest thing in the end and was at the very least out of character.

But he was thinking about it, all the same.

"MY GOD," she yelled into his ear from a foot away; he could just make it out. "THEIR SPECIAL EFFECTS ARE *WONDERFUL!* THEY'VE GOT A BIGGER PRODUCTION THAN *DISNEY ON ICE!*"

Walker smiled grimly and nodded. "It gets better."

"WHAT?"

"I SAID, IT GETS BETTER!"

"I CAN'T WAIT!" She nodded and turned her attention enthusiastically back to the show.

"*She's . . . adorable . . .*" Momma hissed, burning coals that gave off no heat in his brain. "*You can have . . . her by the end of the night. You can have a* hundred *like her.*" He winced; it would be a kindness, after all.

"*AFTER . . .*"—another spasm—"*After. You take . . . care . . .*"

". . . of me."

Walker nodded, deliberately out of pace with the music. The enormous squatting harlot on the stage turned at that moment, leaning back on its haunches and twisting its grotesque head until it seemed to be looking right at him. The jaw snapped open and shut several times. *Snap snap.*

"I wouldn't dream of doing otherwise," he whispered.

8:09:33 P.M. RECAPITULATION

"YEAH! GO, BABY!"

Hook clicked in, on cue, with the taped effects. Stage Three slid effortlessly into the mix: a thousand voices in a digitally enhanced altar call, going, *"Magdhim DIOS! Satanas DIOS! Asteroth DIOS! Ellylldan DIOS!"* in dreadnought-class counterpoint to the established beat. The effect was like the sound of continental plates shifting: huge and grindingly majestic and deadly.

The response was as immediate as it was gratifying. Sixteen thousand voices joined in. The pheromone level skyrocketed on the meters. They were almost there.

"ALL RIGHT!!" Hook laughed like a fucking maniac and slipped on his gas mask.

He never knew sonata form could be so much fun.

8:10:14 P.M.

The four of them were gathered at the mouth of the corridor, hidden behind the piles of road cases. It was Hempstead, Heimlich, Pennycate, and himself. The two dead guys were there as well, but they weren't saying much.

And it was time to talk.

"Very quickly," said Pennycate. "Aside from those two clowns, I saw nobody backstage."

"What does this mean?" Jake asked.

"It means there could be any-fucking-body there," Pennycate elaborated. "The one thing I know is that I saw nobody, and nobody saw me. They got some men up on the front and at the sides of the stage. Lots of techies, but they don't matter. They're busy. Except . . ."

"Except what?" Heimlich said.

"They got three guys up on these things above the stage. It looks like they're running the lights, but they've got some things mounted up there that look like fucking M60s to me."

"Maybe special effects?" Heimlich suggested.

"Uh huh," Hempstead said. "Jes like our buddies here." He jabbed the ponytailed stiff with the suppressor at the end of his Uzi's barrel.

It was hard for Jake to tell his friend from the others, what with their ski masks and all. Just one happy gang of terrorists, invading the local rock concert. He was all too aware of how important it was to keep his head on straight—he was the payroll man, he called the shots—but it was getting pretty hard for him to cope right now.

They had killed two people. That was for starters. They had lifted this operation straight out of trespassing and into Murder One. There was no going back. Only forward and through. To the end.

That rated a big number one.

Then there was the absolute fucking *insanity* of the situation, which was no small change and so ranked number two. Then there was the very real possibility of failure, the possibility that Jesse was already dead, which wasn't bad as number three . . .

. . . except no, wait, scratch all of the above, there was one little soul-blasting realization he'd neglected to mention, which was that he had brought this war onto himself and now he was here and he didn't like it a bit, which led to the biggest realization of all, which was that he might very well be sitting on the last two or three minutes of his life . . .

"Shut up," he said, and instantly knew it was wrong, because suddenly everybody was looking at him, and he didn't need to see their faces to know what they were thinking. *He's losing it.*

Which, in battlefield vernacular, amounted to *Well, he can kiss his ass good-bye.*

"No," he said. "I'm sorry. I'm back."

"Does that mean we can go now?" Heimlich inquired.

Fuck you, Jake thought, then said, "Let's do it."

And then they were up and running, silence not being the issue now, The Scream were making more than enough noise to cover any sound they could possibly make as they ran down the corridor, toward the back of the stage . . .

. . . and they were a death machine, yes, they were, the old feeling was back and Jake felt himself a cog in a larger device that was intrinsically self-contradictory, you were fighting for life and therefore you would kill, you would kill anything that got in your fucking path, you would do anything to save yourself and the ones you love . . .

. . . and the ones he loved the most had already been taken to death's door, it wasn't an abstraction, it was a fact of life, he could still see the faces of Rachel and Natalie and, yes, even Ted, see the terror there and think *I will not be able to rest until I know for a fact that these people are dead, I don't have to look over my shoulder and wonder if one of them is sneaking up behind, they're dead and I'm safe and my people are safe and I never have to worry about them dying again . . .*

. . . and then there was no time to think about it, because they were at the end of the corridor, the music thundering in their ears, and Hempstead went to the right and Pennycate went to the left and Heimlich hung back, guarding the exit, and Jake went straight for the stage. There was scaffolding to either side, scaffolding that held the tons of sound reinforcement equipment aloft. It would do the same for him, give him a bird's-eye view of the stage.

Quickly, silently, he moved to the left.

And began to climb . . .

. . . as the music downshifted into the tightest pocket Ted had ever heard, and everybody around him started bouncing like rubber room rejects, chanting like they meant it, like they were really fucking *buying* whatever the band was selling.

And it was scary. He didn't like the edge they were

walking one bit. He didn't like the look on Tara's face or the way the slash of Mylar across her eyes reflected the lights back at him. He didn't like the huge hulking thing behind her, which was looking less and less like a great stage prop and more like something sentient and predatory with eyes that followed his every move.

And he especially didn't like the hole that was opening up ominously in the floor of the stage right behind Tara's widespread legs. Opening like some secret missile silo.

Or a mouth preparing to scream . . .

"AAHHHHHH!!"

Jesse cried out, as the cross tipped back and sent her swinging. It was lost in the pounding of the stage above them, lost in the roar of the show. "NOOOAAHHHHHHHHHHHHH!!"

The pain was beyond all comprehension. Her whole being strained against the onslaught from the weight of her body sliding down as they hoisted the prop into place. The ligamentous destruction in her wrists and ankles raged against the ropes until the blood ran. They had crucified her, while her own beloved watched, and they had hauled her into a gravitationally excruciating position of blasphemy.

Amazingly enough, she was still lucid. She had remained so throughout the kidnapping, the stripping and the shaving and the insane violation, and remained so right up to this moment.

But she didn't know how much longer she could fight.

"PEEETE!!" she shrieked, hands clawing into utterly useless fists. "PETE, MY GOD!! HELP ME!!"

"Yeah, babay! EEEAYOW!!" he shouted. "Dontcha just love SHOWBIZ???"

The blood pounded in her head like air-sledges to the temples; her arms felt ready to dislocate any second. Her beloved was also shaved and wired at the temples, only he was dressed in a rotted cassock, holding a lethal-looking ceremonial dagger. And he was laughing, alternately cooing and stroking her. And he was rotting, fingers leaving little fleshy smears wheresoever they roamed.

And he was going to kill her. He said so, repeatedly.

Once the platform had fully risen.

"PETE, PLEASE!!" Jesse tried to see his face, but she

couldn't orient herself to the sensory overload. She was clad only in a gauze winding sheet, with her breasts and belly exposed and quivering. Sticky white electrodes stuck painfully to the side of her head where the hair had been sheared away for better adhesion, corresponding to points along the cerebral cortex meridian.

Jesse dry-heaved as an entire reality map overturned, internal gyroscope spinning in a mad dash to reassert itself, the data of dissociation being funneled live to the computers below and the keyboards above.

And the platform rose.

Light and color and sound and heat and death flooded the world into which she was rapidly ascending. *I WILL NOT LOSE IT!* She screamed internally. Externally, it came out a much more fundamental "EEEIYIAAAHHH!!"

She strained against the bonds, feeling the pinch of rope and Pete's dead hand crawling across her exposed flesh. *NOOOO!! NO!! I WILL NOT LET THIS HAPPEN! I WILL NOT GIVE UP I WILL NOT GIVE IN!!*

As vows went, it was downright commendable.

But it didn't slow her ascent one iota.

She felt the sickening lurch of vertigo as the platform edged up. The music punched through to the cochlea of her inner ears with all the finesse of a coping saw. The dread inch-by-inch ascent into madness continued, as Pete cackled and fingered the blade and the platform slid to a pneumatic whooshing halt and Jesse stared in wholehearted bug-eyed disbelief.

Into the faces of sixteen thousand faithful . . .

8:10:23 P.M.

. . . and Tara went into what looked like a trance.

The cross had erected at the apex of the Momma's thighs, just ahead of the drummer and about a dozen feet from the lip of the stage in what was a truly lewd effect, and the naked form writhed under the grasp of a rotting priest that leered like an undead game show host and wielded a knife that made the one in Ted's boot look like a goddamned potato peeler. The priest turned to face Ted's way.

Ted shrieked. He had seen the priest before.

And it didn't take much to figure out who the woman on the cross was.

The music went through a wild series of shifts right then, mutating from Gothic phantasmagoria into lunatic heavy metal power-dirge, as Rod strode purposefully up to Tara's mike and boomed, *"IT'S THAT TIME AGAIN!!* The rhythm section kicked in agreement. *"LADIES AND GENTLEMEN, ONE AND ALL, COME ON DOWN TO THE ALTAR CALL!"*

Ted started half-pushing, half-bashing his way over the hurricane fence on the side of the stage as Rod scanned the waiting hordes and cried—

"When we all come together in blood and bone
In flashing light, in crumbling stone . . .
The Father will spit on all their fears
As the Mother slits the veil of tears . . ."

The audience couldn't agree more. Rod's face screwed up in melodramatic intensity, and he bellowed, "YOU ARE CHOSEN! YOU ARE CALLED! SHE IS RISEN! SMASH THE WALL!"

The chosen responded . . .
"SMASH THE WALL!"
The chosen adored . . .
"SMASH THE WALL!"
All storming the fences . . .
"SMASH THE WALL!"
And climbing on board . . .

8:10:45 P.M.

. . . *and in the hive-mind, the bright spark flared: signaling the end, the opening of the Way, and the last great task remaining . . .*

8:10:46 P.M.

. . . and Mary Hatch could feel the dark thing moving, moving in a hundred different directions at once. From her seat at the top of the balcony, she could taste the frenzy . . .

. . . *the feeding frenzy* . . .

. . . and she fell to her knees as the first supplicant fell to the stage at Tara's feet. She would not watch the obscenity. She would not take it into her eyes. She would not become a part of it. She was praying like crazy to Father and Son and sweet Holy Spirit to save her.

To please, God, save them all . . .

. . . but Buzz Duffy wasn't worried about salvation just then. He was having a blast.

There had been some confusion on the stage for a second: one bouncer in the trough, tripping over the cameramen and looking around confused and screaming for backup, the backup slow enough in coming for *ten* guys plus Buzz to get over the fence and move in, forcing Tara back as the altar call chant built in intensity; the naked chick—*naked*, fer Chrissakes—upside-down on the cross and screaming her head off, the dude in the robes holding the knife up in front of her and laughing, Tara holding her knife up as she motioned them forward, the enormous Momma looming above him and watching it all, and the Buzzer up and over and smack in the middle of it . . .

But then the most incredible thing had happened, because Momma had seemed to look right *at* him, real personal; and before he knew it, a big guy in sunglasses was dragging him forward while three other guys tossed the rest of them back over the side.

It was then that he realized the awe-inspiring truth.

Out of all the limp dicks that had crawled to the stage, he alone had been Chosen . . .

And it was the most wonderful moment of Buzz Duffy's brief life. The taste of victory lay sweet in his mouth. He gave it voice with a full-throated, "EEAYAAOW!"

And they ushered him forth.

He didn't begin to feel the terror until he was nearly two feet from Tara. Only then he could really see what was happening to her belly, and that gave him serious second thoughts. He started to turn, but the guy in the suit had a crusher grip and before Buzz knew what was happening he was flat on his back, pinned on the stage, staring up as Tara moved toward him.

Buzz had time for one last look at the audience. A sea of squirming faces gleamed back.

They certainly seemed to be enjoying the show.

Then Tara was astride him, her ankles to his ears, and she was saying something that he vaguely recalled as being like the wine-and-biscuit shtick from his family's church, the yewka—*Eucharist*, that was it—and he could see up her skirt that she wore no panties, he could see her belly bulge and squirm as she plunged the blade into it, he could see the trails of red worms oozing down her inner thighs as she lowered herself right onto his face.

"TAKE THIS AND EAT," she sang.

He screamed.

"FOR THIS IS MY BODY . . ."

Behind and above them, Alex engaged the digital sequencers.

The last phase of the Great Passage had begun . . .

8:11:13 P.M.

. . . and Pete was just beginning to slit her throat, the silver chalice steady beneath her jugular, the words "THIS IS THE BLOOD POURED OUT IN THE *NEW* COVENANT" booming in her ears, when he jerked and dropped and Jesse never even saw the top of his head exploding . . .

8:11:14 P.M.

. . . and Jake said *Good-bye, Pete* from his awkward, precarious sniper's position on the scaffolding, and he began to aim again before his late friend even hit the floor . . .

8:11:15 P.M.

. . . and Hempstead crashed through the door of the press room and found no Walker and everyone dead, and he *knew* the sonofabitch was backstage somewhere and they hadn't found him downstairs and he *must* be here, and he yanked back the goddamned door to the press box and jumped out into the dark and the noise and there was a six-foot insect turning toward him with a walkie-talkie in its hands, only it wasn't an insect at all, it was Walker with a goddamned gas mask on, pressing the call button like crazy, sending a signal to someone somewhere, and Hempstead raised the Uzi to blow his miserable fucking ass away . . .

. . . and then the whitelight wall of heat slammed home, scorching and blinding him as just under two hundred gallons of homemade napalm went off on the floor of the arena, sending a solid wall of fire rocketing toward the ceiling in great smoking sheets, throwing Hempstead hard against the door and into the black silence of oblivion.

The shock wave hit several milliseconds later, flattening every single person standing in the arena as the air pressure slammed outward, then back in to suck any available air molecule into the growing pillar of fire. Thousands trapped in the uppermost tiers of the stadium blacked out, as eardrums imploded and lungs deflated like toy balloons and thick coils of black poison choked off everything above the exit ramps.

The ramps themselves became miniature wind tunnels, each one funneling fresh, colder oxygen in to feed the firestorm. Over two thousand people died in the first five seconds, from smoke and shock and blast.

Many more followed . . .

By Hook's estimate the nape would spray up and out almost twelve feet on detonation, covering everything it touched in viscous, blistering death. He wasn't far off the mark in his guess. It coated very evenly along its entire circumference, consuming another four thousand in a blazing cylindrical inferno. The stench of several tons of frying human flesh was instantaneous, a vast gaseous presence so incredibly thick and hot and foul-sick-sweet that it brought on a retching gag reflex even through the four-stage filter of his mask.

But he didn't heave. He was ready for it.

It brought back memories.

He reached for the second switch, marveling at the transformation.

The concert hall was gone. In its place was Hell: an instant scale replica, so perfect, so easy, so there for the making. The enclosed vault of the ceiling had miraculously become a Dantean sky, black smoke boiling above them like the wrath of an angry god; the floor before him a roaring lake of fire. He drank in the majesty of it a moment longer.

Then he hit the second switch three times . . .

. . . and two D batteries responded to the overture, sending tiny sparks of electrical current racing through the detonation cord leading to the five steel pillars, each one of which contained mounted within its frame exactly thirty-three for a grand total of one hundred sixty-five claymore antipersonnel devices, each one of which cost exactly sixty-two dollars on the open market and which gave a tremendous bang-per-buck ratio, as each one came packed with approximately four point oh four for a grand total of six hundred and sixty-six pounds of BBs, each one of which promptly blew outward at a sixty-five-degree angle to pulverize and shred absolutely everything in their effective killing range, all of which Hook had artfully deployed to create the shape of a star, an enormous overlapping star-shaped pool of liquified humanity, with some chunks of living flesh

still remaining along each side's seventy-five-foot length but absolutely none left in the middle, where all five paths converged and collided and conspired to reduce every living being within to the consistency of warm, runny Jell-O.

It was a fucking masterpiece.

The backlash of the blast had killed some and maimed more in the shower of chicken wire and plastic and papier-mâchè, of course, but that was nothing, that was the paint flecks that framed the canvas of his great work. It was a marvel of economy: of cost, of construction, of impact. As performance pieces went, it was world-class. How could it not be? It demanded total sensory involvement. Taste, texture, smell . . .

It would be a couple of minutes yet before he could hear clearly, of course, to enjoy the sound.

But sight-wise, it was stunning.

The tinted lenses in his mask afforded him considerable blast protection, for which he was eternally grateful. It would have been a shame to miss the sight of the burning ring, the blasted columns, and the razor-sharp lines of decimation that the claymores had carved through the mass of stoned, swarming wasteoids that packed the floor of the hall. His only regret was that he missed the all-important aerial view.

Of course, it wasn't often that one was afforded a ringside seat at the unveiling of a stadium-sized raw-meat flaming pentagram, and that in itself was really something special.

But he'd still have loved to see it from above . . .

8:13:13 P.M.

Walker stared down from the rim of the press box: his own private box seat for the grand opening of Hell. He could afford the luxury. He was responsible for it.

He was humbled by the spectacle before him.

For this was the Inferno, live at last. A sight to make Dante blanch and Doré turn pale, running mile-wide rings around the visions of Ernst and Bosch and St. Peter and all who had tried to bring that ultimate horror to life. Not even the war, for all its monstrosity, had ever created such a set piece of evil and then granted him such an island of immunity from which to observe it. The smoke, the flames, the pool, the writhing bodies everywhere, the giant demon on the stage, the limp forms surrounding it.

The smoke burned in Walker's good eye. He swiped at it, but the gas mask was in the way. He thought about removing it, knew that was madness, somehow refrained. The pain got worse. His one eye watered, muddying his vision.

"Momma." He couldn't hear himself. It didn't matter. "Momma." If she could hear him, she would speak inside his head.

But no. *This is our last conversation,* she had said, *till we meet face-to-face.* There was no reason to doubt her word, at least with regards to that. She was busy now, busily being born, too busy to be bothered with what he did in these last few strokes of the clock.

So what now?

On the press box floor, Hempstead lay dazed. Walker had stripped the ski mask off. The gun in Walker's hand tracking loosely with the movements of his head. So they had come, after all. *Just like Momma said.* He wondered how many and where. Not that it mattered. Not anymore. A bullet in the face would put an end to him, sure; but for some reason, Walker just couldn't see the point.

In his mind's eye (and wasn't *that* a touch of levity!) he could see himself back at the ambush, all those many years back; he could still see the bloody sap, oozing down the trees.

And it flashed on him then that maybe the snipers had had a point: that maybe—if he'u not given in, if he'd let himself die, as God or Fate or ordinary life had most likely intended—none of this would have happened at all. He had succumbed to the darkness and the evil at each successive turn, and it had returned the favor, in turn, by selling each of them out in a gradually tightening knot of betrayal.

Until there was only himself and it.

Then it sold him out.

"God damn you!" he spat.

The burning in his eye was worse. His brain began to ache.

He looked at the arena. It was bad.

He looked at the stage. Worse still.

He looked at Tara.

And Tara was worst of all.

Because she was still kneeling, the body beneath her no longer twitching, her head and arms thrown back in forever abandon. She was giving birth now, her cargo ripe and ready to deliver at last.

Delivered by self-serve cesarean section.

Millions and millions of tiny tiny worms . . .

They gushed out from the more-than-foot-long gash she had opened in her belly, poured onto the stage, streamed out toward the edge and the floor below. There were more of them than she could have possibly contained.

She had become a doorway.

And the space where his long-gone eye had been began to itch and tingle and *squirm;* the awe he had felt turned swiftly to terror. They were in there—*they were in there!*—and all of the assurances were for shit, his mind and his soul were not his own, they never had been, not since the moment she'd come to him, she wasn't even a *her,* she was an *it,* it was nothing that desperately wanted to be something, and how had he ever been so *stupid* as to think it wouldn't turn on him, too?

The pain squirmed and thrashed in the dead skin of his eye socket, halfway between spirit and substance. He heard the dim nattering of their voices behind the ringing in his ears. *No no no!* He felt the onrushing panic. *It's all in your mind! It's what the fucking thing* wants *you to believe, it's all in your MIND . . . !*

Yes, it certainly was. Squirming and chewing, feeding on the fear and growing, just as the Faith of the Chosen was growing down on the floor. Growing more real by the second, reaching for that point when it no longer needed their belief, until it could reach out and force belief on all it surveyed. The line between imagination and physical reality had gotten very thin indeed, had almost disappeared in fact.

Walker squashed the panic, *hard.* Years of deadened experience were all that separated him from the utter madness that was gaining ground as he tore his gaze away from the red squirming torrent, forced himself to look back at the floor. The Screamers were moving down there now. They had descended in droves, a hundred or more, from the lower grandstand; they waded through the pitiful semiconscious forms of the audience. It looked as though they were howling, but his ears still could not register sound.

Inside the flaming circle, the star began to ripple and glow . . .

And Walker ran out of the box: ignoring his would-be assassin, ignoring the press room and the bodies therein as he barreled down the stairs. The feeling in his head clicked on and off, on and off, intensifying exponentially. If this was it, there was something that he wanted to do very badly.

And he was almost out of time . . .

8:17:11 P.M.

In the hive-mind, a ruptured rapturous scrambling through the widening portal . . .

8:17:12 P.M.

The Screamers stepped into the fading circle of fire, began slashing and feeding bodies to the luminous lake. The shapes hovered at the surface for a moment, some of them thrashing feebly; then, suddenly, they were gone. It reminded Hook insanely of the opening scene from the movie *Jaws:* the hapless blonde, fearfully treading water one moment; the next, vanishing abruptly beneath the waves.

The only problem was that the lake could only be a few inches deep at maximum. There was nowhere for the bodies to go. . . .

Hook had one long moment to contemplate the impossible.

Then the pair of Screamers were upon him, pulling him backward by the throat, down to the floor beside his newly dead assistant . . .

. . . and he didn't even have time to register his betrayal before, with no artistry at all, they slit his throat, dragged him off the platform, across the floor, and into the abyss . . .

8:18:00 P.M.

Pennycate hauled ass up the corridor an instant after the shock and the sound of the first blast hit him. He didn't need to see what was happening; he recognized both by smell. The thick rich stench of petroleum and cordite permeated the air of the passageway, along with the smell of something much, much worse. Death. Lots and lots of it.

Well, this certainly changes a lot of things, he thought as he ran down the backstage access corridor. *I wonder what the big plan is now.*

He heard accompanying blasts of automatic weapons and grenades from up on the mezzanine, and what sounded like some police sirens that ended rather abruptly as what sounded like gas tanks went off. Pennycate decided that somebody better check that out.

He elected himself, tearing up the stairs leading to the promenade as he pulled the bolt back on the Uzi and got ready to just bash through the door and book his butt behind some available cover, when somebody who looked an awful lot like Keith Richards appeared at the head of the stairs, coming down fast, and he had a gun too, and it looked like an impromptu gunfight at the Stairwell Corral, and Pennycate was fast but the Keith-clone was just a little bit faster, and he squeezed off two shots that took Pennycate's knees out from under him and sent him cartwheeling back down the stairs in what he would have to admit was a very unprofessional position, and his neck hit the fourth step from the bottom in entirely the wrong way, sending sparks and pain and then numb black oblivion into every inch of his body . . .

. . . and Kyle jumped over the limp dead form in the ski mask, barely having time to wonder *Who the fuck is that?* because things were getting very hairy up there, and when you start blowing up cops you'd better have some backup real quick and he didn't have enough and he was starting to rethink his commitment to this whole freak show, and he ran like hell down the hall . . .

8:18:31 P.M.

. . . as Ted awoke to the mad ringing in his ears and the crushing weight of bodies on top of him, plastering him to the floor. The blinding thunder was still alive in his head. He couldn't move. He could barely think.

The rain of worms slid over the lip of the stage.

There were five people above him. They took the brunt of the first downpour. They began to twitch and scream; the worms sloughed down in torrents. Most sluiced past, riding the crest of the deepening tide; less than fifty actually came to rest on Ted's arms and back and head in the first five seconds.

Then they started to *bite* him, and his mind cleared dramatically. The pain made him a believer. It threw his body into motion. There was a fleeting pocket of uninhabited space two feet ahead and to the right, flush against the stage. He clawed his way toward it, one thought screaming through his brain.

Jesse.

Ted climbed to the lip of the stage.

Another fifty thousand fell . . .

8:18:52 P.M.

. . . and the music was playing, it was playing *itself*, the coprocessors and sequencers charged with both life and death as they mounted to the first movement's crescendo. They had kept right on going in the seconds it had taken for Alex to regain his footing. He still had a job to do. He was, after all, the ears of The Scream.

Momma's ears, now.

And the voice of Its creation . . .

Alex was the only one still standing on the stage. Tara had passed over, turned to pure inseminoid, her spawn gushing madly out toward the rippling star. Gene and Terry had crumbled, given up their crawling hosts. The bouncers had fallen, unprepared for the moment. And dear little big brother had fallen, too.

"Don't you worry, Rod, baby!" He beamed widely as he spoke. "In a minute, we'll all be together at last!"

The giant Momma-thing had gone dead on stage; no doubt the crew had not been fully prepped. No matter.

It had served its purpose. What was left of the audience lay like newly threshed wheat. They were well on their way to real *believing*.

The second movement would convince them completely.

He watched as the hot tide of Tara-spawn spilled out to grow between the outstretched legs of the star. He watched the center of the star roiling in syncronous accord, the pool bubbling along a thirty-foot central *slit*, a slit that bubbled and frothed and opened in yawning expectation. He watched Screamers wade into the burning muck, dragging unfortunate survivors to the edge and pitching them in. The squirming wave slid closer to the lip of the hole.

Alex's finger poised over the key that would trigger the critical mass. He tipped a loving nod toward Jesse, down on the stage. After all, hers was the ever-important missing ingredient. They were about to make beautiful music together, their symphonies entwined like light and dark. Like Life and Death. They were made for each other.

Alex pushed the button and smiled. He had no clear idea of what would happen next, and he couldn't hear it quite as well as he'd have liked, but he was sure that all was perfection.

He believed.

8:19:00 P.M.

It was time to come out now, come out and take form. All the elements had, at forever last, commingled: flesh and faith, worm and song, all a part of it now. Only one thing remained, one act left to be done.

The supreme act of will.

I AM THAT I AM

As the thing that mockingly called itself Momma began to push its way into the world.

8:19:05 P.M.

In the back of her mind, Jesse heard the Symphony's terrible transmutation. She was still semiconscious from the blast, so it seemed to her more like a resonant echo from the dream. "*Nooo . . .,*" she moaned, drowning in the aura of corruption, fighting the psychotic visions of Pete in her mind as she clawed her way back toward the surface.

Then she felt something give in the vicinity of her ankles, felt the sudden sharp straining at her shoulders and wrists. Body awareness brought her all the way back. She opened her eyes.

And started to scream.

Because she recognized Ted instantly, despite the worms that were burrowing into his body and face. She saw the pain in his eyes and knew that he could not last much longer. Her eyes were on the knife in his hand as he wavered before her, screaming as well . . .

    . . . *and it wasn't just the pain, the tearing of their teeth, or the burning sting of the poison they secreted. It was the fact that they were inside him now. Inside his mind.*
    Saying nasty things.
    He looked at Jesse closely for a second. He had never seen her so nearly naked before. Certainly not trussed up like that. Certainly not while he had his trusty knife in hand. There were so many holes to fill, so many more he could create with a simple homing thrust . . .
    . . . and he couldn't stop the voices, even as he willed the blade to come up, even as he began to saw through the rope that bound her left wrist to the cross . . .

    . . . and she swung forward, still dangling by the other wrist. He caught her before her weight could snap the delicate bone, pressed her back against the cross with his body, awkwardly cut her loose. Her feet touched the floor at last; she collapsed against him for a moment, going, "Oh, thank God . . ."
    . . . and then the worms were biting into her, too, and as she screamed and pushed away from Ted and he fell to the floor she saw that others were moving on the stage now, staggering to their feet, the bouncers and Rod Royale and a fourth man in a black ski mask who appeared from behind her and began to blow holes in the first two men, making them jitter and spray as they fell . . .

    . . . and Rod Royale looked up into the black mask, the eyes without a face, the barrel of the gun, then over at the widening mouth of Hell. They were far too close together, Lord, the black hole and the burning one. There was scarcely any difference at all.
    "BUT YOU PROMISED!" he screamed, one final pointless plea, and then the bullets razored into his belly, throwing him back, throwing him open, cutting him in half . . .

    . . . and Jesse fell to her knees beside Ted, tearing at the worms with her fingernails, tearing them off him, pulling them out. They were in his ears. They were under his skin.

It was clear that he was very likely going to die.

He was spasming now, no longer even fighting; he seemed barely aware of anything but the pain. She kept at it, maniacally, refusing to accept that it was too late, feeling the little fuckers pop under her fingers as she tore them away, ignoring them when they bit her . . .

. . . as the Symphony thundered in her ears, the hideous Symphony of Life beyond Death, cutting through the high-pitched whine at the back of her eardrums . . .

. . . and when the ski-masked man came up to her and tried to wrench her away, she heard the distant sound of her own voice screaming *STOP THE MUSIC, YOU'VE GOT TO STOP THE GODDAMNED MUSIC* as she turned and pointed up at Alex Royale, who stared back down at her, hysterically laughing . . .

. . . and Heimlich understood at least enough to follow her gaze, see the last remaining member of The Scream standing there on the platform, surrounded by his contraptions. It didn't take but a second to aim and fire, reduce the top of the man's skull to vapor and gristle.

But the music kept playing. And the bottom half kept smiling.

A huge, Cheshire cat grin.

He looked back at the girl. She was shaking her head. The word she seemed to be screaming was DIOS, over and over, as she pointed at the platform where the man he'd just blown off had stood. Heimlich didn't understand that at all, but she was emphatic, so he made his way rapidly up the stairs to the keyboard setup. The fucker was still standing, even with the top of his head gone, and there were a lot of controls and a lot of flashing lights up there, dancing waveforms on little green TV screens, a little black box on a massive keyboard.

"Fuggit," Heimlich grunted, and just blew it all away.

The music stopped.

Too late.

8:20:00 P.M.

The great taloned hand was the first thing to emerge from the wide-open crack in the world.

It rose: claws first, five in all, each of them long and dark as coffin lids; fingers, then, surprisingly short and stubby, less than ten feet long apiece, with thin semitransparent webbing between them; the palm next, big as a tractor trailer cab; the wrist, fat and slick and hugely pulsing.

And then the hand was reaching up at the end of an arm too huge for comprehension, reaching for the dead ArenaVision module, the fingers wrapping around it and dawdling with the tons of glass and metal, pushing it like a demonic crib toy, then grasping and wrenching and tightening and pulling as if to hoist itself out farther . . .

All of this Hempstead observed in the moments before he opened fire.

It had been hard, at first, to reconcile himself with the fact that he wasn't dead. New rules were not enough to cover it. Nothing was enough. If this wasn't Hell, then there was no point in even conceiving of one.

But he still had his mind and his body and his gun; and if they still worked, then maybe it was just a matter of new rules after all.

There was only one way to find out.

Hempstead switched to full automatic and proceeded to empty his clip. Even at this range, it was impossible to miss. Thirty nine-millimeter slugs tore an impressive series of spurting holes in the soft red flesh on the flip side of the elbow. They seemed to cause considerable pain.

That was the good news.

The bad news, of course, was that it wasn't enough. It wasn't even close. All it did was piss the thing off. When the arm jerked back in anguish, the hand took the ArenaVision module with it, showering sparks and steel and glass onto the already suffering masses below.

Then the hand cocked back.

And lobbed several tons of death at the source of its pain.

There was time to scream, but no time to spare. He dove through the doorway, rolling toward the stairs, past the anonymous corpses and down, just as the wall of the press room exploded inward in a shower of ruptured cinder block and leviathan steel.

Then he was running, the last several steps disappearing behind him as he raced through the blood-drenched hospitality room and out into the lower concourse, toward the exit and whoever was left to exit it with him, because there was no fucking way to fight anymore, there was only retreat, and it had to be swift, and it had to be now . . .

"Pray!" Mary screamed, grabbing hold of his collar. *"Pray,* God DAMN you!" She'd found Weissman, running like a maniac through the explosions and terrified survivors near ramp LL. And he'd kept right on running, leaving Mary and the pastor to the tender mercies of the Lord.

Mary couldn't leave, though. She didn't even understand why. Common sense and terror said *GO! GO! GO! GO!* through every traumatized circuit on her body. The Horror rising before her confirmed the impulse.

But something else deep inside her spoke. Not in words, but nonetheless. *Stay,* It said. *And fear not.*

For I am with you always.

It was a small voice, but It was growing by the second, and It was not afraid. Feeling It strong and clear in that moment of shattering dread, she realized that all names for It sloughed off like dross. She could not contain It, she could not explain It.

But she believed It, heart and soul.

She found Furniss. She wrenched the spikes from his hands and hauled him up. She shook him like a rag doll with strength she never even knew she had. And she screamed.

"PRAY!!!"

Daniel Furniss's eyes met hers for a microsecond, and they stopped spinning. He nodded his shell-shocked head, and then he started praying, following her words this time, barely making the connection of one word to the next to the next, having but the tiniest grasp of the truth that he had vaunted for so long. He was stripped utterly bare in the face of It and words utterly failed him. That didn't matter, though.

It was the thought that counted.
Together, they prayed. . . .

8:23:00 P.M.

Walker was just coming out of the security room where
Kyle had stowed the ordnance when he ran into Hempstead.
He'd stripped off the eye patch and gas mask and found that
the left lens was smeared with a clot of worms the consistency
of bloody vermicelli. That clinched it. Walker had changed his
mind about a whole lot of things in the past twenty minutes,
and he was damned if he wasn't going to do something about it.
He had to hurry; his grip was slipping, every tickticktick of the
clock finding him weaker and them stronger.

Which is why he got caught in the hall. He wasn't paying
attention to the hall; his mind was fixed on the two heavy
RPG7 missiles that he carted, and the noise coming from the
arena. He was still very much a man in a nightmare. But he
was also, for the first time in forever, a man with a dream. He
stared straight into the eyes of the man with the gun.

"I should kill you," Hempstead said flatly, the Uzi chest-
leveled. The shock of twenty-year-old memories screaming
back like a freight train was a stunner. He saw the scars etched
into Walker's sweat-streaked face. "I ought to kill you right
now." The gun hovered, poised.

Walker nodded and then he smiled, a grim slit of genuine
emotion. "Yeah, I know. So kill me *later*."

He held out one of the RPG7s.

Hempstead weighed the decision another twenty microsec-
onds or so. Then he took the weapon.

"I will, you know," he said. "Believe it."

Walker nodded. "I do."

*There was a God; and if there wasn't, then oblivion had
a real keen sense of justice. Oblivion was the best that Rod
could hope for now.*

Too bad there was no hope.

From where he lay, with his guts blown out, the palace gates were clearly visible. He could see what lay on the other side. He could see where the end of his life was leading.

The end of his life had taken a long time to get here. Gut-shot victims tend to have that problem. Rod knew all about it. It was a great way to prolong the agony: give the squandered past plenty of time to replay while the present went leaking away.

But there always came the moment when the end showed its face.

The face was here.

It emerged the size of a weather balloon, with a skin about as thick, growing thicker by the second. Its head wasn't coated in slime, its head *was* the slime, as viscous as the skin of a soap bubble. It was an enormous outline, filling itself in: translucent, swirling, mutating a million times a second like some humongous claymation creation, boiling and spitting and laughing insane howling rage as it became zygote, then fetus, then baby, then toddler child teen adult ancient twisted inhuman mockery of the world it was struggling to gain hold of.

The other arm came bursting out of the hole like a misfiring rocket, careening up and over and smashing into the floor of the arena, pulping bodies both dead and alive in an expression of its enthusiasm. Victims were grand. Victims were sweet candy. The body followed, trailing huge, bloated breasts over distended belly, reptilian tail and long pulsing phallus and snapping vulva between squat, scaly legs. A long, long umbilical cord trailed back into the pit like so much moist pink rope. The phallus whipped around viciously, its many-toothed opening snapping at the victims under each splayed foot, gobbling them in chunks and hunks, then stuffing one whole into the vulva and pounding him to death in debased coital embrace.

Rod thought about the many sweet victims he'd tasted, let the roll call of their faces take one last quick pass across his fading vision's path. So many eyes, remembering him. Waiting, on the other side of the gate that he'd spent his whole life trying to get through.

Waiting for the chance to return the favor.

And now, as momma closed in on the stage and the mouth opened wide to greet him, that chance had finally come. . . .

8:24:25 P.M.

There was no question as to whether Momma had made it or not. It was herre, all right. The closer it came, the more real it got.

And it was funny, but as they reached the side of the stage and he watched Rod disappear screaming into that leering maw, Walker listened again to a speech he'd made to the late guitarist less than forty-eight hours before.

This is the physical world, he'd said, *and all the physical rules apply. Once she gets here, she's just a bigger and better version of us. You know what that means?*

You know what that means?

"It means your ass is mine," Walker whispered to himself, then turned to Hempstead and said, "Get your people out of here. Now."

"But—"

"Just *do* it!"

Hempstead weighed the situation again. It took even less time now. His people were scrambling off the back of the elevated platform behind the dead cathedral backdrop, and they needed help. He looked at Walker one last time, laid down the spare missile, then turned and bolted for them.

As Walker armed the one-shot he saw Jake stumbling around from the other side of the stage with what looked like a very broken arm. Hempstead caught up to him and yelled something unintelligible, gesturing back at Walker. Jake nodded and looked back at him. There was some justice in the universe after all, Walker thought. It was comforting.

Walker watched as the refugees beat their hasty retreat, disappearing amid the piles of road cases. He gave them a couple of extra seconds to get toward the back door. Momma was busy tearing up the stage and the audience before it, heaving bodies and equipment high into the air and squashing them back underfoot, reveling in its arrival.

That suited him just fine; he had the perfect welcome home present. He shouldered it. *An RPG7 will blow the shit out of a fully armored tank at six hundred yards*, he reasoned. "Let's see what it will do to your face at fifty."

Walker stepped out from behind the speaker column and aimed.

"MOMMMMAAAAAAA!!!" he screamed.

The demon head snapped around to snarl at the sound of his voice.

And Walker fired . . .

They were almost out the back door when the first explosion went off. If they had any intention of stopping, they didn't show it. The blowback from the blast shook the huge steel and plastic and aluminum maze like an earthquake, threatening to send it tumbling down like a giant toddler's building blocks.

They scrambled frantically on: Hempstead pulling Jake, Heimlich helping Jesse helping Ted, a mad follow-the-leader dash for the sanctuary of the back ramp and open air. A tremendous roar followed the blast, sending the teetering boxes smashing down in a jumbling heap, blocking all thought of returning to help fight the beast. There was only the door, and the night, and the wail of distant sirens coming from all parts of the city . . .

. . . and Walker shouldered the second rocket as he stared up into the freshly blasted pit that was the left eye of the demon. He'd missed, striking only a glancing blow off the temple, but it yielded results. The thing was real as real could be now, and boy, it was pissed. Real demon skull had flown in gleaming-white shards across the breadth of the amphitheater; real demon brains roiled in the opened chamber, leaking out to fall and hit the very real floor.

Billions upon billions of tiny, angrily thrashing worms . . .

Momma reeled in the agony of the betrayal, its one good eye meeting his and narrowing to a glowing, bottomless trench, filled with pure ageless hatred. It charged the distance between them in a flash, huge, fanged mouth gaping wide to take him in. Walker sighted straight down its throat as it covered the distance, counting back one fifty, one hundred, seventy-five . . .

"Welcome to Earth, bitch." He smiled.

. . . sixty, fifty . . .

"WELCOME TO THE *FOOD CHAIN*!"

He pulled the second trigger.

The shaped charge round flew straight and true, right into the Demon's howling face.

The explosion knocked it back another twenty feet, sending a brilliant fireball into the already troubled air and joining everything it touched—flesh and blood, body and soul—in that all-consuming, cleansing white light. . . .

8:33:33 P.M.

By the time the second explosion rocked the building, Jake and company had crawled up to the relative safety of the parking lot. Hempstead and Heimlich had picked up Jesse and Ted and carried them, leaving Jake to stand a wounded rear guard.

No one came; not out the back door anyway. The exterior of the Spectrum Sports Arena looked bad: a lot of burning vehicles, a lot of dead or wounded bodies. He leaned against the ramp wall and listened to the sounds that filled the air on the heels of the aftershock.

A long, keening maelstrom of a scream, spiraling up and up and up . . .

Then gone.

The sounds of a world gone mad flooded in a moment later, like water leaching into a bootheel on a beach. Stragglers started spilling out of the distant exits. Sporadic gunfire could still be heard on the far side of the building, but it was answered by gunfire and sirens, and more sirens and more, and somehow Jake thought that, deprived of their source, the Screamers wouldn't last much longer. The world would simply squash them.

The world usually did.

The pain in his arm came throbbing up to meet him as the endorphins burned off. "*God,*" he murmured, collapsing to the ground. He tried to find the words that could phrase the question in his mind, found none that fit, and settled for the basest response.

"Help!! *Shit!* HELP!"

Hempstead came jogging back within the moment. "Yo, Jake!"

"Here!"

"Are you okay?" It was not a casual question; Hempstead checked him for undiscovered damage.

"Yeah, yeah . . . OW! Shit." Jake groaned. "Maybe not."

"Heimlich's already flagging down an ambulance for Ted and Jesse," Hempstead said, relieving Jake of the Uzi. He swung it a couple of times by the strap and heaved it, far down the ramp and into the carnage. "We civilians now, bro'. Ain't nobody comin' outta that door. C'mon, we gotta get that arm tended to."

He helped his friend up, hoisting him by the waist and carrying the bulk of his weight. They staggered away from the ramp, toward the far end of lot SC, where the Philly emergency medical crews were pulling up. The city was responding, pouring manpower and resources into the catastrophe. Slim Jim's Engstrom had already touched down nearby; he could see Jim talking to one of the medical teams, just a concerned chopper pilot landing at the scene of a disaster, sir, does anyone need some help? Jake looked back; tongues of fire licked the inside of the loading ramp door.

"Are Jess and Ted okay?" he said, anxiety tainting his voice.

Hempstead nodded. "I don't know. I think so."

Jake breathed a massive sigh of relief, then said, "Where's Pennycate?"

"Don't know that, either."

"Shit." They stumbled toward an ambulance that looked open for business. Jim caught sight of them and started jogging up.

"I've got a lot of unanswered goddamned questions," Jake said.

Hempstead shook his head. "Save 'em."

"I fucked up."

"You did the best you could."

They walked some more. Jake was feeling dizzy. Hempstead steadied him.

They reached the ambulance. Red lights twirled in their faces; Slim Jim and an attendant scrambled to Jake's side. They grabbed him and eased him over.

"Ow—damn!" he bitched. The medic did a spot-triage and then hustled back to prepare a splint. Jake looked exhausted and crestfallen.

"What the fuck happened?" Jim asked them both. Jake just winced and shook his head.

"Long story," Hempstead said. "You get tired of waiting or something?"

"No shit." He looked at Jake's arm and whistled. "Did we win?"

"Nobody won," Jake replied.

"I ain't so sure," Hempstead countered. He looked at Jake. "We just kicked the titties offa *somethin'*."

Jake didn't look impressed. The attendant came back, started scissoring off the fabric of Jake's shirtsleeve. Jake winced in pain with every snick of the blades.

"Guess I'm not Superman, after all," he muttered.

Hempstead looked at his best friend and shook his head. "Ye-eah," he replied. "I guess not.

"But you still sing real pretty."

AND THE DAYS GO BY

"The recognition that no knowledge can be
complete, no metaphor entire, is in itself
humanizing. It counteracts fanaticism.
It grants even to adversaries the possibility
of partial truth, and to oneself the possibility
of error... In a time of exploding change—
with personal lives being torn apart, and a
the existing social order crumbling, and a
fantastic new way of life emerging on the horizon—
asking the very largest of questions about our future
is not merely a matter of intellectual curiosity.
It is a matter of survival."
—Alvin Toffler

"Same as it ever was.
Same as it ever was.
Same as it ever was.
Same as it ever was."
—Talking Heads

A lot of things changed in eighteen months. The wheels kept right on turning; bringing the end of some things. And the beginnings of others.

The aftermath of the Labor Day Massacre was as lurid as it was predictable. While the survivors offered little in the way of unified consensus as to what had actually happened inside the arena—too many conflicting reports, tales that smacked loudly of mass psychosis and hysteria—the evidence left behind spoke plainly for itself:

The arena itself was heavily damaged, but not destroyed; it got a hiatus and a face-lift and would live to see Disney on Ice yet again. The crowd was not nearly as fortunate. Accurate body counts were, of course, impossible; by the time the fire was brought under control the purity of the human stew on the floor of the arena had been greatly diluted with ash and debris, water and chemical fire-fighting foam. Conservative estimates ran to well over six thousand dead at the Spectrum Sports Arena, killed by blast, fire, smoke inhalation, gunshot wounds, and general mayhem. They were bagged, hoisted and hosed away.

Another hundred and fifty-three bodies found at The Scream's Staten Island estate: some freshly butchered and hanging, most painstakingly exhumed from the walls and grounds over the following months.

Sixty-eight dead at Rock Aid.

And while wild speculation flooded both the press and the Senate subcommittee hearings that sprang up in the wake of the tragedy, in the end, there was only one possible conclusion: that The Scream, for reasons known only to the late band members, had willfully murdered their fans in a series of delusional and apparently satanic rituals that ultimately back-fired, costing them their own lives.

The reason *why*, however, was much less apparent. The members of The Scream were permanently silenced. And their manager, shadowy multimillionaire Joshua Walker, could not be reached for comment; had, in fact, disappeared entirely.

That left everyone else to fill in the blank.

And the legend was born.

Salt Lake City, Utah. Three teenagers are tried and convicted for the ritual slaying of six-year-old Patty Robertson. Police arriving at the scene found the girl's nude body, hideously mutilated, inside a burning pentagram while her killers danced and chanted to The Scream's "Critical Mass." They claim they were trying to "raise a demon" and swear that "Momma will be back." They also claim to have chosen the victim because "her name was perfect." It is the fifth such reported incident in the wake of the Labor Day Massacre.

Detroit, Michigan. The number of Scream-related self-mutilations in this city rises to thirty-seven, culminating in a bizarre wedding ceremony, as twenty-year-old Alvin White and his sixteen-year-old bride, Carrie Cain, exchange ring fingers instead of rings and proclaim themselves "married in the eyes of Momma."

New York City. Despite the passage of a modified version of Congressman Shrake's "Devil Rock" legislation, and the efforts of community groups nationwide, sales of The Scream's Critical Mass album continue to climb toward the ten million mark; and though Bedlam Records has earmarked half of all proceeds for a victims' compensation fund, the legal battle still rages over whether the album should continue to be sold at all. . . .

The struggle was still going on, of course. The struggle would go on forever. Hempstead had been right about that much. You wouldn't think a guy with a mohawk could *be* that smart; but there it was.

Today, the struggle was back where it belonged: on *The Dick Moynihan Show*. Jake was only sorry that he could not attend. There was way too much to do, what with the new album coming out and the new band about to tackle the Rigors of The Road. Bob and Bob were gone, having long since taken that gig with The Del-Rays, but with some searching they had found a new, improved rhythm section, and Hempstead was still on hand and Jesse and even a little of Pete, thanks to the many guitar samples that Jess had made. The band was on its feet again.

At long last, he mused, smiling to himself. *Amen.*

The Moynihan show was still bloodlustingly terrific. Good ol' Yke was back, for one thing: blond and abrasively good-natured as ever, holding the beleaguered rock 'n' roll banner high. So was the fabulous Esther Shrake, looking chipper and smug in the light of her hubby's ace legislative support.

A lovely surprise, though not entirely unexpected, was the appearance of Pastor Paul Weissman, the new director of Liberty Christian Village, defending his ministry's recent appeal for a ten-million-dollar miracle. He had taken over shortly after the Labor Day debacle, when Pastor Furniss effectively disappeared from the ministry and public life. Weissman had always been a cold little shit, and it was obvious that he was getting off on the power of his new position.

Of course, if those allegations of financial mismanagement and sexual abuse at the Village came through, well . . . maybe Pastor Paul would be made to recall that his God was a just God. And a vengeful one, too.

Whatever. Regretfully, Jake couldn't really pay attention to the show. It was hard to concentrate with two crazed midgets in the room, even if one of them hadn't even made it to the toddler stage yet. Little Peetro could scoot like nobody's business, faster even than Natalie at her peak. He was a great kid, no question about it: bold and bright and beautiful. He already made a hellacious racket on his miniature plastic Menudo guitar.

And, yes, he had his father's eyes.

Jesse cruised across the Twilight Zone floor and scooped her nearly-year-old son away from the upside-down sneaker he had begun to chaw. "Nuh-uh, kiddo. Don't eat Uncle Ted's stray Reeboks. No."

"Petey's crazy." Natalie observed, sidling up to Jesse from behind. She was two point three years old now, and precocious as all get-out.

"Who isn't?" Jesse caught a string of little Pete's drool on her forearm.

"Uh-huh," Natalie shot back, then took off in the direction of the kitchen, where the opening of the oven door meant that the next batch of Rachel and Gram's carob almond cookies were ready. Jake and Jesse watched her go; baby Pete was still looking at the rubber-soled object of his passing desire.

Then Jake turned his gaze to Jesse.

Her decision had not been easy. She, more than anyone, had not come away from that night unchanged. When the smoke cleared and the wounds healed, her life was still sitting there: waiting for her to make up her mind about a number of things.

It had not been easy. No way. But somehow, for her anyway, it had seemed right. Too much death already, maybe. Pete's legacy, a living reminder that love was, if not the most powerful force in the world, at least the most persistent.

She had precious few regrets.

And the music was better than ever.

The Symphony of Life, as such, continued to grow almost as fast as the squirming bundle in her arms. She suspected it always would. And a surprising number of the new sounds and textures managed to sneak into the arrangements on The Jacob Hamer Band's new album, Through the Fire. *Whether that accounted for its popularity, she was not prepared to say. It didn't really matter in the end. Credit didn't really count.*

Contact did.

"How's Pee-wee?" Ted asked, walking over and scarfing up the squiggling tot. "Is he ready to rock and roll?"

"Ready as he'll ever be." Jesse smiled, handing him over. A warm glow burgeoned in her heart when she saw Ted handle the urchin. *He looks so much older than eighteen,* she noted, and not for the first time. You could see it in his body, you could see it in his eyes: the child giving way to the man. His skin was still pocked with tiny pitted scars—by now she doubted that those would ever go entirely away—but that only seemed to enhance his character. He took it in stride.

"We'll miss you," she said.

"Hey"—he smiled as little Pete gnawed enthusiastically on his finger—"I'll miss you, too. But it's only three months. You'll be back in time for my graduation even."

"I wouldn't miss it for the world."

"You better not." His eyes sparkled, meeting hers.

Jesse smiled. Seeing Ted holding her child like that, she couldn't help feeling the wash of love, and hope, and quietly biding terror. It wasn't the best time to be coming of age, she thought. There was, after all, a war going on.

But then again, she added, *wasn't there always?*

The letters came every two or three months now. It had been that way since November and his release from Haverford State Mental Hospital. Picking up the jagged pieces of one's obliterated life took time, after all.

Mary Hatch knew all about picking up the pieces.

She sat on the floor of her Diamond Bar bedroom, running her toes through the rust-colored shag carpet, the shower-damp towel still draped around her. Her hair was longer than ever; it fell nearly down to her tail end, completely covered her breasts. They were still little larger than your average tangerines, but somehow that didn't much matter anymore.

She held the envelope in her hands for a moment, picking up the vibes off the paper. Not bad. He had certainly come a long way since the breakdown; it was no longer scary to learn what was going on inside his mind. The frazz factor was gone; he seemed much closer to the peace he had paid lip service to so loudly for so long.

Mary smiled, warm inside the white light that seemed to surround her always.

Then she opened the envelope, noting the Philadelphia postmark, removed the letter, and began to read.

Dear Mary,

The last snow of the season has gone now, God willing. Soon, the streets will be warm enough for my people to go back out and get on with their lives. The hope is, of course, that something will touch them in the course of their stay here. But the Lord, as we both know, works in mysterious ways.

Nonetheless, things are going well here at the mission. We're housing up to forty people a night, and the soup kitchen hands out perhaps three hundred meals a day.

Mildred has adjusted well to our new life-style; she seems much happier now that the trappings of false faith are gone. She is certainly happier with our relationship. We run a Ma and Pa type of affair here. No big stuff: just she and I and a few stalwart volunteers. And of course, the people whose lives we have been charged with.

That's the beauty of true faith, Mary. That's the beautiful thing you taught me, the thing that has sustained me after everything else collapsed. True faith is subtle, not ostentatious. It needs not things; it is the thing. I don't know how many years I preached the Gospel without taking that one most sacred tenet to heart.

For as Jesus said in Matthew 20, verses 27-28: "And whoever desires to be first among you, let him be your slave—just as the Son of Man did not come to be served, but to serve. . . ."

Anyway, God bless you. I hope you are well and wish you all the best in whatever you are chosen to do. The Lord has a special love for you and a special purpose. When the moment comes, I trust with all my heart that you will be up to it.

And that, after all, is the essence of faith.

My love to you,
Dan Furniss

"I love you, too," Mary whispered to the room, and the faraway former pastor. She was, strange as it was to admit, very proud of him. If there was a lesson to be learned, then certainly he had learned it. Yes, the one who served most humbly would be the most exalted; and no, Jesus would not wear a Rolex on his television show. The fact that Daniel Furniss no longer had either was a major step in the right direction.

As for her own role . . . well, he was right again. For now, the things to do were very basic. Finish school. Prepare for college, where she intended to major in theology. There was so much she needed to learn and discern for herself. There were so many versions of the Word of God, after all: each one corrupted at some point along the line, certainly; but nonetheless, all of them were rooted in the sincere desire of the eternal human spirit to understand the eternal questions.

Why we are here.

What it all means.

And what is our ultimate purpose.

She didn't know what her ultimate purpose was, but she was pretty sure that, if there was one, she would be the first to know.

And like the man said: that was, after all, the essence.

The essence.

Of faith.

Joshua Walker sat at the otherwise empty table in the otherwise empty room, staring at the objects laid out before him. They were the talismans of his nightly ritual, the one constant in an otherwise ephemeral existence. As rituals go, it was not entirely unpleasant, filled as it was with an element of mystery and purpose and risk. He had engaged in it every night before sleep, without fail, for the last eighteen months. Every night, for the past eighteen months, he had slept soundly.

The table this evening was in the very back of the hot, solitary *cervecería* of the village of Nahuatla, a tiny dot of backwater civilization carved high into the rocky green hills of the Honduran countryside. It had been his temporary sanctuary for the last few days and depending upon the outcome, might be for the next night or so. Then he'd move on, shape-shifting his way across Central America, once again where he truly belonged. A living ghost, in the killing machine.

The locals feared him as they would any crazy *yanqui*, of whom there were plenty these days. He had money, he had weapons, he was maybe CIA, maybe not. He was scary enough that nobody felt like asking. They served him his drinks and stayed out of his path. This suited Walker just fine: involvement on any scale was a distraction to his purpose, and Joshua Walker was determined to fulfill that purpose.

He surveyed the talismans before him: a shot glass of rum, a .44 revolver, and a single hollow-point bullet.

Joshua smiled.

God is one funny son of a bitch, he thought. He picked up the revolver in his left hand and the hollow-point in his right. The bullet was tarnished from the sweat of repeated handlings. It was a very special bullet, he knew; so special that he'd had it engraved about six months ago in a dusty little locksmith's shop in Mexico City. The surface of the cartridge was scored in tiny, floral script:

Joshua Walker. Paid In Full.

He placed the bullet in a random chamber and spun it. *Yeah, He's a real card, all right*, he thought. *Likes things mysterious. Can't just say it straight out, no* . . . There was no longer any bitterness in the thought, just a sense of incontrovertible realization.

. . . it's got to be a passion play, every time.

Walker stopped the cylinder randomly in mid-spin. He laid the gun down on the scarred, dried wood of the table.

It's got to be Jesus and Judas, right and wrong, heaven and hell . . .

He grasped the gun, as he had every night for the last eighteen months. He gave it a vigorous twist this time, virtually insuring a few extra revolutions. He did that, periodically, just for the added sense of mystery. Not that it ultimately mattered.

While the innocents die, again and again . . .

The gun spun expertly in place. It was American-made, bluesteel, and very well balanced, and he'd had lots of practice. It went round and round, making a scuffling, whirling sound that sent the waiter hustling over to whisper to the bartender. *Crazy goddamned gringo.*

Walker watched the gun go round as his thoughts rolled back over the last five-hundred-odd days. He wondered about Momma, that bitch. Was It a demon? Or was it just an opportunistic sentience, cashing in on our fear? Who knew. All he really knew for certain was that It was lurking out there. Its stink was everywhere. Every new atrocity these days wore Its signature, every undisclosed body dump bore mute witness to Its presence. Walker had even found a blasted cassette of *The Critical Mass* in the blood-streaked mud of his last ambush site. Soundtrack music for a real-life movie. He'd squashed it underfoot and left it there.

Momma was here, no doubt. On both sides, playing each against the other for Its sole aggrandizement. Also here were Momma's fans, in increasing numbers, what with the commitment of fresh combat troops and the escalated fighting that followed the invasion of Honduras. It was a statistical probability that some of them were even survivors from that fateful weekend in Philly. But then, so was he, and in a strange way that sort of evened the odds.

Momma knew it, too, and It was pissed off. It couldn't reach him anymore, even if It could still taint the hearts and souls of so many of the poor dumb fuckers pitched into this geopolitical insane asylum. Emotional scar tissue was funny like that; he'd turned his in like a winding sheet, and found it remarkably protective. He could still feel, oh, yes; perhaps more than ever before, which helped explain his continued sense of mission. But the heart-scars shielded him somehow. Perversely so; the detachment actually gave him an edge, one that It had never anticipated.

That's not much, he amended, *but in hard times that would have to do. More fun from our pal God.* Fucker always stacked the odds in favor of evil, it seemed, giving the one side a David to go up against the inevitable Goliath, then giving that same side only the tiniest shred of hope to hang on to. Not for the first time, he felt himself squarely in the midst of complete and utter madness. Maybe Mark Twain was right: if God existed at all, He must surely be a malign thug.

Or maybe He just liked the odds. Maybe He was a gambler at heart. Walker could appreciate that well enough; he'd seen enough of what was at stake to last a lifetime. And he'd played the long odds every single night for the past eighteen months.

The gun stopped spinning. The barrel pointed straight at his heart, just as it had every night for the past year and a half. *Same as it ever was . . .*

Joshua Walker picked up the gun in his left hand and the shot glass in his right. He scrutinized the glass: an ounce of *Aguardiente,* a vile amber-oily liquid, which seemed to be all they ever had since the *contras* more often then not hijacked the delivery truck that brought in cases of *Salvavida* or *Superior.* Walker liked *Salvavida*—the name meant lifesaver—and drank it when he could get it. As beer went, it was good stuff.

But not for a talisman. Oh, no. For that it had to be tequila or, as tonight, *Aguardiente*—water with teeth. It was fitting somehow.

He scrutinized the rum, so viscous it seemed to cling to the sides of the glass. *Water with teeth.* It clung, but it didn't smile. That was good, like an omen, almost. Oboy. He wondered where it might lead.

But he didn't worry about it.

Walker downed the shot. It burned a smooth track down the delicate lining of his esophagus to nestle in his stomach. A warm, soft glow came back, spreading through his limbs. He welcomed it. It softened the rest of the ritual atonement. What followed was pure discipline.

He picked up the piece and hefted it. Nicely balanced, bluesteeled, American made. Clean. He pushed the barrel firmly into the hollow of his left eye socket and held it there. It fit right in. Joshua pulled and locked the hammer back in two deadly clicks, and he smiled.

The moment of truth, for the five hundred forty-second consecutive time. A purely rhetorical question formed in his head. There was plenty to do in a world like this: a lot of corrupt motherfuckers needing their clocks cleaned, a lot of darkness to be pushed inexorably back. And always, always— far too much innocent blood for one man to ever atone for. *So what do you want from me, anyway?*

Only one way to find out. The deck was shuffled, the cards already dealt. If he lived, there was a supply convoy due in tomorrow on *Uno Norte* that was ripe for derailment. If not, well . . .

Walker pulled the trigger.

And let God sort it out.

MEAT THE AUTHORS

Best known as the inventors of the Florida Yoo-Hoo Spritzer, John Skipp and Craig Spector remain creatures of mystery. Though rumours persist in the nation's tabloids—of extensive plastic surgery, of involvement in the Iran-Contra scandal, and of that fabled 'lost weekend' with Imelda Marcos—in truth, they lead lives of quiet desperation. Shunned by the public they so desperately crave, they are said to have retreated to an eerie estate called Xanadu, where they keep a menagerie of tiny shrunken people in jars and walk around muttering, "Rosebud". Nobody knows what this means. Perhaps it is for the best.

Some facts, however, have emerged. Both are male, Caucasian, and have survived public education. Skipp has a pair of identifying scars near his beady little eyes. Spector dangles little skulls and crosses off of his ear. They are both considered to have arms and dangerness. If you should spot either of these men, do not approach them without offering to buy them a beer. Otherwise, contact your local authorities and turn yourself in.

Their next book is called NIGHTMARE, NEW YORK CITY. They are also editing a star-studded anthology of zombie stories called BOOK OF THE DEAD.

And, yes, they rock and roll.

BANTAM BOOKS
GRAND SLAM SWEEPSTAKES

Win a new Chevrolet Corsica . . .
It's easy . . . It's fun . . . Here's how to enter:

OFFICIAL ENTRY FORM

Three Bantam book titles on sale this month are hidden in this word puzzle. Identify the books by circling each of these titles in the puzzle. Titles may appear within the puzzle horizontally, vertically, or diagonally . . .

D	E	S	T	I	N	Y	
T	A	I	F	Z		M	
H	T	H	I	S		R	A
E	S		E	F	C	L	N
	S	C	R	E	A	M	
A		C		H	P	O	
S	P	L	E	N	D	O	R

This month's Bantam Books titles are:

_____
DESTINY

_____
THIS FIERCE SPLENDOR

_____
THE SCREAM

In each of the books listed above there is another entry blank and puzzle . . . another chance to win!

Be on the lookout for these Bantam paperback books: INDIAN COUNTRY, SOMETIMES PARADISE, and BE HAPPY YOU ARE LOVED. In each of them, you'll find a new puzzle, entry blank and GRAND SLAM Sweepstakes rules . . . and yet another chance to win another brand-new Chevrolet automobile!

MAIL TO: GRAND SLAM SWEEPSTAKES
                        Post Office Box 18
                        New York, New York 10046

Please Print

NAME _____

ADDRESS _____

CITY _____ STATE _____ ZIP _____

OFFICIAL RULES

NO PURCHASE NECESSARY.

To enter identify this month's Bantam Book titles by placing a circle around each word forming each title. There are three titles shown above to be found in this month's puzzle. Mail your entry to: Grand Slam Sweepstakes, P.O. Box 18, New York, N.Y. 10046

This is a monthly sweepstakes starting February 1, 1988 and ending January 31, 1989. During this sweepstakes period, one automobile winner will be selected each month from all entries that have correctly solved the puzzle. To participate in a particular month's drawing, your entry must be received by the last day of that month. The Grand Slam prize drawing will be held on February 14, 1989 from all entries received during all twelve months of the sweepstakes.

To obtain a free entry blank/puzzle/rules, send a self-addressed stamped envelope to: Winning Titles, P.O. Box 650, Sayreville, N.J. 08872. Residents of Vermont and Washington need not include return postage.

PRIZES: Each month for twelve months a Chevrolet automobile will be awarded with an approximate retail value of $12,000 each.

The Grand Slam Prize Winner will receive 2 Chevrolet automobiles plus $10,000 cash (ARV $34,000).

Winners will be selected under the supervision of Marden-Kane Inc., an independent judging organization. By entering this sweepstakes each entrant accepts and agrees to be bound by these rules and the decisions of the judges which shall be final and binding. Winners may be required to sign an affidavit of eligibility and release which must be returned within 14 days of receipt. All prizes will be awarded. No substitution or transfer of prizes permitted. Winners will be notified by mail. Odds of winning depend on the total number of eligible entries received.

Sweepstakes open to residents of the U.S. and Canada except employees of Bantam Books, its affiliates, subsidiaries, advertising agencies and Marden-Kane, Inc. Void in the Province of Quebec and wherever else prohibited or restricted by law. Not responsible for lost or misdirected mail or printing errors. Taxes and licensing fees are the sole responsibility of the winners. All cars are standard equipped. Canadian winners will be required to answer a skill testing question.

For a list of winners, send a self-addressed, stamped envelope to: Bantam Winners, P.O. Box 711, Sayreville, N.J. 08872.

Meet John Skipp and Craig Spector, writers at the crest of a new wave of horror.

"SKIPP AND SPECTOR GIVE YOU THE WORST KIND OF NIGHTMARES."
—George Romero
Director of THE NIGHT OF THE LIVING DEAD

"THESE GUYS ARE AMONGST THE FORERUNNERS OF MODERN HORROR. SKIPP AND SPECTOR TAKE YOU TO THE LIMITS . . . THEN ONE STEP MORE."
—Clive Barker
Author of *INHUMAN CONDITION*

"SLAM-BANG NO HOLDS BARRED HORROR FOR THOSE WITH STOUT HEARTS AND STRONG STOMACHS."
—T.E.D. Klein
Author of *THE CEREMONIES*

☐ THE LIGHT AT THE END
25451-0 $3.95/$4.50 in Canada

It's bizarre graffiti splashed in blood.
Something evil is lurking in the tunnels beneath Manhattan.
Something horrible is hungry for souls.

☐ THE CLEANUP
26056-1 $3.95/$4.95 in Canada

His name is Billy Rowe. Yesterday he was just another talented loser who was chewed up and spat back on the streets. Today he discovered the *Power*. Now he has a mission. Now there is nothing left to fear. Nothing but Billy Rowe.

And coming in February 1988

☐ THE SCREAM
26798-1 $3.95/$4.95 in Canada

Welcome to the heart of the Nightmare!

Look for them at your bookstore or use the coupon below: